everglades

*Also by Randy Wayne White
in Large Print:*

Twelve Mile Limit

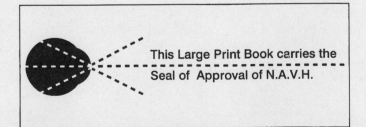

everglades

Randy Wayne White

WHEELER PUBLISHING

Published in 2003 by arrangement with G. P. Putnam's Sons, a member of Penguin Group (USA) Inc.

Wheeler Large Print Hardcover.

The text of this Large Print edition is unabridged. Other aspects of the book may vary from the original edition.

Set in 16 pt. Plantin.

Printed in the United States on permanent paper.

Library of Congress Cataloging-in-Publication Data

White, Randy Wayne.
    Everglades / Randy Wayne White.
      p. cm.
     ISBN 1-58724-468-3 (lg. print : hc : alk. paper)
     1. Ford, Doc (Fictitious character) — Fiction. 2. Everglades (Fla.) — Fiction. 3. Marine biologists — Fiction. 4. Florida — Fiction. 5. Large type books. I. Title.
PS3573.H47473E95 2003b
  813′.54—dc21   2003049682

To Dr. Dan L. White,
a great brother, a great friend

National Association for Visually Handicapped
------------------------ *serving the partially seeing*

As the Founder/CEO of NAVH, the only national health agency solely devoted to those who, although not totally blind, have an eye disease which could lead to serious visual impairment, I am pleased to recognize Thorndike Press* as one of the leading publishers in the large print field.

Founded in 1954 in San Francisco to prepare large print textbooks for partially seeing children, NAVH became the pioneer and standard setting agency in the preparation of large type.

Today, those publishers who meet our standards carry the prestigious "Seal of Approval" indicating high quality large print. We are delighted that Thorndike Press is one of the publishers whose titles meet these standards. We are also pleased to recognize the significant contribution Thorndike Press is making in this important and growing field.

Lorraine H. Marchi, L.H.D.
Founder/CEO
NAVH

* Thorndike Press encompasses the following imprints: Thorndike, Wheeler, Walker and Large Print Press.

Acknowledgments

The islands of Sanibel and Captiva are real and, I hope, faithfully described, but they are used fictitiously in this novel.

The same is true of certain businesses, marinas, bars and other places frequented by Doc Ford, Tomlinson and their friends. When you spend as much time as I have roaming around in a boat, it's hard not to mention interesting people you've met and come to care about.

In all other respects, however, this novel is a work of fiction. Names, characters, places and incidents either are the product of the author's imagination or are used fictitiously. Any resemblance to actual persons, living or dead, or to actual events or locales is entirely coincidental.

This book demanded extensive research in several fields, and I am grateful to the experts who took the time to help. I would like to thank Dr. Allan W. Eckert not only for years of encouragement and friendship, but also for allowing me to draw on his vast knowledge of both the brilliant Shawnee leader Tecumseh and the Everglades. Also invaluable was Dr. Doug Smith of the University of Florida Geology Department. He very kindly replied to my questions about earthquakes with a valuable letter he entitled "Creating Artificial Seismic Disturbance in South Florida."

Equally helpful was Dr. Patricia Riles Wickman, Department of Anthropology and Genealogy, Seminole Tribe of Florida. Her enthusiasm for the premise of *Everglades* was as important as the guidance she provided and her detailed replies to a novice's questions. For any serious student of Florida history, her book *The Tree That Bends* is recommended.

I would also like to thank David Dell and Pedro Chamorro, and the excellent staff of the Colony Hotel for their help while I was in Nicaragua; Tina Osceola; Officer Larry Chilson of the City of Miami Police Department; Sergeant Jim Brown of the Lee County Sheriff's Department; Dr. Rebecca Hamilton, Lee County Medical Examiner; Sue Williams; Renee Humbert; Dr. John Miller; Dr. Brian Hummel; Bill "Spaceman" Lee; Andrey Aleksandrov, administrator of the Russian national baseball team; John and Mitsu McNeal; Bill Haney; Thaddeus Kostrabala, MD; my friend Peter Matthiessen, for allowing Tomlinson to paraphrase his powerful quote about a life that "may not be understood"; Jack Himschoot, for teaching me to drive an airboat; Cindy Abele and Lisa Worthington, for introducing me to windsurfing; and my dear friends Rob and Phyllis Wells, for letting me hide out and write in the boathouse at Tarpon Lodge.

These people all provided valuable guidance and/or information. All errors, exaggerations, omissions or fictionalizations are entirely the fault, and the responsibility, of the author.

Because of deadline obligations, I was unable to participate, as I traditionally do, in the Roy Hobbs World Series 2002, so I'd like to apologize to the members of Bartley's Bombers, a great team: Gary Terwilliger, Stu Johnson, Dan Cugini, Steve McCarthy, Steve Liddle, José Imclan, Victor Candelaria, Tim McCoy, Mike Padula, Dr. Mike Tucker, Dr. Kevin Goodlet, Johnny Delgado, Mike Miller, Rich Johns, Rick Scafidi, Mark Lamers, Mike Radvansky, Don Carmen, Kerry Griner, Scot Harding and Rob Moretti.

Finally, I would like to thank my sons, Lee and Rogan White, for helping me finish this book.

— *Randy Wayne White*
Old Cypress House,
Key West

Hope could not exist if man were created by a random, chemical accident. Pleasure, yes. Desire, yes. But not hope. Selfless hope is contrary to the dynamics of evolution or the necessities of a species.

— S. E. TOMLINSON
"One Fathom Above Sea Level"

I have always thought there might be a lot of cash in starting a religion.

— GEORGE ORWELL, 1938

My letter of yesterday will inform you of the departure of Tecumseh. There can be no doubt his object is to excite the southern Indians to war. [These] include the Seminole of Florida.

The implicit obedience and respect which the followers of Tecumseh pay is astonishing. He is one of those uncommon geniuses which spring up occasionally to produce revolutions, and overturn the established order of things. If it were not for the vicinity of the United States, he would, perhaps, be the founder of an empire that would rival in glory Mexico or Peru. No difficulties deter him.

GOVERNOR OF THE INDIANA TERRITORY,

LATER U.S. PRESIDENT,
WILLIAM HENRY HARRISON,
ON THE SHAWNEE LEADER, TECUMSEH,
WHO ACCURATELY PROPHESIED
THE NEW MADRID, MISSOURI,
EARTHQUAKES OF 1811

chapter one

izzy

Izzy Kline said to Shiva, "Today, she hopped in her Beamer and drove across the Everglades to Sanibel Island. She's got a couple of friends there, so it could be she's looking for help: a marine biologist named Ford, and someone whose name you might recognize."

Shiva was wearing sandals and a Seminole medicine jacket, rag-patched, rainbow reds, greens, yellows, belted around his waist like a bathrobe. Shiva's hair was cut Shawnee style: a fifty-six-year-old male, born to a Canadian mother in Bombay, India — indifferent to the irony.

He was standing in a bedroom that was larger than some of the West Palm Beach homes he could see across the Intracoastal canal through the western window of his beach compound.

In the bedroom was a Buddha-shaped bed with canopy, a gymnasium with sauna, a meditation corner, an office with computers and security monitors. The place was done in white tile and teak, all decorations in gold except for several wooden figurines on the walls. There

13

was a carving of an impressionistic cat, several masks with horrific faces and two rare Seminole totemic masks.

The carvings had been added within the last two years.

Shiva said to Izzy, "I haven't seen or talked to you in a month. So why do you show up now, bothering me with this garbage?"

"It seemed important. She doesn't believe her husband's dead. I already told you."

"You've been working for me for — what? — ten, twelve years. You know I hate details — as if I have the *time*. I don't care about this woman."

"Details — Jesus Christ, are you kidding? If she finds out the truth about what happened to Geoff Minster, say good-bye to your casinos and your development. Three tons of ammonium nitrate fertilizer, explosives grade. Does that ring a bell? It's *my* nuts in the wringer."

Shiva looked impatiently at the Cartier watch he wore on his left wrist. "You need to leave. I have a massage scheduled in a few minutes. There's a new girl among the disciples — with a nice body for a change. I don't want you interrupting."

Izzy Kline: Lean, gaunt-cheeked, with a scar below his right eye, dimples and a dimpled chin — a ladies' man. Ex–Israeli Army, he'd trained with the Mossad, chosen to leave his adopted country rather than face morals charges, returned to America and been hired as security manager by a controversial religious leader, Bhagwan Shiva, founder of the International Church of Ashram Meditation, Inc.

Strictly business.

Shiva had established his first church west of Miami Lakes, the palmetto country between Okeechobee Road and Opa Locka, edge of the Everglades. This was back before he'd changed his name from Jerry Singh. He'd started with forty-some disciples, mostly dropouts and run-aways who'd craved the discipline, and liked wearing robes and growing their own food.

When he'd had cash, he'd bought land. He'd bought a lot of it west of Miami. Cheap swampland.

Eighteen years later, Shiva now had a quarter million followers worldwide, and one hundred twenty Church of Ashram Centers, mostly in the U.S., Great Britain and Europe, though the numbers were declining. In the last five years, his organization had been crippled by lawsuits, IRS investigations and aggressive TV, magazine and newspaper exposés.

He'd been described as the "wizard of religion" because of elaborate miracles staged before thousands. He'd been called the "rich man's prophet," and an incarnate "sex guru."

Kline didn't believe Shiva was an incarnate anything; he knew him too well to fall for his holy man act. Izzy was the only person in the organization who spoke frankly to Shiva. As a result, he was the only man Shiva could be open with, behave naturally around — and who also scared him a little.

Izzy knew *everything*.

Shiva sighed and said, "Okay, okay, so why should we be worried about her two friends on some island? Where'd you say she went?"

Izzy said, "She sent her cousin an e-mail, said she's driving to Sanibel today."

"An e-mail. You have access to her computer? Or did you break into her house?"

Izzy *had* broken into her house. Several times; twice in the last week. He enjoyed going through her drawers. He'd found a couple of fun items hidden away. But he said, "No. I hacked her password. The one friend she's going to see, I think you've probably heard about. Which's why I'm telling you. A guy named Sighurdhr Tomlinson. Or Sea-guard, I'm not sure how you pronounce it."

"Sighurdhr Tomlinson," Shiva said, considering it, but not giving it his full attention. "The name sounds familiar."

"Remember Miami River, the archaeological site where you tried to build the condo complex? That group of protesters who futzed it? Eco-freaks, all the shitty PR they caused. How many millions'd we lose on that one?"

Shiva was nodding now. "Okay, yes, I know who you mean. He was with the protestors, one of the leaders. I remember one of my advisors telling me — *not* you — that he was a kook. Like most of them. A heavy drug user. That's the information I got."

Izzy said, "Really? That's all? There's more. You know me, I'm a fanatic when it comes to background checks."

Shiva said, "I don't think I'm interested."

Izzy said, "I think you should be."

"Why? I don't see the point."

"Because what I found out about this guy is kind of interesting. For instance: Fifteen, twenty years ago, he was implicated in a terrorist bombing at a U.S. naval base. Killed a couple of people."

That got Shiva's attention. "*Really.* A bombing. Hum-m-m-m." Thinking about it, how the information could be used.

"Yeah, but he skated. The feds didn't nail 'im. I'm not sure why yet. I'm still working on that. There had to be a *reason.*"

"But there's a record?"

"Not official, but it's there if you dig deep enough."

"Is there anything for him to find out about Geoff?"

"Maybe. I don't know if the guy was being straight with us or not. It's possible he hid away some papers. Or maybe he had a secret friend. Who knows? What I'm saying is, we're both screwed if his wife figures out what really happened."

Izzy was standing at the bedroom's east

window, looking over the tops of coconut palms, out onto the Atlantic. Seeing jade sea bottom beyond the beach, and a border of purple water way out where a couple of ocean-going freighters moved like long slabs of concrete, floating: the Gulf Stream.

Beneath Izzy, parked on the blue tile drive, were two Rolls-Royces: a 1923 Silver Ghost, and a '31 Landaulette, painted racing green. Shiva loved them; collected them. Maybe because he was born upper caste, in India, British-made cars seemed to represent something. Izzy wasn't sure what.

Less than five years ago, Shiva had owned twenty-three Rollses. But he'd been selling them off — Izzy was one of the few who knew about it — plus some property, some businesses, to augment the organization's sagging cash flow.

His church was in trouble, and the guy was desperate. Izzy knew that, too.

Something else Izzy had realized after all these years with Shiva: All religion was *bullshit*. Religion was nothing more than legend manipulated by carefully staged illusions.

It was his personal water-into-wine theory.

Shiva said, "His wife, the attractive blonde — what's her name?"

"Sally. Yeah, she's a looker."

"Has Sally ever met you? Does she know who you are?"

"No."

"What about Tomlinson?"

"Nope."

"Okay, they're old friends. That's what you said. Sometimes old friends, a man and a woman, they just run off and disappear."

Kline knew what Shiva meant by "disappear." Shiva had paid him bonuses to do it before, and he'd actually kind of enjoyed himself the one time it was a woman. But something about the way Shiva said it now irked him — like it was no big deal; grunt work any idiot could pull off.

Izzy called Shiva by his real name on those occasions when he wanted to underscore the fact that he didn't much give a damn about the man's religious act, or who paid his salary. He used the name now, saying, "Brilliant, Jerry. But she's going to visit two guys, not just one. So maybe what you can do is perform another one of your miracles. Snap your fingers, make all three of them disappear. How's *that* sound?"

Shiva ignored the sarcasm. "This hippie, even if she does try to get him involved — someone like him? I don't see the problem. So tell me about the second guy."

"He's a marine biologist named Ford. Marion D. Ford. Lives on Sanibel Island at a place called Dinkin's Bay Marina. Same place as Tomlinson. Ford sells marine specimens."

"Marine specimens."

"Um-huh. Like to colleges and labs. For research, that sort of thing."

Shiva waited through a few beats of silence, before he said, "That's *it?* Your background check didn't turn up anything else —"

There was a polite knock at the door. Shiva paused, checked his watch again. Time for his massage. He said, "Leave now. The women are here."

Kline said, "Exactly my point. With all the data banks and my resources, that's all there was: where Ford lives, the name of his company, where he graduated from college, some research papers. They play in some baseball league. Nothing else.

"The guy's alive, he exists, but never really lived. He's like an empty body walking."

Shiva smiled, then began to laugh, waving Izzy toward the door, "Baseball. A *children's* game. You're wasting my time for this? If a biologist and some pothead worry you, maybe you've been in the business too long. Get out of here. We'll talk again when I'm through."

Izzy was remembering a maxim he'd learned at the Mossad training complex in the suburbs of Tel Aviv — *Beware the man without a past* — as he considered saying to Bhagwan Shiva, *You really don't get it, do you?*

Not that he was concerned about a man he'd never met, or the woman, or anyone else. It was Shiva's attitude that bothered him, the indifference. Like he was really beginning to believe the lie he'd been telling followers for years: *I am the truth, and the truth is invincible.*

Izzy walked toward the door, thinking, *You're not invincible, asshole. And you're not taking me down with you. . . .*

chapter two

In the green, squall-glow of a Friday afternoon, April 11th, I returned home from the Everglades, and a ridiculous search for swamp aliens that my friend Tomlinson had dragged me on, to find another old friend, and one of the world's bright, independent ladies, Sally Carmel, waiting on my deck.

The recently widowed Sally Carmel Minster, I would soon learn.

She met me at the top of the stairs. When she came into my open arms, it was more of a collapse than a friendly hug. I held her close, feeling her breath on my ear. "Did you see him? You walked right past the guy."

I said, "Guy, what guy?"

"The one who's been following me for the last two weeks. Big guy with a shaved head. Like a pro wrestler. The kind you see on TV."

She stopped me when I tried to pull away. "Don't turn around. He's in the mangroves. I've been pretending like I don't know he's there. It's what I always do when I know he's following me. He's right behind you, watching us with binoculars."

I held her away from me, hands on shoulders, looking her over from head to toe — not an uncommon thing to do if you have not seen someone in a long, long time. And I had not seen Sally in a very long time.

It'd been, what, probably five or six years since she'd visited my little stilt house on Dinkin's Bay. At least three years since our last phone conversation. It was at a time when her marriage was on the rocks again, and she'd nearly accepted my invitation to spend a week on Guava Key, a members-only resort where I'd been hired to do a fish count.

Our friendship dates back to childhood. We both spent early years in the little mangrove village of Mango, south of Naples, Gulf coast of Florida. It was back when I lived with my crazed, manipulative uncle, Tucker Gatrell, and his lifelong partner, Joseph Egret.

Joseph was an Everglades Indian with an enormous heart. He was one of those rare adults who forged friendships with children naturally, sincerely. In later years, it was Joseph who helped rekindle the friendship between Sally and me during her brief separation. It was a tough time for a good lady. Because she was certain the marriage was over, she and I became more than friends.

But the marriage *wasn't* over.

Our relationship ended abruptly when Sally returned to her estranged Miami husband, a high-powered, alpha male named Geoff Minster. He was an architect or a developer — something like that — and he'd lured her back by offering her the chance to help him design some big project.

End of our romance. End of all contact. It is a common, modern phenomenon. Lovers separate, then gradually or abruptly orbit away, trajectories increasingly dissimilar, until one member vanishes, never to reappear. It is a death, of sorts, and it has happened all too often in my life.

When I'd thought of Sally — and I sometimes did — I assumed that it was unlikely her life would ever again intersect with my own. She'd patched a broken marriage. Presumably, she'd been rewarded with the accoutrements of that union: a stable home life, her own work, her own new circle of friends somewhere in or near the concrete swarm that is Miami. Maybe a houseful of babies, too.

But now here she was, standing on the open deck of my little house and lab built on stilts in the shallow water of Dinkin's Bay, Sanibel Island, Florida.

Looking into her face, her lime-blue eyes, I said, "Why in the world would anyone want to follow you. A stalker, you mean?"

"No. A private investigator, or whatever they're called these days. I've called the police a couple of times, but it hasn't done any good. He's been sneaking around, watching me off and on for the last two weeks. Maybe longer, because that's when I first spotted him. Following me across the state from Coconut Grove, clear to Sanibel — this, I didn't expect. It's getting scary now, and I'm sick of it."

I asked again, "But *why?*"

"I think it has to do with Geoff, my husband."

"Your husband? Does he think you're having an affair?"

Why else would he have her followed?

"No, it's not that. I'd never do something like that. My husband . . . Geoff, he disappeared. He's dead."

It took me a few moments before I could find the voice to answer. "*Dead.* Sally, I am so, so sorry. I didn't hear a thing about it."

"I wish I felt the same. But I don't. Six months ago, October twenty-seventh, on a fishing trip to Bimini, Geoff supposedly fell overboard. It was at night, so no one realized it until the next morning. No witnesses. His body was never found."

I said, " 'Supposedly.' "

"I don't believe it. I've never believed it. I don't think the insurance company does, either. If the man out there is a private investigator, they probably hired him."

I said, "Good God," surprised by her reappearance, by the situation, by the implicit obligation. Friendship comes with responsibilities — reliability during crisis being among them. If an acquaintance does not behave accordingly and dependably, he or she is not your friend.

"The insurance company doesn't want to pay off?"

Sally was shaking her head. "No, of course they don't. But they will. They'll have no choice. Not with all the evidence my attorney's presented to the circuit court — which she says is standard in any death settlement case where the body hasn't been found. Otherwise, the state waits five years before issuing a death certificate.

"My attorney's really first rate. She knows how the system works. Which means they're going to have to pay. A big figure with lots of zeros behind it deposited right into a money market account. She expects the court to rule in our favor within a couple of weeks. Two weeks — that's about the same time I noticed skinhead in his car, following me."

"Has he ever said anything? Confronted you?"

"No."

"Have you been getting any hang-up calls?"

If he was a stalker, not a P.I., hang-up calls would be evidential.

She replied, "No. I occasionally get a hang-up, like everyone else, but not enough to worry about."

I put my arm over her shoulder, and began to walk her up the wooden steps toward my house, still not risking a glance behind me.

"What'd he say when the police questioned him?"

"The guy? They've never managed to catch him. He's pretty tricky. They think maybe he has a scanner or something, because he's always gone by the time they show up. Or that I'm nuts and imagining things. So maybe I'm glad he's out there and you'll see him, too. If he's still there. I was beginning to doubt my own sanity."

Standing, holding the screen door wide open for her, I finally turned and took a quick look shoreward.

Sally was not imagining things.

There he was: a large man trying to hide himself in the mangroves, binoculars in hand, using them to scan the area in our direction.

"Nothing wrong with your sanity," I told her. "Maybe the Sanibel police will be luckier. Let's go inside and call."

"Call if you want. 'Far as I'm concerned, though, he can stand in the bushes all night. Let the mosquitoes carry him away. Now that I'm here, back on the island, I feel safe. For the first time in a long, *long* time, I feel safe."

I thought for a moment before I said, "That might not be a bad way to handle it. With this storm coming, let him stand out there and get soaked. Then I'll use the noise, the rain in the trees, to slip around behind him. Maybe he'll be more cooperative, more talkative, if I surprise him."

She held herself away from me. "Storm? What storm? I don't understand what you mean."

Her reaction was disconcerting. Sally's an accomplished sailor. She'd once sailed the entire west coast of Florida single-handedly, yet she hadn't noticed the approaching rainsquall. The storm cell was to the north, sailing across the bay, the rain visible as a precise demarcation of platinum, dense as winter fog.

In a minute or two, the storm wall would collide with the warmer air of the shoreline.

Which was good, because Florida was just coming off one of its driest winters in history. It hadn't rained for nearly a month.

"Doc, before you confront anybody, even try to talk to him, I need to tell you what happened, why I'm here. I don't want you getting hurt on my account, or to cause you any trouble."

Looking back at her, I said, "I don't plan on getting hurt. Or hurting anyone."

"There's more to it than that."

I shrugged. "First things first. You don't like being followed. Maybe it's time someone told him."

"We could both go. I'm a big girl. I can talk to him myself."

Before I could answer, a partition of Arctic wind blasted us, followed by the molecular sizzle of electrical discharge. Then the earth was shaken by a shock wave of expanding, superheated air that rattled the windows of my lab: *klaaaa-BOOM*.

"God, that was close!" She jumped through the doorway, pulling me with her, eyes wide, but what I noticed — to my personal discredit — was that the woman had aged disproportionately to our years apart, and she had not aged well. Gaunt cheeks, skin too loose on her face, frown lines, blond hair frazzled by lack of attention and too much hair spray.

I picked up my backpack — the only gear I'd taken for four nights in the Everglades — and, as I steered her through the breezeway that separates house from laboratory, she said, "The way my luck's been going, I'm surprised it missed."

It took me a moment to realize what she meant. She was talking about being struck by lightning.

I used my fingers to separate the blinds, and took a longer look at the man who was following Sally.

On Sanibel, people use binoculars to look at birds. We get lots and lots of birders because we have lots and lots of birds. Birders are a strange, but likable, type, not averse to standing out in the rain. But this guy wasn't dressed like a birder.

Instead of the L.L.Bean, eco-awareness look, everything in earth tones, he was wearing a hooded blue rain slicker, the kind the yacht-club types wear, and dark slacks. A city-looking guy, standing there bareheaded, bald, in the bushes next to a couple of big buttonwood trees, thinking he was hidden, but he wasn't.

I've been followed and spied upon more than once in my life. An earlier life, anyway. I've spent a lot of time in Third World countries, jungle areas, the remaining dark places on this earth. Which is why I much prefer the peaceful little community of Dinkin's Bay, and my current occupation — a marine biologist who runs a small company, Sanibel Biological Supply. I collect sea specimens of all varieties and sell them to schools and labs and research facilities around the country.

From old habit, I made careful visual notes, then turned away from the window as Sally said, "Geez, Doc, it's been such a long time since I've been inside this place. Like people always say, I remember it being bigger."

I stood and watched her move around the single open room that is my living quarters. She wore sand-colored pleated shorts, a crisp cinnamon blouse and tan sandals. An expensive yacht-club effect. The colors looked good on her; made hers eyes bluer, her hair more golden than I remembered. I watched the lady turn dancerlike, in slow, nostalgic review.

There's not much to see. The kitchen is a galley, really, not much bigger, or differently equipped than a galley found on a commercial-sized fishing boat: propane stove, small ship's refrigerator, pots and pans hanging on hooks suspended from the ceiling.

Adjoining, but separated by a serving counter, is a wall of books, a floor lamp and a reading chair. My ancient Transoceanic short-wave radio, and smaller portable shortwave, both sit on a table beside the chair. My Celestron telescope stands at the north window nearby.

On all the walls, beneath the bare rafters, are copies of paintings that I like, or photographs, and sometimes recipes, tacked at eye level so I can look at them when I want.

What passes for sleeping quarters is a section along the south wall, shielded by a triad of beaded curtains. There's a simple bed, a double stand-up closet, a locked sea trunk beneath the bed, a dispatch box that I also keep locked, more bookshelves, another reading lamp and a table that holds a brass windup alarm clock next to spare glasses.

As she moved around the place, she demonstrated her uneasiness with a rapid-fire monologue. "This whole day's been such a blur, I don't even know how I ended up here. I wanted to get away, so I told myself a weekend at the beach. After that, it was like the car was steering itself, driving way too fast across the 'Glades. Next thing I know, I'm at the Sanibel bridge, paying my toll, then at the Holiday Inn on Gulf Drive, telling myself I wasn't going to bother you. That I had no right to impose."

I stood, twisted the cap off a beer, and said softly, "Old friends are always welcome. Anytime, day or night. That doesn't change."

"You've been on my mind a lot lately. Maybe because of all the weird stuff that's been happening. You, this little house — safe. That's the way I think of you. Just like this island. Safe. So I've been sitting on your porch for an hour, maybe more. Kept getting up to leave, but my legs wouldn't let me. Plus, with him standing out there in the mangroves, this just seemed the best place to be. I'm so *sorry*, Doc."

Hysteria has a tone and, possibly, a pheromone signature. My immediate impression was that this old friend was teetering on the far, far brink of emotional collapse. To interrupt the talking jag, I crossed the room, pulled her close to me, and gave her a slightly stronger hug to silence her.

"Sally? *Sally.* I'll listen later. Right now, let's deal with the guy outside. Is there anything else I should know before I talk to him?"

"Maybe. I don't know. Give me just a couple of minutes to calm down, collect my thoughts. I don't think you realize how hard this is for me. Coming here, seeing you."

She took a few steps and touched her fingers to the old cast-iron Franklin stove in the northwest corner of the room. "This is new. A fireplace. I would have remembered, back when we . . . when we were dating. You put it in afterwards, right?"

I said, "I needed something. In winter, the wind blows up through cracks in the floor. We get a bad cold front, I can see my breath in here. The good heaters, I keep in the lab."

I had to raise my voice to be heard, because the storm cell was now over us, rain loud as hail on my tin roof, water cascading over the windows, the light beyond a greenish-bronze. It was as if my little house had drifted beneath a mountain waterfall.

There was a rumble and boom of thunder, then another that caused the walls to vibrate. Sally hugged her arms around herself. "Whew! I'm cold *now*. It's like *winter* in here."

So I put her in the reading chair, and started to pour her a glass of red wine — once her beverage of preference — but she stopped me, saying, "No. No alcohol, please. I stopped using alcohol more than two years ago. I made a lot of changes in my life two years ago, and for the better, believe me. Maybe some herbal tea?"

Herbal tea I've got. Tomlinson brings me boxes of the stuff, then forgets he's brought it, and so brings more. I keep a thirty-two-ounce screw-top specimen jar filled with a garden variety of bags, identifiable only by their little paper tabs.

I checked the window again. Through a waterfall-blur, I could see that the man was still out there: a dark shape hunkered beneath the buttonwood. If nothing else, he was vigilant.

There was already lighter pine and newspaper in the stove. I took just enough time to light the fire, and put water on to boil, asking her, "What else can you tell me about the guy outside? I don't suppose you know what kind of car he drives?"

"I've seen it enough in my rearview mirror. One of those big shiny cars, luxury American model. It was black, almost new."

"Your car?"

"A blue BMW, the sedan. A present from Geoff just before he disappeared. He was generous. That much I can't fault him for."

"Anything else?"

She shook her head.

I told her, "Then pull your chair up to the fire, wait for the water to boil. Warm up; enjoy your tea. I won't be gone long."

As I went out the door, I heard her say, "Be careful. He's a really big guy."

"I'm going to talk to him, that's all."

"Okay. But don't get hurt. Believe me, it's not worth it."

Something else had been added to her tonal inflections, and it is among the saddest of human sounds: the sound of self-loathing.

chapter three

The rain had slowed, but the wind had freshened, blowing shadows through the mangrove rim of Dinkin's Bay, leaching storm light from a darkening sky half an hour before sunset.

I went downstairs to the seaward deck where I keep my skiff. It's a twenty-one-foot Maverick, a beautiful little boat, with the new Mercury 225-horsepower Opti-Max I'd just had mounted, the combination of which suggested roadster and dragster qualities — for good reason.

I got a couple more peripheral glances as I started the boat and pulled away: The man was still there, still watching.

I idled the short distance to the marina, and tied off at my usual place just inside the T-dock where the fishing guides keep their skiffs. Because of the rain, a little crowd of locals had taken cover under the tin awning by the bait tanks.

But not everyone. Friday is the traditional weekend party night at Dinkin's Bay Marina, so there was a slightly larger group braving the downpour, eager to get things moving because it was already late.

Three of the fishing guides — Jeth, Neville and Felix — were setting up picnic tables, while others, wearing foul-weather jackets, milled around the docks, carrying coolers and platters of food, or strolled and chatted with fresh drinks in hand.

One of the liveaboards had turned the music up loud, so, through her big fly bridge speakers, I could hear Jimmy Buffett singing about one particular harbor, and the day that John Wayne died.

I said a few quick hellos, promised everyone who tried to engage me in conversation that I'd be right back, then walked across the shell parking lot toward the gate that Mack, the marina owner, closes and locks each Friday before sunset.

There were two lone vehicles parked on the other side of the gate, near the trail that leads to my wooden walkway. Sally's BMW was there, a sporty 5-series — an expensive choice that seemed out of character for someone I'd thought of as having simple tastes.

Behind it was a black Lincoln Town Car with gold trim, gold-spoked wheels and Florida plates. I found a stick, and noted the license number in sand beside the gate, before shielding my eyes and pressing my nose against the tinted windows.

On the passenger seat was a Florida road

map, cans of Copenhagen snuff in a cellophane tube (one can missing) and the sort of rubber gizmo that nervous people squeeze to improve their grip. I also noted that the glove compartment was open.

So what do stalkers or private investigators stash in a glove box? Binoculars? Or maybe a handgun.

I used my T-shirt to rub prints off the window, then I stepped into the mangroves, moving quietly over the monkey-bar roots, feet sinking into the detritus bog, mosquitoes whining in my ears.

The path to my wooden walkway channels through limbs and roots, a dark, green tunnel that is a shady conduit walled by swamp.

I was close enough to the boardwalk path so as not to be seen without some effort, but close enough to be aware of anyone approaching or leaving the boardwalk.

If the stalker attempted to leave, I would see and intercept him.

Which meant he was still there, down there in the mangroves, watching my house from the water. Had to be.

So why couldn't I find him?

Mangrove roots are like fibrous, shin-high hoops, half planted in the muck. I stepped over one after another, holding on to limbs for balance, moving steadily toward the approximate area where I'd last seen the man.

I used all the little tricks. Made sure I placed each careful boot-step on a shell or piece of broken branch so I wouldn't sink into the bog. Waited for small gusts of wind to cover what little sound I did make. Paused every few seconds to listen for noise of movement ahead of me, or behind.

Big golden orb spiders thrive in the shade of mangroves, and there wasn't enough light to see or avoid their webs, so I bulled through several insect traps, spider-silk sticking to my face like threads of cotton candy. When I felt a spider crawling on me, I stopped, carefully removed it and released it on a limb.

The whole while, I kept my eyes fixed in the direction where mangroves ended and water began.

Soon, I could see patches of silver and blue through the gloom of leaves. Then I could see the sandy area next to the buttonwood trees where the man had been standing.

He wasn't there now.

Odd. Where'd he gone?

I stopped, waited, ears straining to hear, eyes straining to see.

Nothing.

There was no way he could have left via the trail without my seeing him. The only possibilities were that he had waded down the shoreline, or that he was now better hidden in the mangroves, off to my left or right.

Moving even more slowly, I worked my way

to the big buttonwood at the water's edge. The rain had quit now, though leaves still dripped.

From where I stood, I had an uninterrupted view of my house and the seascape beyond. Could see the top edge of a pumpkin moon, one day before full, a gaseous bubble rising out of the mangrove horizon. Could see Sally through the windows, very busy doing something in the kitchen.

It was the sort of scene that, if I had the talent, I'd want to capture on canvas. I stood in the shadows for another few moments before stepping out onto the sand.

That's where the man had been standing, no doubt about that. The area was stamped with big shoe prints, pointy-toed, flat-bottomed shoes, Vibram heels sunk deep. He was a big guy. Size fourteen or fifteen shoes that carried a lot of weight.

There was an open Copenhagen can there, too. It was tossed down among the roots, silver lid missing, still nearly full.

A guy that big and sloppy should have been easy to track. Coming from the direction of the path, his bootprints were easy to read. But they ended by the tree where I now stood.

Each and every morning, I check the tide tables, which also give solar and lunar information. It has been a lifelong habit, and I do it automatically. So I knew that, on this day, the eleventh of April, low tide was at 7:47 P.M. — balanced, astronomically, between moonrise at

7:45 P.M. and sunset at 7:51. So the bay had nearly emptied, and would soon be refilling.

I stepped out into the shallow water, looking carefully.

Nope. No tracks out there, either. Which meant he hadn't waded down the shoreline. Where the hell had he gone? It was as if he'd vaporized, disappeared into the darkening sky.

Then it came to me. Where he'd gone. Where he *had* to be.

A wise British physician once wrote that, when baffled by a problem, and all probabilities have been eliminated, the remaining possibility — however unlikely — *must* be the solution.

Only one possibility remained, and that probability now entered my all-too-often slow, slow brain.

Sally's stalker was above me, in the buttonwood tree.

He'd been there the whole time, watching, waiting.

I stood frozen for a moment, considering how I should react.

The situation reminded me of something. Years ago, in Indonesia, on a tiny uninhabited island near Komodo and Rintja, a military SAS pal and I decided we wanted to find and photograph one of the rarest reptiles on earth — a giant monitor lizard.

The island was uninhabited, for the very simple reason that the lizards are predators by

40

day and night, very efficient hunters and their flesh of preference is mammalian.

To render a man suitably immobile for easy consumption, the lizards lie in wait, use their dinosaur tail to cut his legs out from under him, then bite his belly open with one slashing swing of the head.

That technique has been well documented, and seldom varies.

Real estate on the island was very, very cheap.

My Australian friend and I found the claw and tail prints of a big animal on a beach beneath coconut palms near a waterfall.

We spent the afternoon tracking it through heavy, Indonesian jungle. A couple of hours before sunset, we were both exhausted and frustrated — outsmarted by a reptile? — and so returned to the beach, and our little ridged hull inflatable boat.

The monitor lizard was there waiting for us. One of the big females, eleven feet long, probably four hundred pounds, tongue probing the air experimentally, like a snake, getting the flavor of us in advance of attacking. Her eyes were black, yet seemed to glow.

She'd been shadowing us the whole time, anticipating our moves.

That's the way I felt now. Like the hunter who recognizes that he is being hunted.

Realizing that the man had to be in the tree above me caused the same sensation of adrenaline rush to move up my spine.

I turned slowly away from the big buttonwood. I wanted to give myself some space before confronting him. In military parlance, he
owned the high ground. I pretended to re-
examine his tracks, puzzled. Then I began to
take slow, small steps toward the path to my
home.

Above me, I heard limbs rustle, then a primal
grunting sound. I looked up reflexively to see a
dark, refrigerator-sized shape falling through
the limbs, dropping toward me.

chapter four

I lunged away, turning, but I didn't react quickly enough. The bulk of the man's weight caught me on the left shoulder, and sent me stumbling into the mangroves. I would have fallen, but I grabbed a mangrove branch as I was going down. Then I used it as a kind of spring to launch me back toward him.

Normally, I'm not a puncher. Punch a man in the face, and you have just as much chance of breaking your hand as you have of breaking his jaw. But I was so surprised, and the adrenaline dump was so abrupt, that I reacted without thinking. He was getting up from his knees, his shaved head turned away from me — a perfect and unexpected target — so I hit him just as hard as I could with an overhand right that should have dropped him to the ground unconscious.

It would have knocked me unconscious. It would have dropped almost *any* man I've met.

Not him. In fact, it didn't even seem to hurt him much.

He gave a little shake of his head. Then he turned his eyes toward mine, his expression slowly translating surprise into anger.

He stared at me for a moment, as if puzzled, before he said, "What the hell'd you do *that* for, Mac? You got any idea what a stupid thing it was you just did? I *hate* it when someone sucker punches me." Talking as if *I'd* attacked *him*, stringing the words together in a heavy, urbanized accent.

Then, before I had a chance to speak, he came charging at me; stuck his shoulder in my stomach like a linebacker, and began to bull me toward the water.

I was in trouble. Lots of trouble, and for a couple of reasons.

For one thing, I hadn't been working out much lately. I was, in fact, in the worst shape of my life. And he was as big as his footprints advertised. *Bigger.* Not tall, but one of the citified, double-wide models. Three or four inches under six feet, but he had to weigh close to two-fifty, two-seventy-five, with freakishly large feet and hands, and a head that could not have been supported by a normal human neck.

Men who are big and quick and hard exude a kind of physical assurance. He had it.

Something else: The guy had been a competitive wrestler — and a good one.

I knew the instant he put his hands on me. It was unmistakable. I knew because, in high school, I'd spent each and every post–football season enduring the brutal practices which that great, great sport demands. Hand control, the variations of classic takedowns and reversals, had all been pounded into my skull by a brilliant wrestling coach named Gary Freis. The moment you hook up with another man in any kind of physical conflict, a wrestler instantly recognizes another wrestler.

This guy had had a pretty good coach himself — unsettling news.

As he pushed me into the water, I used his own momentum to duck under his right armpit, and come up behind him. When I grabbed his throat to take control, though he slapped his huge hand on mine. Then, instead of trying to pull away as expected, he pushed his body back into mine, prying my hand loose as he moved.

Suddenly, he was behind me, his left arm levered under mine, using the back of my head as a fulcrum, his right leg trying to grapevine between my legs.

As I grunted in pain, he said into my ear, breathing heavily, "You want to get nasty, asshole? I'll *show* you nasty."

What I'd learned in those few first seconds was disturbing.

The guy was stronger than I — no question — plus he had to be thirty, maybe forty, pounds heavier. He had those raccoon kind of fingers, steel within hard rubber, that move like tiny, independent little animals, and are nearly impossible to escape.

Something deep inside was telling me to stop, give it up, surrender — but not just because he was capable of beating me; even killing me.

No.

My inner voice and its reasoning were all too familiar: I no longer trust myself in a fight. Simple as that. I can no longer rely on the control I once pretended to have over my own cold temper.

Yet I couldn't quit. Old habit.

Instead, I tried to relax my body, hoping to give him the impression I was quitting. When I felt his grip ease ever so slightly, I swung my hips to the right, then somersaulted forward into the knee-deep water as hard as I could throw my body.

It was enough to break me free. But not for long. He was instantly on me as I tried to get to my feet, pulling me, then turning me with a very effective arm drag.

Then he was behind me again, his left arm wrapped around my throat, the hard edge of his forearm digging into my Adam's apple, severing the flow of oxygen between mouth and lungs.

It is the most basic — and the most effective — of submission holds, and if I didn't find a way to break it, he could hold me there until I was unconscious. Or brain-damaged. Or dead.

"You want to keep dancing, asshole? Or you ready to quit?"

I hammered my head backward. Felt it glance off his nose; heard a woof of pain. It loosened his grip enough for me to drive my elbow into his stomach, but he managed to keep his forearm locked on my throat.

That was the end. All I could do. All I could stand without replenishing the oxygen supply, and I knew it. The world was getting fuzzy, and not just because my glasses were now hanging uselessly, tied around my neck with fishing line.

My head was tilted skyward and I watched the April sunset clouds turn gray, then rainbow-streaked as I began to slip into unconsciousness. . . .

Then I heard: "Oh . . . shit. Oh-h-h-h-h *shit-t-t-t!*"

Was I imagining the distress in his voice?

No . . . because suddenly, I was free. For no reason whatsoever, he released his grip, allowing me to collapse into the shallow water.

I got shakily to my feet, touching fingers to my bruised Adam's apple, pulse roaring in my ears, as I put on my glasses.

Skinhead had already waded to shore where, inexplicably, he was now on his knees at the base of the buttonwood tree that had once been his hiding place.

He seemed to be coughing, making a weird barking sound. It took me a confusing few seconds to understand what he was doing.

He was vomiting, using the tree to steady himself, heaving violently. We've all experienced it: When you're that nauseated, you are absolutely focused on the intensity of stomach spasms, and therefore helpless.

What had I done to cause him to vomit? There was a touch of blood beneath his nose. Otherwise, he was unmarked. Had I somehow caught him in the solar plexus, or the testicles? It made no sense.

As I walked toward him, he held his hand up like a flag, palm out and waving: a universal signal of surrender. He was done; too sick to fight anymore.

Breathing heavily, feeling sick myself, I turned my back to him and waited. I could see Sally crossing the scrim of kitchen window, still busy doing something, almost frenetic in her body movement.

The way she moved seemed out of character — just as some of the things she'd said, her speech patterns, were different.

More indications that my friend had changed.

"Why the hell'd you hit me, Mac? There wasn't no reason for you to coldcock me like that."

The man was still on his knees, pale-faced and leaning against the tree, taking long, slow breaths.

I said, "Are you kidding? You jump on me from a tree and don't expect me to fight back?"

"Jump you? I didn't *jump*, dumbass, I *fell*.

Slipped off that wet limb 'cause I was so surprised to see you down there. Next thing I know, you're taking a swing at me. Just my luck, too — about a billion acres of swamp in this shithole of a state, and I gotta land on a fucking wrestler."

Was he serious? Yeah, he seemed to be sincere, talking in his big-city accent: New York with a touch of New Jersey. Some kind of hybrid combination; almost a parody, it seemed, of a 1940s tough-guy movie. *I didden jump dumm azzz. . . .* The mobster talking to Bogart about a Maltese falcon.

He had a big, wide, citified face, too: Mediterranean skin — Italian blood showing — with birdlike, golden eyes set deep beneath a heavy brow, darker with his head shaved bare. I also noted that his fingernails were thick, pitted like opaque oysters, a condition known as onchomycosis, which is a fungal disease, often associated with people who have their hands in water a lot, or who use steroids. The fungus spores attach themselves beneath the nail, and begin to feed on the nail's cells. Tough to get rid of.

The guy definitely did not fish for a living so, judging from his size, he'd gotten into bodybuilding, juicing himself with shots or pills to get bigger. Maybe.

I listened to him ask, "Where'd you wrestle college, Mac?"

I said, "High school. That was it."

"No way. You had to go further. Or you were a blue-chipper. Nothing national?" He seemed to be marking time, speaking but focusing inward, testing all the internal sensors, unsure if he was going to be sick again. He punctuated every few words by spitting weakly, then sniffing.

"My junior and senior years, I did the AAU tournament in Iowa."

He said, "That explains it. I did that tournament three times, which means you had to be a state champ or you wouldn't'a been invited. You make the finals? Maybe we wrestled before."

I took a few steps and leaned against a nearby black mangrove, relaxing a little. "Nope. Lost in the quarters. I was way out of my league."

He made a baritone gurgling sound, his stomach momentarily spasming, but then he slowly smiled. "Most guys, they have excuses. Tore up their knee or popped a shoulder. But you say it right out loud: just not good enough. I'll tell you something though, Mac. If you made it to the quarterfinals in that tournament, you were good enough. *Plenty* good enough."

I waited a few moments, looking at him, before I said. "You didn't have much trouble beating me."

"The hell I didn't. I wrestled two years college, then three years in the military. I thought you'd be one of those bookworm saps, never

50

been in a fight in his life. Jesus Christ, that was a hell of a Granby you threw. Shocked the shit out of me."

"And you nailed me with one of the best arm drags ever. So it's a mutual-admiration society, except for one little thing. You've been following a friend of mine, and you're scaring her. That's why I came out here — to talk, not to fight." I paused. "You really did fall out of that tree?"

"Uh-huh. What? You think I'm dumb enough to fucking *jump* fifteen, twenty-feet? I climbed up there to get a better angle on your windows — to use those things." He nodded toward the rubber-coated binoculars lying in the mud near some kind of complicated, battery-assisted monocular. Both were camo-coated, the sort of instruments sold in hunters' catalogues. "When I fell, I 'bout busted my nuts on that limb. Climbing a tree in a rainstorm — that's one I need to cross off the list."

I said, "Why the monocular?"

I expected him to dodge the question. He didn't. Like it was no big deal, he told me that the monocular had a passive, infrared motion detector that was triggered by an animal's — or a man's — body heat.

I said, "So you knew I was looking for you, coming through the mangroves."

"Hell, no. You surprised the crap out of me. Once you got in your boat and pulled away, I forgot all about you. Pretty slick move, Mac."

"But *why?* Why're you tailing her?"

He sniffed and spat, thinking about it. "Tailing Mrs. Minster," he said.

"Yes. Sally Minster."

"It's because I'm a private investigator, that's why. A company hired me to keep an eye on the lady, so it's a job-of-work. Nothing personal. She's got nothing to be scared of — not from me, anyway."

His inflection told me more than his words. I said, "You're following her because of her husband. Is that right?"

He shrugged, maybe in affirmation.

I said, "Okay, so I'm guessing it's his life insurance company you're working for. They hired you because they don't believe he's dead. If you follow her long enough, you're thinking she's going to lead you to him."

The man looked up at me briefly. "Just because we both spent time on the mat doesn't mean we're pals. I wouldn't tell you if I could. So stop askin'. Your lady friend isn't in any danger from me, Mac. That's all you need to know."

I told him my name was Ford, not "Mac," before adding, "Then there's something *you* need to know. It might be helpful to your employer, too. My friend Sally doesn't think her husband's dead, either. She's the one who stands to inherit the insurance money — presumably quite a bit of money — but she still doesn't think he's dead. She's not going to take

52

you to him, because she doesn't know where he is."

When I saw the mild look of surprise register on his face, I added, "Instead of sneaking around following her, why don't you just talk to her? You might save yourself some time."

He started to reply, but then stopped, his eyes widening. Speaking softly and very quickly, he said, "Man oh man, I feel like hell. You ever try chewing tobacco, that goddamn snuff? Copenhagen. First time I ever put that garbage in my mouth was just before you showed up. When you head-butted me, I swallowed the crap. All of it. Mac, I don't think I've . . . I've ever felt so sick . . . so damn sick in my life. *Oh-h-h-h-hhh.*"

I turned away and waited while, once again, the man began to heave.

chapter five

He was private investigator Frank DeAntoni, who'd twice made it to the Olympic trials wrestling for the Air Force before joining the NYPD, making detective, and then, a year ago, opening his own firm in Coral Gables.

"Why not?" he told me. "First my mom passed away, then my dad, and then my girlfriend dumped me. So why am I gonna stick around the city? 'Cause I got a great aunt who lives in Jersey? I was *outta* there, Mac."

He sat on the first step of the wooden boardwalk that leads to my house, fanning himself with one huge hand, his face still a pale and sickly gray. His blue raincoat was draped over the railing. He wore a black Polo shirt tucked into the black slacks, both of them stained with muck and sand.

He'd told me a little about himself during our slow walk out of the mangroves. I'd told him a little about myself. When he showed me his identification — an old NYPD badge and new business card — I looked at the card, saying, "Shouldn't there be a drawing of an eye on this thing? Like in the old movies?"

To which he replied, smiling painfully, "Fuck you, Mac. I'm puking my guts out, and you play comedian."

We were of a comparable age. Another similarity was that, as former wrestlers, we'd both worn our headgear religiously. No telltale scarred ears.

"I've never been what you'd call pretty anyway," he explained.

I replied, "There's another thing we have in common."

"Wrestling all those years," he added, "my shoulders, my knees are all so screwed up, I've been having to take steroids. But it's been getting better. I've been working out a lot, making the muscles strong enough to help out the bad joints. Even so, I'm going to be sore as shit tomorrow."

"Me, too," I told him.

Now he sat, holding a bottle of water he'd retrieved from his car, trying to recover, his stomach moving with rapid, shallow breaths.

Why had he chosen this day to try chewing tobacco?

I'd asked him a couple of times.

The only answer I'd received was cryptic: "It's 'cause of my work. We talk, let's see how it goes, maybe I'll tell you. But damned if I'm gonna try snuff again. The crap smells like horse piss and tastes worse."

Groaning sounds. He was still making lots of weary groaning, gurgling noises.

Once, he looked at me and sniffed. "Jesus Christ, is that you who stinks? I thought it was fuckin' swamp gas or something."

I hadn't changed clothes since returning from Tomlinson's swamp ape expedition, and the khakis and T-shirt I wore were still coated with mud, burrs, flakes of duck weed and cow dung, plus the oily residue of something else.

"A skunk," I told him. "I just got back from the Everglades, and I haven't had a chance to shower yet. I got sprayed by a skunk."

"You're shittin' me. I think I saw one in a zoo once. You see 'em squashed on the roads. What makes 'em stink so bad?"

I answered, "They have two musk glands inside their anus. They produce an oil, a chemical compound called *thiol*, which is the same thing that makes a rotten egg stink. They lift their tail and shoot the oil out of their butt."

DeAntoni moaned softly, picturing it. "Their fuckin' anus," he said miserably. He sniffed again, then tried to cover his nose, but it was too much for him to handle.

He was sick once more.

I walked to the marina, got a bucket of ice. By the time I got back, DeAntoni seemed to be feeling better. He rubbed the ice on the back of his neck, as I told him again, "If you're trying to get information on Geoff Minster, it might make sense for you and Sally to sit down and talk. If she's willing."

56

"Hell, yes, I want to talk to her. What do you think the chances are?"

"Give me ten, fifteen minutes and I'll let you know."

He said, "Let's make it an hour. I want to go get a hotel room, get cleaned up first. Brush my teeth, at least. Man, it's like a case of food poisoning I had once. Got some bad mussels in Palm Beach. I heaved so hard it gave me hemorrhoids. Those things, they really itch bad. Hated 'em."

I said, "Okay, an hour. But, before I talk to Sally, I need more information."

He looked at me. "What're you, her fuckin' attorney or something?"

"No, I'm her friend. You give a little, we'll give a little. What's the name of the company that hired you?"

"Whoa, whoa, not so fast, Mac. 'Til we get to know each other, let's talk in whatta-you-call-it . . . generalities."

"Generalities about what?"

"Just listen for a minute, okay? Who knows, maybe you'll learn something." When I didn't reply, he said, "Let me ask you this: You know anything about insurance? About how the companies work?"

I said, "You could fill books with what I don't know about insurance. I'm already assuming you're working for an insurance company."

"You assume anything your little heart desires. But at least it gives us a place to start. Okay . . . what a lot of people don't realize, the way it works with life insurance is, there's a thing called an 'incontestability clause.' A man pays his premiums on time for two years or more, that's when this clause kicks in. The companies never notify you, it's just there. Like in the small print. You know about it?"

"Nope."

I was leaning against a mangrove, looking northward across the bay. It was sunset, now, around 8 P.M.

Through the limbs, the music was louder, the marina's speakers playing Jim Morris singing "Captain Jack is comin' back . . . ," the Friday party just getting under way.

He said, "Insurance bullshit, yeah, I know, boring as hell. But when I decided to open my own agency, I had to learn about it because, let's face it, doing investigations for them is where the money is."

"So you *are* working for an insurance company."

"Damn it, stop *pushing*. I didn't say that. Just shut your hole and listen for a few minutes."

I smiled. All the profanity, the way he used it as punctuation, made the guy oddly amusing, even likable.

"Okay . . ." He paused, getting back on track. ". . . yeah, incontestability clause. What that means is, if you, me, *anybody*, if we pay our premiums for more than two years, just about no matter how we die, the company's still got to pay off.

"Let's say I got cancer and I know it. So I get some — name a company — some Mutual of Omaha agent to write me a ten-million-buck life insurance policy, but never say a word about being sick. They make me take a physical, blood tests, all that bullshit. But if they miss the cancer, and write the policy anyway, all I got to do is survive for the next twenty-four months, and they still got to pay, even though I tricked them.

"Suicide?" he said. "Same thing. I get an agent to write me a big policy, then I make my payments like a good boy." He used his index finger and thumb to imitate a revolver, touching it to his temple, his thumb hammering down. "Seven hundred and thirty-one days later, I can take the Smith & Wesson cure for insomnia, and they still got to pay off. I leave my wife and kiddies rich, and no more sleepless nights for me."

I said, "I didn't know that. I'd always heard that insurance companies won't pay off on suicides."

"That's what almost everybody thinks 'cause that's what they *want* the public to think. Guys would be popping themselves left and right. But it ain't true."

"Are you saying that you think there's a chance Minster intentionally drowned himself?"

DeAntoni shook his head, then rolled it experimentally, stretching the neck muscles, and I could hear vertebrae pop — a mannerism common to wrestlers and football players. "What I'm asking myself is why I should tell you anything. That's a beautiful lady in there. Maybe you two are in on it. Maybe you *wanted* hubby to disappear."

I stared at him for a long, focused moment before saying softly, "I'm telling myself the reason I'm not going to knock the nose off your face is because it's already been broken too many times. But it might really be because I know I'd get my nose broken in return."

He smiled. His turn to be amused. "So you and the lady got nothing secret going on. Men and women, there are only two kinds of friendship: vertical and horizontal. Yours is vertical. That's what you're telling me."

"For the record, it's none of your damn business. But the answer is no, the lady and I have nothing going on."

He sniffed, took a big breath, smiling, and stood. "Okay, okay. Sometimes you got to trust your gut. So I take it back. You don't strike me as the sneaky type. More important than that, she's not the sneaky type. Mind if I tell you something weird?"

"Go ahead," I said. "Weird is something I'm used to. Spend enough time around this marina, you'll understand."

"The weird thing is, I been following her for

a couple of weeks now. She goes to church, she stops and helps these two or three elderly people, brings them food. She goes to the poor neighborhoods and plays with the little kiddies. She works at a local animal shelter. I mean, she's like a fuckin' saint. And pretty, too — not prissy pretty, but kind'a outdoorsy." He stopped for a moment. "What'd you say your name is again?"

I told him.

"Thing is, Ford, she seems okay. As a *person*, understand." He leaned toward me slightly, lowering his voice. "She's been seeing a shrink, you know. Which is too bad, for someone nice as her. All because her asshole hubby decided to disappear."

I said, "So I'll ask again. Do you think he's still alive?"

With his shoulders, DeAntoni gave me a noncommittal reply. "Maybe. It could be I got a picture someone sent that maybe proves it. That's what the insurance company's paying me to do. Check it out."

"You have a photograph of her husband taken *after* he supposedly drowned."

"Um-huh, one of those glossy digital print-outs. Geoff Minster, the big shot, the rich business dude kicked back on some tropical beach, a beer in his hand and a real pretty girl beside him. One of those dark Latin types in a thong bikini."

"Mind if I see it?"

"Depends. Maybe we can do a trade. This is *business*, understand. You work it so I can interview the lady, I'll let you both see the picture."

I told him, "Go get your hotel room, come back in an hour. I'll let you know."

I returned to the house to find Sally busy cleaning. It is not something one expects of visitors. She'd found a brush, had made a bucket of sudsy water and was scrubbing away at my sink and the counter where I prepare food. The house smelled of Clorox and Pine-Sol.

She turned to look as I opened the screen door, and said, "Are you okay? I was worried about you."

"I'm fine. He's a private investigator. He'll be back to talk with you later tonight. If you're willing."

She asked if he got mad when I caught him; if he'd given me a hard time. I gave her an abbreviated account of our meeting, minus the fight and the photo.

"How'd you get so muddy? Whew! You kinda stink, too."

"I'll explain later."

"Is he out there now?"

"No. We've got about an hour."

She returned to her scrubbing. "Good. I'm almost done."

I stared at her, perplexed, as she returned to her work. "Sally? *Sally*. What're you doing? The kitchen may be a little messy, but I'll take care of it. You used to kid me about it, what a neat-freak I am. Remember? I keep this kitchen the same way I keep my lab. Spotless."

Which was a lie. I'd kept the lab up to standards, but, the last six months or so ago, I'd been slipping, doing less and less housework, less and less laundry.

She said, "I'm happy to help. All the beer cans? I put them in your recycle bin."

She continued to scrub as she added, "No offense, but this kitchen isn't what *I'd* call spotless. You've got cobwebs in the corners, grease everywhere. And it could use some paint. Plus some new furniture."

Once again, her voice had a troubled, manic quality that was disconcerting. Made the little hairs on the back on my neck stand up like hackles.

She was still kneeling, so I leaned and placed my hand gently around her left arm. The cinnamon blouse had a silky quality. Her skin was cooler than the April air.

"Sally. I want you to stop now. *Please*. Have a seat. There's no need for you to clean my house. It's not . . . it's not an appropriate thing for you to be doing."

The word *appropriate* seemed to key in her an involuntary response that was like a mixture of distress and comprehension. I watched her glazed eyes clear momentarily, and she touched a hand to her mouth.

"Oh my Lord, I'm doing *it* again. I'm so sorry. My therapist has been working with me — we're doing biofeedback; some hypnosis. She's trying to help me condition myself to recognize the symptoms and stop myself before the behavior takes control. Inappropriate behavior. That's what I'm trying my best to stop."

I was still holding her arm, feeling the gooseflesh sensation that accompanies alarm. I said gently, "What behavior?"

She stood, her expression gloomy, vulnerable. "Something happened to me. I'm not the same person you used to know. They call it manic behavior. Or obsessive. I might even be bipolar, but my therapist wants to get some other opinions before she commits to that diagnosis. I get my mind fixed on something, and I completely lose control. I can clean for hours. Or sew. Or . . . or pray."

I said softly, "Pray?"

She nodded. "I can tell you about it, if you want."

"I want."

"Okay. Well . . . about three years back, Geoff and I began a hard time in our marriage — it was around the time you called and invited me to Guava Key. You don't know how close I came to saying yes."

I said, "I remember."

"You never met him, but he was one of the biggest developers in Dade County. All he thought about was his business. And he was so critical. I just couldn't do enough. I wasn't sociable enough, smart enough. *Pretty* enough.

"He worked twelve, fourteen hours a day, just pushing and pushing until I think something in him finally broke." She stopped for a moment, thinking about it. "Not long after that, something happened to me, too."

"How so?" I asked.

"Geoff — Mr. Dade County Entrepreneur of the Year — got involved with a cult religious group. I've read enough about it to call it a 'cult' now. You've heard probably of it: the International Church of Ashram Meditation. Everyone has. The founder — the guy gave me the creeps from day one — calls himself Bhagwan Shiva, supposedly some kind of charismatic prophet."

She said, "He's got Ashram Centers all over the world, plus a big compound on Palm Beach. You do know who I'm talking about, don't you?"

I said, "He's the one who collects expensive cars, right?"

"Rolls-Royces, yes."

"I read something about his group trying to take control of some western town a few years back."

"Exactly. He sends his followers to live in a small town, enough of them so they become a voting majority. Then they take over the place. Literally. They change the zoning laws, build whatever they want, *do* whatever they want. He did it in Washington State, Alabama, now he's doing it in Florida."

I was nodding. "I know who you mean."

"The Church of Ashram, that's the group Geoff got involved with. He met Shiva at some Palm Beach fund-raiser. At the time, we were having cash-flow problems — later, I can tell you about the housing developments we were building. Shiva's group got financially involved. In a big way, they got involved.

"Next thing I know, my husband was attending Shiva's lectures, taking classes, going to meetings. Then he joined the church. I don't know how many tens of thousands of dollars he gave them, how much property. But it was a lot."

Sally told me that, worse, Geoff insisted that she join him in the church and go through what she called "Introductory Auditing."

"It was like hell," she told me. "They kept us awake day and night, screaming at us, making us memorize Shiva's prophecies, telling us all that we were worthless. I was nobody, nothing. Over and over, they shouted that into my head. That we were dead people. *Meaningless.*"

I noticed that her voice was trembling, on the verge of tears, as she added, "I spent a month listening to it. Finally, I couldn't take it anymore."

I was still holding her arm; had finally stopped her from using the scrub brush. I said,

"Calm down. You're getting upset. There's no need."

"It makes me so furious!"

"I understand. Take all the time you need. Have a seat — stop cleaning, *please*. I'll fix myself a drink, then we can sit down and talk about it."

I felt her eyes on me as I half-filled a tumbler with Nicaraguan rum, added ice, juice from a whole key lime, and topped it with seltzer water.

The marina's black cat, Crunch & Des, sat next to me on the outdoor teak table between two rockers, on the northeastern side of my porch. It's the portion of porch that hangs over my shark pen, and looks out over the bay.

Unseen below us, beneath dark water, two bull sharks and a smaller, seventy-pound hammerhead circled. They were always moving.

The cat was close enough that I could reach over and scratch his ears if I wanted to. He'd never been an affectionate cat, but, in the last half year, he'd become more attentive toward me. Spent more time following me around the house than he did hanging out by the marina's fish-cleaning table.

Unusual.

I'd dismissed Tomlinson's explanation out of hand ("You're fighting demons and he wants to provide comfort") but it *was* nice having the cat around more. Crunch & Des was good company. Tail twitching, he liked to lie on the stainless-steel dissecting table in my lab, beneath the rows of bubbling aquarium tanks, and stare down octopi.

I scratched the cat's ears now, sipping my drink. I'd given Sally the abbreviated version of my encounter with Frank DeAntoni, and told her that he was interested in talking to her. Didn't mention the photo.

While we waited, I sat quietly and let her vent. Told her I'd have one drink before showering, so it was a good time to help me catch up on what had happened in her life. It was a nice night to play the patient, friendly ear. A southern breeze, water-dense, weighted with salt and iodine, drifted out of the shadows while the rim of the moon ascended above mangroves.

I listened to her say, "At first with Geoff, our marriage was pretty good. We live — we *lived* — in Coconut Grove, just off Bayshore, a great view of Biscayne Bay. This little gated community called Ironwood. You have to cross a canal that's more like a moat, and there's not a home under four thousand square feet allowed. Luxury homes, that's the real estate term. Screened infinity pools, boatlifts, everything. Most people's dream place.

"Our next-door neighbor is a U.S. senator. Another owns part of the Dolphins. You add up all the wealth, all the political power, there's no place in Florida that probably compares."

She said, "When my husband got involved with Shiva, he would stand around at parties, barbecues, whatever, telling our neighbors how great Shiva was. *That's* when invitations started dropping off, potential investors started avoiding us. Then our whole business operation began to slide right into the tank."

I said, "The more your husband promoted the cult leader, the more he became dependent on the cult leader's money."

I watched her smile as she lifted the mug of tea to her lips. "Marion Ford. Back when I was a little girl, and you were the big, star high-school jock, people used to say you were strange because you collected bugs and fish and all kinds of stuff. But I always stuck up for you. I told them it was because you were so smart, not weird. My opinion hasn't changed."

Smart? I felt an urge to tell her: *I've done so many stupid things in the recent past that it's laughable.* Instead, I said, "You both went through the organization's programming process. Geoff broke, you didn't. Any idea why?"

She thought for a moment. "I think he was on the verge of a nervous breakdown. He was vulnerable. It was awful, those three weeks. They just about killed my self-confidence. My therapist says it may take me years to recover. But I never gave in because . . . I'm not *sure* why. I used to think I was a fairly strong person. Not the smartest, but fairly bright —"

I said, "You were a strong person. You still

69

are. And you're among the brightest people I know. So there's my answer. You were too strong to be brainwashed. Congratulations."

"It was more than that, Doc. I think . . . I think *God* was there. I think He helped me and I didn't even know it. That's why I pray so much. Even now. You asked me, so I'm going to tell you."

She said, "You've been to Coconut Grove, south Miami. It's kind of an old Bohemian kind of village, so it changes every couple of blocks. That's one of the reasons I love it.

"The reason I know God was with me is, not far from our house, three blocks off Dixie Highway, there's this little Pentecostal church. A couple of days after I got out of Shiva's compound, a Sunday afternoon, I was about at the end of my rope. I was alone, wandering around like a crazy person, and I heard an organ. It was like angels playing. I followed the music to a two-room church. Inside, I could hear people singing. I walked in — just like someone's hand was steering me.

"It's a poor church. Mostly Haitians, Cuban refugee types and poor whites. But that little church changed my life. I've never felt such unconditional love. It became my lifeline, Reverend Wilson and his wife, the whole congregation. Lots of clapping and dancing and hugging. That pretty little white church is still my favorite place in the world."

Sally had been staring at the deck as she

spoke, but now she looked up at me with eyes that were shadowed, dark. "Look, Doc, I know that lots of people make fun of religion. Us Born-Again types. We maybe scare them for some reason. But it's changed my life. I think it saved my life."

I smiled at her, as I said, "A person who makes fun of anyone's religion lacks the brains to be taken seriously."

"It doesn't bother you that I've accepted Jesus as my savior? That I've changed?"

Yes, it bothered me that she'd changed, but only because her transformation exceeded any new passion for religion. There was pathology involved — to what degree, I didn't yet know. But I told her, "We're friends. So, no, it makes no difference. Right now, I'm more concerned with why you're here. Something weird's going on, or the insurance company wouldn't have hired DeAntoni to follow you."

Her eyes widened slightly. "My gosh, I'd already forgotten him. He's going to be here soon, right?"

"If you want to talk to him, yes. If you don't, no problem. I'll send him away."

She said, "That's another symptom, by the way. More inappropriate behavior. A bad memory, a short attention span."

She walked across the deck, retrieved her purse from a teak table and checked her watch. "No wonder," she said. "I forgot to take my medication. The doctor's been giving me

Neurontin, plus some Valium. That's how bad Shiva's group screwed me up. *Shiva*. I even hate the sound of his name."

Her smile seemed too theatrical, her laughter too loud, as she added, "But the pills can't work if Miss Forgetful doesn't remember to take her meds on schedule!"

chapter six

izzy

Lying on a table in a steam room built of herbal wood and tile, Shiva opened his eyes, lifted his left arm toward his eyes and looked at a bare wrist.

He'd dozed during the massage, and now remembered: His watch was outside, on the vanity.

To the oldest of the three women attending to him, he said, "Sister Mary, please check. What time is it?"

The women were naked beneath white robes, but Mary still wore her rubber Timex.

"It's a little after six, Teacher."

Shiva closed his eyes again, relaxing. The office at his Ashram Center in downtown San Francisco closed at five on Fridays, and he had a conference call scheduled with the office manger and two advisors at four-fifteen Pacific time. The *Sacramento Bee* had just published the last of a scathing, three-part series on the International Church of Ashram Meditation Center, in which three former women disciples claimed they had been drugged with something, then raped by "one

73

or more church leaders."

There were quotes from the L.A. County District Attorney's Office promising an investigation, and quotes from an IRS spokesman saying that the personal files of Bhagwan Shiva and the files of the San Francisco Ashram were already being subpoenaed.

Devastating.

But they hadn't ruined him yet, The American legal system, Shiva knew, was a calculator of wile, not a scale of justice, and it could be manipulated — if you had enough money.

He needed cash. Lots of cash. He knew how to get it.

Shiva stretched, irked by yet another problem. He had about an hour before the conference call, then he had to meet with Izzy again, go over some details. So why not enjoy the little bit of free time? One of the maxims he required all initiates to learn was a favorite: *Grasp the moment and you will capture eternity.*

Something to relax him, that's what he needed. Something beyond a massage.

To Mary, he said, "My sister, please tell me. This person, the pale blonde —" He used his finger to point at a girl who could have been sixteen, could have been twenty. "Is she new? I don't remember seeing her in the compound. What's her name?"

When the blonde began to answer, "I'm Kirsten Williams from Lauderdale —," she was shouted down by the older woman, who yelled,

"You may *not* address Shiva directly. Have you already forgotten? Until you finish Basic Auditing, you're not even *alive*."

"Temper, my dear Mary," Shiva said. "Learn patience. Be patient, and our cause will be stronger."

The older woman bowed at the waist, touching both palms to her forehead — an ancient gesture of deference. "I know, Teacher. But I work so hard with these new ones. It's like my words bounce off their idiotic heads."

To the blonde, Shiva said, "You have not yet been given a name."

Sister Mary said, "She is worthless, so she is nameless. It will be another three weeks before she has earned a name."

"How did she come to us?"

"Another runaway. Tired of the imaginary world, no place else to go."

"Have the parents tried to find her? Or friends?"

"The father came twice. We sent him away."

Shiva addressed the girl. "I give you permission to speak to me. Are you happy here?"

"I . . . I think so."

"Do you understand that I care more for you now, about your happiness and spiritual contentment, than your mother or your father ever cared?"

"Yes . . . I'd like to believe that."

Shiva said, "Please remove your robe."

He watched the girl hesitate, then pull the

white robe over her head, willing but self-conscious. He looked at her for a few moments, smiling, before he said, "God has given you a beautiful body. It's a gift to be shared. Your breasts — like white pears tipped with berries. My body desires my hands to touch them. Come closer, girl."

Averting her eyes, the pale blonde moved uneasily from Bhagwan Shiva's feet to his side, her breathing slightly more rapid as the man's long fingers moved up the ridges of her ribs, and touched the underside of her right breast. Then he squeezed her left breast, fingers creating streaks of sweat on the swollen curvature of flesh.

His tone still conversational, he said to Mary, "What level are you now running in your search for enlightenment?"

"I'm at Level Three. I hope to soon advance."

"Excellent," said the Bhagwan.

He looked at the older woman. She'd been his bed partner many times. Though she was never outwardly jealous of other disciples, having her so close was taking the pleasure out of touching the blonde.

"Sister Mary," he said. "Please take your assistant and leave me with this nameless thing."

Two hours later, showered, dressed in white linen, sitting at the desk in his bedroom office,

Shiva listened to Izzy say, "I've decided on two explosions, not three. Each one a chain of several smaller blasts. For *effect*, I'm saying. That's why I came back, to let you know."

Shiva said, "*You* decided."

"That's right, me. I decided. Two's risky enough. I've done the research. I can explain it if you want. Two blasts, seven days, maybe fourteen days apart — no longer. Then I'm out of here."

Using great patience to emphasize his sarcasm, Shiva said, "Do you mind if I know the dates? I should probably know the dates — since I'm risking the future of my entire *fucking organization*."

Used to Shiva, his bullying, Izzy remained composed. "Just give me the word. Sunday, if you want. Day after tomorrow. The first will be small. A series of three or four minor blasts — we don't want too much attention. The second will be the big boom. Earthquake in the Everglades."

The reality of it — it was going to *happen* — startled Shiva. He'd been thinking about the illusion for three years; planning, doing the groundwork, seeding it in people's minds for more than two years.

Now here it was. He said to Izzy, "You're serious."

"Yep. Serious as an undertaker. Did it all by my lonesome, no witnesses, no helpers, no baggage."

Izzy had been busy during his month away, on the road.

Shiva said the word softly — *Sunday* — then louder, showing some enthusiasm. "Okay. *Okay.* Day after tomorrow. April thirteenth, that's Palm Sunday, isn't it? I *like* that. The sooner we do it, the sooner I see results."

Izzy told him fine, invite any of the Seminole and Miccosukee bigshots who would still take his phone calls.

Shiva said, "No, I'm done with them. To hell with those assholes, they treat me like a disease. I'm not trying anymore. Billie Egret's people. The Egret Seminoles, her aunts and uncles. They're the important ones."

Shiva thought for a moment, concentrating, before he added, "We'll let the first blast be a surprise. They're out there in the 'Glades, not thinking about it, when they feel the earth shake. The second time, though, that's when we make sure they're at Sawgrass."

Izzy told him, okay, invite Billie Egret and her relatives, anybody he wanted. Told him to get a couple hundred of his Ashram disciples, too — a thousand if he could — at his resort in the Everglades.

He said, "You start your group meditation. Use the breath drummers, all the bells and whistles. I'll detonate whatever time you say. Morning's good. Cameras going. Act surprised. Then like you *knew* it was going to happen — all that spiritual power focused. You're good with facial expressions. Like a politician."

Shiva said, "I don't have to give any hints. It's prophecy. Seminole prophecy from Tecumseh."

Izzy said, "What*ever*. I leave all that to you. Best-case scenario, they accept you as the real deal. Worst case, you're the victim of another eco-terrorist attack. Public sympathy. Either way, the timing's important."

Shiva was nodding, "Yes, timing . . . which is why I'm thinking . . . what I'd *prefer* to do is make it later in the day. This time of year, we might get an afternoon storm. Lightning would be nice. Lots of lightning and thunder." Shiva paused. "That far away from the blast site, will we hear the explosion?"

"I'm setting it a half mile or so from the resort, but it's all underground. So a rumble maybe, not much. I'm *guessing*. I'm new at faking earthquakes, so who knows?"

"But we'll *feel* it. On the reservations, the Miccosukee and the Seminole, *they'll* feel it?"

Izzy said, "Oh, they'll feel it. At Brighton and Big Cypress, twenty, thirty miles away. A little tingle through the ankles. The National Seismic Network has a monitoring station in Orlando, and the University of Florida has a teledyne, a seismograph, in the 'Glades near Flamingo. Their equipment picks up quarry blasts. So you'll have proof. No one can say it was mass hypnosis, any of that bullshit."

On Shiva's desk were the notes he'd made during his conference call with his San Francisco people.

It had not gone well. They could not speak openly, of course — he had reason to believe that the Feds were monitoring his phone calls. But Shiva could hear the fear in the Ashram manager's voice when he asked, *"Do you know what the average prison sentence is in California for rape?"*

Shiva got the clear impression that the manager would choose to turn state's evidence against the Ashram rather than fight a felony charge.

Shiva looked at his notes briefly, then pushed them aside. He said, "Izzy, there's one thing you need to understand here. We've got to make this work. Nothing — absolutely nothing — we can't let *anything* get in our way."

Izzy was sitting on an orange sofa that had carved teak armrests: elephants and jackals. He'd changed clothes. Was now wearing dress slacks, a satin dinner jacket, black-and-white loafers, his hair blow-dried and sprayed in place.

Coming into the room, he'd checked his watch: eight-fifteen. He wanted to wrap this up; hit the Friday night meat markets, have a few drinks and do some dancing.

Or maybe drive down to Coconut Grove, hop in the boat and check out Sally Minster's house, see if she really had gone to Sanibel.

The woman liked to walk around her bedroom in bra and panties; no idea someone could watch her from the water. He liked the thought of that.

Plus, he'd installed the two minicameras in her bedroom. Those videos could be *interesting*.

Sitting comfortably, showing how relaxed he was, Izzy replied, "I'm not letting anything get in my way, Jerry. I've got a lot on the line myself."

Shiva said, "That means communication between the two of us is damned important."

Izzy waited, thinking, *Oh, shit, here we go again*.

"I'm impressed with what you've got going, all the planning you've done, but I'm going to be frank. I don't like the idea of you changing plans without even consulting me."

"That's what I'm doing now. Consulting —"

"No, no you're not. You're *telling* me. Two blasts, not three. In eighteen eleven, when Tecumseh prophesied the Mississippi earthquakes, there was a series of tremors —"

"Yeah, well, I don't much care about what some dead Indian predicted two hundred years ago." Izzy held both palms out, getting peeved. "You don't need to know all the details, Jerry. I don't *want* you to know the details. I have people in the right places. The whole thing's set. So just take my word for it."

Raising his voice, Shiva said, "*I* make the decisions in this organization —"

"Not when it comes to covering my ass, you don't. You want some stooge, find yourself another guy."

Izzy fumed for a moment before he added, "Maybe it is time for me to quit. Maybe write that book I always wanted to do. Call it *Behind the Curtain with Bhagwan Shiva*. Start off with the gag where you made the one-armed girl whole again. How many people converted that night? Couple thousand? I wonder how they'd feel if they found out the truth — your one-armed miracle girl got paid a bundle . . . and so did her twin."

In barely a whisper, Shiva said, "Don't threaten me. I won't tolerate it. Other men have threatened me, other organizations, and you know what happened to them."

Izzy allowed himself to smile. "Who you think you're talking to — *Jerry?* I'm the one who *makes* it happen. Which is why you'd better be telling the truth about the money."

"You're worried? It's already been deposited into a numbered account. The trustee I've appointed —"

Izzy interrupted, "I've talked to him."

He had, too. The man's name was Carter — a banking tycoon before he'd joined the Church of Ashram and was soon elevated to Shiva's inner circle: the Circle of Twenty-eight.

To Carter, Izzy had said, "If you don't answer your cell phone the instant I call, if the account numbers aren't kosher, guess who I'm gonna come looking for first? Don't even try to hide."

Shiva referred to the money as a "bonus" not a payoff.

Izzy made a good salary working for the church. He'd invested in stocks and property. He'd done okay.

A few years back, he'd done what he'd always dreamed of: bought his own island. Made a sizable down payment, anyway. The island was in Lake Nicaragua, just a mile off the coast from Granada, a fun little town. His island was a hundred acres of palms, waterfalls, a beach so white that it hurt his eyes.

The bonus was big enough that he could pay off the island and build the house he wanted: native stone, tile roof, ceiling fans. Big enough that he could quit, hire servants, enjoy the local women, do anything he desired for a long, long time. Which meant no more hanging out at Palm Beach's Chesterfield Hotel. No more dancing at the Leopard Lounge, seducing aging socialites. No more crossing the bridge into West Palm, searching for hookers.

Which is why Izzy patiently listened to Shiva say, "All I'm telling you is, if it works, we both benefit," before he replied, "The question now is, when do you want the second blast?"

Izzy got up off the couch, adding, "You gave me some dates, if you can stop being pissed-off long enough to listen."

He pulled a spiral notebook from his inside jacket pocket, and began to read, "May second is the last day of Ridvan — that's three weeks from now, a Friday."

He looked up. "What the hell's Ridvan?"

Mulling it over, Shiva said, "A prophet, Baha, found enlightenment near Baghdad in the Garden of Ridvan. That's where God spoke about another messenger. A prophet who would usher in an era of peace for all mankind."

Izzy said, "Meaning you, of course."

Shiva wasn't listening. "May second . . . yes, that could work. It's not a well-known holiday, though. And there's a pretty long gap between it and Palm Sunday. What's the next date I gave you?"

Izzy looked at the notebook. "The eighteenth's Good Friday. A week from now. Sunday's Easter, then Shavuot — that's Jewish. Or we could wait for the Green Corn Dance in late May. You want to impress the Indians, that's the time to do it."

"We can't afford to wait."

Izzy said, "Okay. For the second blast, let's say next week, Easter Sunday, in the afternoon. Which'll give me time to make a quick flyover, make sure there're no people in the area. We'll have to postpone if there are, so maybe the Green Corn Dance can be a backup. In the area where you're building the casinos, you sometimes get airboaters, people canoeing."

Shiva was shaking his head, "No. No postponements."

Izzy had been expecting this. He said slowly, "So you want me to detonate . . . no matter *what*."

Shiva nodded emphatically: *Yes* — no more discussion.

"Ohhhh-kay. . . . which leaves one more little decision — and I mentioned this six months ago. I've read enough geology to know that an underground blast in the 'Glades — a big one — might crack the limestone plate. Limestone's delicate stuff. It could screw up some of the water system between Miami and Naples. That could bring the Feds running."

Shiva was focused on his computer, indifferent, *no big deal*. He replied, "What happens to a bunch of swamp water is the least of our worries."

Then he sealed the subject, saying, "When I go to our Sawgrass Ashram, I want the new girl with me, the blonde. Her name's Kirsten something, from Lauderdale."

Izzy began to grin — the guy was shameless. "That's going to piss off your old sweetie. What'd Mary donate, a couple hundred acres of hubby's Colorado ranch land? That's the way you want to do business?"

More controlled and formal now: "I keep

telling you: I don't run a business. This is a *religion*."

Izzy had heard him say that before. Lots of times.

At the door, remembering one last thing, he stopped and said, "That subject we discussed earlier. The woman who went to Sanibel. What if she and her friends start getting too close?"

Shiva said, "Oh yeah, her friend the old hippy bomber." Giving it a double meaning.

"Umm-huh, the eco-freak who's screwed with us before. I'm already thinking of that angle. If the guy starts sticking his nose where it doesn't belong, what we *could* do is get the two of you together. Find a way to piss him off, get him to threaten you personally. Establish a *motive*, is what I'm saying — an eco-terrorist bomber to throw to the cops just in case things go wrong."

Very calmly, in the deeper voice he used when giving sermons or making prophecy, Shiva said, "The souls of many are worth the lives of a few. Just make it happen, Izzy."

Izzy had heard him say that before, too.

chapter seven

I finished my drink, then ushered Sally inside the house, where I built another tall one. I told her to make herself at home while I got cleaned up. Then I stepped outside, and walked toward the darker, rear section of deck. A single cloud, no bigger than a house, cloaked the moon for a moment, then floated overhead. It was holding water, and it began to rain again, fat, heavy drops. My own little dark cloud hanging over just me.

It didn't affect the party going on across the water. I could hear music; and see Chinese lanterns, red, yellow and green reflecting off the bay. It was 8:20 P.M. Still early for a Friday night at Dinkin's Bay.

My shower is outdoors, a big, brass water bucket of a spray head beneath a wooden cistern, sun-heated through coiled black pipe, gravity creating sufficient pressure.

I walked through the rain, stripping my clothes off as I went, and threw them in a heap onto the deck below — I'd bag them and toss them into the marina's Dumpster later. Then I stood beneath the shower, rain slopping down from snow-peak height, warm water and cold mixing.

Tomlinson had left bottles of counterculture soap, the health-food-store variety — Dr. Bronner's Hemp & Peppermint Castile. I used it to suds away the stink and grime of what had been a weird, but occasionally interesting, four days in the Everglades.

Much to my surprise, I realized that thinking about the trip brought a little smile to my face.

Surprise because, in the last year or so, I hadn't been doing much smiling. Too many bad dreams, too many bad and haunting memories. Too many good people lost.

I am objective enough, scientist enough, to have recognized in myself an uncharacteristic slide toward clinical depression. I kept fighting it, kept thinking that, one day, the feelings of guilt and dread would dissipate.

It didn't happen.

Something else I also recognized: My increasing dependence on alcohol was symptomatic.

On this night, though, I felt better. From any objective aspect, I had reason to smile, and those reasons seemed to be accumulating.

For one thing, anyone who lives on the mangrove coast of Florida, USA, is automatically one of the luckiest souls on earth. Except for going to the 'Glades, I hadn't had to do any traveling for months, and the simple orderliness of a daily routine, awaking each morning on the bay, and doing my work, was helping me to heal.

Professionally, I was doing okay. My monograph entitled *Adaptive Behavior and Problem-Solving Aptitude of the Atlantic Octopus (Octopus vulgaris) as Compared to Selected Primates* had received national attention and was causing interesting debate.

Also, I'd been contracted by Mote Laboratory to help with the organization's massive five-year study of Charlotte Harbor — an ambitious project designed to investigate, then quantitate, the condition of an entire littoral. From sea grasses, to water quality, to fishes, dolphins and manatee, the objective was to assess the ecological health of a complex biota.

I'd been working with them on assessing the ecological role of sharks. Over many miles of sea bottom, we'd anchored forty acoustic hydrophones. They ranged from Sanibel's Tarpon Bay to well north of Boca Grande Pass. Then we'd caught a total of sixty-six sharks and fitted them with internal or external acoustic transmitters. Nineteen of the fish were bull sharks — a specialty of mine. The results were spectacular. We could now precisely follow their movements. Valuable data was piling up.

True, I'd fallen off my normally rigorous exercise routine. I no longer ran daily, swam offshore daily, nor did I lift weights two or three times a week as I have done most of my life. I'd gained some weight and I was nowhere close to

89

the level of aerobic fitness that I'm used to.

However, I *had* found a new recreational passion: windsurfing — a sport charming for its intimate relationship with wind and water, yet one that also consistently kicked my aerobic butt.

There were other good things. My cousin, Ransom Gatrell, had been dating a sane and stable bank president, Marvin Metheny, so there seemed hope the woman was going to abandon her wild ways and give monogamy a real try. Her (and my) quasi–adopted daughter/ sibling, Shanay Money, had passed her high-school equivalency test, enrolled in a local junior college and appeared to be well on her way to a productive future.

Sometimes, her old Labrador retriever, Davy Dog, would spend a night or two with me. Crunch & Des endured him, which is to say the cat ignored him, occasionally staring at him as if he were made of inexpensive glass. Nothing more.

My personal life was going okay, too. I was enjoying a relaxed, sometimes intimate relationship with Grace Walker, a Sarasota realtor friend who made no demands beyond honesty. The chemistry wasn't great, but it was comfortable.

Also, my old pal Dewey Nye had moved back into her house on Captiva. She is still one of my favorite people in the world — despite the fact that she'd been pressing me constantly to get back in shape and become her workout partner once again.

Finally, Dinkin's Bay Marina was now enjoying a new source of quirky, human theater that small, good marinas tend to generate or attract. It was, not surprisingly, thanks to Tomlinson.

Mack, the marina's owner, was the first to notice: Strangers were showing up at the front desk, with no interest in renting a boat, a canoe, hiring a guide, purchasing fresh fish or a fried conch sandwich from the seafood market. But they were very interested in *anything* Mack or anyone else around the marina could tell them about the storklike man with the hippie hair who lived aboard *No Mas*, the sailboat anchored a hundred yards beyond the docks.

"Tomlinson types," Mack told us. Meaning oddballs. "The New Age, touchy-feely kind. Strangest thing is, most of them are from Europe, Asia — faraway places. When they ask about Tomlinson, it's like they're in awe or something. Like he's a rock'n'roll star, and they've come all this way just to get a look at him."

It was an accurate description of an ever-growing number of marina visitors.

At first, the attention surprised Tomlinson. He handled it with humor, and a kind of childlike grace that is at the core of what makes Tomlinson Tomlinson. But, soon, the escalating number of visitors began to upset him.

Then, I think, they began to frighten him —
perhaps because of the devotion they exhibited.
Or simply his dwindling privacy.

He never offered to explain why strangers
were now seeking him out. I asked twice, and
twice I received cryptic answers.

Once, he said, "Start reading at Matthew
seven:fifteen, and keep going until you get to
the part about corrupted fruit."

I answered, "The Bible? I'd have to borrow
yours."

His second reply made even less sense. "I'm
aware that the universe is filled with weird,
wonderful things patiently waiting to be understood. But the whole scene, man, the way the
energy's growing around me. It's like some
karmic snowball getting bigger and bigger —"

He held his palms up: *confusion; worry.* "— I
refuse to encourage it. Or even to participate."

So I did the research on my own. It only took
a night's work on the computer for me to discover the surprising explanation. It had to do
with an essay he'd written while an undergrad-
uate at Harvard. It was formally entitled, "Universal Truths Connecting Religions and
Earthbound Events."

The paper was part of a sociology project,
and it later received a wider audience, and
some acclaim, when it was published in the *International Journal of Practical Theology*, a respected publication out of Berlin.

Professional journals don't have a large readership — particularly when they're in German — so the acclaim was brief. The essay was forgotten. That is, until two years or so ago, when an ecumenical professor in Frankfurt rediscovered it, and reviewed it for the same journal, declaring Tomlinson's writing as "brilliant" and "divinely inspired."

Which was no huge deal until one of the professor's students began to circulate excerpts from the essay on the Internet under a new title: "One Fathom Above Sea Level." The title was taken from a line in the text. A fathom is the nautical equivalent to six feet, so it referred to a universe as viewed from the eyes of a human being. Tomlinson's eyes.

Communication is now instantaneous. The same is true of Germany's surge of interest in Tomlinson and his writing. It wasn't long before enthusiastic linguists began to translate his writings.

Because "One Fathom Above Sea Level" had much to do with Buddhism, it was first translated from German into Japanese, then from Japanese into several Asian languages, then into French and finally (and only in the last few months) into English.

That's when Tomlinson — *our* Tomlinson — began his transformation from a quirky Sanibel character who loved sarongs into an international cult figure. It happened fast. His essay is only about ten pages long, so people read it quickly, copied it and forwarded it along.

I discovered that someone had already set up an Internet Web page where Tomlinson's fans could post little notes about how reading "One Fathom Above Sea Level" changed their lives, saved their sanity, led them toward enlightenment, created friendships, romance, health, laughter, love, all kinds of positive things.

There were several hundred entries.

I found another site where devotees could post personal information about Tomlinson as they discovered it.

A recent posting confirmed the rumor that Tomlinson was an ordained Rinzai Zen Master who lived aboard a sailboat on a secluded bay, Sanibel Island, Florida.

So the explanation was amusing, but also had the potential to cause my friend real trouble down the road.

Which is why I kept the information to myself. Didn't tell a soul. Not even Tomlinson. I decided to let the theater that is Dinkin's Bay Marina play itself out.

So I had some reasons to smile. Life goes that way sometimes. Just keeps getting better and better and better. So maybe my depression, the feelings of loss and guilt, were finally fading.

One of the most powerful laws in physics, however, is the law of "momentum conservation." It states that momentum lost by any collision or impact is equal to the opposite momentum gained.

Which is why, during good times and bad, we need to remind ourselves that just when it seems life can't get any better — or worse — things inevitably change.

Tomlinson refers to it as humanity's seismic roller coaster, his point being that, going up or down, we might as well hold on tight and enjoy the ride — a goofy kind of optimism that he usually exudes, and why I seldom refuse his invitations to travel.

chapter eight

Tomlinson had gone to the Everglades in search of what some Floridians call the Swamp Ape, or Skunk Ape, which is the tropical version of Big Foot or the Abominable Snowman. Because he'd cajoled and pressed, I'd agreed to join him.

I don't believe such a creature exists, of course — no reality-based person could believe it — but Tomlinson is not a reality-based person, nor does he claim to be.

As the man once described himself: "I am a citizen of many universes, many dimensions, and — thankfully — wanted by the law in only a few."

He often cloaks his personal, innermost beliefs in self-deprecating humor.

One thing I could not criticize, however, was the amount of research Tomlinson had done on the subject. When I told him that there was zero possibility of a primate, unknown to science, living in the wilds of Florida, or anywhere else in North America, he smiled his gentle, Buddha smile. Later, he handed me a thick folder of newspaper clippings and print-outs from the Internet.

He'd pulled together some interesting data. Recorded sightings of the Everglades creature dated back to the time of Spanish contact. In the late 1500s, a Jesuit missionary, sent to live among the indigenous people of Florida's west coast, described seeing a ". . . giant man, befouled by a body of hair, running away into the swamps."

Occasional sightings by Europeans and Indians continued over the next four hundred years, but reached their peak of frequency in the early 1970s.

"The reason for that is obvious," Tomlinson explained to me one night, sitting on the stern of his old Morgan sailboat. "That's when construction was booming in Miami and Lauderdale, everything expanding west into what was then the Everglades. The bulldozers and draglines were draining the edge of the big swamp, scraping it bare, taking away all the cover. The River Prophet had to move around, maybe for survival . . . or maybe to investigate the damage being done to the biosphere."

River Prophet — Tomlinson's personal identifier for something that was more or less consistently described as a gorillalike creature, over eight feet tall, covered with hair, and that had a distinctive, sulfurlike odor. Thus the "Skunk Ape" reference.

Tomlinson decided to go to the Everglades in search of the Swamp Ape for reasons that were

97

cryptic and multipurposed — like almost everything else in his life.

It had something to do with a pre-Columbian stone ceremonial circle, chiseled by indigenous people, recently discovered west of Miami. Back in 1998, a similar circle had been found in downtown Miami, near Brikell Pointe. It was a forty-foot archaeological treasure, carved into the limestone bedrock. The location was to have been a parking garage for a $126 million high-rise luxury condo complex, but public protests closed the project down.

This second circle included what Tomlinson said he believed to be small stone stela, not unlike certain Mayan formations found in Central America. He spent weeks at the site, and came away convinced it was both an astrolabe and an uncannily accurate map of the earth. Uncanny because — in his opinion — the map included North and South America, even though the circle of stones was constructed two thousand years before Columbus sailed.

"Extraterrestrials had to have been involved," he told me. "It explains so much. The key, I am convinced, lies in the Everglades."

Years ago, at Tomlinson's urging, I'd read of claims for similar maps — the Turkish Piri Reis map of 1513, for instance, which supposedly shows all the Earth's continents, plus the Arctic and Antarctic.

Misinterpretation of the map is an intentional hoax, of course — research has proven it, though some diehards, such as my friend, continue to believe. Similar hoaxes include Peru's "alien landing strips" on the plains of Nazca, the Lost City of Atlantis, the Bermuda Triangle, the intentional government cover-up of information about UFOs and, of course, all the various legends of the Abominable Snowman or Swamp Ape.

Tomlinson and I no longer argue these things, although they do, occasionally, make for interesting late-night debate. As I've told him, I'd very much like to believe in the things in which he believes. I'd also like to believe in Heaven, visitors from outer space, divine creation, divine providence, divine revelation, predestination, telepathy, guardian angels, ghosts, soulmates, reincarnation, absolution and (most of all) I'd like to believe that order and virtue ultimately triumph over that which is evil, existential, random.

I don't.

I don't believe. I'd like to, so try to remain open, hopeful. I've known Tomlinson long enough to realize that one's spiritual convictions have little to do with one's intellect. His IQ exceeds my own by more than forty points (he's not aware that I was once provided with his entire scholastic dossier). His gift for languages and interpreting nuance exceed my understanding or capability. The so-called intellectual types who assume that spirituality and religion are refuges of the ignorant simply provide testimony that condemns their own stunted intellects.

I'm often dumb, but not that dumb.

Sally was now another example — a gifted person who is also devoutly religious.

Yet, I *don't* believe. Intellectually, I can find no rational, logical foundation for Tomlinson's spiritual convictions. I am incapable of lying to myself, so I am incapable of embracing a spiritual view of the world. I'm hopeful, though. I remain hopeful.

So, I listened without comment as Tomlinson continued, "There's only one Everglades. There's no geographical equivalent to be found on this planet. The River Prophet could be down there doing research, inviting contact. Which is why there has been an unusual number of sightings lately."

Tomlinson had shown me the newspaper stories. A Michigan couple in a Winnebago spotted a huge "apelike" creature near the post office in Ochopee. It supposedly jogged away when they tried to get a photograph. A Budweiser delivery guy claimed to have almost hit a similar creature near Monroe Station. Both places are located on the Tamiami Trail, the asphalt conduit that crosses eighty miles of sawgrass, connecting Miami with the Gulf coast of Florida.

Tomlinson said, "So I propose we assemble an expeditionary team. Mack knows a man who's got a hunting lease in the 'Glades — a couple of hundred acres, plus a cabin and a bunkhouse that sleeps eight. I'll pack some food, make a list of people to invite. Scientists, trackers, psychics, paranormals: the most respected specialists in their fields. Oh yes, and don't let me forget. Alcohol. We're going to need whiskey, vodka, Everclear. All varieties of alcohol, and *lots* of it."

I found the idea of going to the 'Glades in search of an imaginary primate comical, but also oddly heartening. To inspire tales of legendary monsters, wilderness must be sufficiently pristine to lend credibility to the possibility that there really *could be* monsters hiding out there somewhere.

I've never spent enough time in the Everglades to claim to know it well, but it was nice to believe that the region was still wild enough to create fear in outsiders.

So I went to the Everglades with Tomlinson. He planned on spending a couple of weeks. Four days turned out to be my emotional limit. For one thing, I have my business to take care of. Providing marine specimens to schools and research facilities around the country is not a booming industry, but it's what I do, and I try to do it as professionally and expeditiously as I can.

The second reason I bailed out early was more subtle, more personal. I found out that my tolerance for paranormal, lunatic-fringe society is far lower than I expected. Tomlinson is an exception, and will always be an exception.

By virtue of his intellect and purity of intent, I find him an interesting character, an entertaining conversationalist, a dependable travel partner. As a friend, he is as loyal and as thoughtful as they come. Even at his weirdest — and that crosses almost all boundaries — he is, at least, out of the ordinary, and always good-hearted. That wasn't true of the two women and three men he invited to join him in his quest to find the Swamp Ape. Four of the five were academics: college professors in a variety of fields. The fifth had her own cable television show: *Connections with Karlita.*

The alliteration was as impossible to forget as the tune of some inane song.

When the academics weren't talking about applying for government grants or tenure, or discussing convention freebies, they were listening to Karlita ramble on and on about what roles they'd each played together in their past lives.

They seemed offended that I chose not to join them in meditation, or to sit, holding hands in a circle, sending out psychic messages to what they called the "Great Alien Being."

"Doc isn't much of a joiner," Tomlinson explained to them one evening. "You know how the right side of the brain controls all non-linear, intuitive and artistic thought? Doc doesn't seem to have one. A right side to his

102

brain, I mean. Which means he's not exactly what you'd call aura-driven. The man's no social butterfly."

Possibly true, though it didn't seem to mitigate their uneasiness with my behavior.

Not that it mattered to me. There are lots of interesting animals in the 'Glades, land, water and reptilian. I was content to wander off on my own, jotting careful descriptions in my field book, and drawing diagrams when necessary.

There was a canoe available. I used it to paddle sawgrass tributaries deep into the swamp, sometimes as far as the mangrove fringe that marks where Florida's jungle meets the sea.

My nights in camp, though, were not as enjoyable. Their little group would sit around the fire, passing a joint or a pipe, and my consistent refusal was awkward for us all — a situation I've experienced too many times, and so try hard to avoid.

Because the stars in the 'Glades are remarkably bright, and because it's what I preferred to do, I'd return to the canoe carrying a bottle of rum and ice in a little cooler, then paddle far enough away to ensure silence.

I would drift alone, staring upward at the old way points familiar since childhood: Cassiopeia, Ursa Minor with its Polaris handle, Orion, Jupiter and others, all ice-bright, solitary and set apart in the chill of deep space. After that, it was a race between the rum and the depression.

My feelings of guilt and failure are sometimes so power-charged that there seems to be
a chemical source, as if some valve in my brain
has ruptured, and is leaking acid.

Certain memories flashed so vividly, with
such impact, that, floating in the canoe, isolated and insulated by wilderness, I'd groan
aloud until the images passed.

The alcohol helped, even though I knew the
folly of it.

Being in the 'Glades seemed to help as well.

Tomlinson's correct. There's no need to say
Florida's Everglades, because there is no other.
Just as California cannot lay claim to the Pacific, the Everglades is beyond the claim of one
state.

The Everglades region has its own feel, its
own good odor. The odor is created by a fusion
of freshwater flowing slowly over limestone, the
wheat-stubble odor of sawgrass, the lichen
scent of Spanish moss, tannin, wild citrus, and
of tropic sun heating cypress shadow.

To fight the depression, I was also doing
something else: I was using my brain, exercising the cells, *learning* something. I was
making an effort to use all the senses so to
patch together a neophyte's understanding of a
complicated ecological system.

My last night in the 'Glades, Karlita insisted
on joining me on my evening paddle. Despite

Tomlinson's claims, I am not an antisocial person. I didn't know her well enough to have a reason to say no, so I said yes.

Physically, she is an attractive woman by the standards of most: long legged, lean, with a glossy, healthy cowling of Irish-black hair, and the kind of face that looks good on a television screen, or when reproduced on the covers of magazines.

When it comes to the human female face, researchers have identified the five most important components that define our standards of beauty. The male brain, apparently, has been encoded to react both physically and emotionally.

Features include sexual maturity balanced with neonate, or childlike, qualities. Also important are facial expression, the shape of a woman's mouth and lips, plus a measurable ratio between cheek and chin that is similar to the proportional difference in bust size and waist that keys sexual arousal in most men.

Karlita had all of the above. But I found her decidedly unattractive. I appreciate woman as people, so I tend to evaluate them by the same criteria I use to select male friends.

As we paddled into the darkness, she began a nonstop monologue ("I think it's so valuable to invite *oneness* with nature . . .").

It was the kind of introspective discourse that is the hallmark of the self-obsessed. It forbids any attempt at conversation. Her insistence on

105

telling me about my "former incarnations" was a subtle device. It was a way of establishing authority. Her passionate commitment to "spiritual open-mindedness" was a cloaked condemnation of anyone who thought differently than she.

What irritated me most, though, was that she claimed to be an expert canoeist, yet was a sloppy paddler.

I can tolerate pompous assholes in short doses. Fakes and pretenders are a different story.

Even so, I was on my best behavior. Tomlinson's my friend. To confront her would have been to embarrass him.

When we got back to camp, though, I took him aside. I told him I'd had enough. I'd be leaving the next day. "That woman's a phony, old buddy. Your instincts used to be better. I'm surprised you didn't see through her act."

He laughed, and said that he'd invited her along less because of her paranormal powers than for her paranormal body.

I said, "You're trying to get the famous TV psychic in the sack? Just when I think it's impossible for you to shock me, you find a way."

"I know, I know, I'm terrible. But I comfort myself by believing that shallowness is a key part of being a complicated male. At least, that's what I tell myself. There are times when my testicles are nothing more than ventriloquists suspended from one big dummy. Absolutely unconscionable. But it does seem to add a little spice to life."

He added, "I take no pride in admitting that, with the exception of my Zen students, I've never been with a healthy, adult woman in my life when I didn't secretly calculate the chances of getting her in the sack." He shrugged, disgusted. "As long as she wasn't damaged, wasn't vulnerable, it never mattered. Not to me — and usually not to them."

I had to ask. "Do you think Karlita would stop talking long enough to make love?"

"*No.* Play-by-play, the whole time. That's my guess. It'd be kind'a entertaining. Like playing baseball with earphones on, listening to someone describe how you're doing."

I thought that was the end of my days in the Everglades.

I was wrong.

chapter nine

When you shower in the rain, getting dry is not a pressing consideration. The storm cell had spread itself over Sanibel, diffusing intensity, so the downpour had slowed to a steady drizzle and was finally stopping. Big soft drops, the air much cooler now in the tropical moonlight.

I wrapped a towel around my waist, walked to the front door, then paused. I could see Sally through the window, staring at the fire, mug of tea in hand. Across the water, at the marina, there were Japanese lanterns glowing red, green and orange, a bunch of people out there on the docks listening to music, still having fun despite the passing storm.

I tapped on the window to get Sally's attention, then held up an index finger — *Give me a minute, I'll be back* — then clomped barefooted down the steps to the wooden cistern that is my main fish tank. I switched on the overhead lights.

Every morning of my life, my first few waking minutes are filled with mild dread because, more than once, I've lifted the lid of that tank to find a soupy mess of decomposing specimens, the filter fouled, or the raw-water intake plugged. Keeping sea creatures alive is a time consuming, demanding job, and I had yet to check on my collection since returning.

Relief. The system was working just fine. The pumps were sucking in raw water, spilling over-flow out. The hundred-gallon upper reservoir, with its subsand filter, was cleaning the water, then spraying it as a mist into the main tank where sea squirts and tunicates continued to filter, which is why the water therein is too clear to slow the human eye.

Through the water lens, I could see small snappers, sea anemones, swaying blades of turtle grass, sea horses, horseshoe crabs, whelk shells, the whole small world alive. There were five immature tarpon stacked beneath the ex-haust of the upper reservoir, as motionless as bright bars of chrome. There were immature snook, as well, heads turned into the artificial current, a few sea trout, grunts and cowfish, too — strange little animals that look like something dreamed up at Disney World.

My reef squid were the hardest to find be-cause their chromatophores allow them to blend with the sand bottom. But there they were, the entire miniature sea system healthy and well, indifferent to the world of primates going on above and around them.

As I stood looking into the tank, a voice called from the mangroves, across the water: "In that white dress, you look like some fuckin'

109

Fiji warrior. Or a guy in one of them old Tarzan movies. Put some clothes on or I ain't crossing over."

I'd installed shepherd's-crook lamps along my boardwalk, and so I turned to see Frank DeAntoni in the distance, standing ashore in a circle of light.

Smiling, I said, "She's agreed to talk to you, Frank. Come on aboard."

Sally said to DeAntoni, "Before I answer any of your questions, would you mind answering a couple of mine?"

Frank said, "Sure, absolutely. Ask me anything."

The three of us were on the porch, DeAntoni sitting close to Sally, giving her his full attention. He'd been watching the woman for a while, but this was the first time they'd met face-to-face. It put an unexpected touch of shyness in his voice; seemed to make him eager to please.

"I was telling Doc that a lot of weird, bad things have been happening to me lately. Maybe you know something about it, maybe you don't, but I've got to ask. How long have you been following me?"

He said, " 'Bout two weeks. I guess maybe a little more since the company called. Asked if I'd take the case."

"Everglades Home and Life?"

"Yes. Your husband's insurance company."

"Did you ever break into my house? Some-one's been coming in when I'm gone, going through my personal things."

DeAntoni's face demonstrated concern. "It wasn't me. My right hand on the Bible. I've got no reason. You don't have a security system?"

"Yes. Supposedly, a very good one. So who-ever's breaking in is no amateur. That's why I'm asking."

DeAntoni said, "Do they steal stuff?"

Sally said, "No. They leave everything exactly the way they found it."

"Then how do you know someone's getting into your house?"

"That's the same question the police asked me. I'm . . . I'm not sure. It's more of a feeling I have. An awareness. Almost like an odor — I can tell that someone's been going through my things. My files, even my clothing. Plus, all the weird bad luck I've been having. It's being done intentionally."

She told us it began shortly after her husband vanished. She'd get into her car and the battery would be dead. Or the battery cable loose. Or a tire flat. "A brand-new BMW," she said. "What are the chances?"

It was always when she was out. Never at home.

"It's as if someone wanted to make sure I'd be delayed coming back," she said.

Someone had been getting into her com-puter, too. She'd checked the records of her

Internet provider and found that a person had been signing on under her password from an outside computer, and also from her own personal computer. She'd changed passwords several times, but wasn't certain if her e-mail was still being monitored.

"Something else bad happened to my . . . to a pet I had. A dog," she said, her voice beginning to crack. "But I . . . I don't want to talk about that now. Maybe later." She turned to me, regaining her composure. "That's all I wanted to ask Frank. Should I trust him?"

I said, "Yeah. I think you can."

Sally told us she couldn't call the International Church of Ashram Meditation by its official name because she didn't consider it a church. Pagan idolatry. That's what the minister at *her* church called it. The Reverend Wilson.

An example: Bhagwan Shiva taught his followers that, once they were formally accepted, the morality of the outside world no longer applied to them. Everyone on the inside was a chosen person. Everyone on the outside was part of a spiritually dead society, so what outsiders thought — even family members — didn't matter.

"That's a guy I need to talk to," DeAntoni said. "Shiva. I've asked his secretary for an appointment a half dozen times. Even did it in writing. So I may have to try walking into their Palm Beach compound, see what happens."

Sally said, "You won't get far. My husband used to talk about how good the security is. Family members on the outside are always trying to snatch their loved ones, because that's the only way to get them deprogrammed. So Shiva has his own little group of enforcers, like guards. Archangels, that's what he calls them. They dress in black. They're scary-looking, their whole attitude. Men and women both. The ones I saw, they carry nightsticks, and those little guns that shoot electrical darts. What do you call them — ?"

Listening to every word, DeAntoni said, "Tasers."

"Tasers, yes, I think. And his personal staff, his Archangels, they swagger around like they can't wait to use them."

"Talk about one crappy religion. How nice is that? People get in, they can't get out."

Sally said, "Once you reach a certain level — they've got a hierarchy of secret levels — once you get so high in the organization, yes, I don't think you can just one day say, hey, I'm out of here. I don't think they'll let you leave."

"How high did Geoff get?"

"About as high as a member can get. Over a period of slightly more than three years, he went to the top. Probably because he had so much personal interaction with Shiva — their business dealings. He was proud of himself, all his church promotions. He was such a goal-oriented person, so obsessive, that he had to excel at everything."

Frank asked, "Your husband and this religious guy, would you consider them friends?"

"No. I don't think Shiva has friends. He's set himself up like a God, so everyone else is beneath him. Besides, Geoff began to realize that Shiva wasn't all that he pretended to be. I know they had at least a couple of blowups."

"What makes you think that?"

"Because he told me. A few months before Geoff disappeared, he told me he was going to ask Shiva for some kind of resettlement. It had to do with all the money and property we'd given the Ashram. Geoff was about as mad as I've ever seen him."

I asked her, "Did Shiva agree?"

"Yes. My husband said he had no choice. I don't know what he meant by that."

It took her a few minutes to explain that she didn't know all the details, but the resettlement had something to do with a property the Church of Ashram owned on the northeastern edge of the Everglades.

"They're trying to put in housing, hotels and at least three casinos. The casinos have to be built on Indian land for some reason, but that's part of the plan because the church's acreage butts up against reservation property. Even so, I know they were having permitting problems. Geoff told me that."

114

I asked her, "Why would Florida Indians allow anyone to build on their land? That makes no sense."

"Not their property, really. Shiva's property. He'd sell the Indians *his* acreage for some ridiculously low price. A dollar, or whatever it takes to be legal. There's a federal law that says an Indian tribe can incorporate purchased property as part of their tax-free reservation. In return, they'd let Shiva build his development and casinos. He'd pay them a percentage of the gross. That's what he's trying to get them to do."

She added, "But the incorporated tribes — the Seminole Tribe of Florida and the Miccosukee Tribe — weren't interested. That's the last I heard. Geoff told me Shiva was going crazy trying to get them to go along with his idea. Money, political pressure, everything. He even started dressing like an Indian, trying to kiss up. It didn't help. Nothing helped. But, the last time I spoke with Geoff, he said Shiva had an out. A way of making it work."

"Did he give you any details?"

"No."

I sat for a moment, thinking about it before I said, "Your husband. The deal he struck with Shiva. He was to get a piece of the casino development?"

"Yes. A big piece. Enough for him and Shiva to patch up their differences. But then Geoff disappeared."

DeAntoni told her about the photograph.

Hands folded in her lap, the lady shuddered, staring off toward the mangrove circle that creates Dinkin's Bay.

A bright night. Jupiter was like an illuminated ice shard in the April dusk. To the northwest was a dome of foggy light floating on a rim of gray: the stadium lights of Sanibel Elementary School. A Little League game was going on there, or maybe one of the beer-bash softball games.

DeAntoni said, "You don't have to look at it. You already been through a lot. And I'm not the kind'a guy who'd upset a woman for all the fuh . . . fuh . . ."

He paused, flustered, trying to edit himself in midsentence. "For all the, uhhh, freakin' tea in China. So if you don't want to see the picture, you want me to drop the subject, you just tell me, and it's mum's the word."

Touched by his deferential manner — this huge, burly man behaving like a respectful adolescent — she smiled, reached and patted the back of his hairy hand. "You're very thoughtful. If I'd known what kind of man you were, that you were just doing your job, I'd have felt safer, actually."

Unsettled by the flattery, DeAntoni made a flapping gesture with his free hand. "You kiddin'? If I had some dago ugly as me followin' me around, I'd'a called the fuckin' cops myself."

Sally seemed not to notice that DeAntoni slapped his hand over his own mouth, nor did she react to the profanity.

"If you have a picture of Geoff that proves he's alive, I'm more than willing to look."

"Okay. But I got to warn you right now, Mrs. Minster. There's another woman in the picture. She ain't naked or nothing, but she's kind'a naked. Topless, I mean. I don't want your feelings gettin' hurt."

Her voice steady, not giving it much emotion, Sally said, "The picture won't bother me. My husband was having sex with the Ashram girls from the time he became a member. Little zombies is what they're like. It's *allowed*. Even if he's still alive, he'll never be my husband again. So why don't you call me Sally? Or Ms. Carmel, if you want to keep it formal."

When DeAntoni grinned, I noticed for the first time that his upper incisors were a bridge. He'd had his teeth knocked out — no surprise there. "Formal? Oh, no way do I want to keep it formal . . . Sally."

My old friend smiled at his eager manner. "Then go get the photos, Frank."

They were digital photos printed on Kodak ink-jet paper, ultra-glossy, of a man lying on a beach chair, his hand on the thigh of a lean, dark woman. She wore a string bikini bottom, no top. Pink cloth no bigger than the standard dinner napkin. The man looked to be naked but for a billed fishing cap. Both of them comfortable, two lovers judging from the relaxed poses, a couple used to intimate contact.

The photos were similar, both taken from the side, so the man's face was clearly visible. Because her head was turned away from the lens, the woman's face was not. In the first photo, you could see her body in profile, and that her brown hair was sun-bleached copper and salty, tied back with a crimson scarf that protruded from a straw sun hat. In the second photo, her back was to the camera, so all you could see were her hips and the hat's brim.

At the bottom of the photos were a digital date and time stamp: Feb. 2, 4:32 P.M. and 4:35 P.M.

Today was Friday, April 11th. Geoff Minster had supposedly fallen overboard the previous year, somewhere near the Gulf Stream, on his way to Bimini, the night of October 27th.

If the dates were accurate, the photos had been taken three months after Minster had supposedly died.

DeAntoni handed the prints to Sally, who looked at them briefly, shaking her head in distaste or disapproval. She then handed them to me.

"It's like he's gone insane," she told me. "Over a period of three years, he went through a complete personality transformation. Now he does something like this. It's sick. Truly sick."

I held the photos, saying to DeAntoni, "Isn't

it easy to change the date stamp on a digital camera?"

He nodded, "You go to the menu, change it to anything you want. Question is, why would someone fake the date, unless they knew Minster was gonna disappear? Why would anyone intentionally want to cause that kind of trouble?"

I said, "Well, one possibility comes to mind. Not a pleasant one."

"What's that?"

I said, "If someone planned to murder Minster, they might change the date, take the photograph. Kill the man, but make people like yourself keep looking, thinking he's still alive. If authorities continue to search for him, they're not going to waste time searching for the murderers."

As DeAntoni said, "I hadn't thought of that one," Sally murmured, "What an awful idea. It never crossed my mind someone would want Geoff dead."

I asked DeAntoni, "Are these your only copies?"

"No. I got two more prints made. One's at my office. One's with Everglades Home and Life. That's the insurance company that may have to pay Mrs. Minster — Sally here — four million-five. Did she tell you that it seems pretty certain that the court's going to rule in her attorney's favor? Once that happens, the Department of Vital Statistics will issue a death

119

certificate, and then the company will *have* to pay."

I nodded as he added, "So I kind'a feel bad asking you to help me. I'm the one trying to prove you shouldn't get the money."

I raised my eyebrows, looking into Sally's handsome face, seeing the dullness of her eyes enliven slightly, as she said, "Before I found my church, before my life changed, wealth and possessions — all that stuff — social status? They meant something. Now, though, I couldn't care less about the money. So that's the problem. Money. It's one of the reasons I came to see you, Doc. And why I'm happy to help you find Geoff if he really is still alive."

DeAntoni said, "Money's the problem? You lost me there."

"I don't *want* it. If I do get the insurance money, I'm giving it to my church. Most of it. I'll keep just enough to live on. But I can't if there's a chance I got it illegally, because it's dirty money. Or if there's a chance that the insurance company will demand it back."

To DeAntoni, I said, "If they write the check, there's not much chance they'll do that, is there?"

The big man looked uneasy. "I think the *last* they want to do is get their name in the papers for that kind'a scandal. The Feds would have to be involved. But for four million-five. Yeah, they'd take their bruises, suck it up. They'd want the money back."

I asked, "Scandal?"

Sally said to DeAntoni, "I haven't told Doc the whole story yet. He doesn't know."

I said, "What don't I know?"

DeAntoni told me, "About the insurance company. Minster was one of the founders of Everglades Home and Life. The last bad hurricane, whatever its name was, it flattened a couple of big developments that he built. The insurance companies paid off, but they went bankrupt doing it."

Sally took over. "Geoff and some other developers around Miami couldn't get insurance. People who wanted to buy a new house couldn't get insurance. It was a mess. So Geoff and some of his business associates came up with their own solution. He was brilliant in his way. Driven, but brilliant."

DeAntoni said, "What he did was pretty smart. His group did the research and calculated that, when a certain area of Florida is hit by a really bad storm, there's almost always a ten-to-twenty-year gap before it's likely to get hit again. *Statistically.* Those're good odds. How much can you make writing clean insurance over fifteen years? Start in the high millions, then add some nice big numbers at the front.

"So they found investors, formed a company and applied to the Florida Department of Insurance. To push through the kind'a thing they wanted takes a lot of political juice. They had it.

"In June, about three years ago, the state approved them as what they call a foreign property and casualty insurer, and accepted them into the state homeowners' insurance pool. What that means is, that quick" — DeAntoni snapped his fingers — "they were guaranteed to write policies on over a quarter million private homes and businesses. The insurance racket, man, it's got its own language. They were granted a bunch of lines of business: Homeowners' Multi-Peril, Commercial Multi-Peril, Auto, Ocean Marine, Health . . . and life insurance, too."

"Geoff had life insurance through his own company," Sally said.

I asked DeAntoni, "Aside from Sally, were there other beneficiaries?"

"Yeah, and I'll give you one guess who. The company may have to write out a whole lot bigger check to the International Church of Ashram Meditation. More than four times what they would pay to Sally."

"That explains it," I said. Meaning why they'd hired DeAntoni to find out the truth — a small insurance company with a reason to keep things private and quiet, and maybe not have to go bankrupt.

chapter ten

I walked the two of them through mangroves to the marina. I hadn't eaten since that morning — my camp breakfast in the Everglades. Not a very good breakfast, either, since Tomlinson had loaded his goofy little group with health-food types. We'd had bulgur wheat and a slab of some kind of fibrous-looking substance that was supposed to be a substitute for meat.

DeAntoni said, yeah, he wanted to eat, too, but Sally was reluctant.

"It's not that I don't want to see the old marina gang, Mack and Jeth, Rhonda and JoAnn and all the others," she explained, "but I've learned that old friends feel a little uncomfortable when a friend changes."

Referring to herself.

She certainly *had* changed. It happens a lot, and all too often to good men and women. It happens through misfortune, random accidents, the tragedy of disease, the realization of personal failure.

It also happens because the detritus of an unsatisfying life can accumulate like a weight, until even a strong person finally breaks, gives in and seeks shelter in one of the many escapes available to us all. Drugs are a common route of escape. Religion can be another.

Something had happened to this good lady. Maybe for better, maybe for worse. I have no illusions about my competence as a judge. I screw up my own life so consistently, disappoint my own vision of self so regularly, that I have become a reluctant critic of other people, other lives. But it was obvious that she was no longer the woman I had held, laughed with and made love to on the moonlit outside deck of my stilt house.

Surprise, surprise. Tomlinson had returned for the party. Karlita, the television psychic, was with him. Her idea, he said. Totally. Because she wanted to see me.

Tomlinson threw his arm around my shoulder, weaving mightily. Drunk, stoned, nearly out of it, slurring, "The lady likes the cut of your jib, *compadre*. Karlita the Chiquita. She's looked you over port to starboard, bow and stern."

"*Tomlinson*," I said trying to shush him. "Enough with the sailing metaphors. I have no interest in the woman. I already told you that. How'd you get here? Please tell me you didn't drive your own car."

"My car? I've never owned a car in my . . ." He let the sentence trail off, thinking about it. "Wait a minute, I *do* own a car. I bought a

Volkswagen Thing off Bud-O-Bandy. Classic beach transport. It's like a tent with four slabs of drywall built around an engine. My dream car."

"Exactly," I said.

We were standing by the sea grape tree next to the Red Pelican Gift Shop, the docks, the darkening bay behind us, the masts and fly bridges of boats strung with party lights. Tomlinson had a pink sarong knotted around his waist, tarpon and snook hand-painted on silk. Shirtless, he was skin over bone, all sinew and veins, his gaunt cheeks and haunted eyes suspended above his shoulders like a human face perched on the stem of a delicate mushroom.

His hair was longer than ever, scraggly, sunbleached to straw and silver. He'd isolated two shocks of hair with the kind of spring-loaded combs that little girls use: One shock was a ponytail that hung to the middle of his back. The other sprouted directly from the top of his head, a Samurai effect.

He took a deep breath, eyes wide, trying to calm himself. Then he held up an index finger. "Ah-h-h-h, now it's all coming back. I *didn't* drive. I came with Karlita in her black sports car. A hundred fifteen miles an hour through the Everglades. Sawgrass a blur, rednecks in airboats flipping us the bird, screaming foul oaths while I sent out telepathic warning signals to innocent wildlife. Yes, of course. There's

125

no mystery here. I returned to Sanibel like any normal working lug. In a Lexus GS 400, my head mashed to the seat like I'd been Velcroed by kidnappers. So . . . what was your point again, Doc?"

"Karlita," I said. "She's the point. I've got no interest. I don't want her in my house. I don't want her in my lab. I don't want to spend more than a minute or two listening to her bullshit. As long as we're clear on that."

He held up an index finger, asking me to pause so he could ask a question. "Correct me if I'm wrong, but I'm getting a very negative vibe here. You don't like the lady?"

"No. I don't like the lady."

I watched my old friend sigh heavily, eyes drowsy, his whole body drooping as if he were about to fall asleep. Or pass out — a more accurate term.

I hoped it was my imagination, but lately, it seemed, Tomlinson was absolutely smashed after only nine or ten beers — a historically light night for him.

Not a good sign.

I am not a fretter, but, of late, I'd been worried about him. He was killing himself. Slowly and surely, he was destroying his own body, his own first-rate mind, by overindulging in a garden variety of legal and illegal drugs.

He'd gotten worse in the last year or so. My personal guess was that it was his way of dealing with the pressure of his growing notoriety. A way of re-creating an insular privacy that he no longer enjoyed.

So he was staying drunk most of the time. Or hiding out on his boat. Or on the Florida Keys: Key Largo, renting the little apartment overlooking the Mandalay Bar, Mile Marker 97.5. Or in Key West, moored at the Conch Republic Fish Company docks, or staying at Simonton Court, or Old Cypress House, doing happy hour with Dave, then drinking all night with Chris Robinson at Louie's Backyard.

Or exploiting absurd excuses to retreat to the Everglades.

Every day by sunset, he was out of control. Mostly, it was alcohol — which is why the fact the he seemed to be getting drunk on fewer drinks was a troubling symptom.

Chronic alcohol use causes the liver to become fatty. The fat chokes off blood that delivers oxygen to liver cells. Those cells are replaced with scar tissue called cirrhosis. Result? A drinker can tolerate less and less alcohol because there are fewer liver cells to process it.

Of course, it was also probable that he was supplementing his alcohol intake with marijuana, illegal pharmaceuticals, psychedelic fungi, even surgical halothane gas when he could get it.

Tomlinson made friends quickly, and he had a long list of medical professionals he could call on for special fun and favors. Because he knew I didn't approve, he rarely confided in me when it came to his current drug of preference.

The height of paradox was this: A couple of months back, he took me aside and said, "Doc, I don't want to offend you, but I'm telling you for your own good. The whole marina's worried because of your drinking."

I said, *"What?"*

"Used to be, you'd have a couple of beers a night. Now you're drinking that black Nicaraguan rum. Getting drunk, too — that's the rumor floating 'round. That's what I *suspect.*"

Trying my best to be patient, I told him, "Tomlinson, you know exactly what I drink because you're right there with me. Drinking rum on my porch at sunset, or your boat, almost every night. *Geezsh.*"

Which made him pause a few beats, thinking about it, before he replied, "*Oh.* In that case . . . well, you're in the hands of a professional. Enjoy!"

Standing near the marina's picnic tables, where there were trays of crab cakes, bowls of ceviche, steamed shrimp and fried fish, Tomlinson told me, "Last night, when you two were out canoeing, Karlita said she had a psychic vision. That you were destined to become lovers."

I answered, "The lady's wrong. Count on it."

He wagged his finger at me, having fun. "Um-huh, the Ford Theory of Reality. You only accept as fact that teeny-weenie bit of ig-

128

norance that can be measured, weighed and classified.

"One day, though, you'll step through the veil and experience the spiritual world. When you're ready, man, when the *student's* ready, your teacher will arrive. You put out such good vibes, my brother, I'm willing to bet cash money that your spiritual teacher will come complete with a really great ass. So maybe it's Karlita."

"Thanks," I said. "So now I have something to look forward to."

I turned and began to walk toward the docks, where I could see Sally and Frank DeAntoni standing among a group of liveaboards, red plastic cups in hand. Yet, by the way they stood, shoulder-to-shoulder, facing one another, talking intensely, they effectively isolated themselves. Two people alone in a crowded space.

Behind me, Tomlinson said, "If Karlita says you two are going to end up lovers, my money's on her. Might do you some good. Step into the Karlita cage and take a few swings."

First sailing metaphors, now baseball: two of the man's great loves. But all drunks become tiresome after a while, and I was getting irritated.

I told him, "I'm still seeing Grace Walker, just in case you've forgotten. I try to focus on one partner at a time."

"Focus," he said. "I'm with you there. There

are men who choose the vagina as their only telescope to the world. Bad choice. Poor light gathering capabilities and unpredictable resolution." He stopped. "Hey, what's that you got in your hand?"

As I continued to walk, I held up the glossy photo DeAntoni had given me. "Nothing. No one you'd know."

"See? There you go being purely logical, which can be a bummer. That's why you're always surprised by the unexpected."

He took the photo from my hand, holding it up to the dock lights. Stood there weaving, studying it before he said, "This man's name is . . . hum-mmm . . . it's coming back to me. His name is Minster something. Jerry Minster? No . . . Geoff Minster. See? I *do* know the guy."

Surprised by the unexpected. He was right about that. And Tomlinson *often* surprises me.

I said slowly, "Yes. It *is* Geoff Minster. Exactly. Sally Carmel's Miami husband. When did you meet him?"

"Whoa, wait — Sally's husband? That, I *didn't* know. Very weird, man. A very far-out karmic linkage. To meet him yet not know he was married to our old buddy Sal."

Tomlinson has the amazing ability to react as if sober when the subject is sufficiently serious. He's developed what he calls a "lifeguard twin" that is always waiting and ready, hidden within his brain. In an emergency situation, when drunk, Tomlinson calls upon the twin to speak articulately, to walk steadily, to be extremely courteous to law-enforcement types and attentive to attractive women.

He seemed to be sober now, as I said, "Then explain how you know him."

"Remember I told you about the two pre-Columbian circles they found over in Dade County?"

"I remember," I said impatiently. "How does that have anything to do with Minster?"

"Because Minster was the developer who was trying to build some mega-million-dollar highrise luxury condo on the site. Built-in Starbucks, a little mall, high-tech security. You know the place, Brikell Pointe, located where the Miami River joins Biscayne Bay. Right near downtown Miami."

"How long ago was this?"

"A little more than two years ago. I remember telling you about it."

I nodded. "So that's the connection."

"Yep. Do you know where Cassadaga is?"

Cassadaga is one of Florida's stranger towns. It is northeast of Orlando, and well known for an enclave of oddballs who claim to be witches and warlocks.

Tomlinson said, "In Cassadaga, there's a group of mystics. A tight bunch of truly enlightened beings. I can't tell you the name of the group. I took a vow of secrecy. This is an extremely successful, solid bunch. Not the usual flakes that I love so much."

He said, "Unlike the usual ones, the fakes and pretenders, they actually have the gift of telepathy, clairvoyance, all kinds of powers. Which means making money is easy for them. And they've made lots of it. Prescience. Don't you love that word? What it combines and implies?"

"What you're telling me is that you're a member of the group," I said.

"If you choose to come to that conclusion, I'm not going to argue, *mi compadre*. The point is, they — *we* — couldn't allow Minster and his corporation to destroy something that's not only an important archaeological site, but also a major Power Place. It's an earth vortex, both the circles. Very powerful vortices. You're familiar with the term?"

"No, and I'm pretty sure I don't want to hear about it. All I'm interested in is how you know Minster."

Both of us walking again, Tomlinson made a calming motion with his hands. "I'll make it quick. But you need to know what I'm talking about to understand how I met the guy. Okay?"

When I didn't reply, he said, "Okay, a quick lesson in earth energy. There are focal points for electromagnetic power. Hot spots you might call them, or vortices. Sometimes they're rocky areas, water places, whole biospheres. Or sometimes they're built by man. Pyramids or Indian mounds. A deep water spring, for instance. Volcanoes."

"Volcanoes," I said. "That's enough. I get the idea."

"Wait, you need to hear the rest. Vortices have a dominant force, either electric or magnetic. A very few possess both — Power Places we call them. Over the centuries, mystics, psychics — even alien visitors — it's where they go to replenish their energy reserves. The Everglades? The Everglades is one of the world's great Power Places. All those springs and vortices; no other place like it."

"Tomlinson, please don't start talking about the Swamp Ape again. I'm still pissed off about you getting my truck stuck."

"Ahh-h-h. The skunk that nailed you when you were trying to push me out of the ditch. A touchy subject, yes."

I interrupted, "I don't blame the skunk. I blame you. *Only* you. So do us both a favor, please don't dwell on it."

He said, "Okay, okay, so back to the energy deal. It's part of a force field that links everything. The earth. Our own bodies. Our *souls*. The energy's produced by three key elements: iron, oxygen and silicon crystals. Quartz and silicon; it's the same thing. Silicon Valley? That's why computers will ultimately evolve to the point where they have their own spirituality, their own crystal souls."

I interrupted, hurrying him along, saying, "Okay, Minster was going to build on what

133

you'd call a Power Place. I understand that, too. So what happened?"

"What happened is, this group of Cassadaga mystics performed a spiritual intervention. On Minster. Minster and his major partner."

"His partner. Okay, now we're back on track. His business partner, was it a cult leader who calls himself Bhagwan Shiva?"

It was my turn to surprise Tomlinson. His facial expression is normally passive, always congenial. Now, though, his face illustrated an uncharacteristic distaste — maybe even a little touch of anger in there.

"Shiva," he said. "Bingo. That's what he calls himself. But it's not his real name. He chose the name, like . . . like a Halloween mask. A disguise. It's something to hide behind. Bhagwan means 'Blessed one.' Shiva means 'Prophet.' The dude we're discussing, he's neither."

I began to smile. "In all the years I've known you, I've never heard you saying a bad word about anyone. You really *don't* like him, do you?"

"Never met him; never *want* to meet. He's a cult leader, and you know me, man: I've never found a religion I didn't like. Do you know what religion *really* is? Religion, any legitimate religion, it consists of rules of morality linked by love. That's it.

"What Shiva's done is steal the worst parts of three or four faiths, and he uses them to feed

134

on weakness. A lot of it's taken from Scientology; the science-fiction writer deal? There's a very heavy indoctrination program. They do what they call 'cross-auditing,' trying to rid themselves of a kind of virus implanted in humans by space aliens a billion years ago — which is cool. I've got no beef with Scientology. But what Shiva does is use it to control people, not elevate them.

"The guy he really models himself after, though, is Bhagwan Shree — he's dead, now — but he had a couple of hundred meditation centers around the world. He preached free love, that getting rich was *good*. So Shiva's stepped in, made himself the new Bhagwan. He's part carnival act, part like those motivational shysters you see on late-night TV. It's still all about energy, man. Negative and positive. The guy who calls himself Bhagwan Shiva, he's a black hole. A power-zapper, and he just can't get enough. The *non*-Bhagwan, that's the way I think of him. *Evil* — I think of him as that, too."

"You and your group of mystics confronted him and Minster? But you said you never met Shiva."

"I said we performed a spiritual *intervention* to stop construction. The group I'm talking about, they can get into some dark mojo if it's required. You ever hear of a voodoo thing called an 'assault obeah'? Get the right shamans involved, you can suck the life energy

135

right out of your target."

I said, "You can't be telling me your friends are capable of murder."

"What I'm telling you is, someone can die without being murdered. But what they decided to use on Minster was all positive, man. Lots of meditation and some heavy-duty prayers.

"But Minster had been drained by the non-Bhagwan. Shiva, he's like . . . well, remember, in the movie *The Wizard of Oz*? That scene with the witch's soldiers, the ones with the tails and spears? They're marching into the castle, shouldering their spears, chanting what you think is 'OH-eee-ohhhhh . . . weeee-OHHH-one.' "

Tomlinson was singing it now. " 'OH-eee-ohhhhh . . . weeee-OHHH-one.' "

I said, "Sure. Even I know that scene."

Tomlinson said, "What the witch's soldiers are actually singing are lyrics. Only you have to listen close to understand them. What they're singing, over and over, is: 'Oh, we loath-h-h-h-he . . . the OLD one.' We *loathe* the Old One. Meaning the Evil One. That's Shiva. He's evil, man."

I asked, "How do you know this stuff?" I was still back on *The Wizard of Oz*.

He flapped his bony hands at me — *forget it* — as he continued, "What I'm saying is, Minster was under Shiva's control. So mind-zapping him was like trying to drill through

136

solid steel. Which is why we went to see Minster. Two of our group's leaders and myself."

"You made an appointment at his office."

"You kidding? People like us, we'd have a better chance getting an audience with the governor. No, we confronted him at the construction site.

"When he shook hands with me, he had this expression, like he was touching someone's dirty handkerchief. We didn't exactly become chums. But there was one of us, a woman, he really seemed to dig her. So she did most of the talking. A very cool lady — she doesn't want anyone to know she really has the powers she has. She's the private kind."

I said, "It's hard to believe that she convinced Minster and Shiva not to build their condo complex. Not with that much money involved."

Tomlinson shrugged. "I don't know. After the first meeting, I was out of the picture. My services were no longer needed. But construction stopped on the Tequesta Circle — that's what we called it. So something happened."

"You said this was about two years ago."

"Yeah. Maybe a little more."

"Could you contact your lady friend and ask her about Minster? Six months back, he disappeared. Fell off a fishing boat, presumed dead. Now Sally's stuck with a lot of emotional baggage, plus some big financial decisions to make. It would be good to find out what we can. It might help her."

137

"Minster's disappeared? Jesus, you're kidding." Tomlinson had stopped again; sobered even more at the news. "Did they find the body?"

"No. But the court has, apparently, been presented with enough evidence to order that a death certificate be issued."

He was tugging at his ponytail, biting the ends of his stringy hair — a familiar nervous mannerism. "That sounds exactly like it, man. Just what I was talking about."

"I don't follow."

"Sometimes saving a sacred place takes extreme methods. What happened to Minster, Doc, it sounds just like an assault obeah. A very dark and powerful force. The body disappears, right along with the soul."

chapter eleven

Karlita told us, "Why not let me try? Let me hold the photo, tune in on the vibrations. The Key West police, the Dade County Sheriff's Department, they've all used me to find missing people. It's one of my specialties."

We were sitting on the stern of Tomlinson's trunk-cabined, salt-bleached Morgan Out Island sailboat, *No Mas*. He'd recently had her hauled, scraped, painted and refitted for an extended cruise he had planned — another symptom of his desire to escape.

She now had a new little Yanmar diesel (though the man seldom resorted to using power), a high-amp alternator, inverter, wind generator, an autopilot and a very powerful Bose sound system. Even so, the cabin retained the familiar odors of oiled teak, kerosene, electronic wiring, patchouli incense, sandalwood and the musky smell of marijuana.

It was crowded. There were five of us sitting around the stern cockpit and on the roof of the cabin bulkhead: Karlita, Tomlinson, DeAntoni, myself and Sally. Tomlinson was sitting cross-legged, meditation style to my right. When

Karlita spoke, I nudged his knee with mine and, in the glow of blazing moonlight, did my best to glare at him.

The entire evening, I'd tried to avoid her, yet, over and over, Tomlinson had steered her to me, smiling his mild, Buddha smile. Which is how she'd met Sally, then DeAntoni, who, it turned out, was a fan of her weekly television show as well as of her nightly cable TV infomercials.

"I got what you call insomnia, Miz Karlita, so you and me, we've spent lots'a late nights together."

The woman loved that, vamping a little as she replied, "Oh really? You lying there in bed all alone? I bet we've shared some very special moments, just you and me. Am I right?"

DeAntoni missed the implications of that; continued to smile and nod as he told her, "I think you're one of the most beautiful women on the tube. Honest. I'm not just saying that."

Which guaranteed Karlita would be with us the rest of the night, tagging along, listening to everything we had to say and not shy about commenting.

Now here she was on Tomlinson's boat, hair hanging long over her right shoulder, dressed in Arabic-looking scarves, red and black, that showed that she was braless, very comfortable with her body, bare legs and thighs visible when she walked or sat with legs crossed, which she was doing now.

DeAntoni said, "Know what the weirdest thing is? I almost called you. It was the night you had the guy on who could bend metal just touching it. I'm sitting there and it comes to me: Hey, maybe the beautiful psychic could help me with Mrs. Minster's case."

He'd already told her about Sally's husband, and the photo.

Sounding flattered, Sally said to him, "You really seem to care."

DeAntoni said, "Sure, it's my job. Plus, I think you're one nice lady."

"That's a very kind thing to say."

"I mean it. Which is why I've started feeling, well, I guess protective's the word. It's the kind of guy I am. I live alone, not even a cat, so who else I got to look after? All that insurance money involved, you could attract every kind of shark and con man around. Plus, your husband was hanging with a rough crowd. You ever do any reading about the Church of Ashram?"

"Enough to know that the people there scare me."

DeAntoni said, "That's good. I'm glad to hear it. From what I've read, they're nasty when it comes to revenge. People who piss them . . . people who cross them, make them mad. Out west, in this one little town, his followers went to the only restaurant and contaminated the salad bar with salmonella. The whole town got sick, so they couldn't get out and vote. Murder, too — they've been accused

141

of that. Of making people disappear."

"Like Geoff," Sally said softly.

DeAntoni said, "Yeah, like your husband. So I've been keeping a real close eye on you."

To the television psychic, Sally said, "You're right. He's kind."

Then, looking at me, she said, "I'd like her to hold the photograph. If she has a power, it was given to her by God, not any sort of witchcraft. So let's give her a chance."

Holding the photo in both hands, eyes closed, the television psychic did her act.

It took her half an hour to tell that Minster was dead; that he really had drowned.

She ended, saying, "It was his penance, his own way of finding salvation and deliverance. You can rejoice in that."

As she finished, a warm gust of air bloomed out of the mangroves, dense with iodine and sulfur. *No Mas*, at anchor, shifted beneath the stars like a slow weather vane.

I tried to change the subject, but Sally wasn't done with it. After a few minutes, she said, "So Geoff really is gone. I feel bad because we'd become strangers."

"People change," Tomlinson said gently. "No one really knows what goes on in the heart of another human being. We probe and pretend. But few of us ever truly connect with another."

I said, "It seems odd for someone like your husband, the entrepreneurial type — an intelligent guy — to be taken in by a cult leader."

"I would've agreed until I started learning about it," she said. "You wouldn't believe how many successful people join the Ashram. Some of the names — famous people; people with money — I was shocked."

Still speaking softly, in his reflective mode, Tomlinson said, "She's right. The Ashram and organizations like it appeal to two basic types: the successful, proactive sort and the homeless.

"I was telling Doc, a lot of it's stolen from Scientology. If you work hard, stay disciplined, do what they call your 'auditing,' you'll keep moving up the spiritual ladder. Goal-oriented people like that."

He added, "I think for some of them that there's so much pressure in their professions, it's a relief to finally let go. To stop worrying, and have someone tell them what to do for a change."

Sally said, "That's what happened to Geoff. He'd already started building his theme villages. Worked twelve-, fourteen-hour days, then couldn't sleep at night, worrying over details, money."

I said, "Theme villages? I thought he did shopping malls. That sort of thing."

"In the beginning, yes, malls were his specialty. But then he came up with this theme-village idea — he was a genius when it came to marketing."

Geoff's idea was a variation of the theme-park industry that has become synonymous with the plasticized, theaterized and stucco grotesquerie that too many people believe is Florida. It was to buy up large tracts of raw land in Florida and south Georgia, and build gated, turnkey villages. Each village would have a unique theme, built to attract people who shared passionate interests.

He built his first theme community in the rolling pasturelands north of Gainesville. It was called Cross Country — a lush, secure village designed to appeal to fitness hobbyists.

There were miles of wooded running trails and bike paths. There were lap pools and fitness centers. There were artificial rock towers designed to challenge beginner, intermediate and expert climbers. The village employed its own staff of triathlon, marathon and fitness coaches — all part of the monthly maintenance fees.

Cross Country was such a success that Minster began to build three carbon-copy villages — one outside Atlanta, another near Lauderdale, the third, north of Cape Coral.

"It was way too much, too soon," Sally said. "That's when he began to have cash-flow problems. It got worse and worse until he just couldn't handle it anymore. Instead of hustling off to the office every day, he began to avoid work. Hated the mention of it. Same with his obligations.

"He bought a Harley; stayed out all night

sometimes. He began hanging out with what I'd call weirdo types —" She turned and looked at Tomlinson. "Old hippies, no offense."

"None taken," Tomlinson said, amused.

"It was like he went through the adolescence he'd never had. He was smoking marijuana, going to bars, hanging around Coconut Grove and South Beach. Then he took up the martial arts, and started studying meditation.

"By that time, I was in my corporate-wife mode. So I'm the one who actually ran things, took care of all the details. What a strange reversal, huh?"

It was around that time that Geoff met Bhagwan Shiva — the most important "karmic event" of his life, he told Sally. He found the Church of Ashram "fascinating." Better yet, Shiva was looking for big-profit investment opportunities. He had cash, and he was enthusiastic about Minster's theme communities.

Shiva perceived an additional advantage: He suggested that each community also have a "Meditation Center" staffed with Shiva's followers.

"At first, he wanted to call them Ashram Centers, but there were some legal problems with that. So they settled on Meditation Centers, but they were the same thing."

Other theme communities were built. Audubon Estates was designed to attract people who loved bird-watching, natural history, astronomy. There were butterfly gardens, land-

145

scaped sections of rain forest and cypress swamps, all built far inland in what was once cattle and sugarcane flatland, so there was no light pollution.

It was even more upscale than the Cross Country projects.

In the Everglades, closer to Miami, they built their most exclusive community, Sawgrass. Sawgrass was designed to attract the adventurer types, the sporting market. Fly-fishing, hunting and shooting. Several well-stocked bass lakes, quail-shooting from horseback, a landing strip, a hunting lodge, a restaurant with mahogany beams, stone fireplaces, animal heads on the wall.

According to Sally, Sawgrass was Shiva's favorite, and so it became Geoff's favorite.

"The hunting and fishing, it attracted the big-money guys. The heavy drinkers, the gambling and hard-living types. The best Scotch whiskey, the best Cuban cigars and the main restaurant serves nothing but prime beef. It was so exclusive, Shiva and Geoff could both let their hair down a little. He began to spend more and more time there. In fact, the month before he disappeared, he didn't spend more than a night or two at home."

DeAntoni said, "That's where I was headed next. Sawgrass. I'm going to talk to people who knew your husband. There's a little redneck town nearby. I hear they aren't so happy about rich Yankees and Shiva's followers taking over

146

the area. People like that might be a good source of info."

Sally told us that Sawgrass was southeast of Immokalee, in the Everglades region between Alligator Alley and the Tamiami Trail. It was near a crossroads settlement called Devil's Garden, out in the middle of nowhere. There was a bar, a feed store, a couple of houses.

She added, "About the people who live around Devil's Garden — gator poachers and Seminole drunks is the way Geoff described them — you're right. There've been some nasty scenes between Shiva's people and the locals. It's because the Ashram owns most of the land around Devil's Garden; a couple of thousand acres. It's where Shiva wants to build his casinos."

DeAntoni looked at me, and said, "That was my deal with the chewing tobacco. I was experimenting with ways to go down there and maybe blend in a little better with the rednecks."

I said, "Shrewd. No way they'd recognize your New York accent while you're throwing up."

"Funny. Maybe what I need is some local cover. You talk like a college professor, but you still got a little bit of Florida boy in your voice. You want to come along?"

I told him no, I had a business to run, but then Tomlinson spoke up, saying, "Count me in. I'd love to go back to the Everglades. What

147

about you, Karlita?"

As she was telling him, yes, they could go there and try to tune in to Shiva's dark vibes, Tomlinson was staring at me. He waited for her to finish before he said, "I wonder how those gator-poaching types are going to react to two enlightened visitors like me and Ms. 'Lita? A couple of long-haired flower children."

Trying to disguise his distaste, but not doing a very good job, DeAntoni said, "If this guy, your hippie pal, tags along, I can't be responsible."

Meaning I had no choice.

I listened to Frank add, "Sally, I'd appreciate it if you'd drive home and stay there. Just to be safe. Not tonight. Tomorrow, I mean."

I liked the man even more when he added, "I don't want a nice woman like you getting hurt on my account."

As I walked her to her car, I listened to Sally tell me that visiting the marina, seeing my house and lab again after all the years, had really hit her emotionally. Brought back the memories, some of them pretty good.

We were alone.

She said, "Do you know who I miss from those times?"

I had an idea, but remained silent.

"I miss your uncle, Tuck, and Joseph Egret, too. Tucker was such a funny, wild, old flirt. But Joe, I miss him the most. What a dear, sweet man. The gentle giant. Him and his horse, the way he'd ride without a saddle. Cowboys in the Everglades, that's the way I still think of both of them."

"Joseph," I said. "Yeah, I miss him, too."

It was an uncomfortable topic for me, and because it was something I wanted to ask anyway, I changed the subject, saying, "On the porch, you started to tell us about your dog. What happened?"

She slipped her arm into mine — allowing intentional contact for the first time. "It's hard for me to talk about without bawling, and I didn't want to do it in front of a stranger. It's why I had to get out of Coconut Grove. I couldn't stand it anymore."

She'd been doing volunteer work at her local animal shelter. They took in a skinny little golden retriever–cocker mix. He was at the shelter for more than a month. His time ran out. They were going to euthanize him, so Sally adopted him. It was about a month after her husband's disappearance. She named him Mango after the village where we'd both lived, and also because of his reddish-gold color. In her big, empty house, the two bonded quickly.

She was right. She couldn't tell it without crying.

"Last Friday morning," she said, "I went to Publix, came out and found I had another flat tire."

It was hour before Triple-A got the thing fixed.

"I knew right away something was wrong when I unlocked the door, because he wasn't there to meet me. Mango knew the sound of my car. He was *always* at the door. I dropped the groceries and went running, calling for him."

She found her dog floating in the pool. The policemen who took the report guessed the dog had gone swimming and maybe had a seizure.

"That's not what happened," she said. "I told them, but they wouldn't listen. Someone broke into my house again. They killed Mango — and for no reason. He was the sweetest dog. What kind of person would do such a thing?"

I had my arms around her, holding her as she wept. I didn't reply, but I was thinking, *A very, very dangerous person.*

chapter twelve

izzy

Izzy was in a twenty-one-foot fiberglass Bay-liner boat that a disciple had donated to the Ashram, and that Jerry Singh kept at the yacht basin just off U.S. 1 on the Coral Gables Canal, up the waterway from Coconut Grove. He kept the boat there in case he felt like running out and fishing for dolphin, or hitting Miami night-spots by water. It was a good place for that.

Jerry was in a hunting and fishing phase, maybe because of the sporting types he'd been hanging with in the Carcass Bar at Sawgrass.

Carcass Bar — that's the way Izzy thought of it. All those dead animals that reminded him of roadkill, with their glassy stares. Or maybe Jerry was still trying to impress the Indians. Pointless. But who knew?

It was 10:15 P.M. Izzy was still wearing his dancing shoes and satin jacket. So what he *could* do if he wanted was run up the bay to the Biscayne Yacht Club — they had reciprocals with Sawgrass — and check out the waitresses, or see if there was maybe a lonely widow or two looking for companionship.

Izzy loved to waltz. Since childhood, waltzes

were his favorite.

But no. If Sally Minster really had gone away for the weekend, this was a chance too good to pass up.

She hadn't answered her phone the five times he'd called during the drive down.

Standing at the console, seeing city lights reflect off a pale moon, Izzy idled the boat west beneath the bridge at Cocoplum Plaza. Lots of fast, Friday-night traffic clattering overhead — it was a weird feeling to be on water beneath moving cars. It gave him an uncomfortable, drowning sensation that was gone the moment he exited from beneath the bridge.

Ironwood, the gated community where Sally and Geoff Minster lived, was the fifth waterway down on the left, just past Sunrise Harbor, its own little island, right on Biscayne Bay.

Izzy watched an Ironwood security patrol car pass over the bridge. He floated there, running lights off, for a full two minutes before he clunked the boat into gear again, and idled out into the bay, then north past the docks of the lighted mansions.

Minster had built an ultramodern castle on the water, all stucco and glass. It had pointed gables and balconies built over a screened infinity pool, and a lawn landscaped in white quarry rock around islands of palms.

Moonlight on the rock reminded Izzy of when he was a kid in New York, looking out the window at night on fresh snow.

He swung the Bayliner into Minster's dock and shut off the engine. Then he leaned to remove the white cowling of the Johnson outboard — he'd claim to have engine trouble if anyone confronted him.

Izzy paused once more, crouching beneath a traveler's palm as he watched the lights of the same security patrol car sweep by. Then he stood and walked toward the pool door, taking rubber surgical gloves from his pocket.

Sally, the pretty, religious born-again church lady, still enjoyed her private time alone in the bedroom.

Izzy was in her bedroom now, searching through drawers, seeing that certain items had been moved; presumably used.

He liked her bedroom. It smelled of clean linen and body lotion, everything done in white and yellow, very feminine. Like the big four-poster bed with the overstuffed white comforter, pillows stacked in a way that suggested the lady liked lying on the bed watching the flat-screened television that was recessed into the wall.

He checked a final drawer, and thought, *Yep, she's been at it again.* Izzy felt a pleasant fluttering in his abdomen.

Breathing slightly faster, he crossed the room to the electronics control center mounted at eye level behind a plastic cover. It was next to the hallway door.

Beneath the cover, he'd hidden a Mitsubishi 900 MHZ wireless, sub-micro video camera. The camera's lens was smaller than a dime. The entire unit was smaller than the nine-volt battery that powered each of the two mini-recorders he'd hidden beneath boxes in her closet.

He'd placed a second camera on her bathroom ceiling.

Touch any button on the control center — turn on the lights, dim the lights, adjust the air-conditioning, anything — both cameras were activated.

Izzy went to the closet and removed two mini-cassette tapes. Then, as he fitted the first mini cassette into a standard-sized converter, he found the remote to Sally's TV and VCR. When everything was ready, he threw himself onto her bed, turned on the television and pressed *play*. Then he lay back, watching.

Izzy grinned. There she was, Sally Minster, walking into her bedroom, a little wrinkled after dealing with a flat tire, dressed in a peach-colored business suit.

He scooched back, and began to fast-forward, searching for any good parts the camera might have captured. As he searched, he considered going to Minster's study to make himself a gin and tonic. A big one with lots of ice. Or maybe just a nice cold beer, so he could savor the video in style.

But Izzy was too excited.

He got off the bed only once: Went to Sally's drawer and selected blue satin bikini underwear before returning to her bed.

It took a lot of fast-forwarding, but he finally found what he was hoping to find. It was on the second tape; the bathroom camera. He turned the sound up so loud that he could hear Sally breathing.

He watched the screen as she came into the bathroom, wearing a white cotton robe. His stomach stirred as she turned to look at herself in the mirror, paused for maybe thirty seconds, thinking about it, before she loosened the robe, opening it, so that she could see herself.

Then Sally stood with the robe loose, bare skin in the mirror, her ribs showing, abdomen showing, blond pubic hair in the shadows, one white breast bared, her nipple pink and elongated, her eyes intense.

Izzy whispered, "Oh my God," thinking, *What a body*. Pale skin, firm, heavy-breasted over thin hips. It was better than he'd hoped. No way of knowing she looked like that, the way she dressed, the religious woman always covering herself.

He focused on the TV screen, thinking, *Do it . . . do it . . . do it,* as Sally let the robe slide off her shoulders. Then she stood naked, comfortable with herself, alone in her own bathroom.

He watched her shake her hair free around her shoulders, looking into her own eyes. Then he watched her eyes seem to fog, as if her brain

155

had drifted off to some distant place, and the color of her cheeks began to flush as she touched her stomach with long fingers, nails painted with pink gloss.

Now she was relaxing, getting into it. Her head was tilted back, eyes closed, as her fingers moved over her breasts gently, touching them, then massaging the weight of her breasts with open palms, moaning in a voice that seemed high, experimental or apologetic, nipples squeezed long between her fingers.

Izzy whispered, "Yeah. Go for it," as Sally, moving faster now, knelt and removed a plastic, candle-sized object from the pocket of her robe.

He was done, now. He'd cleaned the bedroom, put everything back just the way he'd found it. Everything, including the video equipment.

The tape of Sally was so unbelievable, he'd considered removing the cameras, packing up the recorders. But then Izzy thought, *What the hell,* he'd leave them for one final week. His last week in the States.

There was something about this woman that got to him. More than just her body. It was her face, the way she dressed, the fact that she was a religious priss. *Something.*

Plus, he'd always detested Geoff Minster. A pompous, rich asshole who tried hard not to play the part. The few times he and Geoff were

156

together, Geoff had looked at him as if he were something unsanitary.

Izzy wanted to see the man's wife naked again.

So he decided to leave the cameras in place. He'd pick up the cameras and recorders before he split for Nicaragua. One more look. She was worth it. Just on the chance of getting something better.

But, oh my God, it would hard to get *anything* better than this. He'd made lots of tapes of lots of women, but nothing as good as Sally alone in her bathroom.

Izzy figured he'd give it six months, a year, wait 'til he had everything squared away in Nicaragua, then get a couple of thousand duplicate tapes made. Then he'd go to the Internet, upload a sample and put the tape up for sale. Maybe call it *The Merry Widow*.

What would he make? Sixty, seventy grand easy. Maybe a lot more if word caught on. Because that's how porno sold — word of mouth.

He tried to imagine how she'd react when she found out. Sally Minster, the lady saint. Or maybe a male member of her church, being naughty, playing around in cyberspace, would find her. How would her preacher handle that?

That made Izzy chuckle.

His water-into-wine theory again. All religion was bullshit and fakery. Same with the holy goofs who pretended to practice it.

Hypocrites.

★ ★ ★

Izzy walked downstairs to the pool door, leaving the Minster home the same way he'd entered.

Hurrying.

Maybe hurrying too much because he had so much do tomorrow, Saturday. He had to spend the day making final preparations for the Bhagwan's big magic trick on Palm Sunday. No simple task, which Jerry Singh was too self-obsessed to realize.

Because the Ashram owned interests in many theme communities, and because each community had its own eighteen-hole golf course, collecting several tons of ammonium nitrate fertilizer had not caused Izzy the legal problems it would've most people.

The Feds had been nervous about the stuff ever since a U-Haul truck full of ammonium nitrate nearly brought down Oklahoma City. No way anyone could buy it in large quantities now without filling out forms and lots of background checks.

So what Izzy did, over a period of eighteen months, he regularly borrowed fertilizer from the maintenance barns of every golf course in the organization, saying they needed it at Sawgrass. Then he went to the Ashram's master computer and adjusted the inventory numbers.

Easy.

But now came the shitty part. Tomorrow, he had to dump forty bags of the crap into a cement mixer by hand, then add diesel fuel and mix it until it was the consistency of mayonnaise. Dirty work.

He already had the blasting caps, two dozen six-volt batteries and timers wired, so the only thing left to do after that was transfer the gook to a Sawgrass maintenance truck. He'd had the truck rigged with a four-hundred-gallon skid-mounted tank and a pump that was powered by a Honda generator.

Tomorrow was a full day. So he was hurrying. He wanted to get out and make it to Sawgrass tonight before the bar closed.

Izzy keyed in the security password he'd found in Sally's on-line computer files. He opened the door and stepped out into the night.

Then he froze.

Shit.

He was standing face-to-face with a seventy-year-old man in a brown security guard's uniform. The man had a silver badge on his shirt pocket. He was holding a flashlight, not a gun.

"Can I help you, sir?"

A ridiculous question for the guard to ask. The old man, Izzy realized, was as startled as he was. Scared, too.

Izzy relaxed a little. "Just going out for a walk. See you!" He waved as if saying good-bye, but was really using his open palm to mask his face.

"Are you a friend of Mrs. Minster?" The old

man was following him. Then the old man said, "Hey, hold it right there, buddy," and he shined the flashlight directly on Izzy's face.

Mistake.

Izzy stopped, turned slowly to face the man, and said, "Do you know how fucking *dumb* that was, mister?"

Izzy got to the guard before he could get the handheld walkie-talkie to his mouth. He held the old man, choking him with his forearm, squeezing harder and harder until the man suddenly quit struggling. Went from being a frightened old man to a rag doll.

Just like that. He quit. Or maybe he'd had a heart attack. It was so unexpected.

It was funny how that went. Some people fought like hell when they knew they were dying. Others just gave up, surrendered, as if to get it over with faster.

Izzy was now doubly glad that the woman's dog was gone. The animal would follow him around, lick his hands, bring him a slipper or a towel or something like he wanted to play. Which completely ruined the mood.

Right now, for instance, the dog would have been in the pool enclosure, yapping its head off.

So Izzy was glad he'd gotten rid of the dog — though the damn thing tried to bite him the first time he shoved its head under water.

The dog wasn't like the old man.

The church lady's dog had fought back.

chapter thirteen

Riding in the Freon capsule that was Frank DeAntoni's Lincoln, looking through glass at sawgrass touching April sky, I listened to Tomlinson say from the backseat, "If an infinite number of drunken rednecks pull shotguns from the rack and shoot an infinite number of road signs, I hate to say it, but, one day those bastards are bound to produce a very good haiku in Braille. What're the odds, Doc? It's gotta happen, man."

DeAntoni didn't much like Tomlinson. He made it obvious, ignoring him when he could, shaking his head in reply to questions, rolling his eyes when Tomlinson made one of his eccentric observations.

DeAntoni rolled his eyes now, saying, "As if some blind dude is gonna roam around down here feeling for road signs, searching for something to read." Then after a few more seconds, thinking about it: "Like they could even find the fucking signs way out here in this godforsaken swamp. How stupid can you get, Mac? They'd need a ladder to even *reach* 'em."

DeAntoni was not a man whose life was complicated by an overactive imagination.

At a Mobil station, intersection of 951 and Rattlesnake Hammock Road, east of Naples, DeAntoni pulled me aside and whispered, "Jesus Christ, next time that weirdo takes off those John Lennon shades of his, check out the pupils. I think he might have been smoking *marijuana*."

"Really?" I replied. "Using drugs this early in the morning. Hum-m-m-m. I guess it's *possible*."

"And wearing that crazy Hawaiian dress. I practically had to threaten him to make him change into shorts."

Actually, Tomlinson had been wearing his black-and-orange sarong, swami-style, like a pair of baggy pants. He knew a couple of dozen ways to tie the things, depending on the occasion. I'd had to issue a threat or two myself. Nothing to do with his sarongs, which I've become used to. If he didn't get rid of Karlita, though, he wasn't going anywhere with me.

Which is why he informed Karlita that she couldn't accompany us.

DeAntoni said, "What I don't understand is, you two guys are pals. But you're like exact opposites."

I said, "I know, I know. It's been worrying me for years."

I think DeAntoni decided that the best way to keep Tomlinson quiet was to fill the silence by asking me lots of questions.

162

Speeding east on the Tamiami Trail, the remote two-lane that crosses Florida's interior, all cypress swamp and grass savanna, I explained to Frank that the sawgrass growing out there, ten feet high, got its name from its three-edged, serrated blades.

"Sawgrass is deceptive," Tomlinson added. "Looks like Kansas wheat, but it'll cut you like a razor."

Referring to the thatched huts along the road, and state road signs that read INDIAN VILLAGE AHEAD, I had to think back to the Florida history I'd learned in high school.

Trouble was, I wasn't certain the information was still accurate.

I told DeAntoni that 'Glades Indians were derived from mixed bands of Creek and Muskogees, on the run in the late 1700s, who'd sought safe haven in Florida. The earliest group, Mikasuki-speaking Creeks, became known as the Miccosukee, then Trail Miccosukee, as in Tamiami Trail.

Another group, mostly farmers, were called the Cimarrons, which is Spanish slang for runaway or wild people — possibly because of the runaway slaves who sometimes lived among them. Cimarron became Simaloni in the Miccosukee language, then Seminole.

I told him, "I'm not sure if that information's up to date. Tomlinson's an expert on indigenous cultures, Native American history. He's like an encyclopedia — literally. You should be asking him."

DeAntoni shrugged, ignoring the suggestion, then changed the subject to wrestling.

I could see Tomlinson in the rearview mirror, chuckling, not the least bit offended, enjoying the man, his quirkiness.

We drove past Monroe Station and the dirt road turnoff to Pinecrest, then into the Big Cypress Preserve. At Fifty Mile Bend, in the shadows of tunneling cypress, we approached the cottage that is Clyde Butcher's photo gallery. Tomlinson said why not stop in, say hello, take a look at some of the great man's black-and-white masterpieces, Clyde was a hiking buddy of his.

DeAntoni replied sarcastically, "You got a swamp hermit buddy who's an artsy-fartsy photographer? That's a hell of a surprise," and kept driving.

We didn't slow again until we entered the Miccosukee Indian Reservation east of Forty Mile Bend — beige administrative buildings among pole huts, airboats, brown-on-white Ford Miccosukee Police cars — then the Florida deco tourist attractions, Frog City and Cooperstown.

At the intersection of the Tamiami Trail and 997, DeAntoni got his first look at the Miccosukee Hotel and Casino. It was in the middle of nowhere, elevated above the river of grass, fifteen or twenty stories high.

The casino was a massive stucco geometric

on the Everglades plain, abrupt as a volcanic peak, painted beige, blue, Navajo red. It had a parking lot the size of a metropolitan airport. The lot was already half full at a little before noon on this Saturday. Lots of charter buses and pickup trucks.

"GAMING AND ENTERTAINMENT," DeAntoni said, reading the marquee. "Now, that's one place I *wouldn't* mind stopping. Back in New York, I'd drive to Cornwall — the Mohawks got a pretty nice casino there. Best one's in Connecticut, though, a place called Foxwood Resort, run by the Pequots. You think this Miccosukee place is big? This place ain't nothing compared to Foxwood. It's the biggest casino in the world. They take in one *billion* dollars a year."

Tomlinson whistled, then said, "Far out, man. A billion? You've got to be exaggerating."

"Nope. I read it in the *Times* and the *Post*, too."

"I knew it was big, but not that big."

"Bigger than anything in Vegas. A clean one billion a year, and they're proud of it — which I don't blame 'em for. Man, they got three or four hotels, golf courses, more than twenty restaurants, everything open twenty-four hours a day, and the state doesn't have a damn thing to do with it. No say at all. Not even taxes, 'cause they're Indians. They even got their own police department."

He glanced away from the steering wheel to

speak to me. "Why is that? Why do Indians get to open casinos, but regular people can't? I never checked into it."

"I'm not sure myself." I looked over my shoulder. "Let's ask the expert."

Still smiling, Tomlinson answered, "I'm allowed to speak? I don't want to irritate our driver."

DeAntoni said, "Your weird talk, that's the only thing that drives me nuts. Gambling and casinos — that's something I like. *If* you got something to say."

Tomlinson told him, "I know something about it. I have lots of Skin friends — that's what they call themselves. As in Redskins. The AIM people, man, I was really into their act, occupying Wounded Knee and Alcatraz. The American Indian Movement. The best of their warriors are still out there, fighting their asses off. The right to run gaming businesses, casinos, that's all part of the movement."

He said, "The Skins call it the New Buffalo — casinos, I mean. Tribes used to depend on the buffalo for survival. Get it? Gaming houses are what they depend on now. It's become the same thing. A way for the tribes, their families and children, to live, stay healthy."

I turned and gave Tomlinson a warning look — he tends to ramble and this was not a good time to ramble. But he's also quick to catch on. So he straightened immediately and gave us the concise version. He explained that Indian reservations are on federal trust land, governed only by federal or tribal laws. States have no jurisdiction over Indian reservations, unless jurisdiction is specifically authorized by Congress.

In this way, reservations are actually sovereign nations. Unless prohibited by federal law, each Indian nation can decide for itself what gaming may be conducted. Gaming, not *gambling,* which is considered a dirty word by those involved.

Tomlinson said, "Back in the nineteen eighties, when the state of California tried to screw over the Cabazon tribe, that's what really got the ball rolling. There were less than seventy people left in that little tribe, almost extinct. This little ghost band, out there on the rez, not bothering anybody.

"So what happens? State bureaucrats tell them they can't play bingo on their own rez. Old ladies sitting around smoking, watching Ping-Pong balls fly up the chute. Their thrill for the week. But then the U.S. Supreme Court said, screw you, California, individual states have no say over Indian land. Which is when the idea for Indian casinos started booming."

But that wasn't the end of the controversy, Tomlinson added. Concerned about the Cabazon decision, Congress passed the Indian Gaming Regulatory Act of 1988 (IGRA), attempting to balance the interest between the state and tribal sovereignty.

Tomlinson said, "Roughly, what that law says is, Indian tribes have the exclusive right to regulate gaming activity on Indian lands. The state can't say crap unless *all* forms of gambling are prohibited statewide. For instance, here in Florida, we've got a bunch of state lotteries to generate income because we've got no state income tax. So IGRA says it's hypocritical and illegal for the state to interfere with gambling on sovereign Indian territory."

I said, "That's how the 'Glades Indians got into the gambling business. I didn't know."

"The Seminoles, man. Yeah, they were the first. Their chief at the time, James Billie, he was a genius. An old Vietnam combat vet, and he didn't take any shit. But, in Florida, the Skins have always had to fight."

As an example, Tomlinson told us that, for more than two hundred years, the state and federal government refused to officially recognize the Florida Miccosukee as a tribe.

Every twelve months, Miccosukee leaders filed petitions with the Bureau of Indian Affairs for "tribal confirmation." Every twelve months, their petition was denied.

In the 1960s, the Miccosukee came up with a brilliant finesse. They sent a tribal delegation to Cuba where Fidel Castro signed documents recognizing the tribe as "a duly constituted government and a sovereign nation." It assured them of international legal status.

Embarrassed, the U.S. government had no

choice but to finally "confirm" the Miccosukee as a tribe.

"Florida hasn't made it easy for any of them," Tomlinson told us. "Back in ninety-one, the Seminoles had to sue the state in federal court because Florida refused to abide by IGRA statutes. The state insists it has the right to regulate gaming, so the Skins were all pissed off — Miccosukee and Seminole — and it's still in the courts."

Tomlinson tapped the car window, indicating the casino. "So the kind of gambling you can do in there is low-stakes stuff — compared to other casinos, anyway."

DeAntoni said, "Too bad. Up at Foxwood, the Pequot Indians, they got thirty-some crap tables going day and night. I love to play those double-thunder slots, too. Or get a vodka on the rocks and play baccarat. Man, that's *recreation.*"

Parroting DeAntoni's earlier sarcasm, Tomlinson replied, "You love to drink hard liquor and gamble, huh? A big-city guy like you. That's a hell of a surprise."

At the gatehouse, a guard dressed in tropical whites — including pith helmet — told us that he was sorry, but, unless we were accompanied by an owner, or on a member's list, or unless we had an appointment with a Sawgrass real estate representative, he couldn't allow us to enter.

In Florida, most gated communities hire security people who look like retired wallpaper salesmen. Minimum-wage guys killing time between visits from the grandchildren.

This one was different. He looked like he spent his off-hours in the gym. Had that hard cop formality which is a form of controlled hostility.

DeAntoni opened his billfold, showing his badge. "I'm here on business."

The guard looked at the badge; shrugged like it was invisible. "No, sir, you're not *here* on business. Not unless someone from management notifies me."

"Then call someone in management. It's about one of your deceased members, Geoff Minster. I'm here representing his wife. I can have her call if you want."

The guard thought for a moment, then said, "Back up and pull over. I don't want you blocking the gate if a member needs to drive through."

The gatehouse was sided by high stone walls and an acre or so of landscaped garden, hibiscus, travelers palms, and a life-sized Indian elephant carved of tropical wood next to a fountain. The elephant stood frozen, trunk down as if watering. In front of the elephant, a carved sign read:

SAWGRASS
A PRIVATE MEMBERSHIP
SPORTING COMMUNITY

There was a much smaller sign on the gatehouse wall: OUR SECURITY STAFF IS AUTHORIZED TO CARRY FIREARMS AND AIR TASERS, AND MAY USE LAWFUL FORCE TO INTERCEPT OR DETAIN TRESPASSERS.

As we waited, a new Mercedes convertible pulled up, two middle-aged men in the front. The guard took the phone from his ear long enough to salute, smile and say, " 'Morning, Mr. Terwilliger!" then touched a button to open the gate.

"Friendly little place," DeAntoni said, watching. "The guy in the white jungle beanie — I wouldn't mind slapping him around some. Him and his asshole attitude. What you think, Ford? He looks like a bleeder to me. The kind who stands in front of the mirror with his weight-lifter muscles, but starts to bawl if he gets smacked a couple of times."

I said, "You're not smacking anybody and neither am I. That's not going to get us inside those gates, and it's not going to help Sally."

Tomlinson told him, "Doc's embraced a policy of total nonviolence, which is a major spiritual breakthrough. We've discussed it. He's trying to grow as a human being."

Watching the guard walk toward us, DeAntoni said, "Oh yeah? Then explain why my beezer's the size of a turnip," touching his swollen nose gingerly.

The guard came out, leaned toward the window and handed DeAntoni a card. "Send a

171

fax to this number, stating exactly who you want to interview — we need specific names to make a request — and your reasons for visiting Sawgrass. The office will get back with you within a week to ten days. You know, on whether we can provide assistance."

In a flat voice, DeAntoni said, " 'A week to ten days.' "

"That's right, sir."

"Look, Mac, all I want to do is go to the restaurant, talk to a few people, maybe find someone who knew the late Geoff Minster. It's not like we're gonna filch the fucking silverware —"

I put my hand on DeAntoni's arm, leaning across, and said to the guard, "Thanks. We're leaving now."

The guard said, "That's right, sir. You *are*."

Tomlinson said, "Very, very cool. I don't just like the idea, I love it."

He said it in reply to DeAntoni's suggestion that we park the Lincoln down one of the old logging roads, and sneak onto the property on foot.

DeAntoni said, "Except for Mister Tight-Ass, nobody in there's gonna know we're not friends of members, or maybe just scoping out real estate. Rent-a-cops, Mac. They really bust my balls."

He sounded insulted.

I wasn't as enthusiastic. I've spent a signifi-

172

cant portion of my life working in places I was not supposed to be; places where I would have been shot — or worse — if discovered. Breaching security, compromising security systems, is demanding work.

I was once competent. No longer. Techniques change along with technology. You don't probe a guarded position on impulse. It's something to be researched and planned. *Trespassing,* like *pyromania,* is a word I associate with amateurs.

On the other hand, there wasn't much risk. If we got caught poking around, asking questions about a dead member — and we almost certainly *would* get caught if we starting asking questions — what's the worst they could do? Call the police?

More likely, they'd just tell us to get the hell off the grounds, and that'd be that. In the meantime, we might find a friend or two of the missing man. Having a member agree to talk to us would certainly mitigate matters with local security.

So I told DeAntoni, okay, pull up the road, and we'd work our way back on foot.

It was an instructive decision.

Sawgrass, the exclusive community, was a shaded garden of cypress, bromeliads and swamp maple. The wall that cosseted it was almost always hidden by trees. It followed the roadway for another mile or so before angling back into the shadows of its western boundary.

That's where the wall ended. It is also where the tree line ended, and a new development project began.

Sally'd told us about it. Bhagwan Shiva's theme community for gamblers: a self-contained city that adjoined Indian reservation land where he wanted to build casinos. Several thousand housing units plus a city center, restaurants, recreation centers, all designed to attract people from middle-income brackets; people with enough money to gamble, but not wealthy enough to buy property in Sawgrass.

He was having a lot of permitting problems, Sally'd told us.

From the road, though, construction seemed to be well underway, permits or no permits — although *destruction* seemed a more accurate term. There were several gated, dirt access roads, with modular offices, plastic Porta-Johns, temporary power poles. At each, were signs that read: FUTURE HOME OF CASINO LAKES, AN EXCLUSIVE PLANNED COMMUNITY. PRECONSTRUCTION PRICES AVAILABLE.

The crews weren't working on this Saturday morning. Hadn't been working for several weeks, by the looks of things. The first stage of the operation, however, seemed complete. They'd brought in a fleet of bulldozers and scraped the earth bare. Several hundred acres of black earth were turning gray in the morning sun. Only a few bald cypresses out there were

174

left standing, isolated, sculptured like bonsai trees on a massive desert plain.

The cypress is an interesting, exotic-looking tree, with its connected, tubular base, bulbous knees and leaves as delicate as oriental lace. They grow in distinctive settings: on islands of elevated terrain in sawgrass marshes where, as a community of many hundreds of trees — even thousands of trees — they form a characteristic dome. Green rotundas of shadow out on the sawgrass horizon.

Cypress also grows along floodplains on long, silver strands that can be miles long. South Florida's interior was once an uninterrupted canopy of cypress domes and strands. Up until the late 1940s, they comprised America's last virgin stand of bald cypress and pond cypress: trees well over a hundred feet tall and several centuries old.

At the end of World War II, though, the big lumber companies arrived in Florida, motivated by a postwar construction frenzy that was hungry for building material. Dried and milled, cypress is a handsome conifer wood that is insect- and rot-resistant — perfect for houses. Rail lines were built, spur lines added; labor was imported. It took the companies nine years to girdle, bleed and cut an epochal forest that had been the centerpiece of an ecosystem that dated back to the Pleistocene. Many thousands of loaded freight cars; many millions of board feet.

There're still lots of small cypress trees in the 'Glades. But big cypresses, the old giants are rare. In this area, though, the loggers had missed a few. Now those few trees stood alone on the bulldozed plain, solitary dinosaurs revealed, naked in this new century.

The three of us sat in the car, staring, until Tomlinson finally spoke. "There's a kind of silence that's really more like a scream. *Listen.*" He'd lowered his window. "Hear it?"

DeAntoni turned to me. "What's he mean, because they flattened it like a parking lot? There's gotta be at least two square miles of land out there."

I said, "Yeah. Maybe more."

"Permitting problems, my ass, man."

I told Tomlinson, "What could be happening here — one of the managers at South Seas was telling me about it — is what's becoming a sophisticated developer's device. It's so tough to get permits to build anything, developers know it's going to take them months, even years before they'll get the okay on a project. So they've figured out they'll actually save money by going ahead, building anyway, then paying fines later with inflated dollars. There's a whole generation of bureaucrats out there who behave as if people in the private sector are enemies of the state. Which is just idiotic. So it's become like a war — and everyone's losing."

Tomlinson said to me, "Understand now why I call him a power-zapper? He's a black hole, man, out there trying to absorb all the light he can. He's *feeding*. He's been feeding right here."

Bhagwan Shiva.

A little farther down the road was a crossroads general store, Big Cypress Grab Bag. Shell parking, a pair of gas pumps, rusted tin roof, wire mesh over the windows, peeling yellow paint. *Coke. Bud Light.* Lottery tickets and food stamps accepted. On the other side of the road were two businesses in a single, elongated building built of cement block: Devil's Garden Feed & Supply and Gator Bill's Bar.

Driving by slow, hitting his turn signal, DeAntoni said, "Pickup trucks and Confederate flags. Now you understand why I tried that chewing tobacco shit?"

"Makes perfect sense now," I said as I opened the door, then stepped out into the heat and a sawgrass humidity so dense it was like weight.

It was almost noon. Gator Bill's was a popular lunch place. There were a dozen or so cars and trucks, country music loud from inside, a jukebox, maybe, singing ". . . blow, blow Seminole wind!"

Through the screen door, in the shadows, I could see men at the bar hunched over drinks, a woman with black hair braided long, muling trays.

DeAntoni said, "We'll hit this place on the way back. If they won't let us eat at Sawgrass — one of the hot-shit restaurants they got in there

177

— we'll come back, grab a stool at the bar. That waitress, she doesn't look half bad."

We walked along the road in the heat. There wasn't much traffic: semis loaded with oranges tunneling the heat at seventy miles per hour; dump trucks and tractors with air-conditioned cabs. Their wind wakes created mini-tornadoes in the grass, whipped at our clothes.

Florida is more than beaches and theme parks. It's a major agricultural state and, consistently, the second or third leading producer of cattle in the nation. We were at the southernmost boundary, where pasture meets swamp prairie, the first and final edge of tropical wilderness.

At the beginning of Casino Lakes development, we cut down one of the access roads, then across to Sawgrass. DeAntoni and Tomlinson both wanted to climb the wall, take our chances. But I told them why be obvious and give them an excuse to call the police if someone spotted us?

I said, "Let's try the easy way, first."

Most gated communities have service entrances — they don't want the landscape soiled by all those dirty delivery trucks, or to require members to exchange pleasantries with the hired help. Sawgrass's service entrance was off an asphalt spur at the western boundary: a chain-link fence, double-gated. There was a little guardhouse where an old man sat, feet up on his desk, reading the paper. He looked up from the newspaper as we approached.

To DeAntoni and Tomlinson, I whispered, "Walk like you own the place." A few paces later, I stopped and called to the old man, "Whoops, sorry. I didn't realize this was the service entrance. We'll hike around to the front."

He'd slid the front window open. "Who you fellas with?"

"The Terwilligers, down here for first time. So we don't know the area. No big deal, we'll walk back to the front gate."

Maybe he knew the middle-aged man in the Mercedes convertible, maybe he didn't.

As I turned, the old man called, "Oh heck, go right ahead on in. They got too many rules at this place as it is. Hot as it is, you want me to have staff bring you a golf cart?"

I said, "Nope, walking's a good way to go."

Waving us along, smiling, the man said, "Ain't that the truth? These days, ever'body's in a hurry. You tell Mr. Terwilliger, Freddy says hey."

A nice old guy.

When we were well away, walking on a brick sidewalk among manicured gardens, through tupelo trees and cypress, DeAntoni said to me, "You're smooth, Mac. Very smooth."

I told him, "We'll see."

chapter fourteen

The bartender said, "Mr. Minster? Of course, I knew Mr. Minster. An interesting man. Such a tragedy. We miss him here at Sawgrass."

We were in the Panther Bar, which was part of the Big Cypress Restaurant, a place modeled after the old Rod & Gun Club in Everglades City. It was white clapboard, three stories high, pecky cypress inside with a wide veranda, ceiling fans, pictures by Audubon, Currier & Ives, framed and lighted. There was a formal restaurant — chandeliers and starched table-cloths — a light-fare eatery built on a deck over a cypress hammock, gators basking below in tannin-stained water, plus this ornate bar.

The bar had a granite fireplace, tables of dense wood, walls that were a museum of taxi-dermy: old skin-mounted tarpon, snook, bass and sailfish. There were alligators twelve to fourteen feet long, green turtles, turkeys, coveys of quail, a bear snarling on hind legs and one spectacularly large feral hog with razor tusks.

"Holy shitski," Tomlinson said, eyes swiv-eling as we walked in. "They ought to have a couple of Michiganers tacked up there; human heads just to be fair. Give wildlife equal time. Or a Buckeye or two in travel garb, cameras around their necks. Mount them over there" — he pointed to the largest of the gators — "maybe partially ingested. A leg or two missing, but they've still got that Disney World smile on their faces. Tough-ass Ohioans not about to let *anything* ruin their vacation. A real Florida tableau. Don't you think that'd up burger sales?"

Shaking his head, DeAntoni said, "Jesus, burgers. That's exactly what I was going to order, too. Why you got to be so fucking vulgar?" and left us standing as he walked toward the bar.

The busiest of tourist times in Florida is a week or two before Easter. Even so, the lodge wasn't crowded. At the most expensive clubs, hefty yearly dues ensure lots of personal room, lots of personal attention.

Members and their guests were getting it here. There was a steady luncheon business out on the veranda, a couple more tables occupied inside, but there was only one person at the bar when we sat. A distinguished-looking man with white hair, pleated shirt and slacks. He was peering reflectively into a heavy Scotch glass, but turned long enough to allow us a pleasant nod.

We ordered drinks and lunch; talked among ourselves for a while before DeAntoni attempted to coax conversation out of the bartender. Talked about sports, asked him about the fishing, how was business, how were tips, before he finally mentioned Minster.

The question seemed to surprise the bartender, though he recovered quickly. Bartenders become expert at masking emotion or they don't last long in what is a tough, tough business. He was as muscular as the guard in the pith helmet, but older: clean-cut, tan face beaming as he towel-dried glasses in his white shirt and black vest, with a name tag that read: KURT — LINCOLN, MASS.

But there was something aloof in Kurt's dark eyes, as if he were an actor too good for the role he'd been assigned, and knew it. He and the guard possessed a similar, polite facade that implied a well-hidden contempt.

We listened to the bartender tell us how interesting Minster was, what a loss it was to the club, before DeAntoni said, "The three of us are all friends of his wife, Sally. You ever meet her?"

"No, sir. I don't think I had the pleasure. You're guests of Mrs. Minster?"

"That's right. We're friends of Geoff, too. We *were* his friends. Crummy luck, huh? Falling off the ass-end of a boat. Geoff was one smart operator. He was the guy behind developing this place, which you probably know. Right here where you're working. Sawgrass. Him and some weird religious guru, but Geoff was the real brains —"

For just an instant, the mask slipped a little as the bartender interrupted with exaggerated civility. "Excuse me, sir. Bhagwan Shiva is not some *weird* religious guru. He's a gifted and enlightened individual. A very great man. Shiva comes here often, and we're honored that Shiva has chosen Sawgrass as his personal ashram. In fact, he'll be here this afternoon."

DeAntoni said, "Ashram," in a blank tone that said he didn't know what Kurt was talking about.

"An ashram is a place for spiritual retreat. Like a church, only more than that. At Sawgrass, we have an indoor ashram for meditation, religious instruction. We also have a much larger outdoor ashram, which is at the end of the nature trail. Cypress Ashram. It's an amphitheater beneath a really pretty cypress dome. It's beautiful; seats nearly a thousand. Some people say they find grace and tranquillity if they just sit there alone for a few minutes. I suggest you visit it."

It was a subtle cut that DeAntoni missed. He replied, "Yeah, Geoff was into that stuff, too, meditation, religion —" but the bartender had already turned away, ending the conversation, walking off, telling us that he'd go check with the kitchen because our food should be up soon.

When Kurt was gone, the white-haired man cleared his throat, a mild smile on his face, looking at us with eyes that were bleary, seemed a little sad. "Forgive me, but I couldn't help overhearing that you gentlemen were friends of Geoff. I knew him well. A wonderful guy." The man had the genial southern accent that I associate with moneyed people from Charleston society or, perhaps, old Atlanta.

DeAntoni said too quickly, "Oh yeah, the best. Geoff was a real peach."

"Quite a raconteur," the man said. "Told the funniest stories."

"Hilarious," DeAntoni said. "Made your sides ache when he really got going."

My antennae were up. A lot of little warning bells were going off. I sensed we were being manipulated, even tested, as the white-haired man continued, "So you really did *know* our old colleague. I'm surprised I didn't see y'all at the memorial service."

Tomlinson, typically, had already perceived what I was just beginning to suspect, because he spoke before DeAntoni or I could reply, saying, "My brothers, I think we have badly misjudged our drinking neighbor. Sir" — he turned on his stool to face the older man — "we deceived the bartender. Flat-out lied on purpose. He's a young spirit, an inexperienced soul. But not you. So the truth is, we didn't know Mr. Minster. I met him once — and he wasn't impressed. But we *are* friends of his wife, Sally. Mind if I ask how you knew we were lying?"

The man was swirling the whiskey in his

184

glass, staring into it. I realized that he was already well on his way to being drunk, only an hour past noon.

He said, "The way I know is, I've spent my life starting companies, overseeing corporations, sniffing every kind of man you can imagine. It takes balls the size of pit bulls to be successful in American business — especially these days. So an ol' boy also has to have a finely developed, built-in bullshit detector."

His mild smile broadened as he added, "And you, gentlemen, set off my bullshit detector the moment you walked through the door. The moment your large friend opened his New York mouth" — he used his chin to indicate DeAntoni — "I knew he was full of manure. Besides that, Geoff Minster never told a funny story in his life. I don't think the man knew how to laugh. Although, he was maybe trying to *learn* toward the end."

I expected DeAntoni to bristle. Instead, he stood and held out his hand. He waited as the older man thought for a moment, then finally shook it. "You got good judgment, Mac. The kind of guy who says what's on his mind, which I respect. Truth is, I'm a private investigator trying to help Mrs. Minster. She doesn't think her husband's dead. Neither do I. Which is why I'm down here askin' questions."

The white-haired man considered that through two delicate sips of his drink. His expression read: *Interesting.* Finally, he stood,

185

pausing another moment to be certain of his balance. Then he said, "I'm going to find a corner table — away from that little Nazi of a Yankee bartender. Interested in joining me?"

When DeAntoni said yes, the man told him, "Excellent. 'Far as I'm concerned, the only bad thing about drinking alone is that a fine Scotch never gets the time it deserves to breathe."

"Conversation," Tomlinson replied agreeably, "can be the secret to getting a whiskey binge off to a good start."

" 'Conversation'?" the man said. "Son, I don't waste my time with conversation. No businessman worth a damn talks for pleasure. If I open my mouth, it's either to take a drink or to negotiate. Sometimes, it's to barter. Which is what we're doing now. I'm drinking thirty-four-year-old Blackadder Single Malt. Staff has it flown in special from Ben Nevis at a price that's obscene. If I'm talking, you're buying. That's the agreement. So I hope you brought a walletful of cash."

The white-haired man, who introduced himself as Carter McRae, said to us, "Before we sit down and get real comfy-like, I'd like to ask you a couple of questions. Does Miz Sally want to find out if Geoff's dead 'cause she misses him? Or is it 'cause she's worried about losing the insurance money?"

I answered. "Neither. She wants to give most of the money to her church. Ethically, she can't

186

do that if her husband's still alive."

The older man nodded, apparently pleased. "That there's the only answer I'd have believed. Okay, so now I'd appreciate it if you'd haul out one of those cell phones ev'body carries these days and dial up the lady. Sally knows me. Not well, but she knows who I am. If you're such old and good friends, you won't have to bother lookin' up her number now, will you?"

We were dealing with one tough, shrewd old guy.

DeAntoni had a phone and the number. After he'd dialed, McRae held his hand out, put the phone to his ear, pushed open the double doors, and walked out onto the veranda. I watched him through the glass. As he spoke into the phone, he maintained the same mild smile, but his sad eyes brightened slightly. Beyond and below him were cypress trees knee-deep in water; Spanish moss draped over limbs like blue mist.

"Something's wrong with him," Tomlinson said softly, looking through the window. "Something happened to hurt him recently."

DeAntoni said, "What makes you think that? The guy's ballsy. He likes his whiskey, but there's nothing in the world wrong with a man liking his whiskey."

"It's pure pain. I can see it." Tomlinson started to add something, but stopped because McRae was coming back into the room. As he handed DeAntoni the phone, the older man looked at me, saying, "You're Ford. Sally says you two've been friends since you were kids. Talks about you like you ought to be wearin' shining armor and a halo" — his eyes narrowed slightly as he finished — "but I'd bet a good pointer dog she's wrong about that. The halo part. Which is just fine by me. I don't like saints. Righteousness — that's for people who don't have the spine to live like men."

I told him, "Your dog would be perfectly safe. I've known Sally a long time. She's a good one. A nice person."

"I couldn't agree more, son. Which is why you gave the only answer that was gonna keep me sitting here, drinking your whiskey. I met the lady six, seven times and, each time, I liked her better. Gwendie — my wife — she felt the same. Which is why I'll be happy to talk a spell. You've met those couples who just never seemed to fit? Where you think the wife's got way too much spunk and class and pure built-in funny for the husband? Or just the opposite: The wife's a dud, and the husband's got all the star quality?"

"Sure. Too often."

"Damn right, son, way too often. They got an unhappiness about them that seeps across a room. My point being that I could never picture Sally with Geoff. We ran in the same circles, belonged to the same clubs. To me, what they seemed to be was two strangers who always arrived in the same car. Not like those good couples you meet every now and again. A man and woman who can be at opposite ends of a big party, but're still right there together. Partners joined at the heart."

Tomlinson said gently, "Like you and Gwendie."

McRae seemed to look deeper into his Scotch glass before downing it in a gulp. He was about to reply when the bartender re-appeared, carrying our food. Kurt was visibly surprised to see the four of us at the same table. When he asked, "Is everything okay here, Mr. McRae?" he was really asking if the older man wanted him to get rid of us.

"Fine, Kurt, just fine. Turns out, these gentlemen and I have some old mutual friends. Hell of a coincidence, runnin' into 'em here."

As he walked away, McRae said in a low voice, "One of the choirboys. That's what I call 'em. The Church of Ashram staffs this place with their own people — which is why he got so pissed off when you made that remark about Jerry."

DeAntoni said, "Jerry?"

"Jerry Singh, the head guru. Shiva, the big shot who calls himself Bhagwan. The *weirdo* you were talking about. Only here, we call him by his real name 'cause he found out damn quick that men with enough money to afford membership aren't going to tolerate all his religious nonsense. So he pretends to be just one of the boys. Actually seems to enjoy it."

189

I asked, "Then why do you tolerate his people as staff?"

McRae said, "Why? Because they're superb, that's why. Because they're the best I've ever seen at what they do. Remember that recluse a few years back, one of the world's richest men? He only hired members from this one particularly strict religion. They did everything for him, cooking, all the secretarial stuff, even took charge of his gambling interests out there in Nevada.

"It didn't make sense to me at the time 'til I spent a few weeks at Sawgrass. Same principle applies here. Jerry's people — the choirboys, his choirgirls — really believe in what he says. They don't drink or smoke, and they sure as hell aren't going to steal. They're not employees; they're *disciples*. To them, he's a kind'a God, so they treat us the same way, 'cause that's what he's commanded. Which means they follow orders, no questions asked. You ever see Jerry on stage? Attend one of his services?"

Tomlinson said, "I've read about them."

McRae said, "You won't see a better show in Vegas. Who's the famous magician, the one with the long hair? Lots of smoke and dramatic lighting? Jerry's shows are just as good or better. The man's a hell of an actor. He's got a great sense of dramatic timing. He's fun to watch, and I think that's one reason his followers do exactly whatever he tells them to do."

McRae added, "They work their asses off. They're always on time, always polite. They keep the grounds just like they keep the kitchen — immaculate. Cleanliness is one of the Ashram's tenets. So're obedience and hard work. They're as efficient as little robots. See Kurt? He's bringing me another Blackadder right now. The glass'll be spotless, and it'll be filled with a good, full pour. Never had to say a word. I never do."

McRae paused as the bartender served. Waited patiently until he was gone, then continued, "You can ask 'em to do anything you want — literally almost *anything* — they'll do it. If I tell Kurt, call security and have you gentlemen escorted out, they'd do it so quick and smooth, people slurping soup out on the veranda would never know there was trouble. I wouldn't have to tell them why, give them a reason, say another damn word. Once they got you off alone, from what I've heard, you three'd never *risk* coming back again, either."

He paused, thinking about it, holding his Scotch to the light, seeming to take pleasure in its amber flush. He said, "People like me, men who fought hard to make their fortunes in the world, we *like* that. Unquestioned obedience. Hell, we demand it, but it's getting harder 'n' harder to find with all the damn do-gooders out there, and bullshit laws." McRae leaned toward me, focusing on me with his sad, old eyes, "There's only one thing you can't expect of staff here."

I said, "What's that?"

"Trustworthiness. You can't trust them. Whatever they hear, whatever they see, they'll take straight to Jerry if they think he should know. Which is why I'm sure he'll hear that the four of us were talking about Minster. Tonight at the latest, if that lil' Yankee hasn't called Jerry already."

DeAntoni asked, "So what's wrong with that, Mac? It's a free country."

"I know, I know, I'm just warning you. Jerry's ruthless — you have to be ruthless to run an organization the size of his. He's not going to be happy about a member talking to outsiders — especially me, 'cause he knows how I feel. First time I heard about it, the way Minster supposedly fell off that sports fisherman at night, I never did believe it. Personally, I've always believed Geoff's still alive."

Carter McRae told us he'd been suspicious of Minster's disappearance for a simple reason: He was acquainted with the three men who were with Minster that night. He told us their names. One was a well-known Florida politician, another was an international investment banker, the third a retired State Supreme Court judge. They all lived in the same exclusive little Coconut Grove community, Ironwood.

"Know what else those three had in common?" McRae asked. "They didn't much like

Geoff. Don't misunderstand me — they didn't hate him. Just didn't particularly care for him, which I can understand. Before his religious conversion, Minster was a hard-ass businessman who didn't give a damn about making friends. After his conversion, he was so touchy-feely-spiritual that a real man wouldn't want to waste time talking to him."

According to McRae, he'd spoken with all three after the disappearance. Each of the three men told him that the only reason they'd gone on the fishing trip was because Minster had pushed and pestered until they finally agreed just to fulfill a social obligation they would never have to endure again.

McRae asked us, "Now why would Minster choose three men who didn't much like him to go on that boat?"

"Witnesses," Tomlinson said immediately. "Three of the most respected men in the state. He wanted witnesses. The kind no one would ever doubt."

McRae was nodding, smiling; a man who was at the head of the table no matter where he sat, sober or drunk. "You, sir, have an intellect that is not implied by your physical appearance — unlike your politics. I have a little grand-daughter who uses the same kind'a combs in her hair, and that shirt you're wearing reminds me of Derby Day in Lexington. All the pretty, flowered bonnets."

Tomlinson took it as a compliment. "Thank

you, Mr. McRae. But I can't take credit for the witness theory. Doc was the first to think of it. Invite three solid citizens, then fake your death by jumping overboard. A second boat's in the area, lights out, waiting to make the pickup."

I'd considered the possibility, but didn't remember mentioning it to Tomlinson.

I listened to McRae say, "I haven't followed it that closely. Perhaps you gentlemen know more details. Did anyone ever ask the boat's captain if he had his radar on that night? If there was a second vessel following, or waiting close enough to pick up Minster, the skipper would've seen it on the screen."

DeAntoni said, "I interviewed the captain. So'd the cops. He had radar, yeah, but he told me he didn't notice. It was such a clear night, plenty calm, that he was running the thing all by himself, no need to use the electronics. Plus, he had no idea what time Minster went overboard. The last person to see him was the retired judge, and that was around nine P.M. They didn't realize he was gone 'til the next morning, when they woke up in Bimini."

I asked, "Can you think of any reason why Minster would want to stage his own death?"

McRae said, "There're only two reasons a man disappears on purpose, and both're because he feels he has to escape. He's trying to escape from someone who wants to kill him, or he wants to escape his old life. Too many bills, too much pressure. Leave behind a life he just can't stomach any longer. Or maybe escape into the arms of a different woman."

DeAntoni said, "Minster was sick of his old life, his wife told us that. Was he screwing around on her?"

"Sorry, that's the sort of question a gentleman doesn't answer. Not that I approve of such behavior. I've been married for fifty-two years and was unfaithful to my wife only once. That was a long, long time ago. It was the saddest, sickest thing I've ever done, and the only true regret I have in this life."

After a few moments of reflection, McRae added, "Was Minster screwing around? I will say this. In the Ashram faith, I hear communal sex is allowed. Maybe even encouraged. All I'll tell you is, the month before he disappeared, Minster lived here in the club's bachelor quarters. He almost never went home to Sally. I also know he had a special friend, an Indian woman. That's all I'll say on the subject."

"Would you tell us her name if you knew it?"

"No."

"Is there anything else that suggests to you that he intentionally went missing?"

"As I said, there're only two reasons a man chooses to disappear: to start a new life, or to get away from someone who was trying to kill him. Could be, both reasons applied to Geoff."

That was a surprising thing to hear. DeAntoni said, "He was afraid of being killed? By *who?*"

"Figure it out for yourselves. Toward the end, he and Jerry weren't getting along. They sat here one night, screaming at each other. Kurt about soiled his pants, he was so quick to shut the restaurant down. The holy man, Bhagwan Shiva, acting like a drunken bully. We can't let the faithful see something like that, now, can we?"

"Do you know what the argument was about?"

McRae had begun to weave slightly, his eyes even blurrier. Now, with a slowly marshaled effort, he straightened himself, giving it careful consideration, before he told us, "Gentlemen, I think our little barter session has come to an end. I have reached the point where this very fine Scotch has turned to common whiskey on my palate, and that's a sin against all that I hold dear. Besides, the subject's too serious for drunk talk."

He was pulling his wallet out, from which he produced a business card. "You write your phone numbers on this little piece of paper. Give me some time to think it over. Maybe I'll call. Maybe I won't. Let's just leave it at that."

As we paid the tab, I noticed that Tomlinson had his hand on McRae's shoulder, leaning toward him, talking into his ear.

I watched the distinguished man frown, shaking his head. Then McRae closed his eyes, listening . . . then it appeared as if he were fighting back tears, patting the top of Tomlinson's hand with his own. He spoke a few words as Tomlinson continued to whisper, and then McRae was nodding, smiling a little.

Outside, I dropped far enough behind DeAntoni to ask Tomlinson, "What were you saying to him back there?"

"Mr. McRae's wife, Gwendie, was operated on for a cerebral aneurysm six months ago. She's been in a coma; on life support ever since."

"How'd you know that?"

"I didn't. I had a strong sense that he was in pain. He's a good man, too. Not *my* kind of man. Not the kind I'd choose for a friend. When he described Shiva as ruthless? He was describing himself just as accurately. I suspect you realize that. But a good man, even so.

"His driver takes him to Naples Community Hospital every night at six, where he sits beside Gwendie for as long as he's allowed, holding her hand, whispering into her ear. Every morning, he comes here and drinks single malt until he's drunk enough to go home and get some sleep."

"What did you say to him?"

"I got his e-mail address. Told him I'd send him a paper I wrote a long time ago. Maybe it'll give him some comfort."

I knew exactly what paper he meant — "One Fathom Above Sea Level." But I said, "What paper's that?"

"Just a paper. I'd almost forgotten I'd written

the thing until strangers starting e-mailing me, asking questions about it. Pretty weird, man. The present meets the past. Unfortunately, the brain cells that did the writing are long, long gone. Oh" — he was walking beside me, twisting his yellow goatee into curls — "something else I told him was that my instincts are pretty good. I told him I was getting strong vibes that Gwendie's gonna wake up soon. It might take awhile, but she's going to be okay."

I said, "Do you think that's a responsible thing to do — give the man false hopes? You could end up hurting him more."

"In the paper I mentioned — this is just an example, and I'm paraphrasing. But I wrote something about selfless hope. I said hope is the simplest proof of divine origin. When I told him that, he seemed to appreciate it."

I said, "I wouldn't mind seeing how you come to that conclusion. Why don't you send me a copy. I'll read it."

That much was true. I *hadn't* read it. For some reason, to do so without Tomlinson's permission had seemed an invasion of his privacy. It was something a stranger could do, but not a friend.

"Know what, Doc? Considering all you've been through, I came *this* close to asking you to read it fifty, sixty times. But it seemed like an imposition. Like you'd have to read it just because we're pals." Then he stopped talking and, in a different tone of voice, he said, "Uh-oh.

Here comes trouble."

He meant the golf cart speeding toward us, two men aboard. Pith helmet, the guard from the front gate, was sitting beside a driver who wore a black T-shirt and black cap, SECURITY printed on both in yellow letters.

I remembered Sally telling us about Shiva's Archangels, the security people who always dressed in black.

DeAntoni saw them, too. He stopped, waiting, when pith helmet said loud enough for us all to hear, "There they are; it's them. Those're the ones."

chapter fifteen

The golf cart came at us full speed, then turned in front of DeAntoni so abruptly that it almost hit him. He backed up reflexively a couple of steps as the two men bailed out even before it stopped. Pith helmet was already talking, speaking to us as a group in his cop voice, very officious.

"You individuals are on private property. I warned you. I told you that you weren't permitted on the grounds, but here you are. So we're going to detain you until we've contacted the sheriff's department —"

At the same time, DeAntoni was saying, "Whoa, Mac, stop right there. Not another step closer," because they were coming toward him.

Pith helmet had a leather sap in his hand, and appeared ready to use it. The man in the black cap held what looked to be a cell phone, but the shape didn't seem quite right. Then I realized what it was: a taser gun. A taser shoots twin, dart-pointed probes that produce a pulsing, high-voltage current when they make contact with human flesh.

Pith helmet was saying, "The smart thing for

you people to do is shut your mouths, just come along peacefully. Put your hands behind your heads —" as DeAntoni stopped backing up, his expression was changing; a sort of game-face transformation that I know too well.

"Mac," he said, not very loud, "you lay a finger on me, you're going to be shitting little pieces of that sap for the next three weeks."

Which is when Tomlinson rushed forward, trying to intervene. He was walking fast toward the security guards, his palms held outward — *slow down; stay calm* — telling them, "It's okay, it's okay, we have permission to be here. Call Carter McRae. He knows us. Mr. McRae, or even the bartender, Kurt. He saw us together."

Black hat had been focused on DeAntoni, but now he turned his attention to Tomlinson, holding the taser in his hand like some kind of space-age revolver. Black hat was taller, leaner than pith helmet; had a look of forced stoicism, as if he were trying hard to behave professionally, but was actually excited, enjoying himself.

"You're friends of Mr. McRae, huh? Just like you're good friends of the Terwilligers. I called Mr. Terwilliger and checked. They've never heard of you people. Which is why we're detaining you. So put your hands behind your heads. *Now.*"

At the same time, black hat was talking to Tomlinson, telling him, "Stay back, stay back, don't come any closer — I'm warning you," as Tomlinson continued to walk fast, trying to position himself between DeAntoni and the two guards.

Then black hat shot Tomlinson in the chest with the taser. I heard a blast of compressed air; saw the probes snake toward him. Tomlinson was wearing a Hawaiian shirt, pink surfboards on purple silk. It was very thin material, and I could hear the sickening thud of the darts impacting upon muscle and bone.

It was a grotesque scene to witness. Tomlinson dropped like a rag doll, landed on his side and rolled to his back, his arms and legs flailing, the muscles of his face spasming as his eyes fluttered back in his head.

DeAntoni and I had begun to sprint toward black hat the instant he aimed the taser, but pith helmet intercepted DeAntoni — or tried to. I heard pith helmet give a shriek of pain, but didn't see why because I was concentrating on black hat, who held the taser in his left hand like some macabre puppeteer, Tomlinson twitching wildly at the end of two black strings. With his right hand, though, black hat was now unholstering a revolver.

The sign at the gatehouse had warned that the staff here was authorized to carry firearms, but what kind of idiot would draw a weapon under these circumstances? The answer was unnerving: the kind of idiot who was eager for a reason to shoot someone.

Me.

I vaulted over Tomlinson and drove my

shoulder into black hat's chest, pinning his right wrist against his holster as I pushed him backwards, then lifted him high off the ground, his feet kicking. I held him there for a moment before I turned and body-slammed him onto the brick sidewalk. He hit with such force that it knocked the wind out of him: The wide, bulging eyes were symptomatic. It's a terrifying thing to be unable to breathe, and his expression reflected that terror.

He'd gotten the revolver drawn — a .38 caliber Smith. I kicked it away, into grass, then rushed to Tomlinson and yanked the probes out of his chest. The muscle spasms ceased almost immediately, but it took a few moments before his glazed eyes could focus.

"Are you okay?"

He made a fluttering noise with his lips, his face illustrating dazed wonderment. "Holy shit! What a . . . what a *rush* that was, man. *Wow.*"

To my left, I could hear DeAntoni saying, "I knew it, I knew it. Look'a the tears running down tough guy's cheeks."

He had the fingers of his left hand wedged between pith helmet's throat and jaw, holding him against the golf cart, and was slapping him rhythmically with his open right palm. "Guess what I've decided, tough guy? I'm not going to let you arrest us today. Nod your head a couple times, just so I know you agree."

Pith helmet nodded quickly.

Black hat was recovering, getting slowly to

his knees, so I scooped up the revolver, popped the cylinder, threw the cartridges into the bushes, then the gun. A walkie-talkie lay nearby, and I tossed that, too.

I told DeAntoni to stop, give me a second, and then I said to pith helmet, "Know what we'd appreciate? We'd really like a ride to the closest gate."

Pith helmet's voice was higher-pitched now and raspy. "That's all we wanted in the first place. To tell you to leave the premises. That's all we wanted you to do."

Helping Tomlinson to his feet, I said, "Then you won't mind if we borrow your golf cart."

I told DeAntoni I thought it was a bad idea to drive the cart off Sawgrass property. He said, "Screw 'im. You heard the dude. Gave us permission to use it. Screw walkin' through the field again. I'm driving the damn thing all the way back to that bar. What was the name?"

Gator Bill's.

He did, too. Drove us past the service gate, where Freddy gave us an uneasy wave, down the road to the little crossroads village of Devil's Garden.

Tomlinson sat in the front, still dazed but excited, jabbering away. I was in the back, so I had to turn to listen to him say, "My tolerance for high voltage just keeps getting higher and higher, man. I've been zapped so many times, I'm starting to *enjoy* it — which opens a whole new world of exploration."

He lifted his hair to show DeAntoni, pointing to the tiny lightning-bolt scar on the side of his head. "Mother Nature once zapped me with lightning as a personal favor. Direct strike, man. A very *intense* experience. Years before that, I also spent a couple of weeks doing a little table dance which my old shrink, a Freud-geek, described as 'electroshock therapy.' Didn't have much choice about that one, either. Same this time. Man, when those two darts hit my chest, it was almost like the time I picked up the electric ray. Remember, Doc?"

I said I did, pleased that he was okay; that he didn't seem to be suffering any lasting effects from the stun gun.

He said, "When I got hit, it was like a bright blue light flashed on behind my eyes. I could see a wiring schematic for my entire nervous system. *Seriously.* Like in the cartoons where the mouse electrocutes the cat. Far out, man! In a chemical-electric way, I'm talking about. A really far-out sort of rush."

When Tomlinson added, "Doc . . . I want you to think this one over. If I invested in one of those taser guns . . . if I *asked* you to give me the occasional shot in the ass — controlled conditions, of course. An interesting social experiment is what I'm describing —"

I told him, "Absolutely not. Drop the subject," as DeAntoni, shaking his head, said, "A weirdo, man. How'd I end up dealing with this kind of shit? I'm driving a golf cart through a

205

swamp with a hippie who probably gets his jollies sticking his pecker in a light socket. Unbelievable. After this one, I'm thinking of moving the whole damn operation back to civilization."

When we walked into Gator Bill's, people eating at tables, men at the bar, the waitress, everyone, looked up, as afternoon sunlight trailed us through the screen door.

There's the scene in classic Western films where the saloon goes silent when strangers enter. This room didn't go silent, but it quieted except for the country jukebox. The impression was the same: We were outsiders, and outsiders were neither expected nor welcomed.

At the bar were wobbly, wooden stools. We took the last three at the end. To the woman behind the counter, Tomlinson said, "Maybe you'll know. I just got shot with a taser gun; some *serious* voltage. What kind'a beverage would you recommend as a good chaser? Beer's not going to do it, and wine just doesn't seem appropriate."

She was a tall, wide-bodied woman who wore a blouse outside her skirt to mask her shape. An Indian-looking woman. Most of the people in the bar, in fact, looked Native American. Men, mostly; 'Glades Indians dressed like cowboys in jeans, Western shirts and boots. Working guys, cattlemen and truck drivers, probably, on their lunch break.

To Tomlinson, the woman said, "You drunk? I'm not understanding what you mean."

DeAntoni said, "Just give Mr. Looney a beer," as Tomlinson told her, "The security guards at Sawgrass nailed me with a taser. One of those electric stun guns? Which was actually kind of interesting, but something about it — maybe the electrical current — left a weird metallic taste in my mouth. Probably had to do with the chemical transformation of ions. So I need the right drink to get rid of the taste."

The woman's expression said, *Is this a joke?* but she told him, "Across the street at the Grab Bag, they sell mouthwash. Maybe try that."

"Mouthwash, hum . . . I've tried that under different circumstances, but — I don't want to be indelicate here — mouthwash tends to give my urine an unnatural odor. A little too minty fresh. I'm a *traditionalist*. Can't help it. So, what I think I'll have is" — he held up an index finger to signal his decision — "I think I'll have a double vodka martini. Stoli, if you have it. And pop in a couple of jalapeno olives. No . . . *bleu cheese* olives. That should counteract it. Make me right as rain."

The woman's expression said: *What the hell are you talking about?*

As Tomlinson talked, I'd heard chairs scooching on the floor behind us, and now someone tapped me on the shoulder. I turned to see three men. One wore a sweat-shaped cowboy hat, a straw roper. The other two had their black hair slicked back. Men of size. Wide-shouldered, wrangler-hipped.

One of them, the man wearing the straw Stetson, said, "Maybe somebody forgot to tell you at Sawgrass, but we don't appreciate you staff people coming in this bar. Isn't that right, Jenny?"

The man didn't sound like a bully; just the opposite. Seemed as if he were uneasy having to confront us, even a little shy about it. Kept tugging at the brim of his hat, which was frayed by a couple of years of sweat and sun.

The big woman said, "That sure is right. Your goons have busted enough people's heads in here. We don't want no more fighting, no more trouble. So management up the road said we stay away from your place, you keep out of ours. That's the deal we made."

DeAntoni said, "What? You think we work for those pinheads at Sawgrass. No way. Jeez, Mac, give us some credit."

The man doing the talking turned toward the window, looking outside. "Then why're you driving one of their golf carts? It says SAWGRASS SECURITY on the side. Those're the people we've had all the problems with. The ones who dress in black; carry clubs and stun guns, and they don't hold back usin' them. Which is why the people who live here don't want you around no more."

Tomlinson stood and opened his purple Hawaiian shirt. There were two tiny black burn marks on his chest. "Man, you don't have to tell us about stun guns. Wasn't twenty minutes ago they shot me. There I was flopping around in the dirt like a tuna on the gymnasium floor. They're quick on the draw, those Sawgrass guys." He waited, people staring at his bony chest. "Hey — think if we went back, they'd shoot me again?"

The man doing the talking seemed to relax a little. He took off his cowboy hat and wiped his forehead with the back of his hand. "Why'd they shoot you?"

"Trespassing. That's what they said. Only we weren't — not after we made it to the bar, anyway."

"How'd you get the golf cart?"

DeAntoni told him, "We borrowed it. But we don't plan to take it back, so help yourself. If it ends up in a canal, I'm not gonna shed any tears. Enjoy."

The man looked at his two friends, then the woman bartender, then the waitress — a lean, attractive woman with braided hair and a Plains Indian nose. He'd begun to smile. "Guess we ought to show 'em, huh?"

He and the man to his right unbuttoned their shirts, then pointed to similar twin scars on their chest, spaced as if they'd been struck by the fangs of the same large snake. "It was one of the damnedest feelings I've ever had. Your muscles start twitching and there's nothing you can do. I felt sick for about a week after that."

As Tomlinson said, "Really? You mean you didn't *like* it?" the waitress, who'd moved closer to the window said, "James. *James,* they're here. The Sawgrass people. Call the sheriff, Jenny. Call nine-one-one right now or they're gonna do it to us again."

I was off my stool, trying to get a look through the door, when the man doing the talking, James, said, "I guess they must'a come looking for their golf cart."

He meant the white Chevy van outside, doors open, a half-dozen men climbing out, all dressed in black, SECURITY printed in big gold letters on their T-shirts, carrying saps and stun guns. No firearms in the holsters, though — probably paying scrupulous attention to the law because they were anticipating trouble.

Pith helmet hadn't made the trip. But black hat, the tall, lean one, was among them, although he was markedly smaller than the guards in this new bunch. They could have been a group of linebackers from a small-college football team. Clean-cut-looking bunch, hair squared off at the back, a couple of jock-looking women among them.

Hanging up the phone, Jenny said to the room, "Just like always. The sheriff's dispatcher said it'd take 'em forty minutes, maybe an hour, to get a deputy here from Homestead."

Walking toward the door, his friends beside him, James said, "We already talked about this, what we're gonna do. We're not going to let them come through this door, no matter what. It's gotta stop. It's gonna stop *now*."

DeAntoni continued to impress me. The local men, seven or eight of them, had moved outside, forming a human barrier between the white van and the entrance to Gator Bill's. There were James and his friends, a couple of more Indians and two or three sun-darkened Anglos, Western hats angled back on their heads.

They looked like working cowboys awaiting a rodeo. It would've been easy enough for us to stay behind them, let these two bands of locals battle out their problems.

But not DeAntoni. He edged his way through the group, me trailing along, until we were both at the front, standing on gravel in the April heat, facing the security people from Sawgrass. They were standing in a loose V-formation — a tactical grouping that suggested they'd had some training.

Black hat pointed, saying, "There they are, the ones that stole the cart. Those two, plus the hippie in the back. The short, stocky dude, he's the one who slapped Corey around." Black hat was now pointing at DeAntoni and me, but not getting too close.

One of them asked, "The one with the shaved head?"

"Yeah, Mr. Clean. The one who looks like the fake wrestlers on TV. He got lucky with Corey. I think he hurt him pretty bad."

Expressions on the faces of the guards re-

211

minded me of cops who'd just heard the call *"Officer down!"* Pissed off, united.

Not even a little nervous, like he'd been through this many times before, DeAntoni said, "Sonny, did you just call me *short?*"

"Yeah, so what? You *are* short. Bald and short. You got a problem with the truth?"

DeAntoni said, "Maybe I'll seem a little taller once I shove your head up your ass — give you a different perspective" as, from behind, James was telling them, "You men are on private property and we want you to leave. Jenny in there owns the place. Her and Bill — we all want you off this property."

The guard at the front of the group was not the biggest of the men, but he had an administrative cool that indicated he was in charge. Pointing at us, he said, "These men stole one of our golf carts. Do you want to be a party to that, James? How about you, Bobbie Lee? Grand theft; a felony. Do you really want to help these guys? Maybe spend another couple nights in jail?"

DeAntoni began to walk toward the guards, saying, "They didn't steal your damn cart; no one stole it. I borrowed it. Which reminds me: I've got a complaint for management. The damn thing stops at every bar we come to. I think your golf cart has an alcohol problem."

Which got a nervous laugh from the locals, but tightened the expression on the faces of the guards.

DeAntoni continued to walk as he talked. Didn't stop until he was standing toe-to-toe with the head guard, looking up at the taller man, the kind of physical tension spreading among the group that you sense in pack dogs just before they begin to fight. DeAntoni's voice had gotten softer, more intense, forcing everyone to listen as he said to the man, "Tell me something: Are you the guy in charge of this bunch of candy-ass rent-a-cops?"

The guard was trying to force a professional calm into his voice. "You need to back away, sir. Get *back*. I'm not going to tell you twice . . ."

DeAntoni took two tiny steps closer so that he was, for a moment, standing on the tips of the taller man's shoes. "I've got a proposition for you — sonny. Pick out any three of your guys. Let's fight it out. My pal, the professor, here —"

Without breaking eye contact with the guard, he used his head to indicate me. "— we'll take on all four of you. Tag team, if you want. No clubs, no tasers, just bare fists. You got the balls?"

The guard laughed nervously. I noticed a crisp trickle of sweat begin to river down his cheek. Behind him, a couple of his men were whispering, *Do it, Jason; let's kick their asses. Have a little fun,* but Jason said, "Four of us against two of you? You can't be that stupid. It wouldn't be fair."

DeAntoni edged up onto the man's toes again, his chin nearly touching the guard's chin. "You're right, sonny boy. It *wouldn't* be fair. Okay, here's my last offer. You can have *five* guys. You and any other four you want. There. Like those odds better?"

From behind me, I heard James say, "That's the thing about these guys. Without their weapons, they're cowards."

From the group of guards, a woman's voice said, *"Fucking drunken Indian better shut his mouth,"* but Jason was still in charge, maintaining control, backing away from DeAntoni, telling him, "We're not on the playground. We don't negotiate with thieves. You're gonna have to come with us so we can turn you over to law enforcement."

DeAntoni told him, "Mac, you're dreaming. Not a chance," as I felt Tomlinson trying to push past me. I turned to see him using his fingers to comb his long hair back as he called to the head guard, "Jason? *Jason.* Arrest me — I took the cart. I mean it."

I grabbed his arm. "I'm not going to let them dart you again, if that's what you're hoping."

"They won't touch me," he said, trying to pull free. "You've never taken me seriously, but I've told you that I'm a master of t'ai chi — a completely passive, defensive martial art. Give me a chance."

Looking toward us, DeAntoni said, "Stay

where you are, Tinkerbell." Then, turning back to Jason, he said, "So what about it, sonny boy? You candy-ass rent-a-cops take a hike right now — leave with the golf cart. Or let's you and me roll around on the ground awhile. Unless maybe you want to go crying to the guru geek who pays all you little robots."

That did it.

Three or four of the largest security staff came pushing forward. They'd apparently been talking among themselves; had already decided what they were going to do. They walked toward DeAntoni as a group. As they did, they unbuckled their tactical belts, to which were affixed handcuffs, saps, taser guns and empty holsters.

They handed the belts carefully to their friends, as the largest of them — a huge, black-haired man with winglike trapezoid muscles connecting shoulders and neck — said in a heavy German accent, "Bare fists, yah! Just like you said. Before I am done, you will be saying the name of His Holiness, Bhagwan Shiva, with respect. You will be begging me to let you say his name."

DeAntoni was backing away, giving himself some room, causing a small human ring to form around him. He looked at me, and said, "If they double-team me, I expect you to bust a couple of heads."

Staring at Jason, I lifted my hand and pointed as if my thumb and index finger were a gun.

Speaking loud enough, I said, "I'll start with him."

I expected it to degenerate into a small riot. It didn't — but only because DeAntoni immediately took command.

The German came out with his big fists held high, dancing and pawing at Frank, doing what appeared to be a clumsy imitation of a professional prizefighter. The other guards yelled encouragement — *"Knock him on his ass, Yan!"* — while the locals stood focused, not saying much, not yet willing to risk an alliance with losers, but interested.

Beside me, Tomlinson said, "Keep an eye on the muscle-bound guard. The guy with the biceps. He's trying to sneak around behind us."

He was, too: broad-shouldered man in his late twenties, black hat turned backward, biceps stretching the sleeves of his T-shirt. I watched him move slowly around the back of the little crowd, nonchalant, trying not to draw attention to himself.

Watching him from the corner of my eye, I began to move in his direction, still watching DeAntoni, too.

The German began to throw a fusillade of punches, swinging from the hips. DeAntoni got his arms up over his ears to absorb the first few blows, but, suddenly, he was no longer there to be hit. He ducked under the big man's elbow, then used his open palms to clap the man's ears, cymbal-like — a seemingly harmless slap that, in fact, was excruciating because both eardrums ruptured, judging from the blood that began to trickle down the man's neck.

The German gave a throaty woof of pain and tried to turn, but couldn't. From behind, DeAntoni had already laced an arm around the man's throat, another up between his crotch. He lifted the German off the ground, and then dropped him — not hard — spine-first across his knee, and held him there, immobile, in one of the most dangerous of all submission holds.

To myself, I thought, *They're going to rush him now.*

But the guards didn't.

They wanted to. Adrenaline had taken over. But DeAntoni stopped them in their tracks, saying in a loud voice, "If you assholes take another step, I'll snap his neck. You'll take him home in a wheelchair. Kapeesh?"

After a micro-moment of silence, the guards still thinking about it, DeAntoni added, "Ask your big buddy what he wants you to do."

The German, feeling the pressure on his spine, helpless, called to them, "Yah! Yah! No closer. We are done. We are done fighting! We take the golf cart and go, yah!"

I thought that was it. The end of it.

It wasn't.

I'd lost track of the guard with the biceps. But he hadn't lost track of me. I felt movement close to me; heard Tomlinson yell, "Doc! He's behind you!" and I then felt a sickening blow just above my right ear.

chapter sixteen

Biceps had hit me on the side of the head with a sap. It could have knocked me out, or killed me.

Instead, it sent me jackknifing to the ground, the backs of my eyes strobing with firework colors, cascading reds, greens, golds, my brain deafened by the boom of leather on bone. For an instant, I teetered on the brink of unconsciousness.

There is an ancient mammalian instinct which my forebrain inspected, then rejected: When overpowered by someone or something unknown, play dead. Remain motionless. Maybe it'll go away. Opossums are more strongly coded, but that survival instinct remains within most vertebrates.

As if through a tube, I could hear Tomlinson's voice saying, "Doc . . . *Doc* . . . are you okay?" And to biceps: "You idiot! Why'd you hit him so damn hard!"

Then I was on my knees, eyes open, watching biceps swing the sap at Tomlinson who, to my surprise, parried the blow with a delicate, dancelike movement of his hands. I watched him deflect a second, then a third attack, using biceps' own momentum to turn him away.

I remembered Tomlinson saying something about being a master of t'ai chi — but he was not sufficiently masterful, because biceps finally caught him with a solid blow to the shoulder that sent Tomlinson backpedaling into the little group of onlookers.

James, the cowboy local, caught him, and stepped toward biceps, fists up, ready to fight. But I was already in full stride, driving hard toward the man, making an odd guttural noise that did not seem to originate within me.

It was then that I experienced an internal transformation that I've experienced before. I've come to despise the transformation . . . and to fear it.

In the human brain is a tiny region called the amygdala, a section of cerebral matter so ancient that some scientists refer to it as our "lizard brain." Its purpose is to ensure survival, and all the complicated emotions and behaviors that survival implies. It is here that our basest of instincts thrive: sex, fury, flight — the earliest markers of more than a hundred million years of adaptation and survival. It is here that our atavistic dread of snakes is passed from generation to generation. In this small, dark place lives the killer that is in us all.

The modern portion of our brain has built up around that lizard brain, like a walnut cloaking a seed. However, when sufficiently stimulated, there can be an electrical transfer of behavioral control from the modern, rational brain to the cave-dwelling primate that hides within.

That's what happened to me now.

I felt a gathering, energized chill move through my body; my objective became so pure, so focused, that the progression of events unfolded before my eyes as if in slow motion. I could have been looking through a rifle scope — I could see nothing but the big-shouldered man with the biceps, yet I was aware of *everything* around me . . . everything but sound.

It was as if my auditory canal had been severed from my brain. There was no external volume. None. In lucid detail, I could see the people I shoved to the side, their mouths moving, but no words escaping, as I pursued biceps in a silence created by a surflike roaring in my own head. Nor was there any color. The world had been drained of pigment, leaving a portrait of blacks and grays.

Many animals, as we know, cannot distinguish color.

Yet my vision was acute, even with my glasses now hanging by fishing line around my neck. I could see biceps' eyes squenched in surprise as I caught him from behind, then pivoted him toward me.

I could see his expression with such feral clarity that I knew what he was feeling without having to process my own patterns of induction and thought. He was surprised I was back on my feet . . . he was confident that I was hurt badly enough that he could put me down again without much effort. Then, as I grabbed him, controlling his hands, at first, then his arms, then his entire body, he began to feel consternation, then fear and panic . . . then he began to feel terror.

When the tissue around a man's eyes stretches abnormally wide, it is a sort of ocular scream. Perhaps the brain is attempting to broaden peripheral vision, anticipating rescuers . . . or seeking an escape route to safe haven.

As I wrestled with him, everything I needed to know was available to me instantly; an instinct born within; an instinct exercised often enough throughout my life that it triggered reflex behavior that caused my body to act automatically, with a single objective.

I grabbed biceps by the ears, pulling him toward me as I lunged toward him. I head-butted him once, then twice. It knocked the hat off his head, and mashed his nose flat.

Then I was behind him, my hands and forearms creating a figure-four around his neck and chin, holding him there, waiting patiently, like a boa constrictor, for the perfect arm position that would give me maximum leverage. It's a kind of dance, my body reading the movements of his body, and counteracting immediately, as my hands tightened their control with every small error he made.

His body was unpracticed. It made several mistakes in sequence. He tried to kick me. Missed. He began to thrash. I closed his windpipe until he was out of air and relented. The man was helpless . . . and he knew it.

That's when I began to tighten the figure-four that my hands and arms had created around his throat and skull. Slowly, slowly, I began to transfer my body weight onto the man's neck, applying most of the pressure to his delicate cervical vertebra, which is the stem of bone and fluid between a man's skull and shoulders.

Now I was pivoting, muscles flexed, gradually increasing the weight and the pressure . . . hearing sound for the first time in many minutes as biceps began a meaningless, guttural bleating.

But I also heard a deeper, familiar voice calling into my ear: "Doc. Marion! Please, please . . . *please*. You're going to kill him!"

It was Tomlinson's voice, pleading.

There was another decipherable voice, too: DeAntoni talking to me, trying to pierce the shell of my fury, counseling me to back off, relax, it was over now.

I heard him say, "Let him go, Ford. *Let him go*. It's not worth jail. You're taking it too far."

Then I could feel DeAntoni's hands on me, prying my fingers away from the man's neck — but delicately, as if he were making a request . . . or dealing with a child.

"Easy. Nice and easy. He's had enough. It's *over.*"

It was like being awakened from a nightmare. The tunnel that I'd inhabited broadened into a horizon beneath sky. In the same instant, color returned to the world; sound, as well, as I released biceps. Gave him a little push as I stepped away, feeling oddly groggy — sickened, perhaps, by too much adrenaline dumped into my system, way too fast.

I was aware of my own heavy breathing, and of biceps scrambling away from me, out of my reach, touching fingers to his ruined nose and bruised neck as the cowboy locals, and the Archangels, too, looked at me with troubled, anxious expressions. People who suffer seizures, I suspect, are familiar with the stares I received. Violent criminals, too.

DeAntoni had me by the arm now, leading me away, asking me how my head was, did I need a doctor? Then, in a lower voice, he said, "I want to give you some advice, Ford. No offense. You need to learn to control that temper of yours. If I hadn't gotten to you when I did, you'd've killed that muscle-bound sonuvabitch. I really believe you would've."

I stopped, turned toward DeAntoni; looked at the guards loading themselves onto the golf cart, getting into the van. Biceps was bleeding into a soggy, crimson towel that was pressed to his face, all of them apparently in a rush to return to the safety of Sawgrass.

Then I looked into Tomlinson's sad, old eyes. He was shaking his head, staring at me — no disapproval there, just an expression of helplessness, hurt, worry. Then I turned back toward the door of Gator Bill's bar.

I said to DeAntoni, "I need a drink."

The names of some of the locals inside Gator Bill's seemed oddly familiar.

It wouldn't be long before I understood why.

James was James Tiger, the son of Josie Tiger, he told us. The attractive waitress with the Aztec face was his sister, Naomi Bloom. Behind the bar was Jenny Egret.

Egret?

That was definitely a surname familiar to Tomlinson and me.

Commonality of last names among 'Glades Indians isn't unusual. Among the Seminole and Miccosukee, names such as Osceola, Johns, Tiger, Storm, Billie and Cypress are the equivalent of Smith, Jones, Johnson and Brown in the wider world.

But Egret? It was a name that I associated with only one man.

Tomlinson wasn't shy about asking. To Jenny, the big woman, he said, "I don't suppose you're related to Joseph Egret. Used to be partners with this far-out old redneck cowhunter named Gatrell? He lived west of here, south of Naples, this little ranch on Mango Bay."

Meaning my late uncle, Tucker Gatrell, and

using the old-time Florida term, *cowhunter* for cowboy. Which Tucker and Joseph Egret certainly were. Cowhunters, poachers, whiskeymakers, womanizers, Everglades guides and, in later years, I'm fairly certain, they smuggled their share of marijuana, too. They boated it across the Gulf of Mexico from Colombia and Panama into southwest Florida, the remote Ten Thousand Islands, where not even a helicopter could follow them through the mangrove tunnels and swamp tributaries.

Joe and Tuck were born in the mangroves; grew up in the 'Glades. They knew the wild country better than any outsider could ever know it.

The three of us were sitting at the bar again. Bloodletting during battle usually creates galvanizing bonds, but our second reception at Gator Bill's was only slightly warmer than the first. These were a reserved people, isolated not only geographically, but socially. With the exception of a few, there was racial isolation, too. The fact that we'd beaten off the Sawgrass security team proved that we, at least, had a common enemy. But it didn't mean we were friends — or that we could be trusted.

So our conversation with them was polite, generic. It became slightly more comfortable after a pair of sheriff's deputies arrived, asked us a few questions, then departed. But then Tomlinson mentioned Joseph Egret; asked the tall woman if she were related, and all the Indians in the room seemed to withdraw into a cocoon of their own creation. It was as if we, as strangers, had once again walked through the door for the first time. That's the variety of hush that dominated.

Jenny made eye contact with James, then Naomi — an entire conversation going on among them in that brief silence — before she said to Tomlinson, "I've heard the name Joseph Egret. Ev'body in the 'Glades has. A great big man. Story goes, one time his horse took a stingray spine in the pad of his hoof. Joseph loved that horse so much, he put the animal over his shoulders and carried the horse back to the barn where he had the tools and the medicine. That's how big'a man he was. Only he's dead now."

They way she said it — speaking by rote, slightly theatrical — she might have been talking about some long-gone legend. Daniel Boone. Paul Bunyan. Like she didn't know the man at all, just making conversation. But then, in a different tone, she said, "Why'd you ask about those two? Joe Egret and Cap'n Gatrell?"

Embarrassed by the scene I'd created, the degrading loss of emotional control, I'd gone to the rest room, washed the blood off my face, my gray fishing shirt, and then sat quietly at the far end of the bar. Sat there with my head throbbing, letting DeAntoni and Tomlinson do all the talking, as I finished two quick rums with soda and lime.

Now, though, Tomlinson included me by pointing, telling them my name — an awkward gesture, because he was holding a bag of ice on the ugly red welt swelling just above his bicep. He said, "I'm asking because he's Tucker's nephew. They practically raised him as a kid, Joseph and Tuck both. They were like his father. That's how I met them — through Doc."

The woman, Jenny, turned to me. "You're kin to Cap'n Gatrell, Dr. Ford?"

"Yes."

"You're *Marion* Ford."

"That's right. As a kid, I lived with Tuck for a while. Joseph and I were close. I considered him . . . a friend. A good man. One of the finest men I've known."

Jenny had her own approach to the detection of bullshit. She began to ask me seemingly innocuous questions: "I was at Cap'n Gatrell's ranch once, but that's back when I was a little girl. Was there a horse barn there?"

Gradually, though, the questions became more obvious, then pointed. What was the name of Joseph Egret's favorite horse? (Buster) On which Caribbean island did he and Tucker run a cattle ranch? (Cuba) Finally: Where did Joseph Egret die?

I told her, "The bad curve on the way into the village of Mango. I was there. He and his horse were hit by this idiot in a van. I was beside Joseph at the end. It wasn't a pretty thing to see, and it's not the way I choose to re-

227

member the man. So no more questions, okay? I stopped taking tests years ago."

Jenny's expression softened, broadened. Suddenly, I was no longer a stranger. She told me, "I thought I recognized you."

She looked at Tomlinson. "Him, too — him with his hippy hair and his bony, bird legs. But there had to be three or four hundred 'Glades people the day of Joseph's funeral, whites and Indians. Some famous rich people from up north came, too — his old hunting clients. And lots of women, all of them bawling. The day they buried Joseph."

I said, "You were at the funeral? I'm sorry, I don't remember."

"Yep. I was at Cap'n Gatrell's place, the Big Sky Ranch, back there on the Indian mound. Watched them lower the body down in the old traditional way." She pointed to Naomi, the waitress, and then to James Tiger. "Their daddy's Josie Tiger, and their granddaddy's James Tiger. James started the Famous Reptile Show and Airboat Rides right near Forty Mile Bend. Ev'body knows those big yellow signs with the gator on them. Old James, he played the wind drum at Joseph's funeral. I bet you remember *that*."

I nodded. Yes, I remembered. Which is why, I finally realized, their names were familiar.

For the first time, I heard Naomi speak. "I went with Daddy to hear him play the drum. The day Joseph died, on his way back to

Mango — Joe, I'm talking about — he stopped at our camp. He was on that big horse of his. My sister, Maria, gave him a red handkerchief to wear in his hair, like an old-time warrior. And he gave her —"

She stopped; looked at her brother, James, smiling. Then she walked behind the bar, where she took an old, black beaver-skin cowboy hat from a hook and placed it on her head. "— he gave her his roper's hat, which she gave to me for Christmas. I'll never forget it. He looked so handsome sitting up there on his horse. Even for his age, Joseph was such a good-looking man. I wear his hat nearly every day."

DeAntoni was saying, "See? I told you it was smart to bring you Florida boys along," as Jenny told me, "Joseph had that magic with women. Didn't matter what age, they all loved him, the way he looked, and his great big heart. My mama was the same. She was Rilla Mae Osceola. She and Joseph never married, but I still took Daddy's name."

I touched my hand to the back on my head — quite a lump swelling there. It took me a long moment to realize what she was saying. "You're Joseph Egret's *daughter?* I didn't know he had any children."

"You didn't know Joseph fathered children?"

That got a laugh from the room.

chapter seventeen

Naomi told me, "There was twenty-five, maybe thirty women we know of had children by Joseph. So now, one way or another, we're all kin to him. Joseph Egret could'a populated a whole village with the sons and daughters he sired."

James Tiger said, "Or a tribe. That's the way we think of ourselves now. Pretty soon, it's gonna be official. Egret Seminoles, that's the name we voted to take. Only Joseph wouldn't'a liked that, 'cause he always knew he weren't really no Seminole."

Tomlinson had been following along, nodding, understanding the implications of it all more quickly than I, because he said, astonished, "My God, I understand, now. Your *own* tribe. You're filing to become designated as a tribe. Joseph's offspring; his extended biological family. The *Egret* Seminoles. You really are petitioning the government?"

Jenny said, "Uh-huh. We got every reason in the world to do it, too. And the right. My father had different blood than most of the 'Glades Indians. He passed that blood on to a bunch of us. After more than two years trying to get it done, the federal government's only a month or two from making it official."

Tomlinson said, "Congratulations. That had to take a lot of time, a lot of work," showing her that he knew something about the process.

"When you're dealing with the government, nothing's *easy*. Especially if you're Indian. In the last three, four years, other Florida tribes, like the Tribe of East Creeks, the Oklewaha Band of Seminoles, the United Tuscola, they've all been denied — but they keep right on pushing, filing their petitions. Their clans have been together for hundreds of years. They got their customs, their tribal leaders, but the federal government says they don't exist, so they don't. Not *legally*.

"But the Egret Seminoles, ours is almost a done deal. That's what our attorneys tell us, and the people in Washington, the folks at the BIA's Branch of Acknowledgment and Recognition. They say it like they're doing us a favor. But they got no choice because we *proved* it."

Tomlinson said, "You proved it using Joseph's DNA."

James was nodding, not looking at us, his right hand tugging at the brim of his hat. "The DNA didn't prove it outright. But it sure helped. Maybe you can tell us something about *that*. We heard rumors that you and Dr. Ford are the ones who did the testing. Yanked out hair from Joe's head and took it to some laboratory up north."

231

Then he added quickly, as if to reassure us: "It's not something we talk about with outsiders. We don't use people's private names 'less they says it's all right."

I told him, "Tomlinson's the one who did the DNA stuff. He tested Joseph's hair, not me. He's the expert."

Tomlinson said, "I'm no expert, but a friend of mine is. I took the samples to Mass-Labs, near Boston. They have a Preliminary Chain Reaction processor there; a complete computerized system for testing DNA. Later, if you want, I can tell you the details. What surprises me is that you knew."

"So you *are* the ones?"

"We're the ones," Tomlinson said. "Joseph and Tucker were in trouble. We wanted to help."

Jenny considered that for a moment before she said, "Oh, we *knew*. From the rumors, yes, but that's not the only way we found out. Nearly three years ago, a man showed up here with some papers. They were copies of the DNA report. His lawyers found them in some file up in Tallahassee, and he was all excited. He said there were certain genetic markers that proved Daddy wasn't Seminole or Miccosukee. He said, legally, they were strong evidence that Daddy came from the old Florida Indians, the ones here when Ponce de León came sailing in. The ones who built the shell mounds up and down this coast that Miami, St. Pete, Lauderdale — a lot of big towns — are built on."

Naomi asked, "Do you know about them? The old ones?"

Smiling at her, Tomlinson said, "Tell us."

"They called them the Calusa," she said. "The scientists say the Calusa are extinct now. But they're wrong."

She added, "The Calusa lived here a thousand years before the Seminoles showed up. They didn't have chiefs. They had kings, like the Maya. Only, all the archaeologists, like I said, think they're extinct, killed off by disease. But they aren't all dead. Joseph had the blood. Now we've proved that we got the Calusa blood, too. A bunch of us sent pieces of our hair off in little plastic tubes, and paid for the same kind'a test. We all had the same genetic markers. DNA."

Tomlinson asked, "The man who brought the papers from Tallahassee, was it the same one who developed Sawgrass?"

Jenny was nodding. "Um-huh. This was more than three years back. Before they even broke ground. He told us Sawgrass was going to be a great thing for the area. Some joke."

"The man's name was Geoff Minster."

Once again, James, Naomi and Jenny exchanged a long, communal look, before James answered, "Oh, we *know* Minster. He wasn't too bad. Didn't lie to us no more than most men who want to see this part of the 'Glades developed. Could be, some of us liked Mr.

233

Minster okay. We heard he died. Fell off a boat one night."

DeAntoni said, "If you have the time, I wouldn't mind asking you a few more questions about Minster," but James ignored him, listening as Tomlinson pressed, "If it wasn't Minster, the man who approached you had to be Shiva. The man who claims to be a religious teacher. Or maybe he called himself Jerry Singh. He controls Sawgrass now."

Jenny said, "Yeah, it was Shiva. Came driving up in some kind of big blue car —"

"A Rolls-Royce," Naomi said.

"Yeah, that was the kind of car it was. A tall man wearing robes. Told us God had sent him. That he's a meditator, a mystic, and he said he had a way we'd never have to worry about money again."

James said quickly, "We don't want to talk too much about that now, do we?"

Jenny used a mild undertone to snap at him. "You ever hear me say more than I'm supposed to?" Then she continued, "Shiva was the one who came to us with those papers, saying that, legally, we had a right to form our own tribe. Like it was his idea, but it wasn't. He didn't tell us anything we hadn't already thought of before. But it takes lawyers to file all those forms, to keep pushing the government, and lots of money."

"Shiva promised to provide the money?"

Jenny addressed the implication: "His church

has *already* provided the money. Lots of it, too. Four lawyers, one in Florida, two in D.C., and one out in Oklahoma tryin' to prove there's no Seminoles out there with the same blood as us. But don't think we're stupid. Shiva isn't the first to try and take advantage of us getting tribal status. We know why he's doing what he's doing."

Tomlinson said, "He wants to build a casino."

"It's more than that. When we get confirmed, we'll be our own nation. On our land, if you open a restaurant, a hotel — name it — you don't have to worry about state inspectors, getting permits, state codes, all that red tape. No unions, no Social Security business. Plus no taxes. Or almost no taxes, depending on the kind'a deal you work out with the government."

"But a casino, that's where he'd make his money back."

Jenny was becoming animated, opening up some to Tomlinson, building a rapport. "A little Las Vegas, that's what the man wants to build. A whole city with tall buildings and bright lights out here in the 'Glades. Only he never told us that. We found out slow, from other people. Geoff Minster — he was honest, at least, about what was going on."

"You trusted him?"

Jenny shrugged. "Not much. I liked him better than Shiva. Minster, at first, was just another money man, a developer. No matter what he told us, we knew what he really wanted — profit. But then he began to get interested in us, Joseph's history, some of the 'Glades religions. I believe that about him. He was trying to open up his heart."

She said, "Shiva, though, is different. Even when he's telling you the truth, he's lying, because he wants something more. Something deeper." She thought for a moment, touching fingers to a blemish on her cheek — a touching vanity from a woman her size and shape. "That man, it's like he wants to reach his hand inside you and pull something out of your chest. Something to steal away for himself."

DeAntoni said, "If he's investing money, you can't blame the guy for expecting to make some dough. What else would he want?"

Jenny said, "A lot. Things we're not sure about. He wants our tribal council to make him a member of the Egret Seminoles — which we can do. *Legally.* It's up to individual tribes now, who's an Indian or not. The Bureau of Indian Affairs changed the law 'cause it was so much trouble for them, proving what they call quantum blood. How much native blood does it take to make a person an Indian?"

"Why would you go along with something like that?"

James said, "I'm on the council, and I wouldn't. No way. But our tribal chairman, that's who Shiva's working hard to convince.

The chairman and five elders — old-time 'Glades people set in their ways. Our chairman's a . . . well, our chairman's a mystic . . . a real spiritual person . . . and got a *lot* of power."

When Tomlinson asked, "Who's your tribal chairman?" Jenny began to move around behind the sink, putting away glasses, cleaning ashtrays. Was she getting ready to close so early?

After a few moments, looking at the interested faces around the room, James said, "This is probably a subject we shouldn't be talkin' about in a bar."

Jenny told him, "Plus, you need to be gettin' back to work. If these fellas want, maybe they'd be interested in seeing that new airboat you bought."

She turned to me, a familiar expression on her face — I was being tested again — as she added, "If you don't have the time to follow James, that's fine, too. Come back another day. Or a month from now. Maybe we can talk some more. Or not. Makes no difference, it's up to you."

We were inside DeAntoni's Lincoln, following James Tiger's red Dodge Ram with the high-water tires, the towing package and stainless-steel lockbox in the bed.

We were headed west on the Tamiami Trail, returning to the shade of cypress domes, vultures heavy on hoary limbs, dragonflies and swallow-tailed kites spiraling weightless, riding sawgrass thermals through cumulous vents.

The vultures roosted motionless as gargoyles, their scale-headed cowlings black, like Egyptian priests. Waiting . . . waiting for the first blue-fly vapor of carrion scent. At night, when the swamp air cools, reptiles and mammals are drawn to the sun-soaked asphalt. The fast highway becomes a killing field. Along the Tamiami Trail, vultures never have long to wait.

To our right, the two-lane was bordered by a canal dredged years ago to create the roadbed. The water conduit was a floating garden of yellow pond lilies, Florida violets, pink swamp roses and flag root. Marsh hens — purple gallinules — walked spring-footed on the lilies while alligators sunned themselves on cattail banks, or floated nearby.

Both hands on the wheel, seeing nothing but the road, DeAntoni said, "I wish this guy talked as fast as he drives. Why's it so damn hard getting information out of these people? I ask a couple of questions, they looked right through me. Like I wasn't even there."

Right on both counts.

James *was* a fast driver. This quiet member of the Egret Seminole council drove like a NASCAR fanatic. The only time he slowed was to tailgate the occasional Winnebago, or await the chance to leapfrog a citrus convoy.

He liked outspoken bumper stickers, too.

If DeAntoni stayed heavy on the gas, we could get close enough to the rear of James Tiger's truck to read his bumper:

BIA: BETRAYING INDIAN ASSETS SINCE 1924

CUSTER WORE ARROW SHIRTS

YOU CAN TRUST THE GOVERNMENT. ASK AN INDIAN!

WHERE WAS THE I.N.S. IN 1492 WHEN WE NEEDED THEM?

FLORIDA SEMINOLES — UNDEFEATED! (FOOTBALL? WHAT'S THAT?)

Tomlinson told DeAntoni, "The Skins — Indians, I'm saying — they don't feel comfortable coming right out and answering questions from strangers. It's a cultural thing. Ask a question, don't expect a direct answer, because you're not going to get it. So being pushy, taking the fast approach, is usually a mistake. In some tribes, it's even considered rude."

DeAntoni said, "Jesus Christ. Now Tinkerbell's an expert on manners, too. If I want information on Minster, what the hell am I supposed to do? Send up a fucking smoke signal?"

Tomlinson said, "No, the way to do it is to just let it *happen,* man. Like the universe unfolding. You want information? What I'd do is . . . Let me ask *you* a question. You were a New York cop."

"Twelve years. I already told you."

"Okay, when you were off-duty, where'd you socialize with other cops?"

"We used to hang out at some of the Irish pubs — *real* Irish pubs, where the Guinness's freighted in fresh every day. Not like the bullshit places around here. Most the time, I'd have a few at the Barrow Pub on the corner of Hudson. Good pool tables, plus they show the Yanks *and* the Mets. McSorley's in the East Village. On Seventh Street? What's your point?"

Tomlinson said, "Imagine James Tiger walking into the Barrow Pub, sitting down beside you, and asking a lot of questions about someone you knew, who disappeared and was probably dead."

DeAntoni thought about that, cypress trees flickering by the windshield in a blur. Finally, he said, "Okay, okay. I see what you mean. A guy like that, with a hick accent, comes nosing around, we'd have run him outside into the street. Like, fuck you, pal. Hit the bricks."

Tomlinson said, "There you go. The difference is, at least James is giving us a chance to get to know him a little. If it wasn't for Doc being related to Tucker Gatrell and us knowing Joseph Egret, guess where we'd be right now?"

DeAntoni said, "Hittin' the bricks."

Tomlinson told him, "Exactly."

After a few moments, DeAntoni said, "Know what, Tinkerbell? Sometimes, you actually make a little bit of sense." Then, several seconds later: "The big Indian, the dead one you keep talking about. Why's he so special?"

Tomlinson told DeAntoni that Joseph Egret and my uncle, Tucker Gatrell, were lifelong friends and partners.

Tomlinson said, "I never understood why Joseph stuck by that old redneck. Tuck was one of the biggest racists I've ever met." Looking at me with his luminous blue eyes, Tomlinson added, "Sorry. No offense."

I said, "Are you kidding?"

Then Tomlinson told DeAntoni that, several years back — goaded by my uncle — we had reason to attempt to prove that Joseph had a historical and genetic right to live (and be buried) on the pre-Columbian Indian mounds that were on my uncle's property.

The state of Florida, Tomlinson explained, attempted to annex Tuck's land by exercising its right of eminent domain. Proving that Joseph was among the last of an Indian tribe long thought to be extinct was the only way to keep the state from booting the two men off the ranch.

They'd spent most their lives there, living on Mango Bay, rousting cattle on horseback, fishing, drinking, plotting, spitting tobacco juice off the front porch. Men that age shouldn't be bullied, and that's exactly what the state bureaucrats were trying to do.

"I got bone marrow samples from the Florida Museum of Natural History. Of the Calusa —

bones more than a thousand years old, excavated from the mounds on Gatrell's property. Then took samples of Joseph's hair, and flew them up to a friend of mine who runs a lab outside Boston."

Tomlinson told DeAntoni that they found repetitive genetic markers in the DNA of both marrow and hair that suggested that Joseph was a direct descendant of Florida's mound builders. Those markers, he explained, didn't turn up uniformly in all members of an ethnic group, which is why modern Indians are *against* using DNA to prove anything.

"But the bone marrow from that old Calusa, and Joseph — the markers were right there to read," he added. "The Calusa were an amazing people. Physically — for that time period, back in the sixteen hundreds — they were huge. The Spaniards described them as giants. You see how big Jenny is? Six one, six two, and she's small compared to Joseph. They had a civilization on the west coast of Florida that rivaled the Maya. The entire southern part of the state was their kingdom. They kept slaves, performed human sacrifices. And they scared the hell out of the Spaniards.

"The Calusa refused to convert to Christianity, and literally pissed on anyone who tried to change them. Seriously. As in they *made* the Jesuit priests kneel down and whizzed on them — which the priests wrote about in their journals. Like, to show the kind of savages they

242

were dealing with."

DeAntoni told him, *"Cool."* He'd personally arrested a few priests himself that he wouldn't mind pissing on. Tomlinson continued, "But back to the DNA — we found a double T, double A, double C-G-T sequence in the hair *and* the bone marrow.

"We were focusing on the mitochondrion D-loop. There was also a unique sequencing in the HLA genes — and that's where we found the genetic flags. The state of Florida couldn't argue that. No way. So they let Tucker Gatrell keep his ranch, and they let us bury Joseph in the back pasture, on the mounds where he belonged."

DeAntoni eyes were glazing, getting bored — all this scientific talk. But he was still following closely enough to ask, "So if they were so tough, these Calusa, what happened to them? Why was the old dead Indian, your pal, the last one?"

"Disease," Tomlinson said. "Within two hundred years after contact with the Spanish, the Calusa were almost finished. They went from being kings of the world, to living like animals on the run. When the Calusa started getting sick, losing power, the tribes they used for slaves got their revenge.

"When the United States bought Florida from Spain and settlers started farming the islands, the Maskókî started moving south — Doc was wrong when he told you Creeks.

243

That's a common misconception, still taught in schools. The Seminole and the Miccosukee aren't *Creeks*. They're *Maskókî*.

"Anyway, that was the end of the Calusa as a people. Except for sixty or so who went to live in Cuba. But none were left in the States. Except for Joseph and maybe a few others."

DeAntoni said, "But Joseph had a bunch of sons and daughters. This old tribe is not extinct. So why should anybody even give a damn?"

I was watching Billy Tiger's truck slow, red brake lights aglow, left blinker flashing, as it approached a yellow billboard: a massive alligator, jaws wide. JAMES TIGER'S FAMOUS REPTILE SHOW AND AIRBOAT RIDES.

On the south side of the road was an island-sized settlement of pole houses, thatched palmetto roofs, airboats angled bow-high on the banks of the canal, a parking lot of white coral filled with cars bearing out-of-state license plates — Michigan, Illinois, New Jersey.

A tourist stop. Another Florida roadside attraction.

As DeAntoni slowed to turn, Tomlinson said, "Are you kidding? If Billy Tiger or any of Joseph's heirs can prove the Calusa aren't extinct, that the tribe still exists, they can claim ownership of the whole southern tip of Florida. Everything, West Palm to Tampa, and south to Key West. Because, rightfully, they do own it. They really *do*."

DeAntoni was shaking his head, smiling. "No court's gonna have the balls to order something like that. Give half the state back to a couple of dozen Indians? Yeah, right, I can see it — kick everybody out of Miami, South Beach and Lauderdale. The Cubans would be piling up sandbags, locking 'n' loading, the old Jewish ladies right beside them. It's just not gonna happen."

Tomlinson said, "Personally, I think it *could* happen. Legally, anyway, and then the state would be forced to make some kind of gigantic financial settlement. But just the threat is a powerful leverage tool. Does the state want to risk the issue going to the Supreme Court — maybe lose a couple of million acres of state land, or a few billion dollars? Or, is it better to say, Screw it, award the Egret Seminoles a smaller chunk of land. In return, the state lets them build their houses, shopping centers, whatever they want."

DeAntoni said, "Okay, I'm with you. Shopping centers — or casinos. That's where the big money is."

Tomlinson said, "Precisely."

chapter eighteen

Tomlinson took me aside and said, in a voice too low for anyone to hear, "He's keeping us here for a reason. As packed as this place is with tourists, he wouldn't be wasting his time."

Meaning James Tiger, who had his back to us — barefooted now, still wearing his Stetson — standing with DeAntoni near the canal where there were lily pads and white moonflowers blooming. The two men were on the boat ramp next to a chickee built on poles, and a commercial-sized airboat that was beached near four portable toilets.

An airboat is a weird-looking craft common to the Everglades, though I have seen them in Australia, and in Africa, too. It is a pan-flat boat, stern-driven, powered by an airplane propeller, and can fly over water, grass, even rock. This airboat looked like a red metal sled, bench seats in the middle, a captain's chair bolted atop a massive engine, a Cessna-type propeller mounted aft inside a circular cage.

There were two airboats of similar design tied at a dock. One was off-loading passengers via a short boarding bridge; the other was loading. The boats looked like they could handle nine, maybe ten, people at a time. There had to be fifty, sixty or more people waiting in line, their bodies attached to angular black shadows that moved beside them on the white coral parking lot. There were kids running around, bored, parents shifting from leg to leg.

I said, "I'm not waiting much longer. I need to get back to Sanibel and check my fish tanks. Plus, I've got an order for two hundred horseshoe crabs. This time of year, finding that many crabs is not going to be easy."

Tomlinson said, "Your head's hurting, isn't it? You should get an X ray, as hard as that jerk hit you. We can stop at Naples Community Hospital on the way back."

"Sure, sure, we can both check into the ER. You get your shoulder X-rayed, and they can do my skull while they're at it."

A safe offer to make, because Tomlinson despises hospitals.

Reacting to my impatience, he said, once again, that James would not have led us to his village without good reason, then added, "I think it has something to do with Jenny, the bartender. Joseph's daughter. She's a power woman. Understand what I'm saying? A buffalo woman — very centered, a leader. James might have been doing most of the talking, but she was doing most of the thinking. Maybe she's supposed to call and check on us. Or contact someone else. Who knows, man? What I'm telling you is, the Egret Seminoles have invited us to the outer edge of their inner circle for inspection. We've got old Joe and Tuck to thank for that. Let's not pull the plug now."

I was watching DeAntoni motioning to us, signaling us to join him. Walking toward the canal, I told Tomlinson that I'd give it another half hour, no more, then listened to DeAntoni say, "You guys ever ride in an airboat? I've seen 'em on TV — the bastards scoot."

For the first time, I got a sense of the kind of child he'd been — there was that sort of excitement in his voice. Probably a big, quiet boy; a secret little circus going on inside, but shy for a street kid. He was enjoying himself now; showing it.

Then he said to James, "James, tell 'em about your boat. You guys aren't gonna believe how damn cool this thing is. What'd you say — it can go sixty, seventy, miles an hour?"

Frank DeAntoni, the carburetor-head, talking with his new Indian buddy, who had also gone through a personality change. James, the stoic cowhunter, had now become the racecar speed freak we'd suspected, and was suddenly an enthusiastic talker. We listened to him tell us about his new boat: twenty-one feet long, eight-foot beam, with a big-block aircraft engine, 430 horsepower with a 2:1 reduction system and a seventy-two-inch wooden composite Sensenich propeller.

The hull, he said, was laid upon yellow pine stringers, built up in Cross City by Freedom Craft, modeled after one of the original hulls built by O. B. Osceola, back in the 1930s. The twin aft rudder flaps were foam-filled aluminum, and they'd been custom-airbrushed, green on gold, with the head of a giant snapping gator.

The boat's name, *Chekika's Shadow*, was written upon each in red script.

"It's similar to the newer Kennedy hulls," James told us. "She's a sweet one. The transom's high enough, she doesn't suck in backwash if you lay off the throttle too fast and hit the drag brake. She doesn't porpoise, either, and there's not a hint of hook in her bottom. She's a clean boat. Solid."

He paused, his eyes moving over the vessel, very proud. Then he looked from Tomlinson to me. "You want to go for a ride? I'll run you out in the 'Glades, show you around."

I turned toward the line of tourists standing in the April heat, waiting their turn.

Using my head to motion, I said, "What about them?"

James seemed perplexed by the question. He said, "Why should those people care? It's not *their* boat."

Riding in an airboat, when an accelerant G-force begins to roll your eyes back, causing facial flesh to flutter, your first sensory impression is that you are on a saucer, sliding out of control and destined for disaster.

That's the way it felt when James first hit the throttle. Out of control. Iffy.

And not without reason. In a traditional boat, water is a built-in governor because you have to displace water to move. In a land vehicle, you roll along comfortably, reassured by the limitations of friction. But riding in an airboat is like being vaulted onto a plain of ice, an overpowered airplane propeller strapped to your butt.

It's that kind of wild sensation.

But James Tiger knew how to drive an airboat. That became evident quickly. Had he not possessed great expertise, we'd have died within seconds — simple as that.

After handing us headphones and battery packs — portable communications systems — he took the captain's chair above the engine, then directed Tomlinson and DeAntoni into the two seats in front of, and beneath him.

I had no choice but to sit on one of the bench seats toward the bow — which was fine with me.

I pulled my headphones on, pushed the wire microphone away from my chin — I had no expectations of talking — and listened to DeAntoni and Tomlinson chatter away while James started the engine.

Deafening. It may have been a conventional aircraft engine, but it was as loud as any jet I've ever heard — and one of the key reasons I don't like airboats. I've *never* liked airboats. The noise spooks wildlife while negating solitude gained by the isolated places to which airboats provide transport.

Even jet skis aren't as obnoxious — and jet skis (personal watercraft, they're now called) were once the untreated offal of noise pollution until manufacturers began to quiet them down.

Gatrell built airboats, raced airboats, sold airboats and, for all I know, stole airboats — it wouldn't have been a surprise. I grew up around the things; drove them when I had to, worked on their engines when it was required. Mostly, though I avoided them.

Which is why I already regretted my decision to ride along. In fact, I was giving serious consideration to raising my hand, stopping James Tiger at the dock, and telling him I'd changed my mind. To go ahead without me. That I preferred to walk along the Tamiami Trail; do a little bird-watching and see what kind of fish cruised the surface of the canal.

I never got the chance.

The moment he freed the lines, James swung the airboat a gut-wrenching 380 degrees at full throttle, and then seemed to accomplish the impossible: He used the turn to generate momentum, running his new airboat up the grassy edge of a ramp as if it were a ski jump . . . vaulted about fifteen yards of coral parking lot . . . landed on another patch of grass, gaining even more speed. Then he used the bank of the canal as a second ramp that launched us over two lanes of asphalt — the Tamiami Trail — which would have been sufficiently scary, even if there had not been a truck coming.

But there *was* a truck coming: an eighteen-wheeler loaded with what, later, I would guess to be watermelons.

I could see the box-shaped cab speeding toward us as we careened airborne . . . could hear the diesel scream of the air horn as the driver first reacted . . . could see the driver's eyes widen as he swerved toward the shoulder . . . could see a patina of bugs smushed on the truck's chromium grill as James Tiger performed magic with the rudder flaps, turning us so that the cab passed at eye level . . . and then we landed in a controlled skid that pivoted us into sawgrass higher than our heads . . . and, then, the truck and civilization were abruptly behind us, as if neither had ever existed.

In my earphones, I heard DeAntoni, his voice strained, say, "Was that a Mack Truck that almost clipped us . . . or was it a Peterbilt?"

Calm, unconcerned — *no big deal* — I heard James Tiger reply, "Peterbilt. You didn't see the big red oval on the grill? A Mack Truck, they got the silver bulldog on the hood. That's how you tell."

I listened to Tomlinson say, "Did you somehow make us turn sideways? Far *out*. Man, it was like, suddenly, I had this amazing unworldly conversion. I knew in my heart what it's like to be a *butterfly*, man, bopping down a busy highway. The whole random beauty of it. One moment, I'm feather-light. Next moment, I'm part of a shipment of watermelons, bonded with Detroit, headed for Miami."

James said, "Detroit? If you're talking about the truck, Peterbilt's made out in Iowa someplace, I think. Moline? Is that Iowa?"

Furious because we'd had such a close call so unnecessarily, I moved the microphone wire to my mouth, and said, "Why didn't we stay on the south side of the road, like your other tour boats? Or maybe that's not exciting enough?"

If Tiger caught the sarcasm, he didn't let on. "On the south side of the trail, we got all the tourist stuff. We keep a little village out there on one of the oak islands where we pay our teenagers to wear traditional clothes, pretend like they're cooking. Understand what I'm saying? Entertainment. Then the boats stop and watch one of my cousins wrestle a couple of gators we keep penned. But if you're interested in the tourist stuff, I can give you my little speech if you want. Just sit back and listen. I got it memorized; said it so often I don't even have to think anymore."

Tomlinson said, "Then why *are* you taking us north? Your tribal chairman — is that the reason? Are you taking us to see him?"

James Tiger had a little smile in his voice when he answered. "Could be we're heading that direction. Yeah, we'll see how it goes.

Maybe you *will* get a chance to meet *him*."

The way he said it, I knew what I'm sure Tomlinson immediately knew, and maybe DeAntoni, too: The tribal chairman of the Egret Seminole wasn't a *him*. The chairman was a woman.

James was serious about giving the tour speech he'd memorized. I listened to him recite by rote. Some of it was interesting. He talked about the cast of oddballs, eccentrics, profiteers, predators and zealots who'd lived in the area. Because Florida attracts wanderers and dreamers, Florida's history is as remarkable as it is idiosyncratic.

As we planed westward, running parallel to the Tamiami Trail, he told us about Devil's Garden, that it was named during the Seminole Wars for a famous Indian, Sam Jones, who retreated there after battling U.S. troops, and was never caught.

"The soldiers called him Devil Sam because he just seemed to disappear into a place so beautiful, all the cypress and moss and orchids. After that, white men came and farmed on the same high slough ground that Indians had been farmin' for hundreds of years.

"The strangest folks who ever lived in Devil's Garden, though — this is fact — was a group of people from up north, and they was nudist. They come to the Garden to live in a commune. They bragged to the local folks that they

254

were all so intelligent, they were such perfect specimens of people, the men were going to breed with the women, and start their own super-race — this was back just before the time of the Nazis. Because of the mosquitoes, this is a rough place to go naked. They lasted less than six months."

Through the earphones, I could hear DeAntoni laughing.

Then Tiger told us about other characters who'd spent their lives in the 'Glades near the two-lane highway.

There was a woman he called Mama Hokie, wife of Sam Hokie. The two of them made a meager living selling drinks and bait to passing fishermen — which explained the cryptic sign outside their shack: BEER WORMS FOR SALE.

Her Seminole neighbors called Mama "Alligator Lady," and for good reason. One morning, back in the 1990s, when she went to the canal to dip water for her adopted stray cats, a gator lunged from the bottom, and bit off her right arm. Mama Hokie made her own tourniquet, watered her cats, and went on not only to survive, but to adopt a lot more cats — which she watered every morning from the same canal.

There was Al Seely, a northern artist with an alcohol addiction so severe that, in desperation, he loaded his car with pots and clothes and food, and made his wife abandon him on an island so remote that he couldn't possibly escape to find booze. He lived in a shack in that brackish 'Glades watershed for years, painting striking primitives, and getting roaring drunk on the rare occasions when a passing stranger offered him a ride into Goodland, the nearest town.

There was Buffalo Tiger, first chairman of the Miccosukee, and an Everglades legend who, by flying to Cuba and shaking Castro's hand, guaranteed the sovereignty of his tribe.

There was A. C. Hancock, who was born on Sand Fly Pass, just off Everglades City. He was a master boatbuilder, guide and, for a time, sheriff's deputy, who scrambled to a complaint of "foreigners with machine guns" running a military camp in the 'Glades. He arrived to confront Anglo men in sunglasses: They were CIA officers training Cuban officers for the Bay of Pigs invasion.

"The Everglades is known for its strong women," James's voice said through my earphones — not talking to us, just playing his role as guide, reciting his speech.

I listened to him tell us about the legendary Smith sisters, Sarah and Hannah. Just hearing the name Hannah Smith squeezed at my heart, and caused a familiar sense of loss. I could feel Tomlinson's eyes on my back as Tiger continued to tell us about the namesakes and relatives of a woman I'd known: a strong, good woman whom I had loved and lost.

Sarah was known as the Ox Woman, because

she was the first person — male or female — ever to drive an ox cart across the Everglades. Hannah, who cut firewood and drove cattle for a living, was known as Big Six, because like her sister, she was a couple of inches over six feet tall. The tough men of the Everglades not only respected the sisters; they feared them.

Big women. It made me think of Jenny Egret. It also made me think of my lost girl, a tall woman, legs as long as mine, with eyes that could penetrate a man's head, or his heart.

I was pleased when he moved on to other subjects. He told about Jim Sheely, who so devoutly believed in the Swamp Ape that he set out food for the beast, and about Mrs. Jimmie Robinson, wife of an island crabber, who rallied the men of Florida's fishing community, went personally to Tallahassee and founded the Organized Fishermen of Florida.

It was only when James moved onto other famous 'Glades pioneers — Ervin T. Rouse, composer of the "Orange Blossom Special," Totch Brown, Joseph Egret and Capt. Tucker Gatrell — that I interrupted, saying, "Jimmy. *Jimmy.*"

Getting him to stop in midspeech was like trying to awaken him from a trance.

"Are you talkin' to me, Dr. Ford?"

I told him, "Joseph and Tucker — we already *know* about them. You don't need to tell us. Ervin Rouse and Totch were friends, too. You can skip that part of the talk."

257

Tiger smiled, embarrassed. "Sorry. Once I get going, I can't hardly stop, or I have to start from the beginning again."

I slid the earphones back on my head, tuning him out as he fumbled for his place, listening to him say, ". . . uhhh, another interesting aspect of the Florida Everglades is what scientists call the flora and fauna. . . ."

We were traveling on a trail of sawgrass that leaned as if a tornado had carved a pathway through it. I concentrated on the scenery. There was plenty to see.

As we flew along, the noise of the boat flushed clouds of white ibis, bright as flower petals above the gray grass. We flushed sandhill cranes, a couple of black feral hogs and a herd of a dozen or so white-tailed deer, spotted fawns in tow.

In literature about the Everglades, the point is often made that the region is more of a cerebral pleasure than a visual wonder. This theme, in a stroke, seems to recognize the delicate balance of water and life, while apologizing for the absence of mountains.

There are no mountains, true, but the region is made up of more than just grass and water. The Everglades is a massive biological unit of varied landscapes that once included nearly half the state. It begins just south of Orlando, where Florida settles slate-flat on a porous, limestone base that tilts just enough to keep water flowing toward the Keys.

Once you get south of Lake Okeechobee, beyond cane fields, the land empties. It is veined with creeks, shaded with tear-shaped tree islands and pocked with holes ragged as a moonscape. The Everglades is honeycombed with subterranean rivers and caverns.

South Florida's largest underground river is known as the Long Key Formation.

The Long Key River runs for several hundred miles beneath highways and homes, cities and wild places, mostly through limestone. It begins near Lake Wales, northwest of Lake Okeechobee, and currents southward toward the Everglades.

The river flows beneath State Route 80, Alligator Alley and the Tamiami Trail — the region's only east-west highways. The underground river flows beneath sawgrass, swamp, mangrove fringe and Florida Bay.

The Long Key River then rises to within about 35 feet of the earth's surface at Flamingo, and abruptly descends deep underground as it flows beneath Florida Bay — a freshwater column traveling an isolated course beneath salt water. By the time the river gets to Marathon and Long Key, its limestone conduit is 158 feet beneath the sea bottom.

Limestone can accurately be called a skeletal structure by virtue of having been formed by the calcium remains of long-dead sea creatures. The limestone skeleton upon which modern

Florida exists is porous, delicate, unpredictable. Craters in the limestone can and do appear suddenly. They are formed when the limestone scaffolding gives way, and implodes. Sinkholes, they are called. In South Florida, sinkholes occur commonly. They have swallowed houses, whole business districts and portions of highway.

Sinkholes are an incisive reminder of how fragile our peninsula really is.

We were approaching what appeared to be a sinkhole now — a crater-sized lake surrounded by cypress. As we neared it, I could feel the temperature drop, as if the dome of cypress was absorbing sunlight. Within the dome, the crater was a pool of black water that was carpeted with fire flags and lily pads, white and yellow flowers blooming.

In my earphones, I heard James say, "See the marsh way to the north?"

I looked to see a broad expanse of swamp plain near what appeared to be an abandoned limestone pit.

He said, "We call that Lost Lake. The reason is, there's another sinkhole out there, a lake without no bottom. But you can't see the shape of the lake unless water in the swamp gets real low. Used to be, tarpon would show up there about this time every year. But it hasn't happened for a while."

A tarpon is a saltwater game fish: a chromium-scaled pack animal that migrates into the

Florida littoral each spring. All my life, I'd heard rumors that there were certain inland lakes where tarpon would appear as abruptly as they disappeared — the implication being that the lakes were connect by underground tunnels with the open sea. Some were well known: Rock Lake, Tarpon Lake, Deep Lake and Lake Sampson. I'd visited a couple of them.

We were headed for a tree island now. As James banked toward it, I heard Tomlinson say, "This is starting to look familiar. Man, I think I know where we are. We're getting close to Sawgrass, aren't we?"

James told him, "If you cut straight across the prairie, it's only a mile or so to the back boundary." Then he said what sounded like, "Up ahead is Chekika's Hammock."

Tomlinson repeated the name phonetically, "Che-kii-ka's Hammock."

"Uh-huh. Back in eighteen forty, it's where the white soldiers caught Chekika, an Indian. They said he murdered Dr. Perrine and six or seven other people down on the Florida Keys. Chekika, he was a big man. A Calusa, like Joseph. When the soldiers caught him, they hanged him. Ask her to show you the tree. It's still there."

DeAntoni said, "Ask who to show us the tree?"

Tomlinson answered for James: "Billie Egret. This is where she lives."

Tomlinson, my intuitive friend.

chapter nineteen

Billie Egret, tribal chair of the Egret Seminoles, had inherited Joseph Egret's height, his elongated wedge of a nose and his eyes. She had liquid eyes; black, intense eyes that seemed to add weight to the air when she stared at you.

She was staring at me now, as she said, "My father once told me he considered you more like a son than just some cracker boy. So I guess that could make the two of us brother and sister in a way. He also told me you kept your brain where your heart should be. True?"

There are rare people who exude sufficient confidence that they can direct outrageous questions at strangers, yet make the question sound reasonable, even flattering. She was one of those few.

I said, "Personally, I don't see anything wrong with that."

I watched her smile for the second time since our arrival. "Guess he was right, huh?"

We were standing in a clearing between four pole houses — chickees — that were built around a central fire pit. The chickees consisted of a sapling floor built a couple of feet off the ground beneath a roof of palm thatching. The cooking chickee was open on all sides. There was a pump for water, a wood-burning stove and a porcelain sink that drained onto the ground.

We'd already seen the tree where, according to the woman, Chekika had been hanged a hundred-and-fifty-some years earlier. The "Hanging Tree," she called it, her inflection making it a proper noun.

It was a massive Madeira mahogany, long dead. Put three or four men at the base, and they might be able to circle their arms around it. Most of the upper limbs were broken off; woodpeckers had riddled it with striated holes, but it was still solid. Perched on the highest knob was one of the rarest birds in the Everglades, a snail kite. The snail kite sat one hundred feet above, indifferent to us, a large, hawkish-looking male, cobalt blue.

"When we were kids," Billie told us, "Joseph used to talk about Chekika, because Chekika was his great-grandfather. Which means he's my great-great-grandfather. He was what the old people, the elders, called a Spanish Indian.

"It's because the government sent the last band of Calusas to live in Cuba. They had to learn Spanish. They gave them a spot on a hill just west of old Havana, but it wasn't their home; it wasn't Florida. So they paddled back. More than a hundred miles of open water in dugouts.

"Chekika was different. Like my father. Now like us."

We listened to the woman talk about it. She said if the American military had attacked Indians down on the Keys, it would have been called an engagement. But because it was Chekika who initiated the attack, history referred to it as a massacre.

There is a predictable variety of bitterness associated with the cliché thinking that every conquest-minded European was evil, and all indigenous peoples were noble. But there was no hint of that in her voice.

She told us that there are five hundred and fifty federally recognized tribes in the United States. The largest, the Cherokee and the Navajo, have close to a million members. Some of the smallest tribes have fewer than a dozen men and women left; are on the verge of extinction.

"For the enemies of Native Americans," she said, "extinction has always been the favorite option."

She told us that her band, the Egret Seminoles, were just one unrecognized tribe out of two-hundred-and-forty-some groups petitioning, trying to get the federal government to verify all the research that had been done, to grant confirmation, and make it official.

She spoke matter-of-factly, like an interested historian. She looked the part, standing there in her park ranger khaki shorts and man's rainbow-banded Seminole shirt, strings of traditional glass beads around her neck. An interesting-looking woman: a little over six feet tall, narrow-hipped, flat-chested with good shoulders, high cheekbones beneath velvet cocoa skin, her hair cut short. Plus those eyes. Startlingly intense eyes.

I liked her frankness; her no-nonsense manner.

When Tomlinson placed both his hands on the tree, closed his eyes for a moment, saying, "There's a powerful spirit in this creature; it's still strong and alive —" she cut him off abruptly, saying, "If you're doing that for my benefit, please stop."

As Tomlinson turned to her, smiling, she added, "Sorry. It's just that I don't have much patience with the whole Indian stereotype business. We don't worship nature — never did. We don't all have fuzzy animal names. We've never had shamans — that's a *Russian* word — and the only people who give any credence to that ridiculous book, *Black Elk Speaks*, are New Age whites who have more money than brains. Turquoise Indians, I call them, because they wear turquoise like it's supposed to mean something."

Still smiling, Tomlinson said something heavy and guttural that surprised the woman, then made her laugh. It also seemed to cut through the awkwardness of strangers meeting. Seemed to put her at ease. She answered Tomlinson in the same singsong language, before adding, "I'm impressed. That's a Maskókî maxim I haven't heard since my grandmother died. Very appropriate, too."

Now she didn't seem to mind at all when Tomlinson placed his hands on the Hanging Tree again, eyes closed, and asked, "How often is she struck by lightning?"

Billie Egret answered, "A lot," walking away.

She'd already put DeAntoni in his place, too. The first thing he'd asked her after stepping off the airboat was, "Did you know a Geoff Minster?" To which she replied, "You wouldn't be here if I didn't. And you're not going to *stay* here long unless you agree to talk about it on my terms."

Her terms, it seemed, included getting to know us better before she volunteered information. "She's getting the feel of us," Tomlinson whispered to me as we followed her back to the main camp.

Now she took a seat at a table beneath one of the chickees, and spoke generally, telling us about herself, what she was doing. She owned a condo in Coral Gables — she was working on her doctorate in political history at the University of Miami — but she lived here much of the time with two older aunts and three much older uncles. The six of them, along with Ginny Egret and James Tiger, made up the voting board of the Tribe of Egret Seminoles, Inc., a trademarked corporation formed to ensure that the tribe — once formally recognized — had both a business and political infrastructure in place.

"Under the corporation, we also created the Egret Seminole Land Development Enterprise," she said. "We did it to explore how we can best use the little bit of land we own jointly, and the possibility of purchasing — or annexing — property that adjoins ours.

"That's how I met Geoff. He came to me as the front man for Jerry Singh. They had a business offer. Singh wanted to sell us thirteen hundred acres of adjoining land on a long-term deferred loan, and at a price next to nothing. In return, we'd allow him to build and manage a casino resort."

DeAntoni said, "He wanted to sell you church property."

"Yes, and he still does. Singh bought the land cheap when he was first starting out. Back when it cost next to nothing because it's mostly swamp. A little later, if you don't mind getting your feet wet, I'll walk you to where the property lines meet."

Billie told us she felt the casino idea was plausible and the potential for profit was huge. But, as she explained to Minster, even if she did get the tribe to go along with the idea, it wouldn't be easy. There was a lot of red tape involved; several government agencies to deal with. First and foremost, though, the Egret Seminoles had to successfully petition the Department of Interior's branch of Acknowledgment and Recognition.

So she and Minster had spent a lot of time together, trying to work out the details.

She said, "The main problem is that the U.S. government is constantly . . . daily . . . perpetually devising ways they can erode Indian sovereignty. The gaming industry is their favorite target. Have you ever heard of James Billy?"

"I was talking about him on the way here," Tomlinson told her. "A tough old 'Nam vet who really got the tribe on its feet."

"That's him. When I'd go on a rant about protecting tribal sovereignty, he'd tell me, 'Hell, honey, sovereignty ain't nothin' but who's got the biggest gun!' In the final analysis, he was absolutely correct.

"So now we're working on getting our guns together. Back in the nineteen fifties, when James was growing up, less than a half-dozen Seminoles had even graduated from high school. Today, we dress our warriors up in three-piece suits and pay them to fire off injunctions instead of bullets. So that's how I got to know Geoff."

There was an odd modulation when she said his name, *Geoff*. Was I imagining a hint of tenderness?

No.

Because she then added, "I hope you're right about him still being alive. I don't believe it, but I hope you're right."

The way she said it was like she cared about the guy. Cared about him a lot.

Why was there a Sawgrass maintenance truck backed into what looked to be a long-abandoned limestone quarry?

That's what Billie wanted to know.

It was a white, ton-and-a-half GMC, double tires in the back with a skid-mounted tank in the bed and Sawgrass decals on the doors. A dark-haired man in coveralls was standing at the rear of the truck, doing something with a wrench.

It was the quarry I'd seen on the way in.

"That's odd; he's on our property," she said. "He's got no business being in here. What I don't understand is, Why would he *want* to be there?" Meaning a shallow, marl-looking pit fifty yards or so wide, with an access road that was overgrown with brush. The road ended abruptly where the truck was parked, backed up to the wall of the quarry as if it were a bunker.

I thought, *Dumping garbage,* but said nothing. A man alone, not dozing, not eating. It was the only explanation that made sense.

We'd walked a mile or so north. Had waded through a couple of sections of sawgrass and water, which DeAntoni didn't like. Wild animals, he said, made him jumpy.

"All the snakes and crap Florida's got. Alligators. We've already seen *enough* big gators,

269

sister. So no more, okay? Then you got your black widows, scorpions, plus that hurricane business with a wind that comes blowing down and puts the snatch on people."

Billie chuckled when he added, "Hell, you Indians can *have* the freaking place, far as I'm concerned."

Most of our walk was on high ground. Dry, too, after one of the driest winters in the state's history, but starting to green now that we were entering the rainy season.

We'd followed the woman through pinelands and grass prairie, through stands of young cypress where she pointed out ghost orchids growing wild, swamp lilies and leather ferns. She knew the names of all the birds, too: wood storks, hawks and great egrets with their reptilian eyes.

Once, she stopped, knelt and touched a finger to a paw print that was bigger than my hand. "Black bear," she said. "A big one. Big and healthy."

She said she often found panther tracks in the area, too.

When I inquired, she told me she'd noticed a significant increase in the amount of wildlife in the 'Glades since her childhood, particularly gators and wading birds. "But that doesn't mean the Everglades is back to the way it was when Chekika and Osceola were alive. And there may be a lot more damage to come."

Her reasoning surprised me. She said she felt

the biggest threat to the region now came from the state and federal governments, and a mega-billion-dollar project called the Comprehensive Everglades Restoration Plan.

"But that's a *good* thing," Tomlinson argued. "The scientists, most of them, anyway, say we need to make the 'Glades a free-flowing water system again. Restore the Kissimmee and increase the amount of wetlands by a couple of hundred thousand acres."

That, Billie told him, is exactly what scared her.

In explanation, she first listed a string of environmental disasters masterminded by government scientists and engineers. Back in 1912, they used biplanes to seed the Everglades with a paper-barked, Australian tree called the melaleuca. The exotic tree reproduced like wildfire and displaced whole regions of natural habitat. Then they did the same with casuarinas, or Australian pines. "Environmentally safe windbreaks," state biologists called the tree at the time.

It was government "experts" who transformed the Kissimmee from a hundred miles of pristine river into a fifty-six-mile ditch, renaming it C-38 Canal. The results were ruinous.

Then, in 1957, at the southern base of mainland Florida, government engineers dug the Buttonwood Canal to drain the area north of Flamingo and provide easy boat access to the mangrove backcountry. For the first time in history, the canal allowed fresh water, laden with decaying sediments, to flow directly into Florida Bay.

Again, the results were disastrous. It all but destroyed the fishery in Florida Bay, yet state biologists balked at admitting the truth, or taking responsibility. It wasn't until 1982 that the canal was finally plugged.

"I don't trust them," Billie said. "Government scientists use Florida like a lab rat. They say they want to return the natural flow of water? The Everglades used to include nearly all the land south of Orlando. It's less than half that size now. When they started draining the sawgrass, tree islands like Chekika's Hammock got bigger. The bigger islands provided more habitat for wildlife that'd been forced inland by development.

"So what's going to happen when they cover half the original land mass with the whole, original amount of flowing water? They're going to flood us out, that's what. When water reduces the amount of uplands habitat, where're the bear, the deer, the people're we supposed to go. Miami?

"This has been one of the driest winters ever, but the water's already come up so much here that some of the trees are getting root rot. Our island's shrinking."

She added, "This place is *delicate*. The 'Glades has spent the last hundred years adapting to change, evolving, surviving. Now they want the area to go through the whole process again, but in reverse." Sounding emotional for the first time, she added, "Anything as beautiful as the Everglades *has* to be fragile. Like a butterfly."

Tomlinson was listening to her, not agreeing but not disagreeing, either. In a soft voice, he said, "Everglades. Yes, this place is the real Magic Kingdom."

The man driving the white pickup truck with the skid tank in back didn't want us to see his face.

My interpretation. Something about the way he behaved when Billie called out to him, "Hey, mister! Mind if I ask what're you doing down there?"

She startled him. Made him jump. He didn't expect anyone to come walking up out of the sawgrass the way we did. Ninety-nine percent of the people, they'll look around when surprised.

Not this guy.

He was about fifty yards away and slightly below us. He stiffened at the sound of her voice. Paused as if thinking about what to do. Then he turned away from us, his face partially hidden by an open hand as he waved, maybe trying to appear friendly, but maybe trying to shield himself, too.

Still waving, he called back a gruff, "Howdy!"

My second assessment: He was trying to disguise his voice.

I watched the man duck slightly, keeping the truck between us and himself. He didn't rush, kept it calm, but he didn't waste any time opening the driver's-side door and getting in.

Billie was walking fast toward the access road. Then she began to trot as the truck pulled away. I jogged along with her, for no other reason than the man's behavior did not seem appropriate for the situation.

She was motioning at the driver, calling for him to stop. But he didn't. When he passed within fifteen yards or so of us, he waved again, palm open — shielding his face once more.

"Asshole," Billie said. She was looking at the truck as it bounced away. "And wouldn't you know: There's mud on his license plate."

A few minutes later, the four of us were going over the area where the truck had been parked.

Yes, it was an abandoned limestone quarry, or "barrow pit"; limestone dredged to build roads. The pit was rocky, honeycombed with holes.

I know enough about Florida geology to recognize that this area would be described as a *karst* formation. A karst is a limestone area that consists of sinkholes and abrupt ridges — some as high as fifteen or twenty feet above sea level.

For millions of years, naturally acidic rain and groundwater flowed through these limestone karsts, dissolving conduits and caverns out of rock. Some plates of limestone fell, some rose. Thus the unusual elevation.

This quarry had been dug into the side of a high ridge. Searching around at the bottom of it, we found a couple of daubs of white goo that smelled like fuel oil — insecticide, DeAntoni suggested. Nothing more until Billie held up a large, empty fertilizer bag, and said, "Look at this. He must be one of the golf course maintenance guys. Probably came out here to get away from his supervisor, sneaking in a nap."

She told us her primary worry was that the guy had been dumping trash. She said the Sawgrass staff did that a lot — dumped their junk on Indian property. Old refrigerators, air conditioners, broken bedding and wallboard — anything too bulky or heavy to drive to the county dump.

She said she'd complained to Jerry Singh, but got a sense of indifference behind his promise to speak with his staff. Plus, it didn't stop. They kept right on dumping.

She told us she thought Singh was secretly encouraging the dumping for the same reason he was encouraging his staff to bully the local Indians. If the Egret Seminoles agreed to Shiva's terms, the Seminole corporate board would have the power to hire and fire. It would be a way for the Indians to rid the area of the Ashram's thugs.

Tomlinson asked, "Then why would you

want to go into the casino business with someone like Shiva? I've got to be right up front with you. I think the guy's a slime."

She answered. "I *don't* want to go into the casino business with him. With Geoff involved, it might've been a different story. I doubt it, but at least there was a possibility. Now there's not a chance — as far as I'm concerned, anyway."

"Then why deal with him?"

She thought for a moment, perhaps calculating how honest she should be. Finally, she said, "I'm dealing with him for a real simple reason. We want his land. *I* want his land. Not for a housing development or anything like that. I want to replant it. Make it part of our home again. But just because I was elected tribal chair, that doesn't mean I make the final decision."

She explained that the Egret Seminoles as a tribe were still considering the casino proposal because Shiva had, in her opinion, conned her five older aunts and uncles. Billie said that, as chairman, she could vote only in the event of a tie. So Shiva had effectively captured the interests of a majority of corporate members on a voting board of eight.

She told us, "A year back, Singh sent a limo and drove us all to his Palm Beach Ashram. He gave us the red-carpet treatment; anything we wanted. What impressed my aunts and uncles, though, was his office. On his office walls, he's got these carvings of pre-Columbian masks and totems. They were copies of *Calusa* masks. Masks that almost no one knows about.

"Singh acted surprised when my uncle identified them. It was like Jerry had no idea what they were. He claimed to have carved the masks himself because the images kept coming to him night after night in his dreams. Jerry told us he was a mystic, and sometimes received messages that he didn't always understand right away. Then he told my aunts and uncles that maybe the masks — the fact that he saw them in his dreams — were a positive sign about the casino."

DeAntoni said, "Did they believe him?"

"I think they'd *like* to believe him. I love my relatives, but they grew up in poverty. I think they'd like a reason to justify voting for the casinos, and have some money for once. So, they're still waiting to decide."

"Waiting for what?"

"Shiva promised them another sign. A more powerful sign. Maybe someday I'll tell you what he promised them he'd do — it's actually kind of funny. It'll never happen, of course. So what I've got to do is figure out how to get Shiva's land *without* agreeing to let him build casinos."

As she said that, she handed the bag she'd found to Tomlinson, and he held it up for me to see. It was the industrial variety; triple-thick brown paper. Printing on the outside said that it had contained fifty pounds of ammonium nitrate commercial-grade fertilizer, manufactured by Chem-A-World Products, Bucyrus, Ohio.

As I looked at the bag, I said, "Is anyone doing any blasting around here?"

She said, "No. In the Everglades? They'd never allow it. They used to back when they were digging barrow pits, but not now."

As I asked Billie if ammonium nitrate was a fertilizer commonly used by golf courses, DeAntoni's cell phone began to ring.

She shrugged — *I don't know* — as Frank put the phone to his ear and, after listening a moment, said, "Speak of the devil."

A minute later, he closed the phone, putting it away, and said, "That was our Scotch-drinking pal, Eugene McRae. Jerry Singh already contacted him and asked about our little visit. He's there right now. The Bhagwan, I mean. Mr. McRae said that Singh would be happy to answer any questions we had about Geoff Minster."

chapter twenty

Why did I get the impression that the black-haired man with the dimpled chin and scar beneath his right eye had come into the room for no other reason than to initiate visual contact with us?

In the world of espionage fieldcraft, an individual who is a target for any reason is "made" when the assigned agent contrives a reason to view the target in the flesh. Even a brief, first-hand visual confirmation is more reliable than a photograph.

I had the feeling dimple-chin wanted to be able to recognize us down the road.

Or maybe he did it because he wanted to see if we'd recognize him.

The image of the man in coveralls climbing into the pickup truck, hiding his face behind an open palm, came to mind. The hair was similar. The size was about right.

But why go to such extremes?

He was a lean man, medium height, dressed in expensive slacks and a black, short-sleeved Polo sweater, patent-leather shoes, his hair razor cut, stylish. He carried himself with a kind of easy grace; had the looks and athleticism that most women find attractive. Something else I noticed: He had a pale, quarter-sized scar on his right arm that had probably once been a tattoo.

I found the diminutive size of the tattoo interesting.

We were in the Sawgrass corporate office, which was not far from the main gate, where, this time, security guards waited in golf carts, expecting us. They did a poor job of cloaking their hostility — word that we'd hurt a couple of their brethren had obviously gotten around — but they followed orders. They offered us bottled water, and drove us to meet their leader.

Now we were sitting in an empty conference room, waiting, when the door was opened suddenly. In walked the man with the dimpled chin and scar. He made quick eye contact with each of us, plucked a book off a shelf and left again without a word.

Because I've spent many years in dangerous places, dealing with covert foreign-service types, I have a bad case of the overlies. I am overly suspicious. I am overly cautious. And I am overly aware that 99.9 percent of Americans are easy targets for anyone who wants to take advantage of them for any reason. Why? Because we never expect it. Not really.

So when the man closed the door, I stood and made a quick survey of the room, pretending to look at the same bookshelf, then through a window that opened onto a court-yard where a statue of a happy Buddha served as a fountain, pouring water onto a garden of stone.

On the wall, beneath a modernistic Darryl Pottdorf painting, was a minicamera lens.

When I dropped the book I'd taken from the case, I knelt to retrieve it. Beneath the conference table, I saw at least one pen-sized microphone. Presumably, there were others.

Trying to communicate with Tomlinson and DeAntoni, using intense eye contact — *We're being recorded* — I said, "It's nice of Bhagwan Shiva to be so cooperative. He must be a decent sort of man."

Tomlinson picked right up on it. "Oh, for sure, man, for sure. You read so much negative stuff these days about the religious types, it's kind of refreshing to have the critics proven wrong."

DeAntoni wasn't so quick. "Hey . . . are you two guys out of your gourds? Shiva sounds like a fucking snake-oil salesman to me — and you know how I feel about snakes."

My warning look stopped him. There were just the three of us now. When I'd asked Billie Egret if she wanted to listen to what Shiva had to say, she'd declined. "After five minutes alone with that man, I feel like I need a shower. We don't have a shower on Chekika's Hammock, and I'm not going back to my condo in Coral

281

Gables until Monday afternoon. So thanks, but no thanks."

Carter McRae wasn't with us, either, because he had to drive to Naples Community Hospital to visit his wife.

So now the three of us sat, waiting. I had a strong suspicion that the man with the dimpled chin was now waiting, too. Probably in a separate office, eavesdropping, listening to what we had to say.

To Tomlinson, I said, "Tell Frank and me your theory about how earth energy works. Power places — the whole vortex philosophy. I really enjoy your insights."

Tomlinson's expression was one of surprise, then delight. "Are you serious? Man, I'd *love* to."

I sat back, smiling at DeAntoni's expression: *Oh, God, here we go again. . . .*

I checked my watch, wondering how long dimple-chin could bear listening to Tomlinson's philosophical rambling.

It wasn't long.

The man who called himself Bhagwan Shiva was a sportsman. An outdoorsman — he told us that. A regular sort. He liked getting outside, hitting the ball around on the tennis court, or playing eighteen. He particularly liked shooting trap — which he was scheduled to do right now.

We were in an elongated golf cart that had a

Rolls-Royce grille. Dimple-chin was driving. Smiling, not saying much. He'd yet to introduce himself, deferential in the same way a chauffeur would not presume to introduce himself to people he was being paid to drive.

Shiva was wearing a collarless Nehru shooting jacket, khaki slacks tucked into snake boots, and a purple safa — a turban made from a single, colorful strip of cloth. Several shotguns, in aluminum cases, were stacked at angles on the seat beside him. He might have been a rajah on his way to a tiger hunt on the Punjab.

His tone personable, upbeat, Shiva said, "I'm sure you've known priests, other clergymen — political leaders. *There's* an example — men who've had a strong calling to serve. Underneath it all, though, we're *people*. I'm just a man. Just like anyone else. With certain gifts, of course." He looked at Tomlinson, who was seated beside him, when he added, "We all have our own peculiar gifts, don't you agree?"

Tomlinson answered, "Oh, for sure, for sure. Some more peculiar than others."

Which made DeAntoni chuckle.

There was a perceptible tension between Tomlinson and the Bhagwan, which I found interesting. There was an instant animus, like opposite poles meeting. When Shiva introduced himself, Tomlinson pretended as if he did not see the man's outstretched hand — a subtle refusal that caused Shiva momentary embarrassment.

This was a stubborn, confrontational Tomlinson I'd never seen before.

Now they were trading far more subtle barbs.

"My point," Shiva continued, "is that I want you gentlemen to feel at ease during our visit. I suspect you're aware of who I am, what I've tried to accomplish for the world as a spiritual leader. It . . . it intimidates *some* people. What I'm telling you is, there's no need to treat me any differently. We're all on the same level here."

In the same veiled tone, Tomlinson replied, "Don't sell yourself short, Mr. Singh. You're on a *much* different level."

Which irked the man. Even sitting on the rear bench of the golf cart, I could see the skin of Shiva's face tighten into a forced smile. "Perhaps you have a point, Mr. Tomlinson. It's true that I have — and this is just a rough estimate — but I have more than a quarter-million followers around the world."

Tomlinson replied, "Really? I'm curious. What happens when your followers catch up? Do they still cling to the initial delusion?"

Shiva started to say something, but then reacted with a forced laugh. "Are you trying to insult me, Mr. Tomlinson?"

"No-o-o-o, man, of course not. I wouldn't try to insult you. I wouldn't want to risk being misunderstood."

"I see." Shiva was still smiling, showing us he was under control once again. "You seem so sure of yourself; so quick to judge. That's such an endearing . . . *childlike* quality. I bet . . . I bet that you're the kind of man who still plays children's games."

Tomlinson patted the cased shotguns. "You mean the kind of games that don't involve metaphorical penis symbols?"

"Oh, now, now, now, *please*. I bet that, secretly, you like things that go boom. What child doesn't like an explosion?"

He meant something by that. Which caused Tomlinson to stumble. It set me back a beat, too.

Shiva continued smoothly, "I don't claim always to be accurate, but clairvoyance is one of *my* peculiar gifts. Give me a moment to concentrate. . . ." Shiva had both of his palms pressed to his temples. After a few seconds, he said, ". . . the children's game you play is *baseball*. Yes, baseball. And the position you play . . . I don't know the American equivalent, but in the sport of cricket, you'd be called a 'bowler.' "

Dimple-chin said, "A pitcher. That's the same thing."

DeAntoni said, "Is that true, he's a pitcher? Come to think of it, he does *look* like a pitcher. I'll be damned. How do you people do that?"

I was thinking: *They did a computer search while we were waiting,* as Shiva continued, "I

285

perceive that you feel you are an excellent pitcher. In fact, I perceive that you feel superior in a number of ways. Ego — that's a character flaw you should address, Mr. Tomlinson. In a book, I once wrote, 'A large ego is the favorite habitat of a small mind.' "

Tomlinson replied, "Interesting. So tell me, what's it *like,* having all that room for your brain to move around in?"

Shiva fired back, "You must be speaking of my Palm Beach Ashram. You should come and visit one day, experience it for yourself. You'd have a chance to understand that there's a far more satisfying world waiting for someone like you. Many drug addicts — even unconvicted *murderers* — have found peace and health there. What would you say if I challenged you to come and sit through my Basic Auditing lecture?"

Pulling at his scraggly hair, not smiling and as troubled as I've ever seen him, Tomlinson replied, "I'd probably tell you the truth, Jerry: I'm just too fucking busy. Or vice versa."

On our way to the skeet range, dimple-chin drove past the private airstrip, the Sawgrass minimall where trams were shuttling vacationing members, then into what Shiva called, "our nature preserve and the Cypress Ashram Center."

The nature preserve consisted of several dozen Everglades animals caged in fiberglass dioramas that were constructed to resemble natural habitat. The zoo was on a boardwalk. The boardwalk was part of a self-guided nature tour. There were birds, mammals, gators and snakes. In one of the larger cages, an oversized male Florida panther watched us with glowing yellow eyes as we rolled past.

What Shiva called his "Cypress Ashram" was really an outdoor amphitheater. It was a stage attached to an acoustic dome that was elevated above concentric levels of seating. The place was big; had to seat a thousand or so people. The theater was built at the edge of what must have been a cypress stand, though only a few cypress trees remained growing knee-deep in red water.

At what was the equivalent of a ticket house, a life-sized bronze statue of a bearded and smiling Bhagwan Shiva welcomed visitors. In one hand, he held a lantern, in the other a globe. The statue stood along the cart trail entrance, and Shiva ignored it with a practiced and bored disinterest as we rolled past.

To Shiva, Tomlinson said, "Hey, Jerry! Has there ever been a time in your life when, just once, you'd love to be a bird?"

Shiva reacted as if it were a good-natured joke; played right along. "Do you like birds? Then you'll enjoy our next stop."

Which made no sense until dimple-chin steered us down a gravel service path where a wooden sign read COMMUNAL FARM.

It was an oversized garden, really, laid out in an odd shape — a pentagon, I finally realized. Two acres or so of tomatoes, beans, squash, corn and other vegetables planted in rows. There were compost bins, equipment lockers and a shed for a small John Deere tractor. There was also a long hutch screened with chicken wire.

"We grow a lot of our own food," Shiva told us. "Organically, of course. For our restaurants, and for our church members. Plus, we raise chickens and our own special variety of pigeon."

DeAntoni said, "Pigeons? Those things are like rats with wings. Why'd anybody want to raise pigeons?"

Shiva was getting out of the cart and used his hand to tell us to wait for him. "You'll see," he said.

There were three women working in the garden. All were dressed in white robes belted at the waist. Shiva called to one of them, "Kirsten! You are needed."

I watched an attractive blond teenager hurry to him, her head bowed, not making eye contact. Then she knelt before the bearded man, reached, and kissed the back of Shiva's right hand. She nodded as he spoke to her — I couldn't hear what he was saying — and she remained on one knee as he turned and walked away.

Back in the cart, Shiva said to dimple-chin,

"They'll be ready for us in about twenty minutes."

Then he turned and spoke to DeAntoni, saying, "Now's a good time if you want to ask me about Geoff Minster. I don't know what I can add, but I'll help in any way I can. There's a favor I need to ask in return, however —" Shiva turned his eyes to Tomlinson, then to me. His eyes were an unusual color, I realized — a luminous amber flecked with brown — and they jogged a recent memory.

It took me an instant to make the association. The panther we'd just seen; the caged animal with the golden, glowing eyes. Shiva's eyes possessed a similar lucency.

Shiva said, "The favor I'm going to ask is that you allow us to record our conversation. A legal precaution — I'm sure you understand."

I watched dimple-chin remove a digital recorder from his pocket as Shiva added, "So, if you wouldn't mind stating your names and home addresses for our records . . ."

At first, Shiva said nothing about Minster that was unexpected. His versions of their first meeting, and of their business history were similar to Sally's versions.

He talked along freely, answering all DeAntoni's questions. But his manner was disinterested, almost bored. It was as if he were just marking time, waiting for something more interesting to happen.

There was one small revelation when he said, "Am I convinced that Geoff's dead? Probably, but I'm not *certain* of it. He had a lot going for him here. I was about to appoint him to my Circle of Twenty-eight — a group of my most trusted advisors worldwide. That's quite an honor.

"In terms of business, Geoff was doing better than he'd been doing for the simple reason that he'd turned over almost all decision-making responsibilities to me and my staff. If that sounds immodest, I apologize. But the fact is, we are good at what we do."

Shiva added that, emotionally, though, Minster was having some problems. "I'm not a gossip, and I'm certainly not going to breach the confidential nature of my relationship with a student. But I will tell you what is publicly known: Geoff was not happy in his marriage. It's possible that his unhappiness was reason enough for him to intentionally disappear."

DeAntoni said, "What you're saying to me is that the guy was having an affair. That he maybe ran off to be with another woman."

Shiva said, "I'm suggesting no such thing. We teach that sex is healthy. He had no reason to hide it."

"Then why do you consider it a possibility?"

The blond girl in the white robe was walking toward us, motioning for us to follow — they were ready for us on the skeet range.

Shiva said, "I'm suggesting it because, two

months before he disappeared, he used one of our Ashram computers to transfer slightly more than a hundred thousand dollars in cash to a private account on Grand Cayman Island. I told the police. Check, and you'll see — it's already part of the public record."

chapter twenty-one

The Sawgrass trap range was a professionally designed complex of courses, sporting clays and authentic field stations, all approved by the Amateur Trapshooting Association — or so said the laminated notice on the wall of the range master's office.

There was no range master in attendance, though, which I found odd — until I learned the sort of targets Shiva preferred.

The facility was, in fact, deserted. Shiva insisted on having the grounds to himself, he told us. In hindsight, I understood why. He didn't want witnesses.

We got our first hint as he walked us through the shooting course, briefing us on the history of what he called his newest "path to awareness."

"Are you familiar with the Japanese art of *Kyudo?* It's longbow shooting — a beautiful form of archery practiced by Zen Buddhists. *Kyudo* demands the precision of ballet and extraordinary concentration — yet, to perform well, the shooter must calm himself, empty his mind and allow his body to react automatically.

Mushin is the Japanese word for it. It's a Zen expression that means 'no mind.' "

Tomlinson replied, "I think I've read somewhere or other about *Kyudo,* and *Mushin.*" He said it with a hint of irony so subtle that I was the only one to detect it.

Shiva said, "Then you may be able to appreciate my new love of shooting. To hit a moving target with a shotgun, it requires the same . . . well, the same letting-go of conscious control. If you know anything about how our right brain and left brain work, you'll understand that shooting uses primarily the right brain. That's why it's such an effective tool for meditation."

Shiva added, "As I tell my students, 'You cannot think linearly or logically about shooting. If you do, you will never hit a thing.' When the target appears, you must apprehend the spatial situation instantly and, at the same time, shoot. This truly is the Zen of sport."

DeAntoni said, "You're telling us that you think popping off a few rounds is some kind of religious deal, huh?" His tone, his expression, said, *Jesus, now I'm dealing with two weirdos.*

Shiva laughed. We were walking toward the shooting course. Dimple-chin was already at the trap house, opening gun cases and filling shooting aprons with shells.

Shiva said, "For me, shooting's part of my religious discipline. For you, though, it might be just a relaxing way to spend an afternoon. Even the history of the sport is fascinating!"

Like most men accustomed to being in control, Shiva was prone to lecture. He gave us a brief lecture now, telling us that trap-shooting dated back to the 1700s, when English gentlemen would walk a course upon which their manservants had hidden wild birds in holes. The holes were covered with silk top hats.

"Jolly good fun," Shiva said, demonstrating that he had a puckish side.

"But these days," he added, "the most common targets are called clay birds — although they're actually made of a limestone composite."

He motioned with his hand. The ground was littered with orange shards. "They're thrown from trap houses at a variety of angles. In trap, you shoot from five different positions. In skeet, you shoot from eight positions." He gestured again. "All shooting is done between the two trap houses. It's fun. But it's not my favorite. If you like, I'll show you my favorite. It's called sporting clays."

As Tomlinson and I exchanged looks — *Why is he telling us this?* — Shiva explained that sporting courses were laid out in natural surroundings. Typically, they included ten shooting stations.

"It makes you get out into the bush," he said, "and interact with nature. You have to walk from station to station. The target can fly out from anywhere. Or run — a rabbit or even a deer target. It's exciting. Something else: When

294

I come to shoot, staff always adds an interesting little twist. Just for me."

Shiva was loading what appeared to be a 12-gauge over-and-under Weatherby. When he finished, he looked up and smiled. "I expect you gentlemen to join me. We have plenty of guns and ammunition."

Tomlinson told him, "I've never shot a gun in my life. I don't plan to start now."

"Ah, I'd forgotten — your oversized ego. You're afraid you won't shoot well."

"No, Jerry. Fact is, man, it's the company."

Shiva wasn't going to allow himself to be baited again. He stood with the shotgun, breech open, cradled beneath his arm. "Then come along and watch. Once you get into the spirit of the sport, I'll bet you change your mind."

As they walked away, I knelt as if to tie my boating shoes. Actually, I stopped so as to use two careful fingers to pick up a 12-gauge shell I'd seen dimple-chin accidentally drop. I slid the shell in my pocket, then followed along.

There was something *wrong* about the guy. . . .

Shiva didn't use clay targets on his sporting course. He used live birds. It explained why his staff raised pigeons, and also his insistence on referencing trap shooting's history. It gave the practice veracity.

The first station was at a pond fringed with

swamp maples. Shiva touched a hand to his turban, readying himself, then yelled, "Pull!"

Two birds came flapping out of a camouflaged station, zigzagging wildly, struggling to gain altitude. Shiva shot the first bird cleanly, but wounded the second. It spiraled to the ground, and then lay there, flapping with one damaged wing.

After a moment of dumb shock, Tomlinson began to run toward the floundering bird, yelling, "What the hell are you doing? You *bastard*. You killed them for no reason!"

Shiva popped the spent casings out of his Weatherby, and said very calmly, "All my targets are alive — that's the spiritual component. To create a precise intersection between life and death. Birds, rabbits, deer. That's the *Zen* of it. What possible enlightenment could anyone gain from shooting at miniature *Frisbees*."

Dimple-chin, I noticed was staying close to Tomlinson, walking fast. Why was he still carrying the digital recorder in his hand?

Shiva looked from DeAntoni to me. His expression of tolerance seemed a careful affectation — a mask for elation. I couldn't tell if he was happy because he'd killed something, or because he'd finally infuriated Tomlinson. To us, he said, "I think it's far more humane to give animals a chance to escape rather than simply kill them in their pens."

I heard DeAntoni say, "Oh yeah. You're a

296

real fucking sport," as Tomlinson knelt and cradled the wounded bird in his hands.

Then he walked toward us, carrying the bird, saying, "Guess what this asshole's using to get his little rocks off, Doc. It's a white-crowned pigeon. Singh — are you telling us that you're raising white-crowned pigeons?"

Shiva was reloading, unconcerned. "First of all, I don't appreciate your tone of voice, or your vulgarity. And yes, we *are* raising pigeons. They nest in the mangroves. Staff collects the eggs, and we incubate them. See? We're helping the environment."

DeAntoni didn't understand the significance of it, but I did. Florida's white-crowned pigeon has little in common with the tame pigeon you find in parks. It is a wild Caribbean dove that migrates between Florida and the West Indies, making long open-sea crossings. The gray-blue body makes the bird's white crest conspicuous. I've seen them off the Dry Tortugas, far out at sea. I've seen them in Key West, sitting at the Green Parrot Bar, too.

Up until the turn of the previous century, white-crowned pigeons nested in colonies of thousands. But they were hunted almost to extinction until laws were passed to protect them. Even so, they are not a bird that is commonly seen.

Shiva told us, "I prefer the white-crowned dove to the common pigeon because it's faster. A more difficult target. The challenge is part of

297

the meditative exercise."

Tomlinson was facing him now, and Shiva sniffed, shrugged, indifferent as Tomlinson yelled, "Meditation, my ass, you ridiculous phony. It's murder. Why are you killing these birds?"

Shiva's smugness seemed calculated, an intentional technique to exasperate. "There's a basic spiritual concept," he replied, "that you clearly don't understand. Death is an *illusion*. Meaningless. The bird you're holding — you, your friends, *all* living things — we don't die. We simply change forms.

"The kindest thing you could do for that bird right now? If you really do *care* about suffering. The kindest thing you could do for it is snap its neck. Allow it to move on to its next incarnation."

Shiva turned and looked at dimple-chin. "Or let Izzy do it. He wouldn't mind at all."

Dimple-chin smiled, enjoying himself. "My pleasure."

Izzy.

So the Bhagwan's assistant had a name. The man whose fingerprints, presumably, were on the shotgun shell I'd collected.

I'd never seen Tomlinson so furious. His skin was blotched red, his eyes fierce, as he said, "You're doing this intentionally. You're trying to make me angry. *Why?*"

Shiva said, "I'm trying to instruct you, not

298

anger you. I'm a teacher. Why can't you let go of your ego? Open yourself up to wisdom, and allow yourself to be our student. There's much we can teach you."

"*You* pretend to be able or worthy to teach *me?*"

"Why does that frighten you? You are a young soul. I've been sent here to help people such as yourself. People who are lost."

To Tomlinson, I said, "You're right. He's doing it intentionally. And they're recording every word, so don't say another thing. Let's get out of here."

But he waved me away, holding the bird in one hand, staring into Shiva's face. "You said there are ten stations on this course. Does that mean your going to try to kill eighteen more birds?"

"Actually, there are sixteen doubles — birds, naturally. And two rabbit traps. I was hoping you fellows would shoot with me. So staff has quadrupled the number of targets." Smiling at Izzy, Shiva added, "It looks like I'm going to have a lot of shooting today."

Tomlinson said, "Then why do you have that gizmo loaded with targets?"

He pointed at a manual, spring-operated trap catapult that sat on wheels fifteen yards or so from the shooting deck. In the machine were stacked several dozen clay plates.

"The clay birds are for members. Not everyone gets to shoot live pigeons — it's a rare opportunity that I'm offering. A chance for real spiritual exploration. Are you *sure* you won't give it a try?"

For a moment, Tomlinson focused his attention on the bird he was holding, stroking it as he made a low cooing sound. Then he lifted the dove in both palms, blew softly into its face, and said, "You're not hurt. You're okay, now," and tossed it upward.

The bird flapped unevenly for a moment, came close to tumbling, but then seemed to feel air beneath its wings, and righted itself.

Surprised, I watched the bird fly toward the swamp maple horizon where, I noticed, a much larger bird was perched. It was a snail kite. The snail kite, I noted, was the same size and color of the rare bird we'd seen standing on the mahogany tree at Chekika's Hammock. The kite looked like a blue hawk.

Tomlinson's manner now became oddly buoyant as he said, "Looks like you're only batting five hundred, Jerry. One of your savage animals got away. You say you enjoy sports? I've got a sporting offer for you."

Shiva said, "Really? Sporting. A kind of wager?"

"In a way. How about this: Let me try to break a target. Load a gun with two bullets and let me try. If I hit at least one of the targets, you agree not to shoot any more pigeons."

Shiva began to chuckle. "First of all, shotguns don't fire bullets, they fire pellets from a cartridge. Which is why that hardly seems fair. Even if you've never shot a gun before, it's possible that you might get lucky. One target in two shots?" He was shaking his head now, seeming to relish the circumstances. "No, I don't like those odds."

Tomlinson's voice became steely as he said, "Then how about giving me one cartridge? One group of pellets, and I'll break *two* targets. If I break any fewer than two targets with one cartridge, I'll shoot the rest of the stations with you. I'll kill live birds. I give you my word."

DeAntoni said, "I'd like to get in on some of this action," as I told my friend, "Listen to me just for once. Most experts couldn't make a shot like that. Just stop. Let it go. Let's get the hell out of here."

But Tomlinson wouldn't be swayed. He accepted a shotgun from a grinning Izzy, then a single 12-gauge shell. Tomlinson held the shell in his long fingers, inspecting it. I doubt if he'd ever seen one before.

The shell was the size of a miniature sausage and had a brass cap attached to a red plastic casing. He bounced the shell in his hand, feeling the weight of it.

Then, to me, he said, "Show me how to operate this thing, brother."

The shotgun was a 12-gauge Beretta over-and-under, which means that the two barrels were mounted vertically as opposed to side by side. I demonstrated how to load his single cartridge in the top barrel, then showed him how the safety worked. When he seemed to understand, I opened the chamber and grabbed the shell as it popped out. I handed both the shell and shotgun to him.

As I said to Tomlinson, "You're making a mistake," Shiva, standing off to the side, told him, "Izzy's all set when you are."

Dimple-chin was standing by the catapult, clay targets in place, the spring arms cocked.

I watched Tomlinson pause to tuck his purple-and-pink Hawaiian shirt into his baggy shorts and pull his scraggly hair back. Then he stepped onto the shooting deck, shotgun ready — an incongruous combination and an absurd thing to witness.

I listened to Shiva say, "What an amusing little soul you are."

I listened to DeAntoni say, "Concentrate, Mac. You can do it. Wait until just before the plates cross, then *squeeze* the trigger."

I listened to Izzy say, "Tell me when you're ready. I'm throwing two at once."

Then I heard Tomlinson call, *"Pull!"*

There was the fluttering sound of spring compression as twin clay targets arched high toward the pond — but Tomlinson didn't shoot. Instead, he snapped open the shotgun and plucked out the unfired shell with his big right hand. Then he whirled like the gangly pitcher he is, and rocketed the shell toward the mechanical catapult, narrowly missing Izzy.

But he hit his target. The 12-gauge cartridge had to have been traveling close to eighty miles an hour when it crashed into the stack of clay birds mounted vertically into the machine. Several of them shattered.

In the microsecond of silence that followed, I heard two soft *plop-plops* as the airborne disks landed in the pond.

Tomlinson tossed the shotgun on the ground with theatrical contempt. Then he walked toward Shiva. "No more live pigeons for you, Jerry. You're going to keep your word. Like the big-time religious guru you claim to be. *Right?*"

"Don't be ridiculous. You cheated. You tricked me."

"Nope. I told you if I broke any fewer than two targets with one shell, you win. But I broke five or six. Maybe more. Count 'em if you want. You know what the key is? *Mushin.* That's a Japanese word."

Shiva's smugness was gone now. Beneath the beard, his face was turning shades of ruby, his neck muscles spasming. His voice was more of a hiss as he said, "You pompous, meddling son-of-a-bitch. I want you out of here. I want you off my property. Get the fuck away from me!"

Tomlinson was only an arm's length away from Shiva now, nose to nose, smiling. "No more pigeons, Jerry. You promised. Or don't promises mean anything to you?"

Shiva began to reply, but then he appeared to think of something. The sudden grin on his face was manic. Abruptly, Shiva raised his shotgun, leaned, and fired both barrels.

The snail kite perched in the maples exploded in a smoking swirl of feathers, blue and gray. The corpse of the bird tumbled like a wingless plane. It made a melon sound when it hit the ground.

Shiva lowered his shotgun and yelled into Tomlinson's face, "Okay, smartass! I won't shoot any more pigeons. But the blood's on *your* hands, not mine."

For the first time since I've known the man, I saw Tomlinson break emotionally. Eyes bulging, he lunged toward Shiva. He got his huge hands around the man's neck just as I grabbed him from behind. I had to call for DeAntoni to help — Tomlinson had surprising, freakish strength. I've never experienced anything like it. It took us both to restrain him.

I believe — I truly do believe — he would have tried to kill Shiva if we'd let him loose.

As we dragged Tomlinson away, he was screaming every foul word, all aimed at Shiva, and interspaced with this refrain: "You're ruined, Jerry. The Everglades won't allow it! I swear to God almighty, that we will *ruin* you. . . ."

I noticed that Izzy, holding the recorder, was relaxed. He seemed very pleased about something.

It was on our way home, just after sunset and

while we were crossing the Sanibel Causeway, that DeAntoni's cell phone rang. I looked at a sky that was streaked with iridescent clouds, mango gold and conch-shell pink, and listened to his side of the conversation.

I heard him say, "Hey, Mrs. Minster, good to hear from you. Oh . . . okay, Sally."

We were riding over sand islands, Lighthouse Point an elevated darkness off to our left, as I heard: "You're kiddin' me. And you knew the guy?"

After a full minute of silence, DeAntoni spoke again into the phone, saying, "I'll drop off Doc and Tomlinson and come straight to your place. It'll take me about three hours. Maybe we can have a late dinner. If it's not an imposition."

He closed his phone, and glanced at me. "Ironwood, the gated community where Sally lives, has a night security guard. A guy named Johnson. He disappeared last night, and they found him floating in the bay this afternoon, dead. Sally said the guy took special care of her. Kept an eye on her house because of the break-ins she's been having."

I said, "How'd he die?"

"They don't know yet. Maybe a stroke and he fell off a dock. That's what the cops are guessing. But Sally doesn't believe it. She says someone was in her bedroom again last night. They went through her drawers. She thinks maybe Johnson surprised the guy."

Sitting sprawled in the backseat, working on his seventh or eighth beer since we'd left Sawgrass and already slurring his words, Tomlinson said, "Evil, man. There's something evil in the air. There is a very wicked mojo seeping around Sawgrass. The whole scene. Like swamp gas, man. I can *feel* it."

DeAntoni said, "Um-huh. Have another beer."

"An excellent idea. I think I will."

There was the carbonation *sssush* of a can being cracked.

DeAntoni was chuckling. "I got to hand it to you, Tinkerbell. You stuck it right up that weirdo's cheap seats. The only thing that separates Shiva's lips from his asshole is a couple of feet of tubing — and you proved it."

For the fourth or fifth time, Frank said to me, "The skinny fucker's got an arm on him. I'll never question that again."

Meaning Tomlinson.

Sounding miserable, Tomlinson replied, "Wrong, wrong, wrong. Shiva *won,* man. The way I behaved, it's against everything I believe and stand for. What happened is, he *proved* I'm as much a fraud as he is."

Tomlinson had been talking that way since we left Sawgrass.

To DeAntoni, I said, "When you talked to her about the dead guard, did Sally sound frightened?"

"Yeah. But in control. Not too bad. There's

an ex-cop who works with me sometimes, lives in Hialeah. I'll call him, ask him to hop over to Ironwood and keep an eye on things 'till I get there."

"I think that's a great idea, Frank. We don't want anything to happen to her."

Showing some emotion, DeAntoni said, "If anybody touches that lady, by the time I'm done, they'll need a compass to find all the parts they got missing." Then: "Hey, you know what? She said she'd have dinner with me. Just the two of us alone. That she'd be *delighted*."

He was sounding pretty delighted himself.

chapter twenty-two

The next afternoon, Sunday, April 13th, at 6 P.M., I was working in my lab when I felt the framework of my stilt house vibrate with what seemed to be a series of three distinct tremors.

I was standing at my stainless-steel dissecting table when it happened. I immediately looked to my right where, beneath the east windows, and on a similar table, is a row of working, bubbling aquaria — octopi, squid and fish therein. There are more glass aquariums above on shelves.

In each aquarium, the tremors had created seismic oscillating circles on the surface, and miniature waves.

Nope. I wasn't imagining things. And, no, it wasn't because I'd just built my third drink: the juice of two fresh Key limes mixed with Nicaraguan rum, crushed ice and a splash of seltzer.

To my left, along the east wall, near the door, there are more tanks, all heavily lidded and locked because they contain stone crabs and calico crabs. Octopi, I'd learned, are master thieves when it comes to their favorite food — thus the locks.

The water in those tanks was vibrating as well.

I was working late in the lab because I was running low on supplies. Restocking inventory was long overdue. On a yellow legal pad clamped to a clipboard, I'd written: *compartmented petri dishes (pack/20); Tekk measuring pipets (dozen); Pyrex tubes (mm/various/72); ultraviolet aquarium sterilizer; tetracycline tablets (pack/20); methyl-chrome; clarifier; pH test paper.*

The shopping list wasn't close to being complete. I was leafing through my Carolina Science & Math catalog, thinking about adding a neat little portable water tester to the list when the house began to shake.

At first, I thought to myself, *Sonic boom?* But then I felt it twice more, and I thought, *Construction blasts.*

I walked to the center of the room where I've installed a university-style lab workstation. It's an island of oaken drawers and cupboards beneath a black epoxy resin table, complete with a sink, two faucets, electrical outlets and double gas cocks for attaching Bunsen burners or a butane torch.

I placed the catalog on the table, pushed open the screen door and walked outside, carrying my drink along with me.

I wasn't the only one who'd felt the tremors. The unusual sensation of earth and water shaking had stirred our little liveaboard community to action on this quiet Palm Sunday afternoon. Across the water, I could see Rhonda Lister and Joann Smallwood exiting their cabin door onto the stern of their wood-rotted Chris-Craft cruiser, *Satin Doll*. They were looking at the sky, as if expecting to see fighter jets.

Jeth Nicholes, the fishing guide, was standing on the balcony of his apartment above the marina office. Janet Mueller, I was surprised to see, was standing beside him — a recent development in what has been an old and complex love affair.

Dieter Rasmussen, the German psycho-pharmacologist, and his nubile Jamaican girlfriend, Moffid Seemer, were climbing onto the fly bridge of his classic, forty-six-foot Grand Banks trawler, *Das Stasi*, heads turning. Dieter was in his underwear, and Moffid, I couldn't help but notice, was topless. When people are surprised, they react without considering how they are dressed.

Tomlinson was out, too. Standing on the cabin roof of *No Mas*, a black sarong knotted around his waist, his head tilted, as if listening.

I was surprised to see him. We'd played baseball earlier in the day at Terry Park, a classic old Grapefruit League anachronism in East Fort Myers. After the game, still in his baseball uniform, he'd invited me to drive with him to Siesta Key Beach and join in the weekly drum circle that is held there at sunset.

"Is that the sort of thing where a couple of hundred beach hipster-types stand around a fire, banging on drums?" I said.

Tomlinson replied, "*Exactly*. I know, I know, it sounds almost too good to pass up. Tonight, I've been asked to serve as the lead Djembe drummer. Quite an honor."

So I was surprised he was still aboard his boat . . . or maybe he was just leaving — yes, that was it. I watched him reach into the cabin of *No Mas* and lift a massive skin drum from the hold, his eyes still searching the sky.

Then, as if on cue, everyone looked in the direction of my stilt house, as if seeking an explanation. I held both hands out and shrugged, meaning that I had no idea what'd caused the tremors.

They all made the same universal gesture: *We don't know, either.*

So I walked to the marina, where Joann, Rhonda and Dieter and I stood around discussing it.

"What a weird feeling," Joann said. She's a short, dark-haired woman with a Rubenesque body and a bawdy sense of the absurd. "It was like I was suddenly standing on jelly. I've had the feeling a couple of times, but it was always while I was having good sex. Never when I was brushing my teeth."

When I suggested that the tremors were caused by a construction blast, Dieter said, "Daht does not seem reasonable. A construction blast at six P.M. on a Sunday? Even Germans don't work on Sundays."

I told them, "Well, one thing we know it's not. It *wasn't* an earthquake. Florida's not on a fault line. There's never been an earthquake in Florida as far as I know."

I would soon learn otherwise.

The next morning I was awakened by a heavy pounding on the door. I swung out of bed, checked the brass alarm clock and thought, *Damn. Overslept again.*

It was 8:45 A.M.

Wearing only khaki shorts, I padded barefooted across the wooden floor, gave Crunch & Des a quick scratch in passing and opened the door to find my old friend, Dewey Nye, standing before me. She was wearing Nikes, blue jogging shorts over a red tank suit, blond hair haltered in a ball cap, and she had her fists on her hips — a pose that seemed as aggressive as the expression on her face.

"Goddamn it, Thoreau, you stood me up again! We agreed to work out early this morning, remember? You were supposed to meet me at Tarpon Bay Beach at seven, run to Tradewinds and back, then swim. So I stood around like a dumbass, waiting, when I should'a known all along that you'd screwed me over again."

She made a huffing noise, glaring at me, before she added, "What's this make? The fifth, sixth time you've promised that we'd start working out together? And, every time, you come up with some lame-ass excuse. Or you just don't show — no call, no nothing. What the hell's wrong with you, Ford?"

Yawning, I pushed open the screen door so she could enter. "Dew, I'm sorry. I guess the alarm clock didn't go off. You know how punctual I usually am —"

"That's bullshit. The old Ford, yeah, he was punctual. You could always count on him. But not now. Not *you*. You're almost always late, you've become undependable as hell, and, as far as I'm concerned, a promise from you doesn't mean a goddamn thing!"

I was still holding the door open; could smell the good odor of shampoo, fabric softener and girl sweat as she pushed by me. But, when she finished the sentence, I let the door slam shut. Then I stared at her until her cheeks flushed and her eyes flooded. That quickly, she went from fury to near tears.

She said, "Now I've hurt your feelings. I'm sorry. I don't really mean it. I *do* trust you, Doc. I'll always *trust* you. But . . . damn it —" she had a rolled newspaper in her hand, and she slapped it into her palm for emphasis — "you've got to quit standing me up!"

I motioned her into a chair, and said, "For the second time: Sorry. I mean it. It's inexcusable." I walked toward the galley. "Coffee?"

"Why not? I need something to get my heart going. It's not like I had anyone to push me on my run this morning. Which was boring as hell, not having anyone to talk to."

Another not-so-subtle cut.

I like big, tomboy women, which is why Dewey remains one of my favorites. She's a little under six feet tall, 145 pounds or so, blue-blue eyes, blond hair cut boyishly short, and she has the vocabulary of a sailor. She once also had one of the most beautiful faces I'd ever seen: one of those California-beach-girl faces, all cheekbones and chin with deep-set eyes.

Her face is different now — and for heart-rending reasons — but she's still a striking woman. Because Dewey's had a long and volatile love affair with an internationally known woman tennis star, sex — or the prospect of sex — is no longer a component in our relationship. That it has made us even closer friends is a phenomenon I do not find surprising. The quickest and most common way to end a male-female friendship is to take the friendship into the bedroom.

So she sat in the breakfast booth, reading the paper while I made coffee. The sink was still piled with dishes; the counter was still a greasy mess. Added to the mess was now a single red 12-gauge shell I'd sealed in a plastic Baggie.

There was something about Shiva's assistant, Izzy, that troubled me on a subliminal level. Watching him, I felt a sense of subconscious threat, but also recognition — of what, I couldn't say.

But it'd bothered me enough to want to keep

something that might carry his fingerprints. Which is why I'd stolen the shell.

I put the shell in a drawer. I switched on the coffeemaker as I listened to Dewey make small talk, seemingly trying to reestablish a comfortable mood, which was a sure sign that she had something more serious on her mind.

Finally, she said, "There's something I need to talk to you about. I've been putting it off. But no longer."

"Is it about Walda? If she's still jealous of you and me, I can call her if you want. Explain how it is between us. It might help."

Dewey said, "Yeah, well, that, too. She is such a constant pain in the ass. But that's not what I want to talk about. I want to talk about you."

"Okay. What about me?"

"I don't want to offend you, and I don't want to hurt your feelings again. We've been through a lot together. I love you as one of my best friends."

I said to her, "I'm fond of you, too. So why do I get the feeling this is preface to some more criticism?"

She rattled the newspaper. "It's not criticism. What I'm going to tell you is the truth. But you've got to remember that sometimes the truth hurts."

I turned away from the stove. "Then go ahead. I've got big shoulders. Fire away."

Dewey said, "The truth is, Doc . . . you look

like hell. If you had a decent-sized mirror in this place, perhaps you'd know. You've gained at least fifteen or twenty pounds since we used to be workout partners. But it's not even the weight. You're starting to look soft. Puffy. And look at those circles under your eyes! Plus this weird crap about going from one of the most rock-solid men on earth to being undependable as some goofy teenager."

She stood and held me by both arms, looking into my eyes. "The point is, pal, I'm worried about your health. Maybe something's wrong with you. Maybe you need to see a doctor; get a physical. *Something*. Or start working out with me again. Probably both. And you need to do it soon, because it's getting harder and harder to be your friend."

I said, "That sounds like an ultimatum."

"In a way, it is. I care too much. I've got too much respect for you to watch you go down the shitter. If you're dead set on doing it to yourself, don't expect the people who love you to stand around and watch. It's too painful."

I turned and poured coffee into a brace of Navy-issue mugs, then sat across from her in the booth. I felt tired and empty and disgusted with myself. I said, "Read the paper. Tell me if there's anything interesting going on out there in the real world. After that, let's jog down Tarpon Bay Road to the beach and go for a swim."

She sighed, momentarily relieved, her blue

eyes brimming again. "If there's anything you want to tell me, you can. What's *wrong* with you?"

"A short run and a short swim," I said. "That's enough for starters."

Dewey said, "It's in the paper this morning about the earthquake. I heard the checkout clerk talking about it at Bailey's when I stopped to get a banana and yogurt."

She turned the newspaper's local section toward me so I could read the small headline: EARTHQUAKE? SCIENTISTS INVESTIGATING.

"The clerk said that on Sanibel and Captiva, the only ones who felt it live on the beach. Or on boats. What about you?"

"I felt something. So'd Joann, Rhonda and the rest of the liveaboards. In that way, it makes sense. Water's a better conductor than air."

"Well, at my house, I didn't feel a damn thing — but then, I was on the phone fighting with Walda around six, so pissed off I wouldn't'a felt it if the ceiling caved in."

Surprised, and pleased that we'd been provided an interesting diversion, I took the paper from her and read parts of the story aloud.

Yes, I was wrong about earthquakes in Florida.

Seismographic experts from the University of Florida are investigating the source of three or more earth tremors that were reported yesterday

317

afternoon by South Florida residents from the Everglades to Captiva.

According to seismologist Dr. Smith Douglas, the University of Florida maintains a seismograph network with stations in Gainesville, at the Everglades Beard Research Station and at Oscar Shearer State Park near Sarasota.

"We'll be checking our data, and working with the National Earthquake Information Center in Denver to determine the origin of the tremors," Dr. Douglas said. "It's certainly possible it could have been a small earthquake. According to the Florida Geologic Survey of 1983, Florida's had approximately thirty earthquakes or 'events' that date as far back as 1727. This could be another."

I stopped reading, took a gulp of my coffee and said to Dewey, "I grew up here and never heard anyone ever mention earthquakes."

"Live and learn," she said. "It's kind of interesting."

Yeah, it was.

I continued reading:

According to the National Earthquake Information Center in Denver, Florida is mistakenly considered "earthquake free," yet several quakes have occurred here.

One of Florida's most violent earthquakes occurred in 1879. In St. Augustine, in the northeastern part of the state, walls were shaken down and articles were thrown from shelves. The tremor was strong at Daytona Beach and Tampa, where residents reported a trembling motion, preceded by a rumbling sound. Two shocks occurred, each lasting 30 seconds, and were felt as far south as Punta Rassa and Bonita Springs.

In January 1880, Cuba was the center of two strong earthquakes that sent severe shock waves through the town of Key West. The tremors occurred at 11 P.M. on January 22 and at 4 A.M. on the 23rd. Many buildings were thrown down and some people were killed.

In August 1886, the next serious tremor experienced by Floridians had its epicenter at Charleston, South Carolina. The shock was felt throughout northern Florida, ringing church bells in cities and villages in the northern half of the state.

In recent history, southwest Florida experienced minor quakes in July 1930 and December 1940 that were felt from Fort Myers to the Everglades. In November 1948 an earth tremor caused jars to break and windows to rattle in Lee and Collier counties. Residents reported that the apparent earthquake was accompanied by sounds like distant, heavy explosions.

According to anecdotal stories, however, the deadly Mississippi River Valley earthquakes of 1811–12 rumbled through the American South, and may have caused the most powerful tremors ever experienced in Florida. The anecdotal in-

319

formation comes from Florida's Anglo pioneers, and some Native Americans, both Seminole and Miccosukee.

Usually referred to as the New Madrid (Missouri) earthquakes, they rank as the most powerful and deadly in U.S. history. The area damaged by the New Madrid quakes was three times larger than that of the 1964 Alaskan earthquake, and ten times more violent than the infamous 1906 San Francisco earthquake.

As described by one survivor of the New Madrid quakes: "The ground began to rise and fall, bending trees until their branches intertwined and opened deep cracks in the ground. Large areas of land were uplifted. Larger areas sank and were covered with water. Huge waves on the Mississippi River overwhelmed many boats and washed others high on the shore. Mountains caved and collapsed into the river."

The New Madrid earthquakes traumatized people throughout the South. In his journal, George Heinrich Crist, a Kentucky farmer, wrote: "There was a great shaking of the earth this morning — all of us knocked out of bed. The roar I thought would leave us deaf if we lived. All you could hear was screams from people and animals. It was the worst thing that I have ever witnessed.

"In a storm you can see the sky and it shows dark clouds and you know that you might get strong winds, but with this you can not see any-

thing but a house that just lays in a pile on the ground.

"A lot of people thinks that the devil has come here. Some thinks that this is the beginning of the world coming to a end."

When I stopped reading, Dewey took the paper from me. Folding it, she seemed subdued and reflective, as she said, "Sooner or later, I guess we all experience an earthquake or two. It's inevitable."

I said, "Yeah. Inevitable." Then I said, "Let's go run."

Twenty minutes later, I was standing a little more than two miles from the shell road that leads to Dinkin's Bay Marina, bent at the waist, hands on knees, my T-shirt soaked with sweat and gasping for oxygen.

Dewey stood beside me patiently, not sweating and not breathing much faster than normal. "Sorry, Doc. Maybe I was pushing a little hard. I'll slow the pace way down."

Her kindness hurt me far worse than her characteristic sarcasm.

"How long's it been since the last time you ran?"

I had to clear my throat to form words. "Eight months," I croaked. "A year."

"Oh my God, no wonder. Maybe we should just walk. Have a nice relaxing stroll, then get you back to the house."

She said it sincerely. Like she was talking to her decrepit old father.

chapter twenty-three

On Wednesday, April 16th, three days before an associate and friends reported Frank DeAntoni and Sally Carmel Minster as missing, the wide-bodied former wrestler called me on his cell phone just to talk, he said, but also to ask a favor.

Because my answering machine has a recording that suggests callers try me at the marina's number, that's where he found me.

I was sitting on the stool behind the glass counter next to the cash register where Mack, the owner and manager of Dinkin's Bay, holds court and keeps an eye on the money. Mack's originally from New Zealand; a Kiwi who loves cold cash even more than he loves cold Steinlager.

We'd been discussing the most recent of governmental outrages imposed upon our little boating community. It concerned Captain Felix Blane — all six-feet-five inches and 250 pounds of him — who'd been out in his twenty-four-foot Parker, *Osprey*. He'd had a party aboard when an unmarked flats boat came screaming up alongside, portable blue lights flashing, and forced him to stop.

Two plainclothes U.S. Fish and Wildlife officers then proceeded to accuse him of ignoring the new Manatee Protection Laws that require boaters to travel at idle speed when within five hundred feet of certain mangrove areas.

"One of the Feds had a ponytail," Mack told me. "The smart-ass undercover-agent type, and he gave Felix a lecture about how he needed to learn basic boating skills, and start caring about wildlife. *In front of* his clients."

Captain Felix, who's been guiding around Sanibel for nearly thirty years endured the lecture like the professional he is, then told the officers, "Do you have navigational equipment? Check your GPS. We're more than half a mile from the mangroves. I'm way outside the manatee zone. I haven't broken any laws."

The long-haired officer replied, "In my judgment, we're closer to the mangroves than your GPS says. And that's all that matters. If you want to hire an attorney, I'll see you in Tampa federal court five or six times over the next few months. So you can start canceling your bookings for May right now."

May, the beginning of tarpon season, is one of the busiest times of year for guides on Sanibel and Captiva.

I said, "If that's true, it's terrible. That's a sophisticated kind of extortion. No fishing guide can afford to fight federal attorneys, plus miss all those days on the water over a couple-hundred-dollar ticket."

Mack said, "It *is* true. Almost the exact thing happened to one of the guides out of Cabbage Key. You know Captain Doug. The plain-clothes Feds stopped him twice. The same hippy-looking bugger pointed and told him where he was *allowed* to run his skiff above idle, then a second unmarked boat pulled him over and wrote him a ticket. It's not that they tricked him. It's just that those sots don't know the area, they don't know boats and they don't know the water."

Sadly, he was right — I'd heard too many similar horror stories to doubt it. I was nodding, as he added, "I enjoy the outdoors and wildlife, manatees, as much as the next man, but it's just getting too crazy. Environmental wackos, mate. I think they're tryin' to take over the entire bloody earth."

Because I didn't want to get into an argument with Mack, I shut my mouth tight, walked out to the docks and stepped down into my twenty-one-foot Maverick. I had several five-gallon buckets aboard, and I'd stopped at the marina to fuel up before heading out on a collecting trip.

I don't have much patience with the term *environmental wackos* or the callous, shortsighted philosophy the phrase seems to signal. As a marine biologist, I am also, necessarily, an environmentalist. I take pride in the fact that some of the research I've done, certain papers I've published, have played a role in protecting our dwindling marine resources.

In the minds of many, what is now known as the "environmental movement" began in 1962 with the publication of Rachel Carson's *Silent Spring*. It is a fact that, at the time, America's natural resources were in terrible shape. The Great Lakes were so polluted they were unsafe for swimming. Our rivers were such cesspools of chemicals and petroleum waste that they caught fire and burned. In industrial cities, all six of the most dangerous air pollutants tracked by the EPA measured off the scale.

Private enterprise and a profit-minded government were slowly killing an entire continent. The environmental movement deserves full credit for changing that.

Half a century later, though, what was once a movement has now become the very thing its founders battled. So-called "environmentalism" has become a profit-driven, power-hungry industry in which private political agendas are more important than biological realities, and monetary objectives excuse any perversion of scientific fact.

A few months back, I was talking with someone familiar with Mote Marine, the organization I'm now doing contract work for. He told me that Mote had received an official letter of protest from PETA (People for the Ethical Treatment of Animals) that condemned Mote for housing and studying jellyfish. I'm paraphrasing, but there was a line in the letter that read, "These magnificent creatures should be allowed to roam free in the wild!"

That a national "environmental" organization could pen a letter so stupid, so childishly ignorant of the species that they referenced, is not just sad, it is frightening. Unthinking extremists have taken possession of what was once a noble title, *environmentalist*, and they are destroying our credibility, just as surely as they are giving credence and power to people who use sad phrases such as *environmental wackos*.

In the Everglades, when I'd listened to Billie Egret's short tirade against legislated efforts to save the region, I'd disagreed with her cynicism, but I understood the source of her mistrust: the environmental industry. The En-dustry is made up of governmental agencies, private businesses and "nonprofit" organizations.

Fortunately, each has, in my experience, at least a few men and women who are rational and well-intended, who put the well-being of the environment before their own self-interests. But, like our own natural resources, the numbers of honest ones seem to be dwindling.

I don't trust the En-dustry, either. No thinking environmentalist should.

So I was sitting in my skiff, ruminating over national matters that are far, far out of my control, when Mack paged me over the PA, telling me that I had a phone call in the office.

It was Frank.

As I listened to DeAntoni, I was also aware that Mack, Jeth and Captain Neville were listening, too, and so I told him I'd telephone him from my house.

A few minutes later, Frank answered, saying, "So how's it going with you, Dr. Nerd? You still hanging out with that dope-smoking goofball with the cannon for an arm?"

I told him that Tomlinson had pitched against Naples on Sunday, had given up six runs in three innings, plus done a lot of heavy drumming later that night, and so his "cannon" was probably still hurting him on this clear spring morning.

"Fucking Tinkerbell, man. You could throw a tent over the guy and call him a circus. Weird thing is, though? I kind'a like the skinny little dork."

I had to laugh. It was Tomlinson's guileless candor that made him likeable, and DeAntoni possessed the same rare quality. You couldn't help but like the man.

He was headed for Miami, he told me. Traffic sucked. There were so many Third World former donkey-cart drivers on the road, Cubans and Haitians, that I-95, he said, should have its named changed to the Refugee Express. If he survived, he was going to meet Sally for lunch, then spend the rest of the night in his car, watching her house.

"Stu Johnson, the security guard they found floating? The medical examiner says he died of a cerebral hemorrhage. A vessel in his brain popped. But there was also a nasty bruise on his throat. So they're figuring maybe he hit the dock when he fell. That's what my cop buddies are telling me."

I said, "The question is, why would a security guard get out of his car and go stand on a dock?"

DeAntoni said, "Exactly. Sally swears someone's been in her room, and that lady's word's good enough for me." There was a little smile in his voice, when he added, "Hey, listen to this. We had a great dinner together Saturday night. She was real upset about Mr. Johnson and her dog, too, but we still managed to have some laughs. So we've had dinner together every night since. But this one, you're not going to believe, Ford."

I said, "Yeah?"

"Yeah. I went to *church* with her, Mac. Me, the big wop who stopped going to confession when I started having shit to confess. Sitting there in a sport coat in this little white church with a bunch of jigs and crackers and beaners, but they were all nice as hell, everybody singing and clapping. It was fun, Doc. I enjoyed it."

DeAntoni's voice had a schoolboy quality. He sounded like an adolescent with a crush, but his tone changed abruptly when he said, "But that's not why I called. I'm calling 'cause I need

328

someone I trust. Someone who knows how to take care of himself, and bust a head or two if things get tough. I need a favor."

He then told me that he suspected that one or more men were following Sally. He didn't know who, or why. But he wanted to set a trap for whoever it was, and the trap required a third party to do a careful, long-distance surveillance.

As he explained the circumstances, asking for my help, I felt a sickening tension building in my stomach. Lately, when I have attempted to help friends, the results have been tragic. If I'm involved, the people I'm trying to help are almost always the ones who end up getting hurt.

I said, "Whoever it is breaking into Sally's house, that's who you think's following her?"

"Bingo. I need someone to watch me while I'm watching her. From a distance, understand? That's the only way to nail them. Something else, Ford: Whoever's doing it, he's a pro. And he's very, very damn *good*."

"What about asking your cop pal in Hialeah?"

"He left on a cruise two days ago. You're the only other guy I'd trust. Hey, I'll tell you the truth. Most guys, they're either too stuffy or too Mister Macho, which is to say they're a pain in the ass. But you, I wouldn't mind hanging out with some. Tell you what, come to Coconut Grove, help your old pal Sally, and we'll have some yucks, you and me."

I told DeAntoni that I'd like that — and meant it — but that I'd have to check my work schedule to see if I could take the time off.

It was a lie.

Same thing when I told him I'd call him later that night.

Sailors have an old word for it — Jonah. I was bad luck, a Jonah, when it came to helping friends. I wasn't going to risk contaminating Sally.

DeAntoni finished, saying, "Hell, what we could start doing is find a gym with wrestling mats. Maybe shoot for takedowns, get in a little bit of shape. Roll around a little; get rid of our bellies. We're both carrying a few extra pounds."

I told him that sounded like a good thing to do, too. We chatted for a while longer before I hung up the phone.

It was the last time I would ever hear Frank DeAntoni's voice.

As I headed back to the docks, I noticed that Tomlinson was standing by the Red Pelican Gift Shop, encircled by a dozen or so people — tourists, judging by the number of cameras they carried. When he saw me, his wave was more of a signal — *Wait for me* — and he then began to walk in my direction.

The people with whom he'd been talking watched for a moment, then, as a group, began to follow him.

Glancing over his shoulder, Tomlinson walked faster.

The little gaggle of people walked faster.

Then Tomlinson began to jog.

They began to jog — a mixed group, mostly younger men and women with gaunt, European-looking faces, plus a couple of Asians.

Now Tomlinson was running, his long hair swinging behind him like a flag, barefooted in tank top and baggy surfer shorts. As he ran, he called to me, "Doc! Are you headed out on your skiff?"

I stood for a moment, engrossed by the bizarre scene, then called back, "I'm leaving right now."

"If you got room, I'm going with you!"

"Plenty of room. Come aboard."

I stepped into my skiff, started the engine and popped the lines.

Quick-release knots — I love them.

A second later, Tomlinson swung down onto the deck beside me, breathing heavily. On the dock behind him, his pursuers stopped abruptly, cameras up and snapping photos, as a Japanese-looking girl, her accent heavy, said, "Why do you refuse us, to be our *Roshi?* We have come so far, and searched so long. It was you who wrote the divine *Surangama* of this new century. Our destinies, our desire for *kensho,* we are now all mingled!"

Tomlinson groaned. "My dear, you are wrong. So *wrong.* All of you." His voice sounded pained and apologetic, and he was holding up both palms — *Please stop.* "I'm not worthy to teach you or anyone else. Not anymore. I'm . . . I'm a terrible person. I abuse drugs. I'm a fornicator — *nothing's* beneath me. My God, I tried to strangle a man a few days ago! Basically, I'm an absurd wanderer. I . . . I was sent to this planet to conduct inhuman experiments on the human liver."

Tomlinson put his hand on my shoulder, and pointed to me, adding, "Ask this man. He *knows* me. I'm the island drunk — and that's saying something on these islands."

I was nodding. "Oh, he's a drunk, all right."

"In the entire history of the Sanibel Police Department, I'm the only person to have ever been stopped for DUI while on a skateboard. And the police chief is a distant relative."

True.

"I'm no longer fit to teach!"

We were idling away, nearly out of earshot. Touching my hand to the throttle, I said to them, "This man's scum. Worthless trash that I wouldn't trust with my daughter. Do yourselves a favor. Leave him alone."

Tomlinson said, "That's right, I *am* scum —" but then stopped. Looking surprised and offended, he turned to me and said, "Hey. That's pouring it on a little heavy, isn't it, man?"

Smiling, I said, "Why are those kids following you?"

He sighed and sat in one of the three seats

bolted into the stern platform. "Remember that paper I mentioned? The one I sent to Mr. McRae to help him deal with his wife's condition?"

I pretended as if I had to think about it. "Yeah. That's the one you were supposed to send to me, too. But didn't."

"I wrote it when I was in college. I'd drunk a case of Budweiser, eaten two blotters of acid and a candy-looking substance that might have been mescaline. I'm not sure. Or it was an M&M. Whatever the hell it was, I sat down and wrote this paper for a class I was taking on world religions. The whole thing in one frenzied sitting. 'Twenty Ways to Duct-Tape Your Life.' That was the original title. Then I changed it to 'One Fathom Above Sea Level.' "

I said, "So?"

He sounded sad and concerned, saying, "So someone's been circulating it on the Internet. People all over the world have been reading the thing. It's been translated, for Christ's sake, like, into twenty-some languages. People who read it get the entirely wrong idea about the kind of person I am. There are some — an *increasing* number — who come looking for me, thinking I'm . . . well, that I'm some kind of prophet. *Tomlinsonism.* That's what some are calling it. My own religion. Like Taoism."

"That's scary," I said.

Tomlinson was standing now, rummaging

through the ice locker. "You got any beer in here?"

A few minutes later, a Bud Light in his hand, he said, "You're telling me."

I followed the markers across Dinkin's Bay to Woodring Point, cutting behind the fishhouse ruins. Pelicans and egrets flushed off the spoil islands, their wings laboring in the heat and heavy air, gaining slow altitude as their shadows panicked baitfish in the shallows.

I ran straight across the flats, but at reduced speed, concentrating on the mangrove fringe to my left, then on the horizon of water that opened before me.

My skiff's big 225-horsepower Mercury made a pleasant Harley-Davidson rumble as we sped along, but it was still quiet enough to converse in a normal tone.

Mercury Marine, once a maker of classic American outboards, had had a bad couple of years in which their image and their reputation took a beating. It was not a good time for the company, or boaters who used their product.

Those of us who make our living on the water are necessarily fussy about equipment. We talk freely about what is good and what is bad. A year or so back, I'd begun to hear the rumors that Mercury was back on track. They'd finally gotten it right again.

So I made the switch. A lot of the guides were making the switch, too.

It was a nice day to be on the water. The bay was a gelatin skin that lifted and fell in broad sections; moving with the slow respiration of distant oceans, faraway storms. The air was balmy, scented by the tropics, it had a winter clarity. The sky was Denver-blue, and on the far curvature of sky, beyond Pine Island, were cumulous snow peaks. The clouds were coral and silver: vaporous sculptures, carved by wind shear, adrift like helium dirigibles.

Standing at the wheel, I could look down and see the blurred striations of sea bottom. I could see white canals of sand that crossed the flat like winding rivers, and I could see meadows of sea grass — blades leaning in the tide as if contoured by a steady breeze. Ahead, there were comets' tails of expanding water as redfish and snook spooked ahead of us. The fish created bulging tubes on the water's surface, as if they were trapped beneath Pliofilm.

Behind us, in our slow, expanding wake, the tiny clearing that was Dinkin's Bay Marina — wooden buildings, a few cars and docks, the Red Pelican Gift Shop, my house on pilings — was the only break in the great ring of mangroves.

Sitting to my right, Tomlinson finished his beer, crushed the can in his hand and said, "When's the last time you and I did a Bay Crawl?"

"Bay Crawl" is a local euphemism for an afternoon spent going from island to island, barhopping — or pub-crawling — by boat.

"It's been a while," I said. "Too long. But I have to fill that order for horseshoe crabs. This time of year, it's not going to be easy."

Which was true. Each winter, horseshoe crabs appear on South Florida's mangrove flats en masse; a slow, clattering minion plowing blindly to copulate. Thousands of creatures ride the floodtides into the shallows; the big cow crabs dragging smaller males behind, each tuned in to the instinctive drive to exude and spray; to lay and fertilize. They are animals as archaic as the primal ooze to which they are attracted, dropping bright blue eggs in the muck; hatching one more generation of a species that has not changed in two hundred million years.

Come spring, though, they are not as easily found.

Tomlinson said, "I don't want to go back to the marina for a while. So I'll help you collect the little darlings. Then let's say we start at the Waterfront Restaurant at St. James City, have a few beers and say hello to the twins. Then hit the Pool Bar at 'Tween Waters. After that, work our way up to Cabbage Key, and maybe even Palm Island. The Don Pedro softball team's supposed to play the Knight Island team tonight. Plus, Passover begins at sundown — what better reason to celebrate?"

I touched the throttle; felt the pleasant, momentary G-shock as we gained speed, a jet-fighter sensation, as I listened to Tomlinson add, "Speaking of baseball, I got an e-mail from Marino today."

Marino Laken Balserio is my son. He lives in Central America with his brilliant and beautiful mother, Pilar. Having Marino was unplanned; a surprise to both of us.

I said, "I know. We trade letters a lot now."

"He told me he loves the Wilson catcher's mitt you sent him. Said the Rawlings mitt is a piece of junk, plus he hates the way that Rawlings does business in Costa Rica. Can you believe they're still connected with Major League baseball? Bionts have infiltrated our sport."

I chuckled. "He inherited his mother's intellect, and her heart."

"So there's another good reason to go bay-crawling. You have a brilliant son."

"I'll drink to that," I said, pushing the throttle forward.

Much of what Tomlinson and I did that night remains a blur. Like most drunken intervals, the evening came back to me in a series of lucid snapshots rather than a continuous flow of memory.

After collecting more than a hundred horse-shoe crabs and depositing them in a holding pen near my stilt house, we ran east across the bay to Pine Island, where we had two or three beers at the Waterfront, and ate a bucket of local clams. Then we sped back-country to

337

Pineland and the Tarpon Lodge, where we had more beer, and a spectacular portabello stuffed with fresh oysters.

By then it was close to sunset, so we made a straight shot between Patricio Island and Bokeelia to Boca Grande, and tied off at Mark Futch's seaplane dock. We walked to the Temptation Restaurant where Annie, behind the bar, served us drinks, but refused to read the tarot cards for us.

"Not when you two are together," she said. "I done it once, and once was too much."

Weaving only slightly, Tomlinson told her, "I remember when you did the reading. But you didn't tell us what the cards said. What's our fate?"

He was grinning.

Annie wasn't.

"I didn't tell you for a reason," Annie said cryptically. "So please don't ever ask me again."

The next mental snapshot I have is of us pulling into the Palm Island docks, off Lemon Bay. We had ribs with Swamp Sauce at Rum Bay Restaurant, then borrowed Jill Beckstead's golf cart and drove around Don Pedro Island with a tin bucket filled with ice and beer, feeling a dark, sea-oat wind, smelling Gulf air off the beach.

On the way back, we stopped at Cabbage Key — two more beers with Rob and Terry at the bar — then we were at the Green Flash, drinking Rogerita Margaritas with Andreas, the owner. I remember getting into an intense discussion with a tourist lady from Seattle — her name was Gail — about the important role horseshoe crabs play in cancer research.

As scientists around the world have discovered, I told her, the blue blood of the horseshoe crab, *Limulus polyphemus,* reacts dramatically when endotoxins are introduced. Endotoxins, which are dead cell walls and bits of bacteria, cause horseshoe crab blood to clot immediately. The blood is an excellent diagnostic tool.

I told her, "It's actually an arthropod, not a crab at all. It's more closely related to ticks and scorpions. Fascinating, huh?"

Gail was an attractive redhead with lively green eyes. Turning away from me, she said, "Not really."

Moonrise that Wednesday night was a little after ten, and by the time Tomlinson and I idled into the Dinkin's Bay Marina boat basin, it was adrift above the mangrove rim, a gaseous orange mass in a sky that was weightless, black.

"The paschal moon," Tomlinson said. "The first full moon before Easter Sunday."

When I told him it was a couple of days past full, he said, "Details. It's still the Passover moon."

We'd both sobered on our trip back. Comfortable silence is one of the barometers of friendship, and we rode most of the trip wordlessly, watching the moonrise, enjoying the familiar bay nightscape of strobing channel markers, hedgerows of mangrove shadow, pocket constellations of light on island enclaves such as Useppa, Safety Harbor, Demery Key, South Seas.

As I banked through the mouth of Dinkin's Bay, Tomlinson finally spoke, mentioned the moon and then said, "If I haven't told you already, I'm embarrassed about the way I behaved at Sawgrass. It makes me want to scream, the way that wicked bastard manipulated me. I feel embarrassed. Weak and guilty as hell."

I said, "I can relate," in a tone so bitter that the intensity startled even me.

"That's something I've been wanting to talk to you about, man. Doc, there's something been chewing you down to the core. You're not yourself, and we all know it. A couple of days ago, I walked into your galley. You weren't there. There was a gun lying out, bullets on the table. A square black pistol. Why?"

I waited for a moment before I said, "Cleaning it. That's all."

"Cleaning a gun for no reason."

I didn't reply.

Tomlinson said, "I don't buy it, my brother. That's why I want to tell you this. I'm drunk, but not too drunk to say what's true. I'm aware that you have blood on your hands. *But so do I.* You know it now, you've *always* known it. Since we met, you've always known what I really am."

I said, "Yes."

"And you were assigned to take care of me. Right? *Right?* Like you took care of Jeff Ruben at the Slope Bar in Aspen."

I said nothing.

"Well, guess what, man. I'm guilty. Guilty as sin. But not you. Guilt requires malicious intent. You were an employee. A *messenger.*"

I chuckled. "Tell that to Amelia Gardner. Or about fifteen other people."

Tomlinson put his hand on my shoulder. "Billie Egret called me yesterday. We talked about Shiva. We also talked about you. Because of her father, what you meant to Joseph, she takes her relationship with you very seriously.

"Know what she told me? She said that balance and equilibrium are the central elements of the Maskókî universe, the Seminole world. *Reciprocity,* she called it. If you give bad, you get bad in return. If you take, you have to give.

"Doc, you give as much as any person I've ever met. There're a bunch of us who depend on you, count on you. Goddamn it, you're the *strong* one. It's scaring us that you're acting weak. You've given back a hell of a lot more than you've taken."

I steered silently, the stainless-steel wheel cool beneath my fingers, seeing a sprinkling of lights in the mangrove lake darkness: Dinkin's Bay Marina.

Tomlinson said, "Billie told me to tell you that. I don't know why. Something else I'm supposed to tell you, too: After that little tremor on Sunday, water level in the marsh around Chekika's Hammock dropped. Remember James Tiger saying they could only find Lost Lake when the water's down? Well, the lake's visible now. The tarpon have shown up. She wants you to come with me Sunday, and see it."

I said, "I'd like that. It's something I've always heard about. A hole in the Everglades that opens out to the ocean. Maybe take some dive gear if there's any visibility."

Then I said, "Hey, why Sunday? The traffic will be a pain in the ass, and we can't go by boat."

Tomlinson said, "I don't know. A strong woman like Billie, she didn't leave much room for discussion."

"But we've got a game. Baseball at Terry Park."

"Not this Sunday," Tomlinson reminded me. "This Sunday, we're off because it's Easter."

chapter twenty-four

izzy

On the morning of April 18th, Good Friday, Izzy Kline took a cab to E-Z U-Haul Rental Center off Powerline Road and S.W. 10th street, Deerfield Beach. He used a postal money order, a Social Security number he'd lifted from the Internet and a newly counterfeited driver's license to rent a truck.

He'd already given them his assumed name, a credit card number and expiration date over the phone.

What he chose was U-Haul's four-wheel-drive, five-ton "Thrifty Mover," a medium-sized diesel with a fourteen-foot cargo trailer built over the back. Its maximum load capacity was three thousand pounds. That was more than enough for what Izzy needed.

As he left, the clerk said, "Thanks, Mr. Tomlinson. See you on Monday."

Izzy, wearing a baggy, knitted Rasta hat, and an expensive theatrical goatee, waved to cover his face, and replied, "Save the Earth, brother! Fight the madness!"

The hat and goatee were in a 7-Eleven trash Dumpster before he got back to the Interstate.

After that, he went straight to his condo in West Palm Beach, and moved the last of his personal items — a DVD player, a big-screen TV, similar electronic stuff — into the truck, and drove to Port of the Everglades. He paid three Mexican illegals to pack it all in boxes alongside his Astro van, his Suzuki motorcycle, all his furniture and clothing, in a semi-sized container that was already loaded on a cargo ship. The ship was scheduled to leave tomorrow, Saturday, for Central America.

With the truck empty, Izzy drove south on I-95, headed for Sawgrass. He had the speakers turned loud, playing one of his favorite CDs, *World's Most Beloved Waltzes*.

"Edelweiss" was playing now, the Boston Philharmonic, one of the classics. That one-two-three beat made him want to dance, so he pounded out the rhythm on the steering wheel, feeling good; pleased with himself and smiling, until his cell phone rang.

A minor irritation.

He checked the caller ID. It was Shiva's private number.

Izzy turned down the volume, pressed the talk button and said, "Talk to me, Jerry!"

He could call Shiva by his first name now. The Bhagwan was delighted by the results of the coordinated explosions on Sunday. The two men had never been on friendlier terms.

Izzy listened to Shiva say, "I'm spending the weekend at the Cypress Ashram. We still all set for the second service?"

"Service" meant "detonation."

Izzy said, "I'm on my way there now."

"Easter Sunday at sunset?"

"Yep. Seven fifty-seven sharp. I checked the almanac."

"The church appreciates your dedication."

"Thanks," Izzy said. "One more thing: Make sure to remind Mr. Carter to answer his cell phone when I call. If he doesn't, I'll be seeing both of you on Monday."

They had reason to be encouraged. The first series of explosions had been more convincing, and had received wider attention, than Shiva anticipated.

A reporter for the *Seminole Tribune*, "Voice of the Unconquered," had interviewed a number of people, including Shiva, for a story they were doing on the recent earthquake. Izzy didn't know or care about the particulars, but Shiva had jabbered on and on because the Indian writer knew about Tecumseh right away; what he'd predicted.

The real reason Shiva was so happy? It was because the Seminole Tribe of Florida were at least talking to him. They'd treated him like a con man right off the bat.

That might impress the less savvy tribe of Egret Seminoles.

Izzy was kicked-back, pleased with himself. He'd pulled it off. It had all gone so damn *smoothly.* And so far, the Feds hadn't come snooping around.

Not that it was all luck. No.

First off, he'd taken the trouble to make certain Tomlinson, Ford and the Italian dick — Frank something — hadn't eyeballed him when he was down there in the rock quarry, scoping out where to park the U-Haul while he was filling boreholes with ammonium nitrate. Which was a risky pain-in-the-ass, but had to be done.

They hadn't. Didn't say a word about him when they were sitting alone in the waiting room.

He'd taken his time learning how to do explosives, too. Did all the reading. Found out how to do it *right.* He'd put together a booklet of Bureau of Mines publications describing research on acceptable levels of underground disturbance. Cross the lines, you were inviting scrutiny.

He'd also learned that there was a subscience to achieving maximum efficiency with fewer explosives by drilling several "shot holes" or boreholes in a precise semicircular pattern. The holes had to be five to fifteen feet deep or so, with small diameters. Then the boreholes had to be "stemmed," or packed tight with rock.

No problem.

For his Easter Sunday's fireworks — the grand finale — Izzy had drilled thirteen boreholes in a sequential pattern ("delay intervals," the literature called them) and in the exact semicircle shape of the Cypress Ashram's elevated stage. Even though each of the boreholes was more than half a mile away from the outdoor theater, the series of explosions would rock the place in precisely connecting gradients — and much of the Everglades as well.

This was something else Izzy had learned: Water cannot be compressed. If he extended the boreholes below the water table, the power of the shock waves was quadrupled.

In the Everglades, the water table was seldom more than a few feet beneath the surface. Swampland was a demolitionist's dream. So, this final blast would register way over the government's line of acceptable level of disturbance. Which would invite all kinds of heavy investigation.

Izzy didn't care. He'd be on a plane, gone by late Sunday, never to return. He'd fly to Paris, stay long enough to switch passports, then fly to London, then back to Managua.

Plus, he now had a fall guy.

So there'd be a series of five substantial explosions, followed by a really big boom — the U-Haul truck packed with explosives, backed in tight against the wall of the old rock quarry.

The typical problem with ammonium nitrate, though, was that it wasn't easy to detonate. Use commercial blasting caps, only a third of the stuff would probably explode. Because the truck would be holding six drums of fertilizer

347

mixed with fuel oil, Izzy had decided to use a high-voltage-capacitor-discharge mini-blaster to detonate the rig. That meant he'd have to leave the truck's engine running, hard-wired to the mini-blaster to provide the necessary voltage.

The mini-blaster's timer ran on a single dry-cell battery, but that was okay. He'd mount the timer and the dry-cell battery inside the truck so they couldn't get wet. The other boreholes would be rigged to waterproof individual timers.

All the timers worked on twenty-four-hour clocks. He'd set the first charge to go off at 19:48 hours — 7:48 P.M. Maybe a minute or two earlier or later. It had to seem *random*. After that, there would be five more "tremors" approximately one minute apart.

The last and largest explosion would be exactly at sunset, 19:57 hours. The truck going off. A ton of ammonium nitrate.

To people half a mile away, it would be like the sun exploding.

Religious types were big on sunrise, sunset. Same with the moon.

Izzy liked all of it. Liked the complicated engineering, the precision work, making it happen, fucking with self-important weirdos and geeks like Tomlinson and Ford.

Izzy was mostly happy about the money — his bonus — and moving to his island in Lake Nicaragua where he could afford all the women he wanted; get them to do *anything.*

There was an idea. Start with his sweet little video of Mrs. Minster, the Merry Widow, in her bathroom, then expand the business. Down there in Nicaragua, no one would much care. No one would lift a finger to stop him.

The image of Sally Minster, naked, looking at herself in the mirror, the color of her face changing, came into his mind.

He felt his thigh muscles twitch.

Izzy still had cameras and recorders hidden in her bedroom and bathroom, and he had a LACSA flight to Managua booked for late Sunday.

So why not visit the pretty blond lady's house tonight?

Izzy was in the Bayliner, idling along Tahiti Beach and what looked to be some kind of county park — kids were necking in cars up there on shore, parked beneath coconut palms.

It was sunset. Harsh light angled across Biscayne Bay, coating the high-rise condos and hotels in shades of neon pink and gold, setting windows ablaze. Windy, too. The wind seemed to blow right out of the sun.

Izzy didn't like being on boats when it was windy. It made him queasy, all the odors you never really noticed unless you were on a boat that was rocking. So he shoved the throttle forward and banged and splashed his way back to the marked entrance to Coral Gables Canal.

Shitty, cheap boat. Waves coming over the front got Izzy's sports jacket and gray slacks soaked.

He idled west down the canal, pretending not to notice that the Italian, Frank what's-his-name, was still parked outside the entranceway to Ironwood in his Lincoln Town Car. With the tinted windows and gold rims, the black car looked like some pimpmobile you'd find in Liberty City.

Izzy thought, *Typical guinea,* irked that this guy was screwing up his plans.

He'd rushed like hell mucking around in the swamp, mixing fertilizer in fifty-gallon drums, using a forklift to lift them into the U-Haul. Got all his work done, everything but the timers set. All ready for Sunday — which gave him a holiday feeling. His last two nights on American soil.

So he'd showered and changed at the bachelors' club, hopped in a company car and raced up to Coconut Grove to see if he might discover some more interesting video of the church lady having fantasy sessions in her bedroom. Or maybe even meet her in person.

This late in the game, that would be okay, too.

But now the big greaser was spoiling the entire evening.

Izzy touched his left shoe to the ankle holster in which he carried a .22 Beretta Model 71 — a signature weapon of Mossad assassins.

Why not? Why *not* tap on the window, look into the guy's eye. Say something fun, like "Remember me?" then pop him. Or "Do you really want to find Geoff Minster? I can arrange it." Then pull the trigger.

Under the car bridge next to Cocoplum Plaza, Izzy put the boat in neutral, feeling the vibration of Friday-night car traffic rolling over him. He sat there thinking about it, smelling the exhaust fumes, wanting to do it, but not wanting to risk the noise.

But then he didn't have to worry about it anymore.

He saw the lights of the pimpmobile go on. Then he saw Sally Minster's blue BMW come through the electronic gate, then stop beside the pimpmobile. After a minute or so, both cars drove away, the pimpmobile following the Beamer.

Perfect.

The only trouble was, Izzy didn't know how much time he'd have. So he couldn't lie around on her bed, browsing through the new video. He'd have to snatch the cameras and recorders, then watch the tapes later in his apartment at Sawgrass.

Or maybe . . . maybe he *would* wait for her to come back. When the guinea was on the job, he always stayed outside in his car. So how could he know what was going on inside the woman's house?

Izzy liked that idea. It made him twitch

again, picturing it, imagining meeting the church lady in her bedroom, giving her a special farewell, seeing her naked in the flesh, the two of them together on the bed with the cameras rolling.

How nice would it be to take *that* back to Nicaragua?

And if the guinea followed her in?

Izzy could deal with that, too.

Wearing surgical gloves, Izzy entered through the pool area, jimmied the back lock, stopped and touched-in the security code.

He liked the way the house smelled. It smelled of woman; it smelled like *her.*

He'd been in the place so many times, he knew the layout as if it were his own home. He paused at the fridge, took an apple from the crisper. He walked up the carpeted stairs, munching away.

At the top of the stairs, Izzy stopped. Stopped walking. Stopped chewing. Stopped moving.

The door to the church lady's bedroom was open.

Odd.

She was tidy, consistent in her habits. Sally Minster always kept her bedroom door closed. As if she didn't want unexpected visitors to get a glimpse of where she lived her private life.

There was something else, too. A different odor? Maybe. Something new added to the mix

352

of fresh linen, makeup, shampoo and perfume.

Izzy lifted his head, foxlike, and sniffed the air.

Yep. He didn't know what it was, but it was *different*.

Izzy pulled at his trouser leg, squatted and unholstered the Beretta with his right hand. There was already a round in the chamber — the only way to carry a weapon. He cupped the little semiautomatic in his hand, and moved cautiously through the door into the bedroom.

He stopped again, eyes scanning, ears straining. He could feel his heart pounding in his chest.

The two micro-cameras and both VCRs lay in the middle of the lady's bed, wires black on the yellow bedspread.

Shit.

Izzy had the Beretta up now, locked in both hands, combat-position, as he began to back out of the bedroom. He was almost to the stairs when he heard movement off to the right. He had just enough time to turn slightly when something massive hit him from the side.

It was like being hit by a car. Hands and feet flailing, Izzy felt himself go airborne, the gun tumbling from his hand and over the stairway banister, as he crashed into a wall.

Sitting, dazed, Izzy looked up to see the short Italian private investigator coming at him.

"Get on your feet, Mac. I'm gonna smack

you around a little before I call the cops. You fucking little slimeball."

Izzy rolled hard to his left and stood, backing slowly as the Italian approached. During his four years in Israel, Izzy had excelled at martial arts. He'd once almost killed a man in a bar fight by slamming fragments of nose cartilage into the guy's brain.

Izzy crouched now, his right hand a fist, his left hand a blade, ready. When the Italian was close enough, he did a variation of a swing dance step, and kicked the man hard in the groin — or tried to.

But it was as if the Italian knew exactly what he was going to do before he did it. The man caught Izzy's leg, somehow dropped to one knee, and then, like a fireman carrying a kid, he had Izzy up on his shoulders, off the floor.

Izzy was kicking and clawing, trying to gouge his way free as he heard the man say, *"Oh.* You want me to put you *down?"*

Then the Italian hammered him back-first onto the carpet.

Izzy felt such a searing pain through his spine, he wondered if his back might be broken. But no, he could still move. He began to scramble toward the stairs as the Italian came at him again. The man grabbed him by the belt, lifting him off the carpet like it was nothing. Then the guy forced him to stand on two feet, and shoved him up against the wall, holding him by the throat with one hand. Izzy had to get up on his tiptoes to keep from being choked.

He'd been in five or six fights in his life, and done some amateur full-contact tournament stuff, but he'd never before experienced what it was like to be physically dominated by another man.

It was happening to him now. He was helpless.

Terrifying.

"You fucking little pervert Peeping Tom. On a lady as nice as her. What I maybe might do is break both your arms, then pull your kneecaps off." The Italian was nodding, his expression crazed. "Yeah, both kneecaps. I'll push 'em down by your ankles. Make it so you got to crawl around on your belly."

Barely able to breathe with the man's hand clenching his throat, Izzy was shaking his head desperately. In a rasping whisper, he said, "You've got the wrong idea. Geoff Minster . . . trying to find out what happened to Geoff. *Investigating.* Like you."

The Italian loosened his grip slightly. "Sure, Mac. What the hell you guys care about Minster?"

"He stole money from us. A hundred . . . a hundred grand."

Actually, Izzy had stolen the money; set it up to look as though Minster had done it.

The Italian seemed to be considering it, though; as if it might be true. His grip became even looser as he said, "Bullshit. You hid cameras in her bathroom to find out about her husband? How dumb you think I am, Mac?"

Izzy didn't hesitate. He used the momentary lapse to knock the Italian's hands free, then tried to slam the heel of his open palm into the big man's nose.

Same thing. It was as if the man knew in advance what Izzy was going to try.

He blocked the punch, no problem, then slapped Izzy three times, very fast. The slow smile that then spread across the Italian's face was chilling. He grabbed Izzy's right wrist, saying, "Like those pigeons last Saturday. Let's find out if you can fly, motherfucker."

Then the man lifted him without effort, grunted and spun him over the stairway banister.

Falling toward the ground floor, Izzy screamed — a shrill falsetto — kicking wildly. He landed hard on his left side, and lay there, groaning, hearing the heavy footsteps of the Italian coming down the stairs, in no hurry now.

It felt to Izzy like his left shoulder might be broken. Like there was something sharp sticking out of his own skin. From the first-aid classes he'd taken during Mossad training, he knew the term. Compound fracture. There'd been a photograph in the manual. Sickening to see.

Experimentally, he touched his shoulder with

the gloved fingertips of his right hand, expecting to feel bare bone. Instead of bone, though, he felt the checkered grip of his .22 Beretta.

He'd landed on his own gun.

Fucking stupid guinea!

Izzy pulled the gun into his hands, and was already aiming it at the Italian as he got to his knees, then his feet. When the Italian realized what had happened, saw Izzy standing there, the gun trained on him, the big man's expression changed. It was like a shade being pulled.

He stopped halfway down the stairs. Stood there considering the situation, thinking about it. Then the man's expression changed once more — got that same crazed glare — and he started down the stairs again.

Izzy said, "Stop right there, asshole! You get any closer, I'll shoot you."

Which Izzy didn't want to do. Not here. Not in the house. Way too much evidence. Which the Italian also seemed to know, because he kept walking, his eyes like lasers. "Go ahead and shoot me, Mac. A little sissy gun like that, if I get my hands on you, I'm going to tear your fucking head right off anyway. So make it good."

This guy's a freak.

Now Izzy was backing away, holding the gun, but still afraid of the man who was walking calmly toward him, wanting to end it somehow, make him stop. So he said, "If you don't cooperate, I'll have to kill the woman, too, when she gets back. I'll have to shoot her because you're not giving me any other choice."

That did it. The Italian stopped, furious, but at least becoming rational about the situation. "Then why don't you just get the fuck out of here right now!"

Izzy said quickly. "I *will*. But you've got to do what I say. Stay cool, cooperate, you won't get hurt. The lady won't get hurt. First, you got to tell me — who drove off in your car?"

The Italian paused a little too long. "Two off-duty cops. They're going to be back any minute."

He was lying.

"Are you carrying a weapon?"

"You think I'm going to tell you, dumbass? Why don't you search me and find out."

No way was he going to let the guinea get close enough to get his hands on him again. It didn't look like he was carrying: a refrigerator-sized man with biceps, wearing a seedy white shirt and wrinkled slacks. A guy trying to look sharp, but didn't know how to pull it off. No holster visible.

Izzy said, "Look, all I want to do is get my camera shit and get out of here. So, we're going to find some tape. I'm going to have you tape your right wrist to your ankles. Just to slow you down a little. Then I'm out of here."

When the Italian didn't budge, Izzy used the pistol to motion toward the kitchen. "Goddamn it, move! You do what I tell you to do, no one gets hurt. Fuck with me, I'm gonna have to kill her."

His heart was pounding; he was scared — *Jesus, how am I going to make this work?* But there was still a trace of a smile on Izzy's face as he added, "Trust me, man. I promise."

It turned out, the guy who drove off in the pimpmobile was a chicken-skinny man even older than the security guard who'd surprised Izzy the week before.

He was the guinea's *landlord,* for God's sake. Just some old retired dude who had nothing better to do than hang out, doing favors. Probably wanted to add a little excitement to his life; help the dick set his little trap.

Well, he got it.

When the old dude and Sally came into the house, calling, "Hey, Frank, we're back. Frank! *Frank?*" Izzy waited until they were in the kitchen before he swung open the closet door, pointed the Beretta at them and said, "Frank's kind of tied up right now."

Man, the look on the woman's face. It was like all the blood went out of her. Same with the old guy, whose cheeks started trembling like he might cry.

Both of them looked from the gun to the closet, to the gun again then back to the closet.

There was Frank: His right hand was duct-taped to his right ankle; his left hand was taped to the left ankle so that he was still mobile. He could still walk in a crablike way if properly motivated. There was more silver tape over the man's mouth, and over that big, crooked wop nose, too, just his dark eyes showing.

When Frank looked at Sally, he shook his head slowly, eyes blinking. It seemed a gesture of apology.

Izzy thought: *Pathetic,* but he enjoyed the feeling it gave him. It was an adrenaline feeling; a sensation of power.

Later, after Izzy had robbed the house; trashed it — the cops would be thinking *motive* — and after he got the old dude and the Italian crammed into the trunk of the pimpmobile, Izzy took off his surgical gloves and touched the church lady's face, his skin against her bare skin for the first time.

Soft.

When she jerked away from him, weeping, Izzy told her the same thing he'd told the guinea. "Cooperate with me, do what I tell you, and no one gets hurt."

Feeling better about everything now, he added, "Relax a little; we're going for a boat ride. I *know* things about you. You might even *enjoy* it."

chapter twenty-five

I knew something was terribly wrong the instant I saw the expression on Tomlinson's face.

It was around noon. He came idling across the bay in his dinghy; tied up at his usual spot next to my bay shrimper. Then he came up the steps, shoulders sagging as if he were under the influence of some gravitational force.

I'd been talking on the phone, looking out the window of my lab, when I saw him leave the marina.

Not my regular phone.

I'd received a call on a phone that I seldom use, but always keep charged and hidden away in my lab's galvanized chemical cupboard. I keep it hidden because it is a government-issue, military SATCOM Iridium satellite telephone.

It is a recent addition. Not a welcomed one.

SATCOM is a satellite-based, global wireless personal communications network designed to permit easy phone communication from nearly anywhere on earth. Sixty-six satellites, evenly spaced four hundred miles high, make it possible. The phone is equipped with a sophisticated scrambler. The same is true of the phones used by the only two people who possess my access number.

Its ring is an unmistakable series of bonging chimes. The sound is suggestive of a clock in a British drawing room at high tea.

When I touched the activate button, I was not surprised to hear the voice of a U.S. State Department intelligence guru named Hal Harrington.

Harrington belonged to a supersecret and highly trained covert-operations team that was known, to a very few, as the Negotiating and Systems Analysis Group — the Negotiators, for short. Because the success of the team relied upon members blending easily into nearly any society, the training agency provided each member with a legitimate and mobile profession.

Harrington was trained as a computer software programmer. He'd made a personal fortune in the software industry by sheer intelligence and foresight. Other members of that elite team included CPAs, a couple of attorneys, an actor, one journalist and at least three physicians.

There was also a marine biologist among them. A man who traveled the world doing research. His specialty was bull sharks, *Carcharhinus leucas,* an unusual, unpredictable animal that ranges worldwide, in both fresh and salt water.

We probably would have never met; would

362

have willingly lived the rest of our lives without ever exchanging a word. But, a couple of years back, Harrington's attractive and precocious daughter, Lindsey, got into some trouble. Through coincidence and good luck, I happened to be in a position to help her. Which is how I happened to meet Hal.

By then, he was one of the most powerful and influential staff members at the U.S. State Department, specializing in Latin American affairs. It was Hal who made it clear to me that he and I had more in common than I wanted to admit. He knew certain facts about my past that I hoped no one would ever know. He reminded me of certain events that I preferred to forget.

Unfortunately, once one has participated in a violent, clandestine life, one cannot simply shed it like a skin, or leave it behind like a former job or an old house.

Harrington also made that clear to me. And, because he did know about my past, he had the leverage to guarantee my at least occasional participation in what he referred to as "vital government service."

When I answered the phone, Hal said, "I gather you're alone, Commander Ford?"

"I wouldn't have answered if I wasn't," I told him. "How's Lindsey?"

We talked about his daughter for a while. Lindsey was twenty-five now. She'd been in and out of drug-rehab facilities. Cocaine had a hold on her and wouldn't let go. It was especially tragic because Lindsey, lean and blond, had it all: brains, looks and humor. She would have been spectacular at anything she chose to be.

It gave Harrington special motivation when he went after the drug cartel–types. His hatred of them bordered on obsession. So the subject of Lindsey now provided a natural transition.

"That's one of the reasons I'm calling, Commander. Three weeks ago, my Number Two contacted you with what I considered a perfect assignment. We had good intel that the brother of Edgar Cordero — Giorgio — was going to spend two nights at South Beach, Miami. He's looking for dependable mules. Apparently, the heroin and cocaine business is good.

"Edgar was one of the most ruthless men in Colombia. As far as I'm concerned, he got exactly what was coming to him. Giorgio's no better, and he's taken over the family business. You've got a personal grudge to settle with those people, but you refused the assignment. Why?"

I could see Tomlinson swing down off the marina dock, into his dinghy as I said, "Well, Hal, the way I understand it, I've been conscripted. Redrafted — however you want to put it, as an active, Special Duty Line Officer, an O-5. Which makes it military. It's my understanding that the Posse Comitatus Act makes it illegal for me to accept any assignment that requires action within the boundaries of the United States."

Harrington is not known for his patience. "That's bullshit, Doc, and you know it. That's easy to get around; a simple matter of procedural formality. And let's be honest. It never stopped you before."

As Tomlinson puttered closer, I could see that he was holding a strand of his sun bleached hair in his fingers, chewing at it — a nervous mannerism.

Something was bothering him.

I listened to Hal add, "Which brings us to another subject. Those paychecks the department's been sending. Our records show you've never cashed them."

I said, "When I feel like I've done something to earn the money, maybe I will. Not until then."

"Okay, then, here's your chance. We have hard intelligence that the successor to Sabri al-Banna, head of the ANO, is going to be vacationing in the Leeward Islands in late summer or early fall. Under a false passport, of course. His name is Omar Muhammad. Mr. Muhammad's got a new hobby. He likes to scuba dive. The house he's reserved is on St. Martin, the French side. It has a coral reef right off its own little private beach. Out there in the water, that might be an interesting place to introduce yourself, Commander. Find out how well Mr. Muhammad can swim."

I said, "Omar Muhammad, huh?"

Abul Nidal Organization, or ANO, has carried out terrorist attacks in dozens of countries, killing or injuring thousands of people. Targets have included the United States, the United Kingdom, France, Israel and even moderate Palestinians. They like bombs. The ANO is responsible for putting a bomb aboard Pan Am flight 103 that blew up over Lockerbie, Scotland. Other major attacks included the Rome and Vienna airports, the Neve Shalom Synagogue in Istanbul and the hijacking of Pan Am Flight 73.

The terrorist organization's founder, Abu Nidal, was found dead inside his Baghdad home in August 2002, but the organization continues to spread mindless terror. They have small, secret cells in countries throughout the world.

I felt Tomlinson's dinghy bump against the pilings of my house as Harrington said, "The snake has a new head. We need to chop it off before the group gets active again. Interested?"

I said, "Know what? Yes. That one's a real possibility. I wouldn't mind meeting Mr. Omar," and meant it, even though I felt a nauseating tension in my stomach, thinking about it. Then I said, "Hal? I've got a friend coming up the steps. I'm going to have to call you back."

"You'll give it serious consideration?"

I said, "I already am."

As I locked the phone away, I could hear

Tomlinson calling, "Hey, Doc? Doc, it's me."

I met Tomlinson at the screen door to the lab. Opened it to let him in, but he just stood there, looking at me with his haunted, haunted eyes.

Immediately, I said, "What's wrong? Someone's hurt. *Who?*"

Tomlinson doesn't always need words to communicate, and I've known the man a long time.

He said, "Let's go in the house and sit down."

I touched my palm to his chest; could feel in my spine the neuron burn of panic. "No, tell me now. Is it Ransom? Did something happen to her? Or Dewey. Who?"

I noticed that Tomlinson's hands were shaking as he combed them through his hair. "I just came from the marina. Mack had the news on. Someone broke into Sally Carmel's house last night, or early this morning. Millionaire heiress missing. It's making the headlines. The house was robbed, and there's a statewide search."

He followed me into the lab, and I sat heavily in my old office chair. "Goddamn it! Frank was supposed to be watching her. How could someone get past —"

"That's the worst of it," Tomlinson interrupted. "So far, anyway. The cops found Frank in the trunk of his own car. It was parked in

Sally's driveway. Him and someone else, another man. They haven't released his name yet. They're both dead. Shot execution-style — the reporter's words."

I said, "*Two* men? But why would Frank be with —" I stopped talking, thinking about it, my brain slowed by shock.

I remembered Frank calling me at the marina, then talking to him from my home phone. I remembered Frank saying, *I'm calling 'cause I need someone I trust. I need a favor.*

He suspected that Sally was being followed. Unlike the police, he believed that someone had been breaking into her house. He wanted me to help him set a trap for the guy.

I remembered him saying, *I've got to have someone who knows how to take care of himself. A guy who can bust a head or two if things get tough.*

I was his first choice. His second choice, apparently, hadn't been a reliable one.

I also remembered him saying that whoever was following Sally was very, very good.

To take down someone of Frank DeAntoni's caliber, the man or men had to be more than good. They had to be professionals.

I looked at Tomlinson. I felt sick, disgusted and horrified by the possibility that my inaction had contributed to the murder of two men. One of them was a man I'd come to consider a friend in a very short time. I said, "Frank called me on Wednesday and asked me to help him work a surveillance on Sally's house. I refused.

368

Did the news say anything else about the second man? Was he a Hialeah cop?"

I was clinging to the irrational idea that, if the second dead man was in law enforcement, a trained professional, I was somehow exonerated, and my conscience could be clear.

"Doc, one thing you can't do is blame yourself for this in any way —"

"Damn it, just answer the question! Did they say anything else about the other guy?"

"No. That's all. That's all I heard."

I stood and began to pace. "We've got to do something. I've got to do something. I've got to go over there. We can take my truck."

"And do what? Sit outside Sally's empty house with a bunch of television journalist types? I don't see the point."

"I've got information that's pertinent to the case. I need to find out who's working the case and talk to them. Frank's dead? Jesus Christ — I can't *believe* it. If Sally's missing, you know what that means, don't you?"

Tomlinson said, "I can't bear to let myself think about it. If you've got information, you need to call them on the phone. Call them now, Doc."

I did.

I find it as surprising as I do heartening that law enforcement continues to attract top-quality people despite the daily, predictable critical hammering that law-enforcement professionals take from the media, the public and from special-interest groups of all types.

It took me awhile to find the right agency. The two main ones are the Miami-Dade Police Department and the City of Miami Police. The City of Miami Police was handling all matters relating to the disappearance of Mrs. Sally Minster, and the murder of Frank DeAntoni, licensed private investigator, and seventy-six-year-old Jimmy Marinaro, former carpet salesman and current manager of Pink Palms Apartments, Miami Springs.

I groaned inwardly when I heard that.

The dispatcher put me right through to the Homicide Division when I asked. When I told the on-duty detective why I was calling, she said, "Squad C's handling that one. You need to talk to Detective Fran Podraza. He's heading the investigation. I'll give you his cell-phone number."

Petty bureaucrats devise unnecessary barriers to delay and frustrate outsiders. They prefer inaction because action requires thought. This woman, though, didn't hesitate to make a subjective decision. I sounded credible. That was enough for her. It suggested to me that the Miami Police was a top-notch organization.

I got a voice mailbox when I dialed Detective Podraza's number. I left my name, my number, the marina's number, and added that I was a close friend of the missing woman and had information that might be helpful in the investigation.

Then I began to pace again. I couldn't sit still; couldn't seem to concentrate on any single subject for more than a minute or two. I tried to force myself to review what should have been a simple series of connecting data, but my brain continually misfired.

DeAntoni's voice kept interrupting basic thought patterns, echoing in my skull: *I'm calling 'cause I need someone I trust. I need a favor.*

There was Sally's voice, too. Telling me why she'd instinctively come to me when she needed help. *Being with you, being in this house, it gives me the same feeling Sanibel gives me. I feel safe.*

I felt as if I wanted to run around in circles and bang my head against the wall.

Tomlinson was sitting out on the porch. Sat in one of the deck chairs, but with his palms turned upward as if meditating. I grabbed two bottles of beer from the fridge, went outside and took the chair next to him.

I said, "Do you ever feel like you're going nuts? Like your head's going to explode because you just can't take it anymore?"

My voice seemed to startle him, as if he were in a trance. Then he turned to me with his wise, bloodshot blue eyes, and said, "I passed insane years ago. I'm now on the outer limits of emotional dysfunction. They've yet to define whatever it is I have. Simple psychosis would mean I'm on the path to recovery. I sometimes long to hear the voices of animals speaking to me once again."

I felt like bawling, but Tomlinson got the reaction from me he wanted. I chuckled, feeling the pressure dissipate slightly. "I don't know what to do," I said. "I feel utterly helpless."

He replied, "Have you noticed? In the last year or so, you've begun to react to events in an emotional way rather than an analytical way. I know how painful that must be. But I think it's a good thing for you as a person."

"Oh yeah? I *don't*. I think it's silly, childish and irrational. What we need to do right now is talk about Sally, not me. And Frank, too."

In a musing tone, Tomlinson said, "Did you know that the outdoor temperature can be estimated to within a couple of degrees by timing the chirps of a cricket? You count the number of chirps in a fifteen-second period, and add thirty-seven to the total. It doesn't work in winter. Anytime else, though, the result will be very close to the actual Fahrenheit temperature."

"If that's supposed to mean something, you've completely lost me."

"It means you're right. It's time to be analytical. Time to start counting the chirps. There has to be *some* way we can help them now."

So we drank our beers and discussed it. Tomlinson said perhaps the first thing we should do is contact any family members we could find and offer our assistance.

That made sense.

DeAntoni had told me that he lived alone, not even a cat, but he'd also had an aunt who lived in New Jersey.

I said, "Presumably, she's already been notified or they wouldn't have released Frank's name. When I talk to the detective, I'll ask for her number. We can call and offer whatever help she needs. A guy like him, he's got to have a lot of friends. People are going to need to be contacted; a funeral arranged."

I also knew that Sally had a cousin she was very close to. Belinda Carmel was her maiden name, but she'd married and moved to Big Pine Key.

Tomlinson said, "You find out about the aunt. I'll go back to the marina and hunt around on the Internet. I should be able to track down the former Belinda Carmel. If someone hasn't been screwing with my system again."

At the marina, Mack keeps a little office where the liveaboards can plug in their computers.

I said, "Someone's been using your iBook?"

"No. I've been hacked. Someone got my password. Now I'm getting all this weird right-wing mass e-mail crap. How to build bombs. I'm suddenly on the mailing list of blasting cap manufacturers. Greenpeace and Aryan Nation bullshit."

A joke, I told him.

He said, "If it is, I don't find it very funny."

Detective Fran Podraza called me about an hour later. I was impressed by his professionalism and his attention to detail. After I told him who I was and what I did for a living, he asked for confirmation info — address, Social Security number and mother's maiden name — before he gave me the phone number for Frank's New Jersey aunt.

Then he said, "So we've got a double homicide and an apparent kidnapping. Right now, we're working on the premise that it was probably a robbery that went bad. We know that Mr. DeAntoni was a licensed private investigator, contracted by an insurance company. We know that Mr. Marinaro was Mr. DeAntoni's landlord."

Which is when he gave me the additional data about Marinaro — a seventy-six-year-old man with no law-enforcement experience.

I felt like throwing the phone across the room.

Podraza continued, "Other than that, we don't have a lot. So any information you can provide might be helpful."

I told him everything I knew. Started with how I knew Sally, how I met Frank, about the break-ins she suspected and about Frank calling me on Wednesday, asking for help setting up some kind of trap.

"Why would he call you if he'd only known you for a week?"

"I guess he thought I was the dependable type."

Podraza said, "Any idea what kind of trap it was he had planned?"

"He talked about doing some kind of long-distance surveillance. But that was if I agreed to help. With a man as old as his landlord, I have no idea how he would have tried to work it. Knowing Frank, though, he wouldn't have put an older guy in harm's way. My guess is, Frank would have left Mr. Marinaro in the car while he staked out the house. Maybe inside, maybe outside."

Podraza told me that made sense, because inside the Lincoln Town Car, on the front seat, they found a .45 caliber Blackhawk revolver registered in Frank's name.

"Maybe he left it with Mr. Marinaro so he'd have a little extra protection."

Podraza had already told me that he was aware that, on three separate occasions, Sally had notified his department that she suspected someone was breaking into her house. He also knew that her dog had drowned in her own pool.

I said, "So why are you working this as a robbery?"

He said, "This early in any investigation, you begin with what is most probable. Statistically, the most likely scenario. Then you begin to eliminate things. I try to work from the general to the specific. We find two bodies in the truck of a car, both men shot a single time behind the right ear, the wallets and watches of both men missing. Someone surprised them. Someone robbed them.

"Inside, the house has been trashed. Drawers ripped out, no jewelry or cash left in the place. And the lady of the house is missing. There are other, more specific indicators that I'm not going to tell you about. But go ahead. Toss out another scenario if you want."

I liked this man. I liked his precise, methodical thought process. His friendly, easygoing manner was, of course, a device. Perpetrators often contact the police, pretending to have information. In fact, they are trying to find out how the investigation is going.

Podraza was playing good cop; my affable equal trying to solve a crime. In actuality, he was giving me plenty of room to trip myself up; to hang myself if I was involved with the murders.

I said, "Okay. Here's one possibility. You've got a freak. Some kind of sexual pervert, and he's become fixated on Sally Minster. He figures out her alarm system, and begins to break into her house on an occasional basis. That kind of pathology is well documented. Men like that, they go through underwear drawers; part of the fantasy process. It's a form of sociopathic behavior that's not uncommon."

Podraza said, "You say you're a marine biologist. Mind if I ask how you happen to know all this?"

"I don't have a TV. I read a lot. But let me finish — I'm thinking this through as I go along. Okay, so you have a sexual freak who knows the house well. Violence is probably also part of his fantasy component — he's armed. Check Frank's background. He was an All-American wrestler. Olympic class. The freak had to surprise him, and he had to already have a gun. There's no other way he could have gotten Frank taped and into the back of his own car without a gun."

"A three-time All-American," Podraza said. "It's in his bio. He was one very impressive guy."

"Yeah, I agree. Okay, so the freak surprises Frank and Sally. Or they surprise him. Either way, the freak's suddenly got witnesses, and he has to get rid of them. He wants to keep the cops off the trail as long as possible, so he makes it look like a robbery."

Podraza replied, "That's plausible. I'll keep it in mind. Like I said, we're just getting started. Going from the general to the specific. You get a multiple crime like this, it's usually because someone not very smart to begin with behaves in a really stupid way. Murder is rarely a complicated or well-thought-out crime, Dr. Ford."

For some reason, that keyed a little light switch in my brain. What if exactly the *opposite* were true? I don't believe in conspiracy theories. If I ever meet more than two people who can keep a secret, maybe I'll begin to give them some consideration. But what if the murders, the disappearances, were all part of some larger objective or pattern?

I said, "Do you mind listening to another possibility?"

"Not at all. You have some interesting ideas for a man who says he's a biologist."

His voice had the slightest hint, now, of cynicism. His cop instincts were probably telling him that I knew too much, that I was way too chatty. I didn't mind.

I said, "Okay. Let's review a chain of events that may or may not be related. I'd be interested in your reaction. Nearly seven months ago, Sally Minster's husband, Geoff, disappears —"

"He fell overboard on a trip to the Bahamas," Podraza said. "There's nothing mysterious about that. It's been thoroughly investigated. The court's ready to declare the guy legally dead."

"If you want to move from the general to the specific, you sometimes have to take a step or two back to see the broader picture. So let me finish. Minster disappears, yet his wife doesn't believe he's dead. At some time after his disappearance, she also becomes convinced someone is breaking into her house, going through her private things. Your people check it out, but don't find probable cause."

Podraza said, "Sometimes people in deep grief begin to imagine things. They can get a little paranoid."

Meaning they thought she was a nut case.

I said, "Okay, but let's assume she was right. Next, her dog is found dead in her own pool. A retriever. They're *bred* to swim. Then the night security guard who's promised to keep an eye on the lady's house is also found dead, floating in the bay."

Podraza said, "He died from a brain aneurysm, but I'm with you. We're assuming it was actually foul play. Okay. So Mr. DeAntoni sets a trap for the guy or guys who are doing all this — that's your point, right? But the trap backfires, and they all end up dead or missing. So we've got three-four-five individuals dead or missing. Six, if you count the dog. Interesting."

I asked Podraza if he was aware that Minster had been a member of the Church of Ashram Meditation. He told me he was, and that he was familiar with the organization because the Miami Police had a unit that specialized in cult crimes.

I said, "It might be worthwhile to call them in, and have them take a look. One more thing, Detective? There's a guy who works for Bhagwan Shiva, a guy I think you ought to check out. His name's Izzy — that's what they call him. I don't know his last name. He's like a personal assistant or something to the head guy. His last name shouldn't be hard to find. In fact, I might even be able to provide his finger-prints if you need them."

"Why do you suspect him?"

I paused, my brain scanning around for a cogent response. Finally, I said, "Detective Podraza, when you check me out — and I know you *will* check me out — you'll find that I've been telling you the truth. I'm a working research biologist. I like to think that most of what I do is logical and objective. But when it comes to this guy, Izzy — and this isn't easy for me to admit — my suspicions are purely instinctual. I've got a gut feeling about him. It's an emotional reaction to meeting the man. I think he's dirty. I think he has his own agenda going."

Then I added, "I know you're not allowed to confirm it, but I'm going to ask anyway. The gun that was used to kill Frank and his landlord. Was it a twenty-two caliber?"

Very quickly, Podraza said, "Dr. Ford, I think we need to have a face-to-face interview. And just to make sure you don't decide to leave the area, I'm going to call you back to confirm this phone number. Then I'm going to contact the Sanibel Police to let them know I'm inviting you to Miami for a discussion. Or we can send someone to you."

I told Podraza to call me anytime he wanted, particularly if he got any new information on Sally. I finished, adding, "I'm glad they have someone like you on this case."

chapter twenty-six

I got a hold of Frank's Aunt Juliana. By the sound of her voice, she'd been crying. She kept saying, "In my mind, I still see him as a little boy. He was so quiet and shy!"

She gave me phone numbers for three of Frank's closest friends. I called Harris Washington at the bank where he worked near Trenton. He and DeAntoni had wrestled together in high school, Washington told me. "A hell of a guy," he added.

I said, "I agree. I wish I could have gotten to know him better."

Washington told me that he and another one of Frank's former teammates were taking care of all the details. They were having his body cremated, and the ashes shipped back to New York for the funeral service. Instead of flowers — "Frank hated flowers, man. Something to do with a bad experience he had at the prom" — they were suggesting people send donations to an AAU wrestling program that DeAntoni had been instrumental in starting.

After I hung up, I wrote a check, walked to the marina and mailed it.

I still couldn't stop moving, stop my mind from racing. I went back to the lab, called information, and got the main number for the Church of Ashram Meditation Center in Palm Beach. When a woman answered, I said, "Let me talk to Izzy, please."

I had only a vague idea of what I would say to the guy. Maybe mention the weird trap-shooting encounter, tell him that, unlike Tomlinson, Frank and I liked to shoot so how could we join their interesting club?

If he knew the truth about DeAntoni, that he was dead, I'd be able to hear it in his voice.

But the woman refused to put me through, saying, "It's church policy that we can only take messages for members or staff. It's *their* decision to call you back."

So I took a chance, called the Cypress Restaurant at Sawgrass, and had them transfer me to the Panther Bar. In any organization, the best jobs are awarded in order of rank or seniority. At a place that catered to wealthy sportsmen and big tippers, bartender would be the most coveted of all service jobs.

Kurt, most probably, was a higher-up in Bhagwan Shiva's organization. He'd have insider information.

The stuffy bartender answered. He told me, no, Mr. Carter McRae wasn't in. He told me he couldn't give me Mr. McRae's home number, and he played dumb when I asked him about Izzy.

But he knew who Izzy was. I could tell by his evasive manner.

Then he surprised me by saying, "The Bhagwan and his staff aren't here tonight, but they'll all be here tomorrow for the sunset Easter service. The public's invited. It's going to be quite an impressive event." In his infuriating, superior tone, he added, "You and your friends should come. Perhaps you'll learn something."

I'd been invited to the 'Glades by Billie Egret, anyway, to see the inland tarpon. Now, though, I had a more pressing reason to go — to find Izzy.

To Kurt, I said, "I'll be there. Count on it."

Then, even though it made no sense, I got in my truck and drove across the Everglades to Coconut Grove. It took me awhile to find the exclusive enclave that is Ironwood. There was a Miami Police squad car at the electronic gate, and two uniformed officers. Only residents were being allowed to enter. When I asked to speak to Detective Podraza, they told me he'd just left.

I gave them my Sanibel Biological Supply business card with a brief note on the back.

Please call immediately with any news about Sally Minster.

That I'd visited the crime scene would assure me of special attention from the detective. Which is exactly what I wanted.

I drove past Vizcaya with its formal gardens,

past Mercy Hospital, then headed up the hill into Coconut Grove — clothing boutiques, sidewalk restaurants. On Main Highway, with its tunneling banyan trees, I found a sizable church built of coral rock, then a slightly smaller church, which I guessed to be the church that Sally had described. White clapboard; white steeple. Beside the sidewalk out front was the kind of glass-encased signboard with plastic lettering that can be changed.

In large letters it read: ALL NATIONS CHURCH OF GOD OF PROPHECY.

Below, in letters that were only slightly smaller, someone had recently added, *Pray for our Sister Sally!*

I teared up when I saw the sign. I slowed, staring at it, until a line of cars behind me began to honk.

Then, for absolutely no rational reason, I drove north to Miami Springs and found the Pink Palm Apartment complex where Frank had lived: four rows of stucco condos with numbered carports, speed bumps, a miniature swimming pool, and a couple of kids riding tricycles outside near trash Dumpsters and a mulched playground.

It seemed important to find DeAntoni's apartment. I thought it would take me awhile. It didn't. His was the one with the yellow Crime Scene tape across the door and combination padlock on the doorknob.

I stopped at the door. Peeked through the

blinds and saw a vinyl couch, no other furniture, and the kind of double-handled exercise wheel that people use to do abdominal crunches.

A bachelor fitness freak.

I checked my watch. A little before five. I hadn't eaten breakfast or lunch, but wasn't hungry. I decided that, if I got in my truck and left now, I could be back at Dinkin's Bay while there was still enough light left to get out in my skiff.

Then maybe I'd find Tomlinson, and make a few bar stops by water before watching the moon rise.

That night, something inside me snapped. Something within the core region of my brain. It was ignited by a growing, withering pressure without vent. Intellectually, emotionally, I felt the scaffolding that defines me fracture, then break.

The moment of its occurrence was so precise that I felt it move through my nervous system like an electric shock.

I'd gotten back to Sanibel a little after eight. Lights were already on at the marina, but the sky was still bright with sunset afterglow. To the east, cumulous towers were layered in volcanic striations of rust, Arizona purple and peach.

I checked my main fish tank, the aquaria in my lab, fed Crunch & Des, then took a quick shower.

By the time I idled out of the marina harbor, the clouds had changed to shades of pewter and pearl. I saw that Tomlinson's dinghy was tethered off *No Mas* — he was aboard. I headed toward the sailboat, then decided, no, I didn't feel like company.

I'd made myself a traveler in an oversized plastic cup: ice, rum, fresh lime. With the big Mercury rumbling, I pushed the boat up onto plane, then throttled way back, traveling at a comfortable 2,600 RPM — "wine speed," Dewey Nye calls it, because it's fast enough to get you to dinner, but slow enough so it's still possible to sip a glass of wine. I ran across the flat past Green Point, then Woodring Point.

My cousin, Ransom Gatrell, was out on Ralph Woodring's dock, wearing shorts and a pink bikini top, a sunset beverage still in her hand.

I waved. She waved.

Ransom has Tucker Gatrell's blue eyes, but she's a caramel-colored woman, a color she calls "Nassau chocolate." She wears her hair in braids, tells fortunes, believes in Obeah — a variation of voodoo — and is already making a small fortune selling real estate on a part-time basis. During the day, she works behind a cash register at Bailey's General Store, or at She Sells Sea Shells on Periwinkle.

Ransom tells people that she's my sister. I no longer bother to correct her or them. We've become that close.

Even so, I ignored her beckoning wave — *Come talk for a spell!* — and turned beneath the power lines, then beneath the Sanibel Causeway, seeing the bright high-rise lights of Fort Myers Beach to the south.

One of my favorite places to eat and drink is a bayside café that almost no one knows about, and where only locals go. It's in the old shrimp yards of Matanza Pass, a funky, quirky outdoor restaurant and bar built beneath the sky bridge that joins Fort Myers Beach with tiny San Carlos Island. It's called Bonita Bill's, and it may be the only restaurant in Florida with an unlisted phone number.

Kathy and Barb were working the bar. I sat beneath tiki thatching, drinking rum, staring out at the dark water, seeing the development glare of Fort Myers Beach beyond.

At one point, Kathy said, "You don't seem real talkative tonight, Doc. Something wrong?"

Yes, there was something wrong. Frank DeAntoni had moved into my head and would not leave. His voice had become a refrain:

I've got to have someone who knows how to take care of himself. A guy who can bust a head or two if things get tough.

I told Kathy, "Sorry. I've got a lot on my mind."

Around ten, a bunch of the guys from the Fort Myers Beach Coast Guard station came in. They're a good group. Well trained. Dedicated. I tried to force myself to be jovial, conversational, but my heart wasn't in it.

I bought one more rum for the road, then idled out toward Bodwitch Point, the Sanibel Lighthouse flashing in the darkness beyond.

My next recollection was of standing in my house, staring into the little mirror that is tacked to the wall near my Transoceanic shortwave radio.

The face in the mirror seemed the face of a stranger, even though it was my own.

The Nicaraguan rum I drink is *Flor de Cana* — Flower of Sugar Cane. It is a superb rum; hard to find. I held the bottle in my hand and amused myself by drinking from the bottle, my eyes never leaving the mirror.

See the stranger drink. See the stranger swallow. See how ugly the stranger is with his thick glasses, crooked nose and scars. See what an absurd and meaningless little creature the stranger is.

Still holding the bottle, I walked outside and stood on the deck.

It was after midnight. The lights of the marina created conduits of shimmering brass on the water, linking my stilt house with the darkened trawlers, sailboats and houseboats, and to the solitary lives within.

To the east, a bulbous moon, a week past full, was illuminating far mangroves, creating silhouettes and shadows. With the rising of the moon came a freshening northwest wind. It was blowing an uneven fifteen, gusting out of a high-pressure-system blackness domed with stars — the frail, ancient light of distant suns, incalculable solar systems.

Standing there, I felt as if I were staring into a funneling abyss that began within my own dark soul and expanded into the infinite. I took another gulp of rum, unzipped my pants, and pissed into the darkness below, watching the bioluminescent sparks my stream created; sparks that, in shape and brilliance, were not dissimilar to the starscape above.

For some reason, I found the parallel heart-breaking.

The wind gusted, messing my hair, blowing harder now.

That gave me an idea.

I started windsurfing a little less than a year ago. I keep my sails rigged, hung beneath my house so they are always ready when I want them. On other moon-bright nights, I'd considered windsurfing — but always dismissed it as idiotic. Too many oyster bars, crab pots and old pilings out there to hit.

Now, though, windsurfing in moonlight seemed a superb idea.

I tripped going up the steps; nearly tripped again when I banged my shoulder against the wall, entering my lab. I touched the wall switch, and stared at the rows of aquaria; could smell the sweet ozone odor created by the systems of aerators. I was aware that, from within some of the glass tanks, certain animals — octopi and squid — were staring at me just as intently as I stared at them.

A couple of months back, at a party, Tomlinson and I got into one of our complicated debates. It was about the mandates of scientific method. The debate was unusually heated and, at one point, I told him, "It's the way I've been trained. I'd rather be *precisely* wrong than approximately right about almost anything."

He found that hilarious. A week later, he'd presented me with a wooden sign with the silly phrase engraved on it. I'd tacked the thing on the north wall of my lab.

Now I looked at the sign, reading it — I'D RATHER BE PRECISELY WRONG THAN APPROXIMATELY RIGHT — and the welling heartbreak I felt earlier was transformed inexplicably into fury. An absolute cold and loathing fury.

That's when it happened. That's when I snapped. It was like a flashbulb going off behind my eyes. I took the rum bottle, hurled it hard at the sign, and turned away, hearing an explosion of glass.

In that isolated space between what I was, and what I had become, the stranger within spoke for the first time: *You are insane.*

I wobbled back down the stairs, strapped a harness around my waist, then rigged my surfboard. I chose my favorite board — an ultrawide Starboard Formula 175. It's built for big, clumsy people like me. I locked on my largest, fastest sail, a 10.4-meter Neilpryde Streetracer.

It took me lots of fumbling and falling to get the sail up. When I had the boom under control, I tilted the mast forward to gain speed. Then, as I sheeted in, I walked the board beneath the sail, feeling the wind on my face, feeling the board lift itself off the chop as I accelerated onto plane, the elastic up-haul line thumping rhythmically against the mast. Thumping, it seemed, as if my heart were echoing off the far stars, beating fast enough to explode.

With a little kick, I arched my hips and belted myself to the boom. With my bare feet, I searched the board until I found the foot straps. I wiggled my feet in tight.

Board, sail, boom, mast and I were now a single, connected unit. Tomlinson once told me that the wind does not push a sailboat, it pulls it. I could feel the wind's inexorable pull now as I flew across the water, sailing toward the moon at close to twenty miles per hour.

Then the moon disappeared behind clouds, and I was speeding through mangrove shadow, hearing wind and water in the caverns of my ears. The bioluminescent wake I created was an expanding silver-green crescent. The sensory combination was that of riding a comet across a liquid universe. Off to my right, I saw a mobile galaxy of green streaks: a school of fish. I watched the school explode in a firestream of color; then explode again.

Something big was beneath the fish, feeding.

I turned my board downwind, jibbed, popped the cams to fill the sheet, accelerated quickly and sailed toward the school.

They were mullet — a silver, blunt-headed fish with protuberant eyes. Thousands of them in a tight, panicked herd in waist-deep water. Three or four pounders. As I approached the edge of the school, they began to jump — gray, arching trajectories in the darkness — banging off my board, hitting my legs, landing on the board, then flopping wildly until they were free.

As I sailed through the school, I saw something else. I saw the predator that was feeding on the mullet. It appeared beneath the water as a submarine-shape, outlined in green. It cruised with a slow, reptilian movement as if crawling, tail and head shifting, always at apogee.

It was a shark. In this brackish mangrove lake, it was almost certainly a bull shark judging from its girth. It was the fish that I'd traveled the world studying. It was the fish I often used as an excuse for clandestine work.

The shark was big. Probably nine feet long, three or four hundred pounds. As I passed near it, I watched the shark turn in a whirlpool of light. I saw the shark pause, as if reviewing its options. Then it began to trail me, pushing water in a vectoring, sparkling blaze as it increased speed.

Drunk as I was, I could feel my heart pounding, my knees shaking. A cliché often repeated is that sharks are unpredictable. Seldom true. Like most predators, sharks have a strong pursuit instinct. If something runs from them, they chase it. What this animal was now doing was perfectly predictable: It was tracking me. If I was fleeing, there was a reason. I must be prey.

Watching the fish, my head was turned toward the rear of the board — not a smart thing to do when windsurfing day or night. I could see the shark's bulk creating a column of water as it swam faster, closing the gap between us. I applied pressure to the board and sheeted in even tighter to get maximum speed — an absurd thing to do, because there was no way that I, a land mammal, a novice surfer, could outrun the muscled culmination of a million years of perfected genetic adaptation.

Then the shark was on me, behind the board, its fin cleaving the water, tacking back and forth with every thrust of its tail. I pulled my back foot out of its strap in an attempt to kick at the thing, and nearly lost control of the boom; almost went flying over the sail.

For several seconds, the shark matched my speed, both of us streaking through darkness, stars above, bioluminescent stars below. Then I felt the board jolt beneath me once . . . twice . . . then a third time.

The bull shark was bumping the board with its nose. It was testing, feeling, sensing what I was, interpreting the *why* of me.

Few know that a shark's most powerful sensory organ is not its sense of smell, even though the sensory apparatus is located on the animal's nose. If you ever get a chance, take a close look at shark's head. You will see that the snout area is covered with tiny black dots. These are, in fact, pores that are filled with a complicated jelly. The jelly accurately detects bioelectric impulses. Quite literally, a shark can sense the precise location of a human heart beating from many hundreds of yards away. It is a remarkable sensory ability, and I know of no other animals that are equipped with it.

By touching its snout to the board, the fish was monitoring my physiology: pounding heart, electrical circuitry on panicked overload, mammalian blood pressure lowered by alcohol then spiked by fear.

I was flesh. I was eatable.

For a micro-instant, I felt a tremendous weight on the back of the board — perhaps the fish had mistakenly bitten the skeg. Then the fish passed beneath the board at twice my speed, its tail-slap creating an unexpected wake.

In the same instant, my big sail was hit by a gust of wind.

I was drunk. My balance isn't great to begin with. It was enough to catapult me over boom and board. I landed atop the slowly sinking sail, still hooked to the boom.

My hands were shaking as I fixed my glasses back on my face and tried to free myself. Frantically, I looked ahead: The shark, turning, had created a swirling green vortex with an exit streak like an arrow.

The bull shark was returning. Its sensory receptors were attuned. The sound of my pounding heart had to be unmistakable, nearly deafening. It knew exactly where I was, what I was.

Windsurfing sails are made of see-through plastic, a kind of monofilm. I watched the shark cruise toward me, and then beneath me — me atop the thin skein of plastic, it below. I could feel the pony-sized girth of the animal lift both the sail and me briefly; could hear the rasp of its rough skin abrade the boom. I sensed a rolling movement — had it turned to bite?

Then the shark exited from beneath the sail. Confused, it cruised a few meters beyond, and turned toward me again.

I was free of the sail now, standing in waist deep water, trying desperately, pathetically, to right my board and get back atop it. But I was drunk and disoriented. I was too fat, too winded, too slow. I kept slipping, falling off.

That's when something in my brain ruptured once again. It was the same sensation: a flashbulb exploding behind my eyes.

And, once again, the result was a cold and loathing fury.

"Fuck it!"

I shoved the board away from me, and turned to face the shark. I could see the column of water rising as the animal gained speed, coming at me. I could see the silhouette of its dorsal fin trailing star-bright streamers. In my crazed state, there was a single, stabilizing truth that fueled my rage: Why run? We are *both* predators.

I began to walk toward the shark. Then I charged it, creating my own wake as the stranger in me screamed aloud, "Come on, you big bastard. Hit me. You're doing me a favor!"

When the bull shark was three or four body lengths away, I dived hard toward it, both fists extended. I expected to collide with the fish; to feel its jaws crush my arms.

Instead, my fists touched only soft bottom.

I came up, searching the surface through blurry glasses.

I could see that shark's wake plainly.

It was swimming away at top speed. Spooked.

I took my time sailing back. I'd not only sobered; I felt as if I'd experienced some elemental transformation. What had occurred was powerful beyond any encounter I'd anticipated or imagined.

I thought about it on the long reach home, trying to figure out what had happened, why I felt changed. The lights of the marina glittered in the near distance. The windows of my house and lab were yellow rectangles, uniform and solid. My tin roof appeared waxen.

To live fearlessly, one must first invite death. It's one of Tomlinson's favorite maxims. That may have been a tiny part of what I was feeling, for I had certainly accepted the inevitable when I charged the shark. If the shark had rolled and locked, I would have been killed. I would have died quickly or gradually, but I certainly would have died. I would have bled to death.

It was a strange disconnected feeling, as if I were suddenly free of all emotion, fear included.

It was unexplored territory. I felt energized.

What I felt was more than just the absence of fear. I'd spent the last year or so reacting to past mistakes, punishing myself — or so my inner voice claimed. After my shark encounter, though, self-flagellation seemed an absurd justification for allowing the circumstances of my life to control me. We've got to be suspicious of that little voice. Our innermost voice sometimes lies to us. It is a necessary revelation if a man or woman is to take the occasional leap of faith and invite the courage necessary to live an aggressive, creative and satisfying life.

I'd known that before. How had I lost the thread?

Maybe it happens to us all, sooner or later. Maybe we all stray off the path, driven by incremental events, great or small. Or maybe it's just a secret laziness that seeks an excuse to escape the daily discipline, bravery, endurance and plain hard work that it takes to live up to our own idealized image of self.

I'd certainly strayed from the path.

I despised what I'd become. I didn't like the way I looked, didn't like the way I felt. There had been growing in me a bedrock unhappiness and discontent that I could never quite define.

Now, though, I was struck by what seemed to be a rational explanation: For the last many years, I have been at odds with my own past. In my previous work, in what I think of as my former life, I'd been required to demonstrate what I prefer to define as extreme behavior.

I was ashamed. Ashamed of what I'd done. I'd hidden it from others, which was not just understandable, but a legally binding mandate. However, I'd also attempted to hide the truth from myself.

Why? What did I have to be ashamed of?

Alone, beneath stars, buoyant, water light and moving with the wind, the answer to that question seemed to ring like crystal in my innermost being.

Nothing. You have absolutely no reason to be ashamed.

It was a transcendent moment. A few minutes before, I'd confronted what is truest in me

— We are both predators.

It was true. I am predatory by nature. I also like to think that I am ethical, kind, selective and generous. But, at the atavistic core, I am a hunter, a killer.

I am a *collector.*

It has always been so with me. It will always be so.

In accepting that truth, I felt a delicious sense of freedom.

I steered my surfboard home. I hung the sail, washed the board — a kind of workmanlike penance. The bottom half of the skeg was missing: Ragged fiberglass in a half-moon shape. No surprise.

Then, after a quick glance at my fish tanks, a quicker hello to Crunch & Des, I went to my galley and placed upon the cupboard every bottle of booze I owned. It was an impressive stash. Five unopened bottles of *Flor de Cana,* two unopened bottles of Patron, which is a superb tequila, plus a complete stock of other whiskeys, gins and vodkas.

I also stacked up two and a half cases of beer . . . thought about it for a moment before deciding to keep the beer for Tomlinson's visits.

I put the bottles in boxes. It took me two trips to carry it all to the marina. It was a little after 2 A.M. Aside from the hiss of the bait tank aerator, and the flapping of sail halyards against masts, all was still. I opened the ice machine and buried fourteen bottles therein.

Finders, keepers. If someone wanted the bottles, there they were for the taking.

I'd brought a flashlight. The marina's commercial fish scale is out back behind the marina office, next to the cleaning table. It had been more than six months since I'd last weighed myself. I stepped onto the scale, touched my fingers to the poise counterweights, moving them.

It took awhile. Was the damn thing broken?

When the suspension bar was finally balanced, I whispered, "Jesus Christ, this can't be right."

I was still wearing my wet T-shirt and shorts. I stepped off the scale, stripped naked, then stepped back onto the scale plate.

After a few more seconds, I whispered, "You fat son-of-a-bitch."

I walked back to my stilt house.

Every human being should have at least a half-dozen people that he or she can call day or night when they are sleepless, goofy drunk, feeling lonely or in emotional need.

Dewey Nye is on my short list.

When I got back to the house, my rubber wristwatch said it was 2:39 A.M.

Feeling totally sober, now, I dialed the lady's number. The phone rang twice before I heard her groggy voice answer, "This better be fuckin' good, Walda."

She expected it to be her longtime, off again—on again roommate and lover.

400

I said, "Dew. It's me."

I could picture her sitting up a little, focusing. "Doc? What time is it?"

I told her.

"Are you drunk? You've got to be drunk."

I said, "In the morning, seven A.M., I'll meet you on the beach at the end of Tarpon Bay Road. We run, then swim. Three miles, then swim a half mile. No — make it a mile. You don't have to swim the whole way."

I listened to the lady yawn. "Oh, Doc, you *are* drunk. Go to sleep, sweetie. I'll stop by around noon. We can go for a walk."

Not raising my voice, I said, "You need to listen to me, Dewey. It's important. I'm not going to explain it to everyone, but I'm going to tell you because I need your help. Starting tomorrow, we work out at least five days a week. And no more alcohol. Period. Not for me. Twenty, twenty-five pounds from now, maybe I'll reconsider. Or maybe I won't. I'm making you that promise. Hold me to it."

"You're serious."

"Yep. It's time I quit feeling sorry for myself. Seven A.M. on the beach. I'll see you there."

"What time's the sun come up?"

I said, "Seven-oh-one."

"Our own private sunrise service. I'll be there."

I hung up, found a pencil, then walked to my outdoor shower. On the outside wall of my house, I wrote my weight: 247.

Then, in parentheses, beside it, I wrote my minimum objective: 220.

It seemed to formalize the change that had taken place in me. Because I had written it, I now had no choice but to achieve it.

I showered, walked into the lab and looked at the stranger in the mirror for a long moment before I said, "You're done."

Then I went to bed.

For months, I'd been plagued by nightmares or dreams of frustrating inabilities. On this night, though, I dreamed of the face of a child whose photo I kept in a moon-shaped locket. Then, in my dream, the child's face became the face of an old, old love.

She was a woman with waist-length blond hair, dressed in white crinoline. Her face was luminous and comforting, a woman so beautiful that seeing her caused me to linger upon detail: lighted portions of chin and cheek, strong nose creating shadow, perceptive eyes unaware and uncaring of her own beauty.

Her voice was a kindred chord as she said, "I have waited so long for you, my dear. So many, many years. Now, once again, you've come back to me. . . ."

chapter twenty-seven

Tomlinson said, "The way these people are be-
having, it's more like a rock concert for fascists.
Or a magic show. I'd say a kind of Grateful
Dead deal, but that'd be an insult to Jerry.
They're giving me the creeps, man."

He meant the several hundred Church of
Ashram members who were moving along the
boardwalk, filing toward the outdoor amphitheater, Cypress Ashram, on this Easter Sunday
late afternoon. They were men and women of
various ages, but there did seem to be a
strange, almost mechanical, similarity in the
way they moved, the way they behaved.

Many wore robes: orange or white or green.
There were far fewer orange robes than green,
and fewer green than white, so the colors were
suggestive of rank. Others were dressed in
neatly pressed slacks or skirts, hair trimmed
short. They traveled in tight groups, sometimes
creating human chains by holding on to each
other's waists — slow conga lines — or walking
in step, calling odd phrases back and forth as if
in some cheerful competition:

"We're running Thetan Three over here."

"We're running Thetan *Four* over here!"

"Bhagwan Shiva's version of Scientology," Tomlinson told me when I asked. "Don't worry about it."

Frisbees were popular, too. The church must have designed its own. Each plastic disc was a black-and-white yin-yang symbol stamped with *CAMI*, the church's initials. The air was filled with their slow, arching ascents. Prayer wheels, I heard one person call them.

The Archangels were maintaining high visibility. Shiva's security people, dressed in black, weight-lifter types, male and female, were cruising in their golf carts, letting their authority be seen.

So far, I hadn't seen any guards that I recognized.

Not that I would have minded.

I was in that kind of mood.

I'd talked to Detective Podraza twice during the day. They'd found no sign of Sally, no witnesses, no clue to where she might be, despite press conferences and expanding media coverage. They were, however, accumulating some crime-scene evidence. He'd also told me that he'd spoken to the Sanibel police. They'd vouched for me, so his manner, though still professional, was slightly friendlier.

"The security camera at the front gate shows Frank and Sally's cars leaving, then both cars coming back," he said.

I said, "They came by boat. Whoever shot

Frank and the old guy, they were smart enough to come by water. Unless you've got something else on the security cameras."

Podraza said, "That's a possibility we're considering."

I didn't expect him to provide any other details, and he didn't.

I added, "I'm no expert, but I've read that a kidnap victim's first twenty-four hours are critical."

"I'll tell you the same thing I told Mrs. Minster's cousin, Belinda. If the lady was our own sister, mother — name it — we couldn't be working this case any harder. A double homicide and a kidnapping. That's about as bad as it gets. And you're right — the longer she's gone, the less chance of finding her alive."

When I said that, if she was already dead, her body was probably out in Biscayne Bay, Podraza replied, "We have boats looking. And you're right again. In an abduction-murder, getting rid of the body is always the biggest problem, because it's evidence found on the body that usually nails them."

What he *wanted* to know was why I'd guessed that both victims had been shot with a .22 caliber.

I told him the truth: Like my suspicions about Izzy, it was a hunch. Something about the way the guy looked, the way he handled himself. Israeli intelligence, the Mossad, uses the .22 Beretta as its signature weapon of assas-

sination. Only a sociopath would put two innocent men in the trunk of a car and execute
them, and the Mossad signature was the sort of
touch a sociopath might try to imitate.

Podraza said, "I'll be honest. The first time
we talked, I got the impression you might be a
kind of kook. But the Sanibel police chief told
me that if you had some suggestions, I'd be
smart to listen. So I did try to find out about
the guy.

"I contacted the church's main office. But
cult religions, law enforcement, we don't get
along. Family members are always asking us to
help get their sons and daughters out. I didn't
expect the church to be cooperative, and they
weren't. There's no way I can check the guy out
if I don't even have his last name."

I told Podraza, "Izzy's last name. I can come
up with that. I'll call you tonight."

I'd looked out the window of my lab, and saw
that Tomlinson's dinghy was tethered to the
stern of *No Mas*. I got on the VHF radio, hailed
him, and we switched channels. He'd told me
earlier that he was going to Sawgrass to view
what he called "Shiva's Easter sunset carnival
show."

He sounded shocked when I said I wanted to
go along.

"I thought we were going separately because
all you wanted to do is see the tarpon. That you
were going way earlier."

I replied, "My interests have broadened."

On the drive down, he told me that Billie Egret, Ginny Egret, James Tiger, her aunts and uncles were also attending the Cypress Ashram, all as Shiva's special guests. Them, plus some members from Tomlinson's secret group of Cassadaga psychics, who weren't invited but were going anyway. He said they would be sprinkled among the crowd.

"We have no choice. Something big's going on, so we've decided to do another spiritual intervention. The Non-Bhagwan has Billie's people conned. They're almost convinced they should go into partnership with him. All of them except Billie. She's still standing strong, but she needs our help. She'll be really glad you're there."

I had a different kind of help in mind.

That morning, during my run with Dewey, I'd nearly collapsed from exhaustion. But I'd completed the three miles — and at her brutal pace. The swim didn't go much better. I stopped twice to vomit salt water.

But I finished the swim, too.

I was tired; still had a trace of hangover shakes. For the first time in months, though, I felt focused, energized by purpose.

So now it was 6:30 P.M. The parking lot adjoining Sawgrass's outdoor amphitheater was jammed, and we were being swept along by the crowd. Tomlinson had come for his reasons. I'd come for my own. I was going to find Izzy.

Once I found him, if I got the slightest whiff

of suspicion that he was involved with Frank's death and Sally's disappearance, I would devise a way to separate him from the group, isolate him, and I would then do whatever was required to make him talk.

It was something I was good at.

Why had it taken me so many years to admit it?

As we walked along, Tomlinson said, "We're plenty early. Billie told me the main show's supposed to start a little before sunset. That's at eight, right?"

He knew that, every morning of my life, I check the tide tables.

I said, "Around eight, yeah. Seven-fifty-seven, to be precise."

Actually, the show had already started. The Cypress Ashram had become a mini-stadium. The stepped levels of seating were already half full, and more people were rivering in, trying to get as close as they could to the stage.

The stage was attached to an acoustic dome that looked like a giant clamshell. The first time I'd seen it, the theater had seemed to consist of nothing more than tile, wood and stucco, built at the edge of a cypress pond. What was not readily evident was that the structure was a technological marvel, loaded with computers, lights and sophisticated electronic equipment.

I remembered Carter McRae telling us that Shiva's show was better than anything we'd find in Vegas. I now got the first inkling of a confirmation.

The stage was bare, yet it was not bare. Standing, facing the growing audience, were three translucent men, twice normal height. They had glittering skin and flowing, brightly colored robes. Yet, you could look through them and see the wall beyond. One was Jesus — the standard image you see in children's Bibles. The other was of a smiling, then laughing, Buddha. Standing between them was an equally happy Bhagwan Shiva.

The men were animated. Walking. Hugging. Spreading their arms wide as if to embrace the audience.

Orbiting above the three was a perfect miniature solar system; nine planets revolving around a smoldering sun, the earth a brilliant, lucent blue-green. The planets orbited to the slow wash-and-draw sound of waves on a beach. The sound seemed to come from every direction — behind us, from the stage, from the tops of the cypress tress as well, even from the ground below.

As I stopped, trying to comprehend what it was I was seeing, what I was hearing, Tomlinson said, "They're holograms, man. Animated laser photos. And they got this whole place wired for sound. Disney World in the Everglades. Amazing."

We were standing at the top of the bowl of seats, near the life-sized bronze statue of Shiva.

The sound of the waves was hypnotic. If I allowed my mind to drift even for a moment, the pace of my own breathing began to match the rhythm of the waves.

I noticed that men and women in the stands were all sitting quietly, hands folded with palms upward in their laps, as if eager to join the rhythm, to give themselves over.

We stood and watched for a couple of minutes. As we did, a recording of Shiva's deep voice joined the sound of the waves. I listened to his voice say, "A hologram is a three-dimensional photograph created by lasers. Like all things, it possesses a spiritual lesson to be learned. To create a hologram, an object is first bathed in the light of a laser. Then a second laser beam is bounced off the reflected light of the first before a third beam is added.

"Three-dimensionality is not their only remarkable characteristic. If the hologram of an apple is cut in half and then illuminated by a laser, each half will still be found to contain the entire image of the apple. Every part of a hologram contains all the information possessed by the whole.

"The nature of a hologram provides us with a new way of viewing the nature of existence. Western science and religion have always labored under the bias that the best way to understand the physical world, whether a frog or an atom, is to dissect it and study it. Like our faith, our brotherhood, the hologram proves that separateness is an illusion. . . ."

As the recording continued, I said to Tomlinson, "He sounds like you."

Tomlinson replied, "Yeah, but do you know what the difference is? I live it. He *uses* it."

Apparently, even the wealthy residents of Sawgrass were attending Shiva's show. Or maybe they just went home; locked themselves away from the devoted.

The Big Cypress Restaurant had a few tables seated for dinner, but the Panther Bar, with its granite fireplace and walls adorned with skin-mounted fish, was nearly empty. Four men were sitting at a table, bottles of beer and a basket of nachos between them.

I was hoping to find Kurt behind the bar. On the phone, he'd evaded my questions about Izzy. In person, I'd be more persuasive.

I'd left Tomlinson back at the outdoor theater, next to Shiva's statue, where he was to meet Billie, Ginny Egret, James and the other board members of the Egret Seminoles. I told him I was going to visit the bar and later, if we couldn't find each other in the crowd, I'd meet him back at the truck.

As I walked away, he'd said, "Have a rum for me."

I didn't smile. "Nope. I've had enough."

So I was alone. Which is exactly what I wanted. But Kurt wasn't working. Instead, there was a haggard-looking woman in her early thirties — maybe younger — wearing an apron and sleeveless blouse, a butterfly tattoo visible on her right shoulder.

She didn't have the manicured look that I'd come to associate with Shiva's followers.

When I sat at the bar, she said, "What can I get for you, hon?"

I told her iced tea would be just fine, then I said, "Where's Kurt?"

Walking away, she said, "Give me just a second, hon." A moment later, when she returned with a pitcher of tea, she said, "Kurt's off tonight. The whole staff, they're all off because they got some big whoop-de-doo going on. It's like this religious thing they belong to. So we're all temps. We work through a Naples agency. The restaurant's only doing a limited seating, and they told me to close the bar at nine. Easter Sunday, the place should be packed, but look at it."

She shrugged in a way that passive-aggressive people do. "But I guess they don't want the business. And what do I care? It all pays the same to me. Accept for the tips. I'm not gonna make crap for tips."

I said, "You've got to wonder how some places stay in business."

"Can you believe it? A holiday weekend, they close the bar early."

I sipped my tea. "Too bad. This guy I met — his name's Izzy something — he told me to stop in, say hello to Kurt. We're both from the Boston area."

Kurt's name tag had read: *Lincoln, Mass.*

I added, "I don't suppose you've got a staff list back there. I could give him a call, say hello."

"They gave me a list just in case there's trouble, but it's not going to do you any good. They already told us. In staff housing, they don't got phones. So you can't call 'im."

I had my billfold out. I decided a twenty would make her suspicious, so I put a ten on the counter. "Can I have a look at the list? I'll walk over and surprise him."

Kurt's name was on the list. He was in Cell B, Apartment 103.

Izzy's name wasn't.

Sawgrass staff housing consisted of a circular village of small, modular apartments positioned in three clusters, at the center of which was a swimming pool and barbecue area.

The place looked deserted. I worried that I was too late; that Kurt Thompson was among those already taking seats at the outdoor theater. From the direction of the Cypress Ashram, I could hear a muffled heartlike pounding, as if hundreds of people were beating drums in unison.

The sun floated above the canopy of cypress trees. I checked my watch. It was 7:05 P.M.

The middle cluster of apartments was labeled B. I found 103 and touched the doorbell.

413

I waited through a long moment of silence before I heard a rustling within. I stepped back to let the door open, then I quickly stepped forward, blocking the doorway so that the door could not be closed.

Yep, Kurt was one of the higher-ups; a senior member in this strange church. He wore an orange toga with a ruby sash. His hair was brushed to a sheen, tan face glistening, and he held a towel in his hands, as if he'd just finished shaving.

When he saw me, realized who I was, his expression changed briefly from indifference to surprise, but he recovered quickly.

"Yes? May I help you?"

He said it in his infuriating, superior tone.

"Remember me, Kurt? On the phone, I told you I'd be here." I smiled broadly. "So here I am!"

"Is that supposed to be funny, sir? Just because I told you about the service doesn't mean I invited you. What I suggest is that you go to the restaurant and ask anyone. They can tell you how to get to the Cypress Ashram. Perhaps I'll see you there."

He tried to close the door, but I blocked it with my shoulder.

I said, "Naw, Kurt. I'm looking forward to going with you. We can have a little talk on the way. I'm really interested in the church. I've got lots of questions."

He'd heard about our fight with the Archangels. I could see it in his face, a mottled paling of skin: fear. "Mister, I'm not going to ask you again. Please leave immediately, or I'll call security. I'm late. I don't have time for this kind of silliness."

Once again, he tried to pull the door closed. When I blocked it again, he tried to push my shoulder away. I lunged forward and hit him so hard in the chest that he backpedaled across the room and fell backwards over the couch.

I stepped into the miniature living room, closed the door behind me and locked it with the deadbolt.

"Why are you *doing* this?"

Kurt was on one knee, getting to his feet. He held his hands up, palms out, as I walked toward him. I grabbed his left wrist with my right hand, yanked him to his feet, spinning him at the same time so that I was behind him. I had his left arm levered up between his shoulder blades, applying pressure, but not much.

"You're hurting me, goddamn you!"

Into his ear, I said, "Language, Kurt. Pretty rough language for a man dressed in a robe."

I was walking him across the room, moving slowly, in control, and then I pinned him against the wall.

"I want you to answer some questions. If you answer my questions, I won't hurt you, Kurt. If you don't answer, or if you lie to me, I *am* going to hurt you. I'm going to hurt you bad."

415

For emphasis, I took his left pinkie finger and twisted it.

"Stop. Please *stop!* You're going to break my fucking hand!"

I said, "That's right. One finger at a time. I'm going to break your hand."

Kurt, the aloof and superior bartender, suddenly became an eager, nonstop talker. Most people are strangers to violence, and so behave unpredictably, often oddly, when subjected to it.

He wanted to be my *friend*. He wanted to *understand* why I was interested in Izzy. When I told him, "He may have had something to do with a friend of mine who disappeared," Kurt's sympathetic expression said, No *wonder* you're upset.

Truth is, he was terrified.

He sat across from me in a chair and told me about Izzy Kline. For a time, Izzy had been in charge of organizing church security. Then he became Shiva's special assistant — Kurt wasn't certain why.

"I've been with the church for six years," Kurt said, "and Izzy has always been kind of a mysterious figure in the brotherhood. We almost never see him at the Ashrams or services. He's not a believer and doesn't pretend to be. He spends a lot of time away. What he does, I don't know. But he's close to the Teacher — our Bhagwan."

I said, "I've heard rumors that if someone

pisses off Shiva, he finds ways to get even. Maybe that he's even had some people killed. Would that be part of Izzy's role?"

Kurt began to move uncomfortably in his chair. He'd been maintaining a kind of fraternity-boy eye contact. No longer. "Our Teacher is a man of peace. He's one of history's greatest prophets. I've heard those same rumors — and there is Ashram scripture that tells us that the souls of many are worth the lives of a few. But I don't believe our Teacher would resort to violence. I've never believed it and never will."

"But if he did, would that be part of Izzy's job?"

After a long moment, Kurt said, "Yes. That would definitely be something that Izzy would do."

"Where's he now?"

"I saw Izzy this morning. I was surprised because I didn't see him here last night. He was driving a big U-Haul truck."

I said, "A U-Haul? Why?"

"I can't say for certain, but it's almost impossible — we're all very close — to keep a secret from the brotherhood. I heard that Izzy resigned his position. That he was leaving for Europe. So maybe he had some personal possessions here and he was moving them."

"When's he supposed to leave?"

Still eager to please, Kurt said he didn't know, adding, "If I knew, I'd tell you. I really *would.*"

chapter twenty-eight

I was right about the drums.

Several dozen men and women, wearing green or white robes, formed a semicircle on the highest steps of the amphitheater. They held skin drums between their knees, and used their hands to pound them in a slow, deliberate rhythm. About one beat every three or four seconds.

The rhythm reminded me of night markers flashing on the intracoastal waterway. A similar space of time.

The percussion of the drums vibrated through the ground, through the speaker system, through the tops of cypress trees and into a bronze-bright late-afternoon sky.

As I got closer, I could see that there wasn't an empty seat in the theater. Had to be more than a thousand people.

Shiva's people were recording the event, too. There were no fewer than four videographers moving among the crowd, holding small, digitized cameras to their eyes.

Despite the crowd, the little Seminole contingent was easy for me to pick out: four or five men and women in traditional dress, seated on the aisle in the front row, their rainbow-colored shirts and blouses much brighter than the robes worn by the people around them.

I didn't see Tomlinson, though. And it didn't look as if Billie Egret was among them, either.

A minute or so later, I realized why. On the outskirts of the arena was a grassy area landscaped with cypress and oak. It had a good view of the stage. There they both stood among trees, several people nearby.

Karlita. She was with them, too — and looking reasonably normal in jeans and a white blouse, her long black hair braided like a rope down her back.

The three of them, I noticed, were holding hands, joined in a chain with six or seven others.

Billie was the first to notice me approaching. She nodded at me, her eyes intense, then nodded toward the amphitheater.

Shiva was on center stage. He wore an elaborate purple robe with orange, green and white bands on the sleeves. His turban was golden, and he sat in full lotus position on a red cushion the size of a mattress. Behind him, in a semicircle, were several dozen men and women, all in orange robes, carrying candles and what appeared to be bundles of red sticks, walking in slow step to the pace of the beating drums. One of them, I noted, was the attractive blond teenager named Kirsten.

She and the others were filing off the stage. They were leaving Shiva alone.

The laser hologram of the solar system was still being projected. It was eerily beautiful. It now revolved above Shiva and around him.

On a small platform in front of the stage, another videographer had a much larger camera mounted on a tripod. It was fixed on Shiva. Perhaps they were broadcasting the event. Maybe some kind of in-house cable production.

As the drums pounded, and the orange robes marched down the steps of the amphitheater, Shiva's amplified voice spoke to his audience live for the first time since I'd arrived. In the momentary silence between drumbeats, he said, *We will* . . .

In the next silence, more than a thousand voices replied: *Move the earth.* . . .

Boom!

We will . . .

Boom!

Move the earth.

Boom!

I will . . .

Boom!

Make the earth move!

Billie Egret caught my eye again and motioned with her head. *Come closer.*

She was standing between Tomlinson and Karlita, both of whom, I could now see, stood with eyes closed, their breathing shallow, as if

420

they, too, were in trances. Billie then joined their hands, stepped away from the little chain of people and walked to meet me

"Why don't you come and join us?" she whispered. "We're trying to fight him. His power. It won't be long until sunset."

I shook my head: *No,* but in a way that also apologized. I whispered back, "What's supposed to happen at sunset?"

"He's told my aunts and uncles that he can do it again. Make the earth move. Like last Sunday, the earthquake. They're ready to join him now. He's almost got them convinced."

I said, "*Earthquake?* You're . . . you're not *serious.* The idea that he had anything to do with that little tremor we had is absurd. Plus, why would they care?"

The woman took my arm in hers — Tomlinson was right. Because of my relationship with her father, Joseph, her acceptance of me was instant and seemed unconditional. She said, "It's because of something that no outsider would know about. Or understand. Have you ever heard of Tecumseh?"

I said, "Yes. The Indian leader. Most people have."

She was holding my arm tight.

"In eighteen eleven, he tried to organize all the southern tribes to help fight the whites. On November sixteenth, in central Alabama, he told our people that, one moon cycle later, he would stomp his foot, and the earth would move. It would be a sign to join him."

Still keeping her voice low, she added, "That prophecy spread across the country, village to village. It's well recorded. It *happened.* Exactly twenty-eight days later, the New Madrid earthquakes began. The worst in American history. He was also a genius, a prophet. He was a Shawnee; an Ohio tribe. What almost no one knows is that Tecumseh's mother was core Maskókî — some called us Creek. She was what they'd call a *Seminole.* So it's part of Seminole legend. To my aunts and uncles, an earthquake is a tremendously powerful sign."

From the amphitheater, the chant continued:

We will . . .

Boom!

Move the earth.

Boom!

I will . . .

Boom!

Make the earth move!

I said, "Then you've got nothing to worry about. Because there's no way a human being can cause an earthquake. Shiva, the Bhagwan, whatever you want to call him, that fraud can sit down there and meditate, chant, whatever he wants to do, all night long. The ground's not going to shake just because he promises that he can —"

I stopped, feeling a sudden, dizzying sense of suspicion, then of realization. I said, "Wait —

when did Shiva make his prediction about the earthquake. Was it prior to Sunday?"

"Long before that," she replied. "Remember me telling you about the meeting he had with us? About the wooden masks he told us he'd seen in a dream, and carved himself? That's when he said that he'd also dreamed he would one day make the Everglades tremble. As a sign; a sign that we should join together. He pretended that he didn't know anything about Tecumseh or our connection with him. Which I never believed."

Now I was shaking. My mouth was dry. I felt a flooding sense of panic and urgency. I was walking toward Tomlinson, my brain connecting what had seemed to be random events, meaningless sentence fragments:

A man Izzy's size standing beside a maintenance truck in an abandoned limestone quarry, leaving behind an empty bag of ammonium nitrate, and a couple of blobs of goo that smelled of fuel oil.

Me asking Billie if someone was blasting in the area. I'd asked because there is a commercial explosive jelly called Thermex. It consists of little more than ammonium nitrate and diesel fuel.

I remembered Izzy tape-recording a furious Tomlinson. Remembered Tomlinson telling me that he was getting e-mail from manufacturers of blasting caps and explosives, and from eco-terrorist organizations. Remembered Tomlinson saying that, if it was a joke, he didn't think it was very funny.

I remembered Detective Podraza telling me that, in an abduction-murder, getting rid of the body is always the biggest problem. How can you destroy the evidence? Remembered Kurt, the bartender, telling me that he'd seen Izzy that morning, driving a U-Haul.

Walking faster now, I said to Billie, "Shiva's prophecy. What time is it supposed to happen? The earthquake."

"At sunset. That's just a few minutes from now."

I checked my watch. Seven-forty P.M. We had seventeen minutes until sunset.

From the amphitheater, the chanting seemed louder.

We will . . .

Boom!

Move the earth.

Boom!

I will . . .

Boom!

Make the earth move!

"Billie. I've got to get back to that rock quarry. The place where we saw the white truck. Did James come in his airboat?"

She'd stopped following me. "Marion? What's wrong with you? Why're you acting so strange?"

"Did he come in his airboat!" I said it so loud that she jumped.

424

"*Yes.* It's right over there. At the edge of the cypress head."

Tomlinson was still standing, eyes closed, holding Karlita's hand. I grabbed him roughly and turned him around. I said, "Let's go. I need you."

"Doc? Why? I can't go. Not now."

Karlita had turned her head; was staring at me. "It's *you.* I want to go. *We belong.*"

I told her, "Not a chance," as I took Tomlinson by the shoulders and shook him. "Damn it, I need your help. I think I know where Sally is!"

I couldn't figure out how to get the airboat started.

Tomlinson and I had sprinted far ahead of Billie; found the big twenty-one-foot airboat banked at the edge of the sawgrass. On the boat's twin aft rudders, its name, *Chekika's Shadow,* glowed a metallic crimson in the late sunlight.

We were both aboard, Tomlinson in a lower seat, me standing at the stainless-steel control panel where there was an ignition key tied to an oversized float, and three rows of unmarked toggle switches.

When I turned the key, nothing happened.

There were twin automotive batteries beneath the captain's chair. I checked to see if there was a cutoff switch. There was. I twisted the dial to "On" and tried the key again.

Nothing.

"*Goddamn* it!"

I looked my watch. Saw that my hands were still shaking: 7:46 P.M.

Tomlinson said, "Maybe I should run back and ask Billie. Or try to find James."

I'd refused Billie's help, and her offer to fetch James because, if I was right, and I allowed them to come with me, I might well be responsible for their deaths.

I answered, "We don't have time."

I took a deep breath, told myself to stay calm and to think. All those years with Tucker Gatrell, I'd learned more than most about airboats. Some were powered by standard car engines, others by aircraft engines.

Then I realized: *That's the problem.*

All the toggle switches were flipped down — the off position.

I flipped each switch momentarily, experimentally, until I heard the steady hum of what I guessed to be an electronic fuel pump.

At least two of the toggles had to be magneto switches.

They have to be.

I flipped them until I found the right combination, turned the key, and the huge engine fired like a mini-explosion.

I swung myself up into the captain's chair, pulled on the headphones. Tomlinson had done the same, his scraggly hair sticking out. I said into the transmitter, "Hold on tight.

It's been awhile."

I heard him reply, "Let 'er roll, brother!"

I touched my foot to the accelerator pedal, pushed the control stick forward, and the boat pivoted to the right in a fast, tight circle. When we were bow-out, the boat straightened itself as I gradually backed off the stick, accelerating like a dragster as I pressed the pedal toward the deck.

I had to keep reminding myself: To turn right, stick forward. To turn left, stick back. At sixty-plus miles per hour, we went sledding through sawgrass, southward.

To the west, only a few degrees above the horizon, the sun was the smoky orange of a hunter's moon. Because it was precisely bisected by a band of purple stratus clouds, there was a ringed effect — as if Saturn were ablaze and spinning on a collision course toward Earth. The harsh light flattened itself across the prairie, horizon to horizon, turning feathered sawgrass to gold, turning the mushroom shapes of distant cypress heads to silver.

I checked my watch once again: 7:48 P.M.

I'd just returned my attention to the trail ahead when I felt the first tremor rock the boat — an explosion so close the hull was bounced by the seismic shock. It lifted us up, then slammed us hard to earth.

In my earphones, I heard Tomlinson cry, "What the hell was *that?*" Then: "Oh, dear God, that was it. We're too late. If you're *right,*

427

if you're right, that's it, we're done."

I said, "Maybe. But I'm not stopping now."

I steered the airboat toward the abandoned limestone quarry, into the heart of the Everglades.

chapter twenty-nine

izzy

Izzy finished dialing the number he had saved months ago on his Palm Pilot, then checked his watch: 7:49 P.M.

It was Charles Carter's private cell number, the wealthy banker who'd dedicated his life — and his money — to the Church of Ashram.

What a moron.

Miami International Airport is built in the shape of a horseshoe, Dolphin and Flamingo parking barns in the middle. Izzy was in Terminal H, the Crown Room, sitting in one of the secluded cubicles provided for members who want to use the Internet or make phone calls.

His membership was under the name of Michael Mollen, same as the name on the passport he was using. Once he got to Paris, after he'd spent a week or two relaxing, letting things cool down, he'd fly to London, then to Managua with a different passport, Craig Skaar.

He liked that name.

Izzy had his Dell laptop plugged in, signed onto the Web page of Bank Austria, Georgetown, Grand Cayman Island. He'd already checked his e-mails, and updated himself on the local Miami news: HEIRESS WIDOW STILL MISSING.

Not exactly. But soon. Very soon.

That made him smile.

He had a Bloody Mary on the desk to his left — one of the reasons he preferred Delta and loved the Crown Room. Free drinks, all you wanted, and bar snacks that weren't too bad. Even on this Easter Sunday, it wasn't crowded.

As he finished dialing, he placed his hands on the keyboard of his laptop, and used his shoulder to cradle the phone against his ear.

Carter answered immediately; knew who it was going to be.

Into the phone, Izzy said, "Has the service started yet?"

Used the code word: *Service*.

Hearing drumming in the background, and impassioned chanting, Izzy listened to Carter exclaim, "Two of them so far. Unbelievable! Magnificent!"

Izzy said, "Well, you have four more to go, and the last one's a biggie." Then he added, "Carter — I didn't call to chat."

As Izzy listened, he typed an account number into a blank rectangle provided by the Bank Austria Web page. Then he typed in the password that Carter gave him. The password was *Tecumseh*.

Hilarious.

But there it was. The account opened right up: Isidore T. Kline, who, as of that instant, had access to more money than he'd ever had in his life.

Now hearing what sounded like thunder in the background, then something else — screams? — Izzy said to Carter, "Hey, just for the record, I always thought you were a fucking idiot."

He hung up the phone, immediately changed the password, then he closed the laptop.

His flight to Paris was already boarding.

Standing in line, waiting to hand his first-class ticket to the attendant, Izzy couldn't make himself relax. He'd had a couple of beers with lunch at Cheers in the main terminal, then three Bloody Marys at the Crown Room.

They didn't even dent the tension in him. Until he was in the plane, off the ground, some cop or Fed could come up any second, tap him on the shoulder and say, "We need to ask you a few questions."

As long as he was still in Miami, still in U.S. airspace, it was all right there with him.

That fucking Italian!

The Italian, surprising him the way he did, had nearly screwed up all those months of planning. Izzy was a perfectionist. Had always been a perfectionist. He hated improvising last-minute changes. But he'd had to do it. And until just now, when he'd successfully received the account number and password from Carter, nothing had gone the way he'd wanted.

On Friday night, getting the two men taped and loaded into the truck of the pimpmobile was a nightmare. He'd been scared shitless that some security cop, or some neighbor, was going to come snooping around.

So how should he do it? Drive them to some secluded place, and pop them? Or risk the noise and do it ghetto-style, like someone high on crack who really didn't give a damn who they killed or how, just as long as they found money for drugs?

Even with his mouth taped, the old man was bawling like a baby when Izzy touched the Beretta to the back of his head.

But not the big guinea. With those black eyes of his, the guinea had looked at Izzy like he would have ripped him apart and eaten him if he could have gotten his hands free. One scary son-of-a-bitch.

No fear, either. Not a whimper. Even as Izzy put the barrel behind his ear, and said, "I'm gonna count to three real slow, then your fucking head's coming off."

The guinea had shrugged, like he didn't much care.

It took the pleasure out of it; the power-feeling it normally gave Izzy.

Same with the Merry Widow. She'd been the biggest disappointment. Turned out she wasn't so merry. Like the wop, she wasn't afraid, either. Not after she got herself under control, anyway.

For most of Saturday, he'd kept her in the back of the U-Haul, tied and gagged. He had so much work to do! But, every now and then, he'd pull into some secluded spot, remove the gag, and try to have a little fun.

She wouldn't cooperate. Even after he'd slapped her a few times, she'd steady herself on her knees, eyes turned skyward, repeating over and over, "The Lord is my shepherd. I shall not want. He maketh me to lie down in green pastures. He restoreth my soul . . ."

Which sure as hell ruined the mood.

Plus, she wasn't afraid. Nothing he did, nothing he threatened, frightened her.

Cold bitch.

So, as far as enjoying himself, the whole deal had been a bust. But that was okay. He had Nicaragua to look forward to. His own tropical island paradise, and plenty of money now to enjoy it.

When the attendant took his ticket, and passed it through the scanner, Izzy felt his heart rate increase — he'd been worried they'd cull him out into the security line. Not that he had anything on him to hide. It was the delay he dreaded.

Now, though, he grinned at the attendant, shouldered his briefcase, and walked down the ramp, feeling a little spring in his step.

One Bloody Mary later, Izzy was lounging in

his first-class seat, looking out the starboard window as the plane lifted off, ascending and banking. He was looking west into a blazing aftermath of a sunset sky. He could see domino rows of houses that thinned, then ended abruptly on a demarcation of unbroken light that he knew was the edge of the Everglades. It was a golden void connected to a golden sky, prairie and sky linked by a thin black tether of horizon.

He checked his watch.

Eight-twenty P.M.

He'd left the Merry Widow, Sally Minster, with her hands and legs tied, mouth taped, in the front seat of the U-Haul, doors locked, engine running so to produce the necessary voltage to detonate the barrels of ammonium nitrate loaded into the rear.

Hey — if she'd been more cooperative, he'd have gone easier on her.

So much for the evidence.

The Feds, though, would be all over it. The underground stuff would be harder to find. But chunks of a U-Haul lying around?

Too bad for the supercilious hippie. Too bad for Jerry Singh.

Izzy had grown to despise the man.

Now he held up one finger to get the attention of the lean, redheaded flight attendant — service was always so much better in first class. He smiled his lady's-man smile, dimples showing, as he said, "When you get some time, how about another Bloody Mary?"

Then Izzy Kline sat back and released a long, slow breath, the tension flowing out of him, replaced by a feeling of liberation so powerful that it seemed a mix of serenity and deliverance.

chapter thirty

We rounded a stand of cypress, the hull of *Chekika's Shadow* skidding, then catching on its starboard chine. A half-mile or so ahead, I could see the elevated rim of the abandoned limestone quarry.

We were back in karst country. For millions of years, rain and flowing water had created conduits, caverns out of rock; a slow geologic cataclysm that showed in the gray limestone piled high above sawgrass.

In my earphones, I heard Tomlinson yell, "There it is! We've got to go faster, man. Can't you go faster?"

No. Running at sixty miles per hour in an airboat is like turning a boat with a flat hull into a hurricane wind. I'd already come close to wobbling out of control a couple of times. Any faster and I feared we'd hydroplane into the air, then pitch-pole to disaster.

Within the last four minutes, we'd felt the boat rock with two, perhaps three or more tremors. Hard to tell for certain, because these explosions — and that's undoubtedly what they were — seemed to come from behind us, at opposing spots on the perimeter of the outdoor amphitheater, Cypress Ashram.

Long ago, I'd spent months training with various explosives, and I'd used them, when required, for several years afterwards. Pros with explosives have zero tolerance when it comes to the people whom they teach. You learn, you remember or you get the hell out. So I'd learned.

Izzy Kline had, apparently, bracketed the amphitheater with underground charges. He'd staggered the timers to go off every one or two minutes. With the shock of each tremor, Tomlinson would cry out as if in pain, but I found the pattern of explosions encouraging. If the first explosion occurred at 7:48 P.M., the last explosion would almost certainly occur as predicted by Shiva — at sunset. Maybe a minute or two later, just for better effect.

I checked my watch again: 7:52 P.M.

If I was right, we had five minutes. With luck, we had a little longer.

Against my better judgment, I pushed the accelerator closer to the floor and held it there. I felt my cheeks begin to flutter with wind torque; felt the hull beneath me rise as if elevated by the razor edge of sawgrass.

Standing between us and the limestone quarry was a marsh of swamp maples, cattails and arrow plants. The trees and cattails were coated in golden light, casting black shadows eastward. If there were old lighter pine stumps in there, or hidden cypress knees, and we collided, we were dead. Even so, I kept the accelerator mashed flat, right hand sweaty on the joystick.

Instead of hitting stumps, though, we flushed a hidden populace of wildlife. Two gigantic gators bucked out of our way, one of them hitting the hull so hard with its tail that he nearly flipped us. A cloud of snowy egrets flushed before us, too: white wading birds that angled away, banking, then igniting as a single, flaming pointillism in the burnished light.

In my earphones, I heard Tomlinson say, "Panthers! Two of them!"

There they were: two flaxen-colored animals the size of retrievers, running fast, their long tails swinging like rudders.

I kept my eyes fixed on the rim of the abandoned quarry, and noted that there was something different about the area. It took me a moment to identify the change, and then connect it with what Billie Egret had already told me.

The previous week, the quarry had been on the edge of a shallow marsh. Now the marsh was dry but for a small, crater-shaped lake. The lake was several hundred yards from the quarry, at the terminus of a descending ridge of limestone that was overgrown with scrub grass and small melaleucas. The perimeter of the lake was as round as the rim of a volcano. It held water that mirrored a molten sky.

James Tiger had also told us about it. *Lost*

Lake. The lake that was visible only when the 'Glades were nearly dry. The lake to which, Billie had said, tarpon had returned. She'd wanted me to see it.

Maybe I would. Later.

Still traveling near top speed, I angled the airboat toward the access road that climbed the ridge. Then I turned hard onto the road, banging our way up marl and limestone, the hull shuddering. As we breached the top of the ridge, Tomlinson was already shouting, "It's there. The truck's there!"

A medium-sized U-Haul, with a bed that extended over the cab, was backed in tight against the wall of limestone where, a week before, we'd seen the white GMC pickup.

Sliding to a stop, I yelled, "We'll gut the hull if I try to jump across that rock. Stay here; I'll run for it."

But Tomlinson had already bailed while the boat was still moving, throwing his earphones off, sprinting hard down the incline toward the truck.

I looked at my watch: 7:54 P.M.

Three minutes until sunset.

Tomlinson has always been faster than I. Now, though, in the worst shape of my life, he left me far behind as he sprinted the hundred yards or so to the U-Haul.

"Doc, she's here! She's in the truck!" He was pulling at the door handle on the driver's side.

It was locked. Still pulling at the door, he banged on the window. "Sally. Are you okay? *Sally!*"

He ran around to the other door, saying, "Oh God, I think she's dead!"

I ran harder, feeling an appalling sense of loss and failure; was also aware that, in three minutes or so — maybe less — the truck was going to blow up. I'd made Tomlinson come with me. I was responsible, and now I was going to get him killed, too.

Still running, I yelled, "Are you sure she's dead? Get *away* from there. I'll try to get her out."

He was pulling at the passenger door now — it was also locked. I leaned and picked-up a baseball-sized chunk of limestone and was coming around to the driver's side of the truck as Tomlinson, banging on the opposite window, yelled, "Sally! We're going to get you out." After a pause, he then said, "Doc, she's *alive.*"

And there she was, my friend from childhood, lying naked on the seat, her hands and feet tied, her mouth and most of her face covered with duct tape, a purple swelling on her left temple, her jade-blue eyes wide, tears welling — an expression of joyous disbelief — staring back at me.

I yelled to her, "Close your eyes!"

The chunk of limestone broke in my hand when I smashed it against the door's window, but the glass shattered. It became a pliant, plastic shield. I used the remaining chunk of rock to knock the window open, calling to Tomlinson, "Check the back of the truck. If it's not locked, I might be able to disconnect the detonator."

Unconsciously, I'd already assessed the situation; the steps I'd have to take. The truck's engine was running — there could be only one reason: voltage. If the bed was full of ammonium nitrate, Kline had probably rigged some kind of high-voltage detonator to back up, or assist, a standard, timer-rigged blasting-cap-type detonator.

With the truck's engine running, there would be a small boom followed by a horrendous explosion. Shut the engine off, the nitrate would still blow, but a markedly smaller portion of it.

Tomlinson yelled, "The back doors are padlocked! I can't get in."

Damn it.

I used my hands to rip the sheet of glass away, reached in, found the lock and yanked the door open. Tomlinson was already behind me as I took Sally by the shoulders and pulled her out. He took her gently into his arms as I said, "Try to find some cover. Get her away from here."

I jumped behind the steering wheel, and reached to shut off the engine — but the key wasn't in the switch. It took me a long, dull moment to realize why: Kline had broken the key off in the ignition. If the woman managed to get her hands free, he didn't want her to be able to foil the explosion.

I glanced to the west. The sun was gone; vanished behind a scrim of distant cypress trees. I looked at my watch: 7:56 P.M. Less than a minute remained.

Feeling a sickening sense of unreality, I considered opening the hood and disconnecting the battery. But that would not disable the secondary timer switch. At this distance, any explosion, big or small, would kill all three of us anyway.

That's when it came to me. What I had to do.

Suddenly, I didn't feel sickened or frightened anymore.

Tomlinson had Sally cradled in his arms, struggling beneath her weight, trying to get her away from the truck. I called, "Stay here. Get down and cover her with your body." Then I put the truck in drive, floored the accelerator and began to bounce and jolt my way up the access road.

The back of the truck was loaded to maximum. I could feel the weight in the sluggish, teetering way the truck handled. As I drove, I checked to see if the transmission was in four-wheel drive — it was — then tried to calculate how far I'd have to move the truck so that, when it did explode, Sally and Tomlinson wouldn't be hurt.

You can't get far enough in sixty seconds.

That was the inescapable truth. Which is

when another idea popped into my brain.

This detonator system is electrical.

It was my only chance. *Our* only chance.

When I got to the top of the quarry, I turned off the road, onto the ridge, and steered directly toward Lost Lake. It was a couple of hundred yards away. The water color had changed from molten red to molten bronze, and the lake's surface seesawed before my eyes as the truck's tires banged over rocks and small trees. Traveling at thirty . . . then forty miles per hour, the steering wheel vibrated and bucked so hard beneath my hands that it was a struggle to maintain control.

Seven fifty-seven P.M.

Did I hear an electrical click from behind me?

Still accelerating, I scrunched down in my seat, expecting to feel a blinding white pain that marked the explosion, and the end of my own life. I was still ducked low, accelerator floored, when one of the front right tires blew.

Bang.

Stunned, I released the steering wheel momentarily, and the world tilted crazily as the truck careened sideways, then rolled.

Suddenly, water was pouring through the broken window, gushing like a river, filling the cab. Then I was underwater, in a familiar, slow-motion world.

For a few moments, the escalating speed of

the truck's descent toward the bottom of the lake kept me mashed to the roof of the cab. I reached, found the steering wheel. I pulled myself toward the broken window.

I have wide shoulders. For a terrible, claustrophobic moment, I got stuck in the window, but managed to bull my way through. Then I was ascending toward what appeared as a silver lens, thirty or forty feet above . . . slowly ascending, exhaling bubbles, right arm extended toward the surface out of old habit.

When I breached the surface, I sucked in air, filling my lungs. Then I paused, sculling, for a reflective moment. If the water hadn't shorted the electrical system, the nitrate might still explode.

I looked at my watch: I saw 7:59 P.M. become 8 P.M.

Not likely.

I began to do a relaxed breaststroke toward shore — and got another unexpected shock when several big fins cut the surface ahead of me, then disappeared.

Sharks?

I was still spooked from my recent encounter. Then I smiled.

No. The tarpon, a prehistoric fish, can supplement its oxygen supply by rolling at the surface and gulping surface air.

Billie Egret was right. Tarpon had returned to Lost Lake. Tarpon had come back to the Everglades.

People were screaming.

Why?

The screams we heard were coming from the direction of the outdoor amphitheater. Men and women yelling, falsetto shrieks, their voices echoing through the shadows of cypress trees.

I'd driven the airboat up onto the manicured grass of Sawgrass, as close to the parking area as I could get.

Sally kept telling us, "I'm okay, I'm okay. There's no need to hurry."

But she wasn't okay. She was faint from dehydration, already starting to cramp. She had a swelling subdural hematoma on her temple, and she was probably in shock, too.

And she kept repeating, "The Lord was with me. I was never afraid. All the things that creep tried to do to me; all the things he said. I was never afraid. The Lord put His hand in mine and never let go."

It was like a dream, she said, opening her eyes and seeing us. For a moment, she thought she was in heaven.

All good boat captains keep a little bag stowed aboard, well stocked for emergencies. Billy Tiger was a good skipper, and I found his emergency bag in the forward hatch. Along with packages of freeze-dried food, a first-aid kit, candles and bug repellent, I found two half gallons of bottled water, and a military-issue blanket.

Tomlinson tended to Sally, wrapping her in the blanket, helping her hold the half-gallon bottle so she could gulp the water down.

I ran the boat. Our return to Sawgrass was not nearly as fast as our trip out, but I didn't tarry. We needed to get Sally to the hospital. And I was eager to confront Jerry Singh.

Sally's physical description of the man who assaulted her, and who also murdered Frank and his landlord, left no doubt that it was Izzy Kline — Bhagwan Shiva's personal assistant. So I wanted to find Kline. I wanted to find him *tonight*. I wanted to get to him, snatch him, take him to some lonely spot, then eliminate him.

It was irrational. I knew that. Contemplating revenge is always irrational. Besides that, anyone smart enough to simulate an earthquake is smart enough to run far and fast after committing at least two murders and attempting a third.

The bartender said he'd heard Kline was going to Europe — probably a red herring. But I didn't doubt that Kline was leaving for somewhere.

The last time she'd seen him, Sally told us, was late that morning. She said he'd smiled at her and said, "Give my regards to St. Peter," and slammed the truck door, timers set, engine running.

So he was probably out of the state. Maybe already out of the country.

If anyone knew Kline's whereabouts, though,

it would be the man Tomlinson called the Non-Bhagwan.

I was eager to look into Shiva's face and make him talk. So I steered a rhumb line toward Sawgrass, running at speed.

I watched the sunset sky fade to bronze, then pearl, as the far horizon absorbed light. To the east, the vanished sun still illuminated the peaks of towering cumulous clouds. A commercial airliner, banking away from Miami International, became an isolated reflector, mirror-bright, connected to a silver contrail. Below, white birds became gray as they glided toward shadowed cypress heads to roost.

Tomlinson was in the seat below me, holding Sally. Every now and then, he'd stroke her blond hair. Her hand would find his, and squeeze.

Now, back at Sawgrass, I switched off the engine of *Chekika's Shadow*, swung down out of my seat and helped Tomlinson get a wobbly Sally Carmel on solid ground.

"We've got to find something better than this blanket," she told us. "I can't let anyone else see me naked."

After what she'd been through, her modesty was touching.

That's when all three of us grew silent, our brains trying to translate and identify the strange, distant sounds coming to us through cypress trees.

Terror has a tone; an unmistakable pitch. We were hearing the screams of terrified people.

I said, "It sounds like there's a riot going on over there."

Tomlinson waited for a few moments, head cocked, listening, before he replied, "Something's happened. Something powerful. I can feel it, man."

We could also hear the wail of distant sirens.

As we walked out of the trees, we could see people running. Men and women in their bright robes; some in regular clothes, too. Some seemed to be running aimlessly, as if panicked or crazed. Most, though, were running toward the parking lot where a line of cars had bottlenecked at the exit. Horns blaring, some drivers were cutting cross-country to escape the line and get back to the main road.

One thing was clear — people were fleeing the area out of fear.

Holding Sally between us, we walked against the flow of people toward the amphitheater. We headed that way partly out of curiosity — what was happening? — but mostly because we wanted to find Billie or James. They both had cell phones, and I wanted to notify law enforcement just as soon as possible. Kline might be at an airport right now, waiting to fly out.

I also wanted to call an EMS chopper for Sally. I'd checked her eyes. Her pupils weren't dilated or fixed, but that didn't guarantee that she hadn't suffered a concussion.

As we approached, we could see that the amphitheater had emptied. To the right, though, off in the cluster of trees where I'd first found Tomlinson, the Egret Seminoles had gathered, their colorful shirts and blouses dulled by the fading light. Karlita was with them.

She walked toward us, saying, "I'm sorry, Tomlinson. I know you don't approve, but we had no choice."

Behind her, in a somber tone, Billie Egret said to us, "He's gone. The Everglades took him. It had to be. If you give bad, you get bad in return. If you take, you have to give — and Shiva, he took *souls*."

None of which made any sense to me until I looked where Billie was now pointing. The amphitheater's concentric levels of seating remained. But where the stage and acoustic dome had once stood, there was now . . .

I had to stare to be sure, brain scanning for explanation.

. . . where the stage and acoustic dome had once stood, there was now a circular lake, water roiled and murky, lots of trash and flotsam on the surface.

Billie told us, "When the first tremors started, the Ashram followers were so excited. I thought they'd won. I thought Shiva had won. But then, after the third tremor, chunks of the dome began to fall. Then the whole stage collapsed and fell, like going down a waterfall. The earth collapsed beneath it. A sink-hole."

Karlita added, "People were terrified. They panicked. It was frightening to watch."

His voice subdued, perhaps in awe, Tomlinson asked, "When it happened, was he alone? Was Shiva the only one on stage?"

"Yes. He was alone. I wish you had been here to witness the . . . *power* of it."

We *would* witness it. Worldwide, anyone with a TV could witness what happened that Easter Sunday over and over because Shiva's film crew had captured it on video. The segment became standard fare for reality-based disaster shows: Jerry Singh — Bhagwan Shiva — in his purple robes, still leading his followers in that metonymic chant.

We will . . .

Boom!

Move the earth.

Boom!

I will . . .

Boom!

Make the earth move!

Then there is a close-up of Singh grinning triumphantly as the camera lens begins to vibrate with one . . . two . . . three earth tremors . . . his followers cheering but still chanting; chanting faster now:

We will . . .

Boom!

Move the earth.

450

The close-up continues as Shiva's expression changes from joy to a kind of stunned surprise as chunks of stucco begin to fall on him from the acoustic dome. He'd been sitting in full lotus position, but he gets quickly to his feet, perplexed.

Then all color drains from his face — an illustration of fear, then horror, as the rear of the stage collapses. The initial collapse created a momentary, marble incline, water already boiling up to take it.

The last shot shows Shiva clawing desperately, trying to keep from sliding into the pit below. He's screaming something, but there's so much peripheral noise, his words are indecipherable.

Above him, the laser hologram of the solar system continues to orbit, unaffected.

Then he is gone; the stage, dome, the prophet of Ashram, all swallowed up by a flooding darkness.

Three days later, *The Miami Herald* reported that a charter captain, his boat loaded with tourist scuba divers, found Shiva's body floating off Marathon and Molasses Reef, more than a hundred miles south of Sawgrass.

Geologists from the University of Florida provided an explanation. The sinkhole created by the series of explosions had collapsed into an underground river — the Long Key Formation. The river had swept Shiva's body along beneath sawgrass, swamp, mangrove fringe and

451

all of Florida Bay, before jettisoning him into open sea.

Billie Egret had a more succinct explanation for me: *"Reciprocity."*

chapter thirty-one

Eleven days later, on Thursday, the first day of May, two FBI agents came to the marina, asking for Tomlinson. They had a warrant to search *No Mas*, and they impounded his computer.

Aboard his sailboat, in the icebox, they found a sandwich bag filled with what appeared to be cannabis.

The agents used the discovery as leverage. They told Tomlinson that they were investigating what may have been an eco-terrorist bombing at Sawgrass in the Everglades. They said they had cause to believe that he might have been a participant. If he cooperated, talked freely, they'd forget they found the marijuana. If he didn't, he was going to jail *now*.

He requested a few minutes alone with me before he decided.

"What'll happen if they arrest me?"

"Ask a lawyer, not me."

"But I *am* asking you."

I said, "If they arrest you, you'll be taken to the jail in downtown Fort Myers. Tomorrow, you'll have your first court appearance, where the judge will consider bail — which you won't get. Not if they have you pegged as an eco-terrorist. Then you'll go back to jail until your hearing, where you'll be formally charged. After that, you'll go back to jail until your trial's over, which will be a very long time. Call an attorney."

He said, "I think I'll talk with them. They've got to know it was all Izzy Kline."

I told him, "Call an attorney! That's exactly what you should do."

He thought about that for a moment, twisting a lock of hair with his long, nervous fingers. "I don't know. Jail might be kind of peaceful. It's getting worse and worse, you know."

He meant the number of daily visitors the marina now received; devotees of *Tomlinsonism*.

Long before the events of Easter Sunday, unknown to any of us, several of Shiva's own followers — now former followers — had been deeply touched by Tomlinson's paper. It was they who were now spreading the word, via the Internet, that Tomlinson had been in attendance at the Cypress Ashram that amazing night. That he had personally exposed Bhagwan Shiva for the fraud he was.

It was also Tomlinson's powerful aura, they suggested, that had catalyzed Shiva's doom. So, ironically, Tomlinson had won the devotion of a growing number of people who had once followed the only man that I feel he genuinely despised.

"Get a lawyer," I repeated.

But Tomlinson was shaking his head. "Nope. I'm going to sit down and tell them the truth. Frankly, I'm pulling for some jail time."

He didn't get it. Two weeks later, one of the agents phoned him, said that he was no longer considered a suspect, and he was free to travel anywhere he wanted.

The next day, Tomlinson slipped his mooring before sunrise, and sailed for Key West.

I'd been carrying on an investigation of my own. Quietly. Privately.

By Fed Ex, I'd sent the shotgun shell that, hopefully, carried Kline's fingerprints, to Hal Harrington. No one had more varied intelligence assets available than Hal — not even the FBI.

I enclosed a six-word note: "Find him before the Feds do."

The FBI was looking for Kline. I knew that from my own intelligence assets. Working with Interpol. They'd lost his trail in Paris, but they were pretty sure he was still somewhere in Europe.

Harrington replied via e-mail with a six-word note of his own: "Will try. But quid pro quo."

I knew what he meant by that.

Mostly, I worked hard at becoming the individual I'd once been, but had somehow allowed to slip into physical and emotional decline. It had happened slowly; taken nearly a year, and it was frustrating that recovery seemed doubly slow.

I cleaned and rearranged everything in my house and lab, and updated all my files. I was meticulous. I took great joy in obsessive attention to detail.

I worked out every day, seven days a week. Hard.

Dewey Nye, and my cousin, Ransom Gatrell, became my tag-team partners. Every weekday at noon, Ransom and I would ride our bikes, pumping furiously, always keeping the pedal revolutions between seventy-five to a hundred a minute according to our little handlebar computers. Twice a week, we rode to the gate at South Sea's Plantation and back — 27 miles. Three times a week, we rode to Lighthouse Point and back — 10.5 miles.

In the afternoons, Dewey and I would alternate between running, lifting and swimming. Years ago, we'd started an informal group we called the Teaser Pony Swim Club. Now, we revived it, and did a long offshore swim every Sunday.

Saturdays, I worked out alone. Those became the hardest, most dreaded workouts, because that is when I punished myself for past indulgences. In the morning, I'd swim toward the horizon for twenty minutes. I would then turn and fight to beat my time coming back.

Memories of my encounter with the bull

shark were always with me. He was still out there, on a feed.

Ignoring the fear, forcing myself to stroke and kick in rhythm, was a kind of penance.

Once ashore, after chugging a quart of water, I'd run on the beach until it felt as if my heart were going to explode.

I ate protein. Mostly oysters, scallops and fish I'd caught myself. I threw the cast net a lot. I ate a lot of broiled mullet.

I also ate a steady diet of grouper, sheepshead and snapper. I used mask, fins and speargun. When it comes to those three species, if you know where the random, rocky places are, it's like going to the grocery store.

I drank nothing but water. I didn't allow myself food after 10 P.M. Once a week, I weighed in and noted the weight and date in pencil on the wall.

By the last week of June, I was down to two twenty-three — close to my goal. But I decided to keep working, keep driving and see just how far I could push the physical envelope.

I hoped soon to rendezvous with Izzy Kline. He'd somehow managed to overpower a far better man than I — Frank DeAntoni.

I wanted to be in top shape for the meeting.

Because she visited Tomlinson regularly, I got to know Karlita better, and actually came to enjoy her company. She really *did* have extrasensory powers, Tomlinson told me. In truth, she was the leader of the Cassadaga group, but didn't want anyone to know.

"A television psychic," he explained. "Can you think of a more brilliant cover for someone who actually *does* have the gift?"

I didn't believe that she had extrasensory powers, of course, but now that I knew she was part of the Cassadaga group, she didn't behave like such a pompous flake. Not surprisingly, that made her more physically attractive: long legged, lean, with glossy Irish-black hair and good cheekbones. We had some nice talks.

Karlita stopped by the lab so often that Dewey, I think, began to get a little jealous. I found that surprising.

Dewey and I have had a strange relationship. We've been lovers, and we've been friends. In the end, friendship seemed to be winning out. I'd never felt closer to her. On our long runs, we'd discuss every subject imaginable.

Once, I caught her staring at me. When I asked why her expression was so intense, she'd replied shyly, "I was having impure thoughts about you. Thinking maybe the two of us should hop in the shower and suds up."

I thought she was kidding. So I'd laughed, and reminded her that I was still occasionally dating Grace Walker, the busty, mahogany-dark realtor from Tampa. We had an exclusivity agreement, so I'd have to tell her first. I did not care to invite that woman's wrath.

At least once a week, I drove to Coconut

Grove and spent time with Sally. She seemed undamaged by what had happened; was doing lots of charity work for her church, spreading her money around. She'd accepted the insurance check for her husband's death, and he *was* dead. Izzy Kline had told her that.

"How that creep knew about Geoff," Sally said, "I have no idea. But the way he said it, I believe it's true."

On the way back from Coconut Grove, I fell into the habit of stopping to visit with the Egret Seminoles. I got to know Billie Egret much better; felt a familial closeness to her. In July, she and her people received formal notice from the U.S. Department of the Interior, Bureau of Indian Affairs, Branch of Acknowledgment and Recognition, that they were now confirmed as a legal, independent tribe — with all the rights, privileges and obligations that went along with it.

"My only regret," she told me, "is that my father isn't here to see what he created."

Some people live in a way that they are forever missed. Joseph Egret was one of those people.

Billie showed her business savvy, as well as her dedication to the Everglades, by forming a fast alliance with the new chairman of Sawgrass's board of directors — Carter McRae. He'd gotten the board to agree to sell the tribe the massive acreage on which Shiva had planned to put his casinos, and also to help

459

them plant and restore the land.

"Mr. McRae's a nice man," she said. "I'd always heard what a tough businessman he is, but I've never met anyone so generous. I think it's because his wife's out of the hospital. He's happy, so maybe there's no reason to be tough anymore."

It was around then that I read a satirical piece by a *Tampa Tribune* columnist that supposedly explained the sudden absence of Swamp Ape sightings. It was hilarious. But when I told Tomlinson about it, he said, "That's not the reason. In your heart, I think you *know* the reason."

By late August, Dewey and I were running at a pace that was consistently under seven-minute miles, and I was bench-pressing a hundred pounds more than my own weight — which was now down to two-oh-five.

It was the least I'd weighed since a couple of years after high school.

So I was fit and ready when, one day, I checked my e-mail to find a two-word message from Harrington: *Granada, Nicaragua.*

Three days later, I flew American Eagle to Miami, and then COPA to Managua.

chapter thirty-two

izzy

Izzy knew Ford was in Granada the day after he arrived, the big, nerdy biologist who'd behaved like such a smartass know-it-all on the skeet range.

That's one of the reasons Izzy loved Nicaragua. If you had money, you could buy anything, including security.

Izzy had the money, so he had spies everywhere. Had his own efficient intelligence network that kept him informed. If anyone new came into town, anyone suspicious, Izzy got the word pronto.

He hadn't eyeballed Ford personally. But one of his staff — the kid who did his legwork in town — had sneaked a digitized photo of the man sitting at the pool bar of the Colony Hotel, right next to the park in the old part of the city.

It was Ford, all right. He looked thinner, almost gaunt in the photo, but not sick-looking. Just different.

At first, it had shocked the hell out of Izzy. Those first few seconds looking at the photo, he'd thought, *I'm out of here.*

But then he told himself to hold on, slow

461

down. *Think* about it. He'd been living peacefully on his little island for more than three months under the name of Craig Skaar, not a hint of trouble. The way Izzy had worked it, covering his trail every step of the way, not even the FBI could have found him. So what were the chances of some dopey biologist accomplishing what the FBI couldn't?

Nil.

So Izzy had one of his people, Giorgio, talk to a couple of the staff at the Colony. Turned out, it was a total coincidence. The nerd was in Granada to study some kind of weird freshwater shark that lived in the lake.

"What the hell's a bull shark?" Izzy said when Giorgio told him.

He'd been swimming off his beach in the lake every day, and hated the idea of sharks being out there.

Smiling, Giorgio had clacked his teeth together, and said in Spanish, "The kind that bites, Chief."

So Izzy had nothing to fear. Not from Ford, anyway. But his being in Granada was a big pain in the ass for two reasons: One, living on an island, Izzy had learned, was boring as hell. And, two, Granada really was a *fun* town.

Izzy enjoyed walking the streets and open markets, looking for young girls. He liked the Spanish architecture, everything painted in Caribbean pastel blues, corals and greens. He liked the feel of the old mansions, the way they were built around a central park that had a bandstand where marimba groups played almost every night.

Izzy liked eating and drinking at the Mediterraneo and Dona Conchi's, where the American adventurer William Walker had supposedly dodged a firing squad. He especially like a quirky little bar outside town, Restaurante Aeropuerto 79, that served excellent and unusual food, such as crab-and-iguana-tail soup.

When he got bored with Granada, he'd hop in the Land Rover he'd bought and drive to Masaya, a little village famous for its two massive markets — that was always interesting. There were lots of bars there; plenty of women.

Nicaragua was also famous for its volcanoes. There were dozens of them; maybe hundreds. At night, from his island, he could see them glowing in the distance.

Once, Izzy decided to have a look at a volcano just to see what it was like. Masaya supposedly had one of the largest, so he'd driven miles up the mountain road, got out and stared into the mouth of the volcano for which the village was named.

Mah-SIGH-uh — that's the way the locals pronounced it.

The crater was huge, smoky. It smelled of heat and sulfur. If he really leaned over and looked, he could see orange lava way down there, nearly a thousand feet below.

No more volcanoes after seeing Masaya, Izzy

decided. If there really was a hell, that's the way it'd look. Plus, there were plenty of other things to do around Granada.

But not with Ford around. Ford being in town was a pain in the ass because it made it impossible for Izzy to leave his island. Granada was not a large town, and he couldn't risk being seen.

Which meant he'd just have to wait patiently until the nerd got on a plane and left. Which he almost certainly would. Soon.

As an extra precaution, though, Izzy had his people spread the word: Let him know immediately if the biologist rented a boat, a canoe, anything that floated. If he was on the water, Izzy wanted to know *where*.

Otherwise, he was safe, and hidden away. After all, Izzy's island was more than a mile offshore. What was the guy going to do? *Swim?*

Ford arrived in town on a Tuesday. Now, five days later, Izzy was going stir-crazy. Every night, he had his staff bring out different women; two, sometimes three at a time — so it wasn't too bad. But today was Sunday, and nobody in the whole country worked on Sunday, not even the hookers.

Fucking Catholics.

It was the only day of the week when Izzy was alone on the island, so he'd come to despise Sundays.

So what he did was work on his Internet

stuff. He had to keep the generator running outside to do it. The massive *casa* he was building wasn't done; he hadn't yet gotten the electric cable laid from Granada, so the wood-and-tile house in which he now lived was primitive but comfortable.

Izzy was careful about the way he used the Internet. He knew that it was one of the few ways he could be tracked. An individual's Internet habits have a signature, so he varied what he did, the sites he accessed; kept a low profile.

He hadn't put the video of the Merry Widow on line yet. Same with the two dozen porno tapes he'd made since he'd arrived in Nicaragua. He kept all the tapes in his office, neatly cataloged on wooden bookshelves.

No. He was taking it slow, getting his new identity established, playing it cool. He'd begin to market the tapes soon, very soon. And the money would start rolling in.

At dusk, Izzy went for a walk; walked the entire perimeter of his island, looking at similar islands to the south, then the red tile roofs of Granada to the northeast. He did the walk nearly every afternoon, partly for exercise, but also for security reasons.

No boats out there anywhere.

Then he stopped at the boathouse and checked the lines of his new twenty-six-foot Mako. Same thing. Habit. He did it every night.

As he returned to the house, there was a silver, crescent moon, he noticed, floating above a horizon of volcanic peaks.

Izzy was still sitting at his computer at a little after 10 P.M. when the computer, the lights, everything went out.

Shit.

Because it wasn't unusual for the generator to run out of diesel fuel, he had glass oil lamps all over the house. He lighted one now.

Goddamn Pablo didn't fill the tank before he left like I told him to do.

Pissed off, bored, Izzy carried the lamp to the back door, opened it . . . and dropped the lamp, he was so shocked to see who was standing there.

The glass shattered, spilling kerosene across the tile floor. The room was immediately bathed in the eerie light of spreading flames.

A deep, articulate voice said, "Hello, Izzy. Hey — you need to be more careful. Or maybe you never learned not to play with fire."

Izzy took a step back.

Jesus Christ, it was the fucking nerd biologist, standing there in a black sweater and black shorts, his face painted green, a watch cap pulled down to his ears, water dripping from him. He was smiling. It was like he was an old friend or something, happy to see him.

Not in his eyes, though. What he saw in Ford's eyes was scary.

Izzy turned to find water, a blanket, something to stop the fire, as the biologist said, "Hold it right there. I'm a little cold after my swim. So let's just let 'er burn. Okay?"

"Fuck you, mister!" Izzy was still walking away. Where he was really headed was his desk to get the Beretta. *After* that, he'd worry about the fire. "You just don't show up without an invitation, come into a man's house and start giving orders."

Which is when he felt the man's big hands grab him from behind. Just as he'd been trained in martial arts, Izzy swung back hard with his left elbow, already pivoting to slam the palm of his hand into Ford's nose — but Ford had somehow managed to remain behind him.

Christ, it was like fighting the Italian all over again.

Izzy had the same kind of feeling — overpowered, helpless — as Ford took him to the ground.

"You've got no reason to do this to me. Why are you doing this?"

Ford said, "I want to have a chat, Izzy. A little come-to-God meeting you might call it."

As he talked, with not much effort at all, he got Izzy's right arm behind him, then his left.

Izzy heard a ripping sound.

Fuck! He's taping my hands.

"I want to talk about Geoff Minster, and what you did to his wife, Sally. And I want to talk about Frank DeAntoni. The guy you put in the trunk and shot execution-style. Remember?"

Izzy grunted at the terrible pressure the man was now putting on the back of his neck.

"Remember?"

Barely able to speak through the pain, Izzy said, "I'll pay you. Anything you want. I'll tell you anything, give you money. Just let me go."

"The only thing I want you to tell me right now is where you keep the key to your boat."

Izzy pictured the Beretta, thinking, *I'll pretend it's in the drawer,* and said, "Let me go. Let me stand up. I'll get the keys for you. I promise."

Ford stood over him. The room was bright now, flames moving up the wall, crackling, the wood catching fast.

Izzy listened to him say, "The boat keys, Izzy. Or I'll tape your legs and leave you here. Burning to death. Personally, I think that would be the second worst way to go."

Second worst. What did he mean by that?

Izzy told him where to find the key.

Now Izzy was in the trunk of a rental car, his legs taped, his mouth taped, and he was thinking, *The son-of-a-bitch is going to do the same thing to me I did to the wop and the old man.*

He'd never felt such fear. He was trembling, heart pounding, panting through his nose. When the biologist beached the boat in what appeared to be jungle, opened the trunk of the car he'd hidden there, and lifted him in, Izzy had lost control of his bladder — that's how scared he was.

They'd been driving now for nearly an hour. Lots of curves and bumpy roads. Lots of long, uphill climbing.

Izzy wanted the car to stop, but dreaded stopping because he felt certain that he knew what Ford had planned.

But Ford still hadn't asked the questions he said he wanted to ask. And that was good, right? Right?

If he takes the tape off my mouth, I can talk my way out of it. I can talk my way out of anything. Anything! Please, God, let him take the tape off and give me a chance to talk.

It had been true all of Izzy's life. So that's what he decided to do. Stay calm, use his brain, tell Ford anything he wanted to hear. *Think.*

But when the car stopped, and Izzy saw where they were, he thought, *Dear God, no. Please dear God, no, please.*

Izzy lost control of his bladder again.

At an elevation of more that two thousand feet, Masaya is Nicaragua's most unusual and isolated active volcano. It is rough rimmed, like a gigantic barnacle, with steep-sided walls that are home to a rare subspecies of parrot. Masaya has been frequently active since the time of the Spanish conquistadores.

The volcano's northwest basin is filled by more than a dozen rocky vents that smoke constantly and erupt occasionally. On its opposite side, though, where the walls are steepest, it is a straight drop into molten lava more than a thousand feet below.

It is on the southeastern side of the volcano that Nicaraguan seismologists maintain a gate-like structure built of galvanized metal, a fifteen-foot steel arm connected to a turnstile with heavy hinges. It is cemented into the ground. On it are fixed a variety of instruments that record heat, sulfur emissions, seismic activity.

Swing the gate out, the instruments are suspended above the lava a thousand feet below. Swing the gate back, and the instruments can be read.

It is checked monthly.

As Ford tied Izzy to the gate, Izzy was thinking: *This can't be happening.*

But it *was* happening.

Ford had him tied to the galvanized arm of the gate, legs and hands, back to the ground, so that he hung helplessly, like a pig on a spit. Ford had used some kind of complicated knots that Izzy didn't recognize. Some kind of quick-release knots. The way it looked, the biologist could pop all the knots by simply yanking on the end of the line that he held in his hand.

Izzy was panting, heart banging in his temples, as Ford said, "Izzy. It's time for us to have that talk."

He ripped the tape off Izzy's mouth.

Still holding the end of the rope, Ford then pushed Izzy as if he were on a merry-go-round. The gate swung out over the abyss.

OhhhHHHHH God!

Izzy began to cry; felt as if he might vomit, as Ford said, "Let's make this quick. It can't be pleasant, hanging out there, so save us both some time and stick to the truth. For starters, what happened to Geoff Minster?"

Shaking, his teeth chattering, Izzy said, "Please tell me you're not going to pull that rope. Please don't let me fall. I'll do anything. I promise. *I swear.*"

"Answer the question."

"Okay, okay, okay!" Izzy was talking fast, not even having to think about it because he *was* telling the truth. "I stole a hundred grand from the church. I did it through the computers. I'm good with computers. I set it up to look like Minster stole it.

"Jerry Singh — an asshole — he told me to kill Minster. The two of them hated each other by then. Plus, we suspected Minster had found out about our plans to fake earthquakes. We weren't sure, but Shiva couldn't risk it.

"So I went to Minster and cut a private deal. Minster paid me ten grand, and he set it up to look like he'd fallen off a fishing boat. I was supposed to be behind him in my boat. Minster carried a waterproof light to signal me when he was going over the side.

"Once he'd disappeared, I was supposed to

go to the cops, agree to be wired, and get Jerry on tape telling me what a good job I'd done, killing Geoff. Jerry'd go to prison. That way, Minster figured he'd get all his money, his property back."

Izzy said, "Minster also figured he could lie low for a couple of weeks; have some fun. I think he had a thing for some Indian woman down in the 'Glades. A big, ugly woman. A guy with his money, it was weird."

Izzy paused for a moment, before he added, "Hey — don't tug the rope like that. You're scaring me."

After a longer pause, Ford said, "He went overboard, but you didn't pick him up. You'd already misdated a digital photo of him in case someone suspected you, and they started to get close. A way of buying time."

Izzy was sobbing now; weeping as if from his soul. "I'm so ashamed of some of the things I've done. I *mean* it. I really am. That's one of the reasons I came to Nicaragua. There are so many poor kids here — I want to *help* them. I want to make amends for some of my terrible acts."

"Did Shiva often ask you to commit murder?"

"Four times. I regret every one. I'm going to church now. *Confession.* I've been talking to a priest, trying to get my life in order. I *deserve* to be in hell. But I want to do some good before I leave this earth."

"You murdered Frank and Jimmy Marinaro. Shot them in the back of the head. And you tied up Sally, locked her in the truck with your homemade bomb."

"Dr. Ford, I feel so much guilt, I can't tell you. I'd do anything to bring them back. I'd give my life for theirs in a second. One thing I can tell you about Mrs. Minster, though. I never laid a hand on her. I made sure she went peacefully. She was a nice lady. So classy. I'm surprised you know about that."

Ford thought about it for a moment before he said, "Do you want to know what a smart cop recently told me? In any abduction-murder case, getting rid of the body is always the biggest problem. That's because it's evidence found on the body that usually nails the killer."

Hanging from the galvanized pipe, Izzy said, "I'm not sure what you mean by that, but I know this: My life is in your hands. The guilt I feel's going to haunt me forever. I've got to live with it. But you *don't*. You're too good a man to do the kind of things I've done. You're too good a person to do what you're thinking about doing now. I can *tell*. It's an instinct I've got. First time we met, I knew you were a stand-up guy. There's something about you. Solid."

Marion Ford replied, "Izzy, we have both badly misjudged my character and my conscience."

Then he pulled the rope's bitter end,

473

springing all four knots.

The biologist didn't linger. He turned away from Izzy Kline's descending, echoing scream . . .

epilogue

On an equator-heated, blue-bright tropical morning, November 14th, a Thursday, I walked away from our rental cabana, and our private, secluded patio toward the beach, but the lady stopped me by wagging her finger: *Come here*.

She said, "Where do you think you're going, mister? It's going to be another hot one, and I need to be coated with sunscreen. Do you mind?"

No, I did not mind.

She lay on her back in a lounge chair, beside the blue-tiled plunge pool, a tall drink and a book within easy reach. She wore sunglasses and an orange bikini bottom, nothing more. Even after six days of this — lots of nude sun-bathing — her breasts were pale orbs, flattened by their own weight and softness.

I checked my watch before I sat beside her. She trembled slightly as I began to apply sun lotion to her abdomen and thighs, her pink areolas flushing, nipples erect, blue veins beneath the milk-white skin deepening in shade.

Her eyes closed, the lady placed her hand on

my thigh, and began to massage my leg with the precise, slow rhythm that I used to apply the oil.

She murmured lazily, "I think we need to go back to our bedroom for a little bit."

Smiling, I thought, *Again?*

That good woman, Grace Walker, the Sarasota realtor I'd been dating, had told me something interesting and true a month or so before. It was over dinner — a nice restaurant on St. Armand's Key, just off the circle.

She'd said, "Doc, here's what I've learned about men and women. If the sex is good, it's about thirty percent of a solid relationship. If the sex is bad, if the chemistry isn't there, it's about ninety percent of the relationship. It's just not going to work."

It was her way of telling me it was time for us to start dating other people.

I was neither surprised nor disappointed. I was, in fact, relieved, because I'd driven north to meet her with plans to end it myself.

We'd remain friends — always friends.

And Grace was certainly right about sexual chemistry. With this lady, the chemistry was there. It was unmistakably, obsessively, irresistibly there.

That morning after making love for the second time, we'd lain naked, sweaty and spent, beneath the revolving shadows of a ceiling fan, and I'd listened to her say, "Maybe it's true. Maybe we should stop fighting it. Maybe we *are* destined to be more than just friends."

I replied, "An exclusive relationship. You and me. I'm willing to try — if I have enough energy left after a couple of weeks vacationing with you."

She chuckled, and said, "Maybe more than just a dating relationship. We've both lived alone for a long time. Do you think you'd be willing to try? Down the road, I mean."

I nodded. "Yeah. Yeah, I think I would." I meant it.

"Something's changed in you, Doc. Something's changed in us both. Do you feel it? It's different. *We* seem different. I've been thinking . . . well, maybe it's because of the paper Tomlinson gave us to read. Maybe it really *has* had an influence. I checked the Internet. It's changed the lives of a lot of people."

We'd brought "One Fathom Above Sea Level" along on the plane for something to read. The lady had spent far more time pondering it than I. She'd even used a pink highlighter to mark her favorite quotes.

She'd made me review them:

The absurdity of a life that may well end before we understand it does not relieve us of the duty to live it through bravely and generously, with passion and great kindness.

Another was: *Humanity has a limited biological capacity for change, but an unlimited capacity for spiritual change. The only human institution incapable of evolving spiritually is a cemetery.*

Another was: *Pain is an inescapable part of the human experience. Misery, however, is not. Misery is an option.*

Another: *Hope could not exist if man were created by a random, chemical accident. Pleasure, yes. Desire, yes. But not hope. Selfless hope is contrary to the dynamics of evolution or the necessities of a species.*

I'd marked my own favorite in green: *Never underestimate the destructive power of small, mean people joined together as a larger group.*

Lying in bed, her long legs thrown over mine, she had said, "You can't read what Tomlinson's written and still doubt that spirituality — having *faith* — is important. So maybe it *is* our destiny."

I told her, yes, that was certainly a possibility — although I didn't believe it.

I found Tomlinson's paper interesting for the intellectual depth and perception it demonstrated, but nothing more. I am incapable of lying to myself, so I am incapable of embracing a spiritual view of the world. I'd come to accept who I am, *what* I am. It's unlikely that I will ever believe — yet I still retain hope. Even so I no longer engage in that debate, or risk undermining the beliefs of others.

So now, lounged back in her chair, the lady arched her back slightly, moaning, as I rubbed oil on her heavy breasts, her hand moving beneath my running shorts, searching.

Breathing faster now, she whispered, "Doc.

Let's go to the bedroom. Now."

I checked my watch: 10:27 A.M.

I thought: *Damn.*

Her fingers had found me, and I was certainly ready.

I said, "Stop, wait. Let me check something."

I stood awkwardly, and jogged barefooted down to our little section of private beach on St. Martin's in the French West Indies. I used small but superb Zeiss binoculars to look across the bay that separated our rental house from a big, Mediterranean mansion half a mile away. The mansion was built into the side of a cliff, connected to the main road above by a gated access drive.

Security there was tight for a reason. The house was being rented by Omar Muhammad, the successor to Sabri al-Banna, and the new head of Abul Nidal.

There was Omar. I could see him plainly through the binoculars. He was a tall, bearded man with hollow eyes. He was lugging his scuba gear down the steps from the house to the beach.

Omar was a man of habit. Every morning for the last three mornings, exactly at eleven, he'd put on his gear, and swim out to the shallow reef a hundred yards away. Always alone.

Quid pro quo, Hal Harrington had told me.

I sighed, turned and walked back to the patio. I placed the binoculars on the table, sat and kissed the lady on the lips. "Honey, give me a little time to rest up, okay? I'm going for a swim. I'll be back in, oh, a little less than an hour."

For the first time, she opened her sleepy eyes, sat up and said, "You want to swim? Hell, I'll go with you. We've been eating like horses all week. I could use the exercise."

To my right calf, I was strapping a stainless-steel Randall Attack/Survival knife in its leather scabbard. I strapped it tight, and tied the safety lanyard around my ankle.

I leaned, kissed Dewey Nye once more. Then I looked into her good eyes, bright and true, and said, "No, my dear. This swim, I should probably go alone."